Praise for USA TODAY bestselling author

Christie Ridgway

"This sexy page-turner [is] a stellar kick-off to Ridgway's latest humor-drenched series."
—*Library Journal* on *Take My Breath Away*

"Emotional and powerful…everything a romance reader could hope for."
—*Publishers Weekly* (starred review) on *Bungalow Nights*

"Kick off your shoes and escape to endless summer. This is romance at its best."
—Emily March, *New York Times* bestselling author of *Nightingale Way*, on *Bungalow Nights*

"Sexy and addictive—Ridgway will keep you up all night!"
—*New York Times* bestselling author Susan Andersen on *Beach House No. 9*

"A great work of smart, escapist reading."
—*Booklist* on *Beach House No. 9*

"Sexy, sassy, funny, and cool, this effervescent sizzler nicely launches Ridgway's new series and is a perfect pick-me-up for a summer's day."
—*Library Journal* on *Crush on You*

"Pure romance, delightfully warm and funny."
—*New York Times* bestselling author Jennifer Crusie

"Christie Ridgway writes with the perfect combination of humor and heart. This funny, sexy story is as fresh and breezy as its southern California setting. An irresistible read!"
—*New York Times* bestselling author Susan Wiggs on *How to Knit a Wild Bikini*

CHRISTIE RIDGWAY

make me
lose
control

HQN™

Recycling programs
for this product may
not exist in your area.

ISBN-13: 978-0-373-77871-3

Make Me Lose Control

Copyright © 2015 by Christie Ridgway

www.HQNBooks.com

Printed in U.S.A.

In memory of my brother, Matt, the best of family men.

Dear Reader,

It's time for another visit to Blue Arrow Lake, surrounded by peaks, pines and sunshine! Just a short uphill drive from Los Angeles, the resort area is a popular place for city-dwellers to explore mountain life. The people who make their home there year-round consider themselves the luckiest of souls, even though it means often dealing with the flatlanders who are mere short-timers to the area.

Shay Walker, one of the Walker mountain clan, is content most of the time…except once a year when her birthday rolls around. She has issues on that day, and this time she indulges with a delicious stranger as a way to forget her woes. But when that man shows up on her doorstep—uh, *his* doorstep, as she's ensconced in his lakeside estate as a live-in tutor for his estranged teen—she realizes her life has become quite a bit more complicated. Jace Jennings spells *difficult d-a-u-g-h-t-e-r*, and now he has her sexy tutor to reckon with, as well. He considers himself no kind of family man, but he's going to discover he has hidden talents!

It takes an open heart to love, as the characters in this story come to learn. They resist, they rebel, they flat-out pretend not to see how wonderful they are for each other, and I enjoyed every minute of writing their journey toward becoming a pair…and then a family. Come on board, sit back and revel in the ride. Destination… romance!

Christie Ridgway

A life without love is like a year without summer.

—Swedish proverb

CHAPTER ONE

SHAY WALKER WATCHED the twentysomething man slap a cardboard coaster on the polished wooden surface in front of her. His long sun-streaked hair hung about his shoulders in the careless style of a guy who snowboarded on the nearby peaks in winter and kayaked on the deep lakes in summer. "What can I get you?" he asked.

"A change in the calendar?" she murmured, looping the strap of her purse over the convenient hook on the underside of the bar. The small leather bag brushed her knees, bared by the new summer dress she wore. Though the late May evenings might still be cool in the Southern California mountains, Shay had opted for the filmy floral garment anyway. It was sleeveless, and the hemline was asymmetrical, nearly mini in the front and then flowing to midcalf in the back. It also revealed a minor amount of cleavage, which even in its relative modesty seemed to be captivating the bartender.

"Um, what?" he asked, his gaze slowly lifting from her chest to her face. "I don't think I know that drink."

"I was kidding," she said. "How about a martini? Vodka. Straight up." Though chardonnay was more often her order, tonight she needed a stronger beverage.

Birthdays didn't bring out the best in her.

In no time, the boarder-slash-bartender slid the requested drink onto the coaster then watched as she picked it up and sipped. Tiny slivers of ice melted on her tongue and the alcohol pleasantly heated the back of her throat. Okay, she thought, as she took another swallow. Maybe this celebration wouldn't turn out so bad, after all.

"You here alone?" the guy on the other side of the bar asked.

"For the moment. I'm meeting a friend." She glanced at the TV mounted above the glass shelves of liquor bottles, pretending a fascination with the news program playing.

Whether Boarder Dude would have taken the hint or not, she didn't know. A waitress approached and fired off a long order that claimed his attention, allowing Shay to give up her pseudofascination with the consumer reporter's fight to get a pothole filled in a city thousands of feet below the mountains.

She glanced around, taking in the adjacent restaurant. Exposed wood, an enormous chandelier made of antlers, warm lighting. People were dressed in peaks-and-pines chic, meaning they wore everything from denim to silk. A meal at the Deerpoint Inn's grill had been her old friend Melinda's idea. She'd recently moved to a tiny cabin a couple of miles from it and said she'd heard good things about the food.

Since the place was fifteen miles of winding mountain road from where Shay was currently living, in Blue Arrow Lake, she'd decided to book one of the inn's six rooms in case the birthday blues triggered some over-imbibing. Thinking of the key already tucked away in her purse, she took a hefty swallow of her drink. No reason not to get all warm and fuzzy as soon as possible.

It beat the heck out of what she could have been doing tonight—sitting alone in a massive lakefront mansion. And didn't that just sound whiny and pitiful? But it wasn't *her* massive lakefront mansion—she'd always lived in much humbler abodes—and the house would seem much too empty without the presence of the teenager Shay was charged with looking after until the end of summer. For the previous three months, she'd been a governess of sorts for a girl who colored her hair inky black, who exclusively draped herself in dark shapeless garments and who walked around with the jaded air of a thousand-year-old vampire. It made for interesting times.

But the teen was otherwise occupied for the night. In a show of rare enthusiasm, she'd opted to attend the Hollywood premiere of a much-anticipated animated movie with Shay's sister, her sister's young son and her sister's fiancé. They would spend the night down the mountain, too.

So when Melinda called, suggesting a get-together, Shay had agreed.

The bartender strolled by and glanced at her glass, and she gave him the nod. *Yes, sir, I'll have another.* She wanted more warm and fuzzy.

Birthdays were her bane not because her age upped a digit, but because the occasion reminded her of the circumstances of her conception. She wasn't a Walker, really—not by blood. When strained finances had put a rift in Dell and Lorna Walker's marriage, Dell had headed for a mining job in South America. Lorna's subsequent affair with a wealthy visitor to the mountain resort area had ended when she found herself pregnant. But not long after Shay was born, Lorna's husband returned to the States, reconciled with his wife and accepted another daughter into the family as if Shay were his own. There were adoption papers somewhere to prove it.

Still, she'd always felt a step or two outside the family circle, even though her older brother, Brett, and her big sisters, Mackenzie and Poppy, had never once made her feel like only half their sibling.

She lifted the fresh martini and took a swallow. Maybe her throat was numb now, because the burn there was gone. Instead, the drink sparked a bright idea in her brain. She should locate those adoption papers! Frame and display them as a daily reminder that she was actually one of the Walkers. Legally anyway.

With her parents deceased, however, she didn't know how to find the documents. Maybe Brett would have a clue where to look, she thought, digging her phone from her purse. When he didn't answer, she sent him a text, realizing her fingers were a little clumsy on the tiny keyboard.

Another swallow of mostly vodka eliminated her concern over it.

She'd nearly drained the second martini when the phone buzzed in her hand. The display read Mel.

"Where are you?" Shay demanded through the device. "It's my birthday and I'm all alone."

"Your birthday's tomorrow," Melinda pointed out.

"Oh, yeah." Shay had been going glum a whole day early. But that was okay, she decided, tilting back her head to shake the last drops of her drink into her mouth, because there was enough glum to spread across the calendar. Not all of her sibs could do cake and ice cream—their usual tradition—tomorrow so that was being postponed to yet another time.

Poor Shay. Poor Shay, who was not really a Walker.

"Uh-oh," she said to Melinda, signaling the boarding bartender that she needed a refill. "You better speed over here, stat. I'm drinking martinis and getting morose."

"About that…"

"Noooo." Shay began to shake her head, then quit, because the movement made her dizzy. When had she eaten last?

"I'm sorry, but—"

"This was your idea, Mel. I need an un-no, a munmo… An un-moroser!" She finally spit out the made-up word with a note of triumph.

The bartender replaced her glass with a fresh one. She pointed at him with her free hand. "I bet you really tear it up when you're shreddin' the gnar," she said to express her appreciation of how he'd anticipated her need. "And you never biff, do you?"

"Are you talking to me?" Mel said in her ear.

"Nope." Probably her friend didn't understand snowboard lingo any better than Shay, but that didn't stop her tonight. "That was to BB—Boarder Bartender."

"Oh, dear." Mel sighed. "You *are* drunk. And alone in a bar, where I can't get to you."

"Which I'm still waiting to hear what for." Shay frowned. "How. I mean, why."

"A wildfire has caused local road closures," her friend said. "They're diverting cars from the highway, too."

Shay blinked, somewhat sobered by the news. Fire

was a constant danger in their mountains. "Structures threatened?"

"Not so far. But the closed roads mean I can't reach the inn…and you can't get home, either."

"I booked a room here." She drew the martini closer, and, thinking of fire, took it up for a hefty swallow. "So's all's good."

"You're slurring," Melinda said.

"I'll order food. What goes with martinis?"

"Olives?" Mel suggested.

"Oh." Shay inspected her glass. "Mine came with those twisty lemon peels."

"I was kidding," the other woman said. "Get something with protein. And order bread. That's good to absorb the alcohol."

"But I'm enjoying the alcohol," Shay protested. Her gaze shifted to the TV screen as the bartender upped the volume. The picture was from a helicopter and showed the dark mountains and a glowing orange snake of flames. A shiver rolled down her back. Fire had taken a lot from the Walkers and she didn't appreciate the reminder of it.

Again, she brought her glass to her lips, hoping to drown her discomfort.

"Shay?" her friend called.

"Oh." She'd forgotten about Mel. "I wish you were here."

"Me, too." The other woman's voice went stern. "Now promise me no more martinis."

"Um…" Shay closed one eye to better inspect the clear liquid left in her glass. The yellow curl of peel was so delicate and pretty. Who needed olives? "No more martinis." Maybe.

"And try to have some fun tonight," her friend said. "That's an order."

Fun? All alone and with no more martinis? That wasn't the way to make Melinda's command come true.

THE VOLUME OF noise from the patrons of the Deerpoint Inn amplified as more of them became aware of the fire and tuned into the coverage on the TV over the bar. The manager struck a glass with a fork and when the voices around him died down, he announced which roads were blocked. New people trickled in, having been rerouted from the now closed highway. The long-haired bartender got busy filling drink orders as many guests figured out they likely wouldn't be driving anywhere that night.

Trying to tamp down her nerves, Shay sipped at the last of the third martini, ordered a plate of chicken quesadilla appetizers, then threw caution to the wind and asked for another alcohol concoction.

Mel had told her to have fun, hadn't she? When the front door of the restaurant opened once again, bringing with it the disconcerting scent of smoke, Shay didn't hesitate to reach for her new glass.

She needed to block the fire from her mind.

A body slid onto the bar stool beside her. Shay looked over, the glance automatic, but her response was anything but.

As she took in the man on her right, it was as if a cold pail of water had been dumped on top of her head—an icy surprise. Following that, a rush of heat crept up from her toes all the way to the roots of her hair.

He was gorgeous.

And no boy, she thought, with a mental apology to

BB, the boarder-bartender who had, after all, been so ably supplying her with vodka and a splash of vermouth. The newcomer was tall, his build rugged, with heavy shoulders and muscled arms, a broad chest, lean waist and strong thighs, all signaling a more than passing familiarity with manual labor. Linking his fingers on the bar, he ordered a beer, and Shay directed her gaze to his hands. They were big, too, and wide-palmed. She could see tiny white scars scattered on the tan skin.

Then, under the cover of her lashes, she took a second look at his face. At the same time, she tilted her head, just a little, as if trying to get a better view of the television and not his fine, fine features.

Wow.

His hair was mink-brown, thick and straight. It was shorn fairly tight, revealing a broad forehead. His cheekbones were high, he had a straight blade of a masculine nose and his lips were full. His strong jaw was edged with just a hint of dark stubble.

She stifled the urge to fan herself, afraid to draw his attention. What would she say to someone like him?

And then, before she could redirect her eyes, his head turned. His gaze cut straight to her face.

Like a lion's, his irises were golden. Also like a lion's, they seemed preternaturally aware of the weaker creature—Shay—in the vicinity. The tiny hairs on her body lifted, her senses warning he was supremely aware of her tripping heartbeat and all the delicious warm blood rushing below her skin.

Though her belly fluttered, she remained as she was—frozen, and feeling like an impala just now singled out by the biggest predator on the savannah. One of his dark eyebrows winged up.

And Shay blurted out the first thing that came into her head. "I'm supposed to be celebrating my birthday tonight but my friend couldn't get here."

The corner of his mouth twitched as the second eyebrow joined the first. "Okay."

"This is my third martini." She gestured toward her current glass, then frowned. "Or my fourth."

"All right."

"I've had nothing to eat yet." At that, she ran out of things to say. None of what she'd already shared, she realized, gave any rational explanation for why she'd been staring at him. *Damn.*

"Is it a four-martini birthday, then?" he inquired conversationally. He murmured thanks as his beer was placed before him. His gaze turned assessing. "I can't imagine it's one of the more painful ones."

"Oh, um, well." She shifted her attention to her drink and drew it closer. "Maybe it's the fire."

"Aren't we safe?" He sipped from his beer. "The highway patrol seemed to know what they were doing when they shuttled me in this direction. They said I might be stuck here for as little as a few hours, though possibly longer."

"We'll be fine." There was no need to pass along her skittishness. "The fire protection people and the other authorities have a lot of experience."

Her quesadillas arrived and the smell of them tickled her taste buds. She could feel the man at her side eyeing them with interest. Enough interest that she felt compelled to offer, "Help yourself. There's too much for me to eat all by myself."

"Oh, I—"

"Go on," she said. "We're fellow refugees of a sort, after all."

There was another moment's hesitation, then she saw his hand reach toward the platter. She pushed half the tall stack of paper napkins that had been delivered with the food toward him.

What she didn't do was look at him again.

Never before had she found a man so attractive, Shay decided. She wasn't a nun; she'd dated and had been in a couple of longish relationships. But one-night stands were on her Not Ever list.

Living in a small tight-knit community meant that everyone knew everyone's else's business. Since Shay was the product of an extramarital affair and the father of her sister Poppy's son had hightailed it at the words *positive pregnancy test*, there was more than enough Walker tattle for people to tittle over. Shay had never been tempted to add to it with a casual hookup.

Not that the man on the next stool was in the market for a hookup with her. He could have anyone. Though he didn't wear a ring, for all she knew he was married to the most beautiful woman on the planet.

"Hey, birthday girl," the man at her side said. "You really are down in the dumps, aren't you?"

She risked a look at him. Whoa. Still unbelievably handsome. His golden gaze swept her face, dropped just briefly, then came back up to meet her eyes.

That was good, because her nipples were tingling as they tightened into hard buds just from that quick glance. With masterful effort, she resisted squirming on her seat.

He was still staring at her expectantly and she couldn't help but notice the faint white lines radiating from the corners of his eyes. Clearly he spent a lot of time outdoors squinting into the sun. They could be laugh lines, she supposed, but he didn't look like the type who succumbed to hilarity on a habitual basis.

A question, she remembered now, as he continued staring. He'd asked a question. "Um…" Clever or charming was really beyond her at this point, whether it was due to the martinis or his rampant masculinity. "I really don't like my birthday," she confessed.

"That's too bad. No good memories about it whatsoever? Not one?"

Shay's brow furrowed as she thought back. "I had a pony party when I was eight. We went out on a trail ride and at the end my dad barbecued and my mom served a cake in the shape of a horseshoe."

"Sounds like fun."

"It was." She smiled a little. "When I was thirteen I had a pajama party. My older sisters treated me and my friends to facials, manicures and cosmetic makeovers. That year, the cake was shaped like a tiara." Also fun.

"So, when did the day go from tiaras to tragedy?"

The very next year, when she was fourteen. It was the year her father died and at her birthday party one of the guests had whispered loudly to another that Shay was a bastard and her mother a whore. Though that mean girl had been summarily sent home, in that moment Shay had become very self-conscious of who she was and who she wasn't.

Not that she would tell the stranger all that. So she shrugged instead and turned the tables on him. "What about your birthdays? Pizza and laser tag? Cakes shaped like footballs or Super Mario?"

"We didn't celebrate birthdays in my house."

Shay's eyes rounded. "What?"

"My mom was gone early…I don't remember her. My father, a former Marine, was a hard man. At my house, the showers were cold, Christmas was just another day and the date of your birth was only something to put on a medical form or a job application." He said it all matter-of-factly, no shred of self-pity in his tone.

Shay stared at him a moment. Then she swiped up her martini glass and swiveled forward in her seat, unsure how to respond.

"I'm sorry." He sounded genuinely apologetic, not to mention a trifle embarrassed. "Too much information, right?"

His discomfort eased hers. She threw him a little pretend glare as she took another sip of vodka. The look was ruined by the hiccup that bounced up her throat. As she swallowed it back down, she caught sight of the corner of his mouth kicking up in that small, amused and very attractive smile of his.

She tossed another brief glare in his direction.

"Okay, Birthday Girl, what's wrong now?"

"What's wrong, he asks?" she said, shifting to face him while rolling her eyes. "I was into my four-martini, poor-me birthday routine, though still sharing my appetizer, you'll recall, when you released the air from my gloom balloon by telling me about cold showers, no Christmas and a complete lack of birthday cake."

"Gloom balloon?" He started laughing, husky and low, showing a wealth of even white teeth. The sound of it rolled over her like honey.

She was *so* over being intimidated by his good looks, she told herself as she sucked down the rest of the vodka in her glass. You could be gorgeous and built and have the world's most powerful-looking hands and the warmest surprise of a laugh, but if you'd never had birthday cake…well.

That had to be fixed immediately, she decided with half-drunken logic.

Boarder Bartender—in his own immortal words—was "down with that." Mere minutes after her whispered aside, a server came from the kitchen bearing a big hunk of chocolate cake topped with a lighted birthday candle. As the room erupted in song, Shay realized she didn't know his first name.

"Jay," he said over the loud singing. There was a bemused grin on his face. "You're crazy, you know that?"

And maybe she was. Or maybe it was the vodka. Whatever the reason, she felt reckless and carefree as they both cozied up to the bar around the piece of multilayered cake. He tried to tell her he didn't like sweets, which caused her to roll her eyes again, and him to let loose another round of that rough-warm laughter.

They dueled forks for the last bite of cake.

Jay ordered another round of quesadillas, so she had more to eat to counteract the effect of the martinis. The night wore on, the crowd around them drinking freely while Shay switched to sparkling water. From somewhere, the management dredged up a motley collection of games. It didn't surprise Shay that the king of the jungle snagged the only deck of cards for the two of them.

It was useful to have a predator at her back.

"You would have been good on the *Titanic*," she mused.

Lifting those golden eyes from the cards he was shuffling, he glanced around. "Is that what this feels like?"

Shay looked, too. In one corner, some men were

playing dominoes with ruthless concentration. In another, a group of middle-aged women, with a bouquet of now empty wine bottles working as the centerpiece for their table, launched into a rendition of Beyoncé's "Single Ladies."

"Hmm, maybe Rick's Café from *Casablanca*?" Shay suggested.

"I guess I'd rather be Bogie than the kid who turns into an ice cube." Then Jay dropped his hand to her bare knee and gave it a brief squeeze. "So…what should we play?"

Shay stared down. The large palm and long fingers covered her skin like a warm and slightly raspy blanket. The calluses were a workingman's, just as she'd guessed. Though she supposed she might still register fairly high on the tipsy scale, the alcohol hadn't desensitized her flesh. It prickled in reaction to his touch, hot chills rushing from the point of contact northward. Involuntarily, her thighs pressed together, prolonging the small thrilling ache she felt between them.

"Birthday Girl?" he called again.

Her gaze moved up to his. His golden eyes studied her face. She felt it like another touch, a fingertip, maybe, following the arch of her eyebrows and the profile of her nose. He looked lower, and her lips started to tingle, her mouth going dry inside.

Her tongue snaked out to her lower lip.

Jay jerked, his attention jumping from her face to the cards. His hand moved from her and he began dealing them out.

The sexual hum in her body did nothing to help her brain. It only muddled her thinking, which meant while she should have been edging away from him or sliding off the stool altogether and making tracks for her room, instead she leaned closer, her shoulder bumping his.

She intended it in a friendly way, but the tap became kind of a rub, and when he glanced at her there was another charged moment of energy passing between them. An exchange.

A sexual exchange.

Wow, she thought again. He was the most beautiful, masculine man she'd ever met. Her sister's fiancé, Ryan, was classic-cinema-star handsome—when you looked at him you thought you should have some popcorn on hand. Watching him breathe was pure entertainment.

With Jay, it was different. Shay wanted to watch him move. Or better yet, move things. Do things. He was a man made to operate a forklift or lay railroad ties or rig a suspension bridge.

He'd separated the cards into two piles, one of which he slid toward her. When she gathered them closer, their fingers touched. Again, Jay flinched.

The sexual spark stung her, too.

"What are we going to play?" she asked.

He gave her a grim look. "War."

Shay sighed. She could have told him it wasn't going to work. It was completely clear to her, even after chocolate cake, quesadillas and martinis.

There was no way to battle this pull between them.

And at this point, she didn't want to.

With another forbidding glance, he slapped down the first card. A deuce.

Hers was a king.

Several minutes later, when the game was over and all the cards were piled in front of Shay, she began to stack them neatly.

"Round two?" he asked. There was a tense note to his voice.

Likely because he thought they'd have to sit here all night playing cards instead of having another kind of round two…around dawn.

In her room at the inn.

They could do that, though, couldn't they?

Her heart started beating faster and she could feel her pulse thudding in her throat and at her wrists. She'd never propositioned a man before…but now she wanted to. Really wanted to, and hadn't she promised Mel she'd have fun? Glancing at the clock on the wall, she noted it was after midnight.

It truly was her birthday now. "You know, there are rooms here…" she began.

His gaze was trained on her face. She had the impression he was counting each and every one of her eyelashes. "I was told there's no vacancy," he said.

Shay's hand crept toward her purse, still hanging on the hook. From it, she pulled out the plastic key card, which she placed on the bar's surface and then slid toward the man at her right. He was turned toward her on his stool, his elbow on the bar. "I reserved the last one," she whispered.

Hesitating, she ran her gaze over his rugged shoulders, his wide chest, his powerful thighs. If she scooted closer, she'd be between his legs, surrounded by him. Closer to the clean scent that she'd been aware of for hours.

Shay cleared her throat and reminded herself she was due a present. "The bed's big enough for two."

CHAPTER TWO

JACE JENNINGS STARED down at the innocuous rectangle of plastic. Birthday Girl's fingers touched one edge, the nails short and painted with clear polish. Transparent, the same as her face.

He'd been able to read every expression flitting across it all night long.

At first, she'd been shy. She was younger than he was, by a decade, he supposed, and he'd had no intention of even engaging her in conversation. But then she'd launched into her martinis-and-birthday confession and he'd found himself drawn in...then drawn to her.

When he'd shared that bit about his childhood—and what had prompted him to do so, he couldn't say—her quasihuffy, amusing response had tickled his funny bone. Not many people managed to do that.

But Birthday Girl and her "gloom balloon"...

Shaking his head, he felt a grin tugging on the corners of his mouth again.

"You're leaving me hanging here," she said now.

He glanced up. She was beautiful. That had struck him immediately. Her shoulder-length hair was a mix of red, gold and brown. Her eyes were an arresting shade of pale blue, her skin creamy, with just a faint spray of tiny golden freckles peppering her small nose.

As a builder, he had an interest in and appreciation of the bones of things, and those of this woman were both delicate and elegant. Her mouth was lush, though, its unpainted color a pale rose.

"Well?" she demanded.

And he could read her again, the slight truculence a defensive position. "This could be a dangerous habit, Birthday Girl."

"This?"

"Propositioning total strangers."

Her mouth dropped, and she yanked the key card back toward her. "I don't—"

"Wait." He placed his fingers over hers. "That came out wrong."

She was staring down at his hand. Jace knew why. The instant they touched, heat snapped like an electrical shock, then ricocheted through his body. He supposed she felt something similar. All night, he'd been half-hard and her flesh beneath his was taking him the rest of the way.

Slowly, as if retreating from a skittish creature, Jace lifted his hand. Her gaze lifted, too, and those blue eyes zeroed in on his face.

"I don't make a habit of this kind of thing," she declared.

"I shouldn't have said that." And why the hell would he care if she propositioned a new man every night? But for some stupid reason he'd wanted to hear her say she didn't out loud. He'd wanted to know that this... connection was something unusual for her, too. Different. Special.

Because it felt damn special to him.

Holy hell, she'd bought him birthday cake.

"We don't know each other," he heard himself say, though he'd never told anyone else about those daily frigid showers. It was true. His father had believed in cold water as the cornerstone of making a man out of a boy.

"Are you married?" she asked.

"Divorced." And his ex was dead now, a recent circumstance that had wrought a huge change in his life. Just the thought of that made him toss back the rest of the whiskey that he'd switched to when the cards came out.

"Girlfriend?"

"No." He paused, then lifted a brow. "Boyfriend?"

"If I had one, wouldn't he be the one spending my birthday with me?"

Which made Jace think about what he'd been calling her. Birthday Girl. She hadn't offered up her real name. He hadn't corrected her when she misheard his as "Jay."

This beautiful young woman was really offering up no-strings, one-night-only, stranger sex.

God knows he didn't deserve it, but—

"Okay, then." Birthday Girl slid off her stool and onto her feet. He was close and turned in her direction, so she landed between his knees, and swayed there a moment. To steady herself, one hand reached out and clutched his thigh.

Uh-oh. Those martinis were still in her system.

That thought didn't stop another piercing zing of heat from rocketing from her hand to his crotch, just a few inches north. And it wasn't only her touch that got to him. There was that sweet little dress she wore that showed a whole hell of a lot of bare leg in the front, then flowed lower around the back.

"I'm going," she said, still looking a bit woozy. "It's up to you whether you come with me or not."

Jace sighed. Of course he was going with her. Whether he crossed the threshold of her room, well, first he had to make sure she got to it safely. He hopped off his own stool, feeling a twinge as his newly healed left ankle found the ground. "I'm right behind you, Birthday Girl," he said.

Actually, he took her hand, as well.

That was weird. He wasn't a toucher. When he was with a woman he didn't worry about keeping her close. But this one was tipsy, he reminded himself, and though he'd been raised by a distant and unfeeling man, in this instance he wasn't going to take after the old bastard.

Drawing her nearer, Jace could smell the sweet scent of her hair. Now *he* went a bit woozy.

"It's this way," she said, tugging him toward a steep staircase off the foyer. Judging by the architecture, the Deerpoint Inn had to be about a hundred years old. On the way inside earlier that night, he'd glanced at the framed magazine article about the place that hung on the entry wall. The building had started life as a boardinghouse for area loggers. Now they'd converted the original fifteen rooms upstairs to just six, each with its own bath.

Birthday Girl would have a comfortable night.

She wobbled on her heels as she mounted the first step, causing him to drop her hand and grasp her hips instead. Birthday Girl would have a comfortable night if she could make it to her door.

Jace, on the other hand, had a very uncomfortable few minutes as he was forced to watch the bunch of muscles in each fine ass cheek as she continued upward. He breathed easier when they made the narrow hallway. It smelled of old wood and roses.

With his fingertips hovering a quarter inch off the small of her back, Jace followed her to a door bearing a brass 6. He took the key card from her hand and inserted it in the slot. The mechanism flashed green and he heard a small *snick*. He turned the knob and checked out the environs over her shoulder, the room illuminated by lamps at each end of a long table centered beneath a narrow window. Papered walls, dark wood floor covered with a thick area rug with a floral design. A nightlight gave him the glimpse of a tiled bathroom through a half-open interior door.

Birthday Girl stepped inside.

Jace realized it was now or never.

Hell, she was beautiful. Alluring. Tempting.

But…

He had a pile of regrets on his plate and using the circumstances—birthday, flames, liquor, lust—to get a quickie shag out of this pretty young thing would be just another black mark on his soul. In the morning, he didn't want to be something she was sorry for.

There'd been enough of that in his life. From his father, his ex and, most likely, his daughter.

Her head tilted, and the room's light caught the warm fire in her hair. "Well?"

He couldn't help but lean toward her. She took a half step, getting closer, and then her eyes closed as she offered up her mouth.

Jace's cock turned to steel at the anticipation of a kiss written all over her face.

She was more than halfway drunk, he reminded himself.

Too young for him.

Too sweet.

And yet…

She was too appealing not to touch one more time. He pressed the pad of his thumb to her lips—God, so soft and lush—and whispered in her ear. "Many happy returns."

Then he strode away, cursing himself, the constricting denim of his jeans and his suddenly discovered streak of decency.

Downstairs, the management was trying to make the refugees comfortable in the dining room. Jace opted for his SUV instead, reclining the seat and trying to get comfortable on the stiff leather. By leaving that lovely offer of a night with Birthday Girl on the table, at least his conscience couldn't nag him, he decided.

Except that it could, of course.

There was still the small matter of his daughter to consider. She was mere miles away, at his house situated on the shores of Blue Arrow Lake. Though he hadn't seen her in a decade, Jace wasn't as frustrated as he should have been that their meeting was postponed for another day. Truth to tell, he was grateful for the reprieve.

A lousy night's sleep seemed a fitting punishment for that.

At first light, when he smelled coffee emanating from the inn, he climbed from his car. His muscles were stiff and he limped inside, his left foot not long out of its soft cast and not yet completely normal. His head ached, too—though not like it had after the debilitating concussion he'd suffered that had made focusing on paper or screen or even spoken words sometimes impossible—and reminded him he'd downed plenty of beer and whiskey the night before.

He wondered how Birthday Girl was faring.

And then he saw her, the back of her anyway, sitting on the same stool she'd occupied yesterday evening. She was dressed in jeans this time, but her auburn hair was unmistakable. Jace paused, uncertain how to proceed. He looked for an open spot at one of the tables in the restaurant, but it wasn't a big space and some of the patrons were still sleeping, stretched on two chairs.

The only seat free was the one beside her. Why not take it? He'd done the noble thing, hadn't he? It would have been much more awkward to wake up on the neighboring pillow, after all.

As he approached, his gaze caught that of the bartender's. He signaled the need for java by miming a mug to his mouth and then he slid into the empty place beside Birthday Girl.

Though she didn't glance his way, her body stiffened.

Jace hesitated again, his gaze focused on the gleaming wood grain in front of him. Good manners dictated he should at least look at her, not to mention express a friendly "good morning." But during the course of the night in the SUV, he'd begun to rethink the hours they'd spent sitting together and the unprecedented appeal she'd had for him.

It was just some birthday cake and card games, he'd told himself and the moon, its beam shining through the windshield. Too much booze. In the light of day, she probably wouldn't be as pretty as he'd thought.

The intense attraction was likely overblown in his mind as well, Jace had decided then. And…

And for some reason right now he didn't want confirmation of that.

Stop being ridiculous. Just get out a greeting and let reality assert itself. "Good morning," he finally said, sliding a look at her.

Her face turned toward him. Icy-blue eyes. A faint flush obscuring the tiny freckles on her nose and edging her fabulous cheekbones with a delicate pink. Her rosy lips pursed. "Really?" she said, her voice frosty.

Okay.

Okay, fine.

The booze, the fire and the cake had not caused him to exaggerate anything. She was just as beautiful as he remembered.

Just as sexy.

She made him just as hard.

But the disdainful expression on her face communicated clearly that she was no longer as sweetly dispositioned as she'd been before he'd rejected her generous offer and left her with only the touch of his thumb at the door. He winced. "Birthday Girl—"

She slid from her stool and, with her coffee in hand, stalked off. He stared at the insulted line of her spine and the angry sway of her hips. Oh, yeah. She still made him hard. Very hard.

Jace sighed, shifting on his stool to adjust the fit of his jeans. Damn.

And he'd thought taking her to bed would result in regret. Instead, he'd learned that being a good guy left him feeling no more satisfied than being a bad one.

HALF HORRIFIED AND half humiliated, Shay escaped toward the stairs that would take her to her room. She glanced back at the bar and saw Jay still in place, his head turned to watch her go.

Another wash of heat rose up her neck and burned her cheeks. In the morning light he wasn't any less masculine. Still had that charisma in spades, too. She could feel the pull even from here, as if he'd lassoed her waist and was steadily drawing on a rope held between his big capable hands.

The hands she'd wanted on her last night.

But he'd refused her.

Whipping her head around, she stomped up the steps. Until she was free to head back to Blue Arrow, she'd hide out between the four walls of her room at the inn. Inside, she flipped on the television and found the channel offering fire coverage. At the bar, she'd learned the road closures were still in place, but there could be better news at any moment...

Ten hours later, nothing had changed.

Not her confined circumstances, not her humiliation over last night's rejected overture.

She bounced on the mattress, she punched a pillow, she flung her body across the bed and hung her head over the side. The actions didn't alter the news on the television—but they did serve to underline her restlessness. If she didn't get out of this room—soon—she'd go stir-crazy.

But *he* might still be downstairs. The jerk.

Several times between last night and this afternoon she'd replayed their moments together: her nervous chatter, his birthday cake, the card battle. Too bad the hangover she'd been suffering from hadn't obliterated her memory. For hours, she'd had a dry mouth and an aching head, as well as instant recall of his amused smile at her half-drunken ramblings, the heat in his gaze as he'd stared down at her before his "many happy returns," his calloused touch against her upturned mouth.

Without thinking, she pressed her fingertips there. It was as if a brand still pulsed on her lips.

Damn man. He'd walked away from a tipsy stranger and likely considered himself the hero in the scenario.

Jerk.

Her conscience tried to reason with her ire—in truth, wasn't it actually a decent-guy move?—but she shut down that part of her brain. It was her birthday and a girl should get a pass on logic for at least one twenty-four-hour period a year.

Still, she had to get some fresh air. In her jeans, a simple T-shirt and a pair of sneakers, she crept down the stairs, a bottle of water in hand. The bar and dining room held a scatter of refugees, but no Jay. On a sigh of relief, she pushed open the front door and set out along the quiet streets of the tiny hamlet surrounding the Deerpoint Inn. While she'd never been to the town, which was little more than a crossroads, she'd seen enough of the fire coverage to have gained a general sense of direction. She took every turn uphill and hiked along the narrow roads while committing her route to memory.

Though she didn't actually venture far, she was moving steadily upward, surprising chipmunks and squirrels who skittered across the asphalt to ascend the trunks of the towering conifers lining the road. Black ravens sailed among the top limbs while blue jays flitted at the lower levels. If she wasn't used to elevations that were over five thousand feet, she might be laboring for air. As it was, she appreciated the cool breeze on her sweat-dampened skin and welcomed the chance to pause when she came to a break in the trees that offered a glorious view.

From here, there was no sign of fire. The wind must be carrying the scent of it away, too. And spread out before her were miles of craggy pine-covered peaks and a slice of blue that signaled one of the many local lakes in the distance. She breathed in double lungfuls of the air that was just starting to come down from its afternoon high temperature. It had probably been seventy-five at some point today.

Already she felt calmer, she thought, as she took in more fresh oxygen. She might not have true Walker blood in her veins, but the mountains were still her place. The foundation beneath her feet.

A twig snapped, the sound loud enough to make her whirl and her heart jump to her throat. She put her hand there as she stared at the man who last night and this morning had been seated on the neighboring stool. "You," she managed to choke out. "Did you follow me?"

Jay held up both hands. "Not exactly. I wanted to stretch my legs. I thought by trailing you I could have a guide of sorts."

"Unwilling guide," Shay muttered under her breath.

"Yeah. Sorry." He paused to suck in air, then half turned. "I'll go."

"Wait." Narrowing her eyes, Shay took a closer look at him. His breath was more ragged than it should be for such a fit man. Altitude, she thought. Clearly, it was getting to him. Stifling a sigh, she held out her unopened bottle of water. "You need a drink."

He inhaled sharply again. "I think that's where one or both of us went wrong yesterday."

Ignoring that comment, she stepped closer. "Seriously," she told him. "You need water. You're feeling the effects of the elevation."

He took the proffered bottle but his expression was dubious. "It wasn't that long a walk."

"We're near seven thousand feet here. Where you came from…?"

"Sea level."

She nodded. Beach. His tan already announced it. Glancing around, she saw a fallen log a few feet away and gestured to it. "Sit down. Drink. Rest a little."

He didn't look happy as he followed her direction.

Shay shook her head, reading his mood. "Don't worry. Your macho will bounce right back once you descend a few hundred feet."

"I don't know," he grumbled. "Last night I lost at War. Now this."

His disgruntled tone made her almost smile. "I'm lousy at gin rummy," she said. "If we played that it would shore up your ego in an instant."

He glanced over as he settled on the log and stretched out his long legs. "You're offering another round of cards? Thought you were mad at me."

Shay shoved her hands in her pockets. She *was* mad at him—except when her conscience reminded her that he'd done the more honorable thing by refusing her. She'd been under the influence of birthday and booze.

Now that she thought about it, she and her half-tipsy offer had probably been less than flattering—and she had maybe been not all that alluring. *Great.* The pulsing sexual energy she'd sensed was likely a one-sided figment of her own inebriated imagination. "Can we forget about that?"

His eyes on her, he took a long swallow of the bottle, then lowered the plastic. "I probably can't forget a moment of it," he admitted.

Heat crawled up Shay's neck and she looked down. Okay, so not one-sided? "Um…"

"And I also can't help thinking it would have been damn good," the man continued.

The words had her gaze leaping back to him. She stared at his face and into his golden eyes as the sexual attraction spun between them again, the line of it thrumming with energy. She could feel the heated effect of it in her chest, in her belly. Lower.

With a wrench, she cut the connection and turned away, to once again take in the view. *Say something*, she thought. *Something inconsequential. Something to cool this down.* She was sober now, and this wasn't a safe or sane sensation.

"So…" Shay swallowed. "What is it you do at sea level?"

"Construction, mostly."

Of course. Just as she'd figured. He was a man made to wear low-slung carpenter bags.

"Yourself?" he asked.

"This and that. I'm mountain-born and-bred. Lots of us have to do a variety of jobs in order to meet the alpine-resort prices." This was all true. The schools in the area were small and though she had a credential, a teaching job had yet to open up. So she kept herself busy—and paid her bills—by tutoring and running some college test prep boot camps. Sometimes she helped out with her sister Mac's maid service. The temporary live-in tutor job she'd scored until summer's end was kind of a combination of all three.

Redirecting her gaze to the northeast, she thought about her sister Poppy's pet project. "And my family has a tract of land and some cabins we're refurbishing there. We're hoping to create a quiet and very exclusive retreat for people who want to get away from it all."

It wasn't clear whether the idea would come to fruition, though. Her brother and Mac were still unconvinced, claiming to hold on to the outlandish idea that the property was cursed. Shay was on Poppy's side, but as the non-Walker Walker, she kept quiet about her wishes on the subject. Because that outside-the-circle feeling was impossible to leave behind. The whispers she'd first heard on her fourteenth birthday had rooted deep in her heart and it didn't help when to this day she caught old-timers going over the old gossip.

Behind her, she sensed Jay rising. "Well," he said, "I guess I'll head back."

She swung around, risking another glance his way. "Are you going to be—"

"I'm better now. Fine."

Looking him over, she decided on a small suppressed sigh that yeah, he was fine. Very fine. Tall, broad, all heavy muscles and long bones that came together in one package that just…just hit her someplace deep. Someplace…private. "Goodbye," she said softly as he moved onto the road.

One stride away from her. Two.

Suddenly, he turned back. "Let me buy you dinner."

Her heart jerked at the command in his voice. "I—"

"You owe me that game of gin rummy, remember? My macho needs shoring up. You said it yourself."

She couldn't help but roll her eyes. He was at least

six feet four inches of hot-blooded male, elevation effects or no. "I don't think—"

"It's still your birthday. We'll have more cake."

Oh, there was that pull again. Her mouth was curving upward and inside she felt a dangerous fever jacking up her temperature and overriding her good sense. "And fewer martinis?"

"Whatever you want."

Shay sucked in a breath, remembering what she'd wanted last night. What she'd offered, and how he'd rejected her. How low that had brought her.

Now, though, with him looking at her with those warm golden eyes, she felt light, free, like a kite that could soar over the mountaintops and float through the blue, blue sky.

Then the expression in his eyes became more intent as his gaze roamed her face. She was no kite, now, but a woman, sexy and beautiful.

Rubbing her damp palms against the side of her jeans, she moved toward him, unable to do anything but. "All right," she said. "Dinner."

Upon their return, they made arrangements to meet in the grill in an hour. Though he still didn't have a room, the inn had opened up an employee area where the refugees could wash up. Shay took a quick shower then appraised her outfit choices. It was a replay of the jeans or a repeat of last night's dress. And while she knew it would be wiser to stay casual—and more fully covered—she put on the filmy garment anyway.

When she took the stairs to the restaurant and turned the corner to see him waiting at a secluded corner table, she was glad she'd changed. He was in slacks and a dress shirt, an expensive watch strapped around one strong wrist. He looked confident and successful and when he lifted his gaze to her, once again she felt lit up inside.

While still trembling, just a little, on the outside.

He stood as she approached, his mouth curved in an assuring smile that nonetheless delivered a jolt of nervous anticipation. Surely she'd never felt this dichotomy around a man before. There was a familiarity about him—as if he were someone she recognized—that was at odds with her wary response to the immense attraction he held for her. He pulled out her chair and touched the small of her back to direct her into the seat. It sent a flurry of chills up her spine that tumbled down the front of her in a hot wave.

For a full five seconds, she couldn't breathe.

There were no martinis. Nor birthday cake or gin rummy. Instead they shared a bottle of wine with an appetizer platter that was a delicious mélange of carmelized Brussels sprouts topped with shavings of a tangy, salty parmesan cheese. Then it was two dinners of seared halibut, rice pilaf and crunchy steamed vegetables.

They didn't talk of anything consequential, including themselves. At one point he said he was on the verge of asking her name—but that "Birthday Girl" had kind of grown on him. So she didn't say a word about it. Instead, they made up stories about their fellow refugees. That man in the opposite corner was an antler chandelier salesman, Jay proposed: he sold them off the rack.

The grandmotherly woman at the bar was a Mafia boss's wife on the lam for offering counterfeit knitting patterns on the internet. Shay added, she'd bought herself a skein of trouble.

Finally it was getting late and the tables were cleared and those patrons without rooms were collecting blankets and arranging themselves for the night. When someone took the extra chairs at their table in order to create a makeshift bed, Jay cleared his throat. "I guess it's time to turn in."

During dinner, he'd told Shay he'd spent the night before in his car. She cleared her throat, too. "You know…"

"I know what?"

Her fingertip made an aimless pattern on the tablecloth. She pretended it fascinated her. "The bed upstairs is king-size."

Silence welled between them when she didn't say any more.

Then Jay broke the quiet. "Birthday Girl," he said, his voice low. "Can you look at me?"

Of course she could. It was easy, because he still really didn't know her—not even her name. But it took a couple of seconds before she managed to comply. His golden eyes studied her, but she couldn't read the expression in them.

Her face heated as she forced herself to continue meeting his gaze. "I'm saying we could just share it… you know, sleep," she clarified. "Nothing more than that."

He reached over and captured her wandering finger, then took her whole hand in his. His thumb, that work-roughened thumb that had pressed against her mouth the night before, rasped over her knuckles, back and forth, making the journey down the shallow valleys and up the low hills slow and hypnotic.

Shay felt the touch everywhere. Feathering along the

groove of her spine, ghosting over her tight, tingling nipples, teasing the tender insides of her thighs. Her body was melting, and if something didn't happen soon he'd have to scoop her out of the chair with a spoon.

"Jay," she whispered. It almost sounded like a whimper.

"We could try sleeping, I suppose," he mused. "But we should probably be realistic about our chances of 'nothing more.'"

Who wanted to be realistic? Who wanted to calculate odds? Not Shay. She only wanted *him* and this time, this time out of her normal world, her usual ordered, good-girl, scandal-averse existence.

Rising to her feet, she turned her hand to clasp his. To tug him up, too. "Let's go to my room."

It was near dark inside the space that seemed dominated by the bed. The only illumination came from the glow of the night-light in the attached bathroom. They halted just inside the entry door and Jay cupped her face in his warm hand before lowering his head.

At the touch of his mouth, she jerked, her body moving into his of its own accord. His other arm curled about her hips, keeping her against him and the hardness that pressed into her belly.

She shivered, and he murmured something soothing as his lips feathered over her cheek, down her neck, before returning to her mouth. This time, the kiss went from gentle to greedy. Shay made a low sound in her throat and stood on tiptoe to get closer to him.

He made an approving noise and then swung her into his arms and strode with her to the bed.

What happened next was hot and sweet. He was a tender lover, and gentle, despite the size of his hands and the strength of his body. She supposed he was holding back—a man like him would have ravenous appetites, yes?—but that was all right with Shay, because she was holding back, too.

It felt as if they were encased in a fantasy and she didn't want to pop its soap-bubble exterior by holding too tight or crying out too loud. With slow, patient touches, he rolled her up and over the orgasm, and when he followed, he buried his face in her neck, his big body shaking against hers.

They drifted to sleep without words.

In the gray light of early morning, they came awake to the sound of car engines revving. Shay gathered the covers close around her shoulders as his eyes opened and he looked at her from the other pillow. "Sounds like the roads have reopened," she said, her voice quiet.

He ran a hand through his hair, and she remembered the cool, thick softness of it as she'd held his head to her breast the night before. Her nipples sprang to life against the cotton sheet and her face heated, but she didn't make a move and hoped he didn't sense her kindling desire.

Their time out of time was over.

He sat up, the sheet pooling at his hips. Through the screen of her lashes, she ran her gaze over the ripples of his chest and abs and stifled a sigh. She'd had her night with all that muscle and skin. It was time to let it go.

Let him go.

He took a shower and while he was occupied she rose from bed and wrapped herself in her robe. When he emerged fully dressed from the bathroom, she was standing at the window, staring into the street and the cars that were cruising by.

The world moving again. Moving on.

He stood close behind her, not touching. "Well," he said. "Thanks for sharing your evening with me."

"You're welcome." Shay refused to let herself look at his handsome face.

"And your bed," Jay went on. "I think I owe you for sharing that with me, too."

Melancholy tried tugging at her, but Shay refused to give in to its grasp. "Maybe someday I'll demand payment," she said, keeping her voice light. "Have you lift a hammer or something at our family cabins."

"Sure," he said, then he swept her hair off the back of her neck and pressed his lips there in an obvious farewell. "You name the time, Birthday Girl."

The nickname, of course, just underscored how that would never happen. They didn't have any way to make further contact. He had no idea who she really was. She considered changing that. One side of her wanted to grab a pen and write her name and number on that wide, calloused palm of his. The other side of her, the wary side that didn't trust easily, hesitated. And while she was arguing with herself, he left the room.

Like that, it was decided. By him, who hadn't pushed to know any more about her.

She made her own decision as she heard the quiet click of the door swinging back after he exited. Not regretting a moment of what they'd shared. Her neck still tingled where he'd placed that goodbye kiss. The memories of their singular attraction and single night together would last a long, long time.

It might have been her best birthday gift ever.

CHAPTER THREE

SHAY TOOK THE highway turnoff that led to the family land and traveled the four miles of private road, all the while pushing the Deerpoint Inn adventure into the far recesses of her mind. It was time to go back to normal, become the unruffled, circumspect woman who mostly kept to herself—and who held her fears and dreams close to the chest, too. A precocious and sometimes impossible fifteen-year-old was under her care and Shay needed a calm temperament to do her best for the girl.

Maybe she'd done something out-of-character on her birthday, something self-indulgent and possibly a little reckless, but it was over now. In the very short period of their acquaintance, Jay couldn't have made any permanent change to her.

Pressing her foot to the accelerator, her car climbed the steep drive that led to the cabins. Her sister Poppy had exchanged her battered SUV for another in decent shape—at the insistence of her fiancé, Ryan—and it was parked near a cluster of five cabins. Shay braked beside it.

Climbing from her vehicle, she took in the view. The last time she'd been out here had been weeks ago, just as winter was giving way to spring, when the snow was melting on the ground around the dwellings, but still abundant on the tree-free slopes rising above them. It was the last of the property held by the Walkers that had been secured one hundred and fifty years before, when the pioneering men and women came to the area in search of timber to harvest. In recent times, before the fire that took out the chairs, lifts and lodge, the family had run a small but popular ski resort.

While the snow was completely gone now, the cabins didn't look much different than in March. They were run-down, with dirty windows and sagging porches. Shay assumed the seven she couldn't see, those nestled in the surrounding woods, weren't in any better shape. Still, she smiled as her sister emerged from the closest bungalow. Poppy and her five-year-old son, Mason, had lived there until a torrential rainstorm had destroyed part of its roof and sent her into the arms of the man she was now promised to marry.

"Hey," Poppy said, the smile that, of late, seemed to reside permanently on her face brightening a few more degrees as she caught sight of Shay. Her honey-and-brown hair hung around her shoulders and she slipped dark glasses over her gray eyes as she stepped into the sun. "You made it."

Shay nodded. "Once the roads reopened I left as quick as I could."

"Did you get my Happy Birthday text?" her sister asked as she came closer. Then she hesitated, tipping up her shades to send Shay a sharp look. "What's happened?"

"Happened?" She hoped guilt—and why should she feel guilty about a single night of commitment-free passion?—wouldn't show on her face like a blush. "I don't know what you're talking about."

"You look different," her sister said, now nearly toe-to-toe with her.

Shay shuffled back. "How was the premiere?"

"We talked to you on the phone about that," her sister reminded her.

"Yes, but I only heard about it from Mason's little-dude, naturally hyperbolic point of view. How's London?"

Poppy propped her glasses on top of her head, an appraising light in her eyes. "Let's see. She was Memphis the first day, Raleigh the next. Today she's Omaha."

Meaning she was much the same. The teen had taken a keen dislike to her first name and Shay had indulged her request to try out different city names as alternatives, telling herself it was good geography practice. Not to mention she would be heeding the old adage about choosing one's battles. "Where is…Omaha, did you say?"

"She and Mason are exploring the woods."

Shay looked over her shoulder to peer in the direction of the close-growing trees. Pines and oaks and dogwoods covered the landscape surrounding the cabins. As a girl, she'd loved to hike among them herself. Until the fire thirteen years before. A shiver rolled down her spine and she rubbed her hands over her suddenly cold arms. She still had ugly dreams about that day.

"Shay, what's wrong?" Poppy demanded.

"Not a thing," she lied. "What's been going on around here?"

With a grimace, Poppy glanced about the clearing. "Maybe now that we have decent weather, I can make some real progress."

"That's got to be a little tough, what with you being busy with your fancy Hollywood fiancé."

"Ryan realizes how important this is to me."

"And Ryan loves you so much he'll do whatever it takes to make you happy."

"I know." Poppy smiled, clearly delighted that Shay had noticed. "But I want to do what makes him happy, too, which means a lot of shuffling between here and LA, so I can't work on the cabins as much as I might like."

"You're not the only Walker able to wield tools."

Poppy's mouth turned down. "The three of you aren't enthusiastic tool-wielders when it comes to this place."

"I…" Shay hesitated. Poppy had good reason to believe that. When Mac and Brett had put down their sister's idea to tackle the decrepit cabins and make them into something good, Shay had stayed on the sidelines, aware it wasn't a legacy that came to her through DNA.

Poppy's eyes narrowed again. "You…?"

For some reason, the truth spilled out. "I do like it here. Love it. I always have." But she'd always felt the destruction of the resort was partly her fault. "Seeing it come alive again…if your father was still here it would make him so happy."

"*Our* father," Poppy corrected. "But are you serious? You'd stand with me in the face of Brett and Mac's opposition?"

"They're persuadable, I think," Shay said.

A small smile curved Poppy's lips. "So if you explained to them it's as important to you as it is to me— is it really?"

Even though she knew the land wasn't her birth-

right, Shay couldn't refuse her sister again. She nodded. "Really."

Poppy swooped in for a fierce hug. "Thank you.
Thank you!" She pushed Shay away, her fingers still
curled around her biceps. "See? That wasn't so hard.
Telling the truth. Saying what you want."

Shay couldn't resist returning her sister's sunny
smile. "I guess not."

Poppy's grip tightened. "All right, then. Spill the
rest."

"Spill?"

"You have another secret. What happened on your
birthday? What happened to you at that inn? Something
did. I can see it."

Another guilty flush heated Shay's skin. "Noth—"

Her denial was interrupted by a young boy's shout.
Mason came rushing out of the woods and into the
clearing, his hair disheveled and his hands clutching a
ragged collection of weeds. "Flowers!" he said, shoving them at his mother. "I brought you flowers, just
like Duke."

"Duke" was his name for Poppy's groom-to-be. London, aka Omaha, sidled up behind him. "Mace," she
said, "I told you not to squeeze them so tight."

Shay looked over at her charge. She wore her usual
black jeans, a black T-shirt and black high-top sneakers. Her hair was dyed black and she wore such thick
black liner and mascara that just looking at her could
make Shay's own eyes itch. There didn't seem to be one
soft thing about the girl…except for the gentle way she
treated Poppy's son.

If only for that, she would have been endeared to

Shay forever. But London/Omaha had other qualities, too. Her parents had divorced when she was small and she'd lived with her mother in Europe. From what Shay had gleaned, the woman had put little time into parenting, and the teen had largely raised herself with the aid of household help.

Now her mother was dead and her father absent from the scene. Yet the fifteen-year-old was keeping it together, despite the dark wardrobe. Shay had to imagine London felt alone. But Shay understood loners because of her own outsider feelings, and so tried to give the girl space, as well as boundaries. Companionship when the teen would tolerate it.

The girl tousled Mason's hair, the smallest of smiles tipping up the corners of her lips. Yes, London was a survivor, and Shay had to admire that, too.

"Did you have a good time?" she asked her now.

Her mask of boredom resettled firmly in place. "Sure."

"Are you ready to go home?"

"Whatever." But the world-weary facade again slipped a little as they said their goodbyes. Mason was impossible to ignore when he gifted her with a ferocious little-boy hug, and she again ruffled his hair while expressing polite thanks to Poppy.

The four drifted toward Shay's car. As London stowed her belongings and then climbed into the passenger seat, Poppy stayed by the driver's side. "We need to have lunch," she said through Shay's window.

"To discuss the cabins?"

Poppy shook her head. "To discuss *you*. Something's different about you."

Buckling her seat belt gave her an excuse to avoid

her sister's comment, and soon she had the car turned in the direction of Blue Arrow Lake. Her sigh of relief was lost in the hum of the car engine and for the first time she actually appreciated her teen charge's usual dour silence.

So she was completely gobsmacked when the girl shifted in her seat and willingly addressed Shay for maybe the first time ever. "Yeah," she said. "What happened to you? Something's changed."

SHAY AVOIDED THE teen's question by employing a trick she'd learned from her mother: she pretended she didn't hear it. Lorna Walker had used that ploy often and it was easy to understand why. What with four children, a spouse who'd wandered away and then wandered back, and a daughter conceived in scandal, Shay's mom had likely been often plagued with uncomfortable—or just plain nosy—queries.

Luckily, London didn't seem interested in bestirring herself to insist on an answer, so the ride home continued in silence. It gave Shay time to think over their upcoming schedule. After a couple of eventful days that had relaxed their usual routine, it was time to get back to normal.

Soon they were passing through the small town of Blue Arrow Lake, with its European village atmosphere that drew tourists up the hill from the big Southern California cities in the valleys and the beaches below. Small shops, boutiques and bistros catered to a crowd with money to burn on fine cheeses, fancy wines and casual, yet chic, designer apparel. The businesses appeared to be busy, even midweek, though on Saturday and Sunday they would be packed when the owners of the mansions surrounding the lake visited their vacation homes at the end of the workweek.

Blue Arrow Lake was a private body of water, and only those who owned the exorbitantly priced frontage properties were allowed docks. As they left the town behind and turned into the estate-lined narrow streets, she caught glimpses of deep blue water and the occasional powerboat or sailboat cutting across the surface. No one walked the streets. They didn't encounter another car.

Still, Shay couldn't help her recurring fancy from popping up, the one that revolved around London's absent father. She'd never spoken with the man. After the death of his ex-wife, he'd apparently turned over his daughter's care—temporarily, she was told, while he finished up some business in the faraway country of Qatar—to a factotum in his company. The aforesaid factotum, one dry and gray Leonard Case, had interviewed Shay via Skype. Then, he'd brought the stoic teen and her plethora of belongings to the cavernous mansion where Shay had met the two in person.

Leonard Case had lasted forty minutes before he returned to wherever he'd come from.

Ever since that day, she'd imagined herself running into her employer, Jace Jennings, accidentally. Not that she'd ever admit it to anyone, but she'd drummed up this idea that it would happen like governess Jane Eyre coming across her as-yet-unknown Mr. Rochester when he and his horse fell on an icy causeway almost at her feet. Of course, now wasn't the time of year for frosty conditions, and the entire idea was beyond ridiculous, but still Shay couldn't help herself from keeping a lookout for a frowning, rough-looking traveler.

There was no sign of anyone, of course.

And the house they now approached was no Gothic Thornfield Hall.

Instead it was a massive modern two-story, all steel and glass, with two walls made entirely of windows and a sleek deck that wrapped the entire structure. The prow of it jutted toward the lake, giving the impression of a ship preparing to set sail on the water.

It was butt ugly.

There wasn't a homey touch about the place.

As they came to a stop in the drive, London sighed, as if she were thinking the same thing. They both pulled their belongings from the backseat. As the teen hitched the strap of her laptop bag over her shoulder, Shay felt another ping of guilt. Not over her brief fling this time, but because she'd left her own computer behind at the house while on her birthday adventure. Not once had she thought about finding a way to check her email. What if Jace Jennings had responded to one of her reports about his daughter at last?

Though that seemed highly unlikely.

Since taking over London's care, she'd delivered weekly missives to the email address provided by his factotum. At first they'd been news-filled and professional—the topics they'd covered during school hours, his daughter's excellent progress on catching up to grade-level standards— but at his continued silence she'd begun writing more and more outrageous things in order to provoke a response.

I've decided to replace our trigonometry lessons with tango instruction.

Yesterday, we studied literature by reading *Celeb!* magazine from cover to cover.

Our chemistry field trip was a trek to the local chocolate factory.

So far, no reply.

Inside the house, together they mounted the stairs to their separate bedrooms. "It's your turn to dust," Shay reminded the girl, noting the sparkling motes dancing in the sunshine streaming through the windows.

London paused and turned her head, her black-lined eyes narrowing. "I dusted last time."

"Nope," Shay said, her voice cheery. "That was me. Of course, if you'd prefer to vacuum—"

"God, no," London said, and stomped off, each heavy footstep communicating her mood.

Shay let it roll off her back. "Before dinner, all right?"

There was a mumbled answer.

When they'd first moved in, the factotum had said he'd arranged for a weekly housekeeping service. She'd told him not to bother. Cleaning up after oneself was its own lesson, and she'd guessed correctly that it was a lesson the teen had yet to learn. So they split the chores and Shay was unmoved by the eye rolling, the grumbles and the can't-I-do-it-tomorrow? pleading. Lately, she'd even caught a small smile of satisfaction on London's face at a well-swept floor or a lemon-wax-polished table.

Inside her bedroom, she caught a whiff of that pleasant scent. It was a large room, with views that overlooked the lake. The four-poster bed was modern in design, but its stark lines were softened by a white lace-edged duvet she'd brought from home. On the cube table beside the bed sat a photo of the Walkers, from when both her mother and Dell Walker had been alive. Shay paused to scrutinize it now. She often did, looking for similarities between her and her siblings, and her and her mother. Shay's hair color was different from everyone else's in the family, and she'd always assumed she'd gotten it from the man who'd made her mother pregnant.

The one who'd never bothered to reach out to Shay.

She'd never reached out to him, either. Not even with an innocuous email, let alone an outrageous one.

I've decided to replace our trigonometry lessons with tango instruction.

Remembering that, Shay glanced toward her laptop. Out of obligation more than expectation, she turned it on and clicked to her email program. New posts popped up and she ran her gaze down the listing. Something from a high school friend. Another sent to her by an acquaintance she'd made on the homeschool message board she visited. And then her eyes caught on a brand-new sender: JJennings.

Her finger jerked on the mousepad; she blinked, then she clicked to open the email. *Oh. My. God.*

Shay dashed from the room. "London," she yelled, forgetting the name of the day. "We have an emergency."

The girl took her sweet time to saunter to her doorway. "What? Is this about my paper on *Romeo and Juliet*? I know it was a little trite to compare and contrast the play with that Taylor Swift song—"

"Your father is due to arrive here today."

London's insouciance shattered like a glass hitting the floor. Her jaw fell, too. "What?"

"Anytime now. Well, he didn't give a time, so who knows when?" Shay forked her fingers through her hair. "Or maybe he came by already and we missed him. Do you think he came by when we weren't here?"

She was aware she was babbling and that the teen was staring, but Shay couldn't help her jangling nerves and the acute, uncomfortable awareness of those emails she'd been sending.

I've decided to replace our trigonometry lessons with tango instruction.

Yesterday, we studied literature by reading *Celeb!* magazine from cover to cover.

Our chemistry field trip was a trek to the local chocolate factory.

Crap. What had she been thinking?

And a little voice answered: *you were thinking about how your own biological dad ignored you and how you don't want that for London.*

Erasing the thought from her head, she sprang into action. "Dust, okay?" she said on the way to the closet where the vacuum accessories were stored.

Then she went to work. It took a few minutes to notice that London wasn't actually doing her share, but was instead watching Shay flit about. She turned to the girl. "Hop to it. Please."

"Give me a good reason I should try to impress him."

Shay could see her point, she really could, since the

man had been out of London's life for years. "Because the care of the house is a reflection on me," she said. "Your father signs my check so *I* want to make a good impression."

The appeal seemed to work. The human-sized crow pushed away from the wall she was leaning upon and did the cleaning without further complaint. Finally, they were both done with their half of the chores and both looked disheveled, with mussed hair and pink cheeks. Shay caught sight of their dual reflections in the hall mirror. Their eyes met in the glass.

"Showers," they said together.

But before they could repair to separate bathrooms, the doorbell rang.

Really, Shay thought, as her stomach and her heart jumped, *I shouldn't have made that crack about the tango.* Her inner organs seemed to be doing the dance themselves.

London stared at an unmoving Shay, the panic in her eyes warring with the blank expression she was trying to keep on her face. "Aren't you going to answer the door?" she whispered.

"Of course." Shay smoothed her palms over her hair, then over the sides of her jeans. As she stepped toward the entry, she licked her dry lips. "It might not even be him," she reminded the girl.

As a precautionary measure, she peeped through one of the porthole-styled windows that flanked the front door. Her whole body froze.

"Well?" London said.

Shay couldn't make a sound. How had he found her? Why was he here?

It was Jay on the front step, his attention focused on the door.

Gladness, as bright as sunlight and as buoyant as a pop song, poured through her. He'd come after her! The happy feeling was accompanied by the same kind of relief one felt upon waking from a bad dream to discover the test hadn't been failed or the tumble from the steps had been averted.

She wasn't the only one who wanted more time together.

Could that be true? Did she really want to see him again? It didn't seem right to yearn for someone after a mere handful of hours and a one-night stand.

But she remembered his guiding touch as he directed her into her chair at the restaurant table, a gentleman's move that had nearly brought her to her knees. Then there was the way his calloused hands had brushed her naked shoulders as he'd removed her dress in the dark bedroom. She remembered his golden eyes laughing at her in the candlelight and the tickle of his thick lashes as they fluttered against her skin while he kissed her throat when they lay together on the bed.

"Aren't you going to let him in?" London demanded.

She already had, Shay thought, her mind whirling. She'd let him into her body precisely because she'd never expected to set eyes on him again—and yet she was thrilled to find him here.

London muttered something, then brushed past Shay to open the door herself. She flung it wide, and Shay's heart jolted again, every instinct wanting to shout out: *go slow! Be careful! Protect yourself!*

Then there was no barrier between the three of them. Shay was still formulating the right question to ask the man who was staring at both her and the teen. Which came first? Was it *Why did you track me down?* or *What do you want from me?*

Then, as his gaze shifted between her and her charge, once, twice, a horrible, dreadful thought struck.

No. No, it couldn't be.

It was London who spoke Shay's fear. "Well, well, well," she said, her flat voice expressing neither happiness nor hostility. "You must be dear old dad."

CHAPTER FOUR

FOR A MOMENT, Jace thought he'd fallen, as he had weeks before in Qatar, and taken another blow to the head. The last time he'd been knocked out, but though he was surely still conscious, his world was rocked all the same. That…that inky-haired, more than half-grown human being was his *daughter*?

The last time he'd seen her she'd been a chubby-cheeked, irrepressible child, who wore pigtails and shirts with cartoon characters on them. In the intervening years he'd pictured the same, ribbons and Roadrunner, only taller. Never had he expected to find a teen wearing…wearing whatever you'd call that dark garb.

And just as unbelievable…

Birthday Girl.

Birthday Girl! She was standing behind the teenager, looking stunned. She reached out a hand and placed it on the girl's shoulder. To steady which one of them?

"You're…" the woman began.

"Jason Jennings. Jace." He cut his gaze to the teen. "Her father."

There must have been some question in his voice, because Birthday Girl nodded. "Yes. Right. And this is Om—"

"London," the youngster interrupted. The black

around her eyes and the heavy coating of the same color on her lashes was startling.

"I know your name," he said. His ex-wife's selection, of course, chosen after the city she'd run to upon leaving him when she was four months pregnant. Jace, tied financially and morally to the sick old man who'd given him a leg up and his very first job, had remained in the States, frustrated and confused and just beginning to realize that the woman he'd married might have never expected them to grow old together.

He looked at the auburn-haired female behind his daughter and felt his head spin again. It really was the woman from last night. *Shit*. From the first, he'd known regret would be the outcome of their encounter. Still, he had to carry on. "May I come in?" he asked, wincing at the sharp edge to his voice.

The two females stepped back.

"Of course," Birthday Girl said—no, he recalled her real name now. Shay Walker. Or S. Walker, as she'd signed the succession of emails he'd finally managed to read last week when his head issues had cleared up at last.

At first he'd thought her talk of tango lessons and celebrity magazines was something his mind was misinterpreting. A few emails later, he'd realized she was either putting him on or was a terrible mentor for his kid.

It had been only one more reason to seethe at the delays—caused by injury, crappy means of communication and his isolated location—that had postponed his return. But he was here now, he told himself, and it was time to implement the simple plan he'd conceived when he'd learned of his daughter's situation: a summer of getting to know her before school started in September.

He crossed over the threshold, then glanced around the massive foyer, with its thirty-foot ceiling. "Good God," he said, staring up at the walls of unrelieved concrete. The staircase was more gray cement, with a tubular metal banister painted a janitorial blue. "Is this place butt ugly, or what?"

Both London and Birthday Girl stared at him like he'd sprouted another head. He lifted an eyebrow. "Problem?"

Birth— *Shay* met the eyes of his daughter then looked back at him. "Um, this is your house."

"Yeah, but I never saw it before in my life. I needed something in So-Cal, somewhere quiet, I thought, and my man Leonard Case found it. I got it for a song."

"Which must have been 'Anchors Aweigh,'" Shay muttered, and his daughter snickered behind her hand.

The sound sliced at Jace's conscience. She didn't look like she laughed often. When he'd been told the fifteen-year-old had lost her mother, he'd felt sorrow for her loss and a deep uncertainty about what it would mean for him. Of course he was going to step up and do his duty, but he'd expected to find... He didn't know.

Not this dark-clad teenager whose expression was near deadpan.

Quashing a rising sense of suffocating panic, he reminded himself he had a plan.

"Why don't you show me around?" he asked London. "After I see my room, I'll collect my luggage from the car."

She glanced over at Shay, who nodded. "We'll both show you," the woman said. "Come this way."

Foiled already, he thought, as he followed their lead. He'd hoped to get his daughter alone and determine exactly how things were with the tutor. Though, hell, didn't he already know Shay—

No, he did *not* know Shay. The woman with whom he'd spent the night at the inn was someone else altogether. He'd left that person behind in the room, including his memories of her lithe body, her delicate fragrance and the softness of her skin beneath his lips. If he were going to follow through with his idea of taking this time with London, becoming acquainted with her even as she continued her studies, then he had to forget all about last night and see the tutor in a completely businesslike light.

He could do that. He'd always been a businessman first, after all.

They showed him around the downstairs area, which had an open floor plan containing some midcentury modern furniture that looked to be all angles and uncomfortable cushions. The kitchen was large enough to feed the navy and the best thing you could say about it beyond that was it was clean.

The view of the lake was stupendous, but even the sun streaming in the windows didn't warm the atmosphere of the place.

Without much optimism, he mounted the stairs. The top landing opened into a large gallery that contained a long center table. Textbooks sat in neat stacks on it, as well as a desktop and a laptop computer. "This is where London studies," Shay said.

The girl was already at a computer, drawn to it like a magnet, and as the screen powered on, its pale light washed onto her face, making the darkness surrounding her eyes even more stark. Jace shoved a hand through his hair, keenly aware of being out of his element. Panic tried digging its claws in him again.

Feeling a gaze on him, he glanced over at Shay. She was staring, and when she noticed *he* noticed, her face colored and she looked away. "What do you know about website building?" she asked, then hurried toward the table without waiting for his answer. "London, why don't you show your dad what you're working on?"

The girl's frozen expression didn't animate, but she obligingly moved her fingers on the keyboard. Color splashed onto the screen, brilliant-colored flowers and the words *Build a Bouquet*.

"It's a multidisciplinary project," Shay explained. "She's developing a website for a pretend florist business. Visitors to the site are able to select flowers and greenery to custom-design a floral arrangement. She's setting it up for three disparate locations throughout the country, so she's had to research local flora and seasonal availability along with the computer programming aspect."

Shay reached around the teen to hit a key. The screen switched from bright photography to rows of incomprehensible—to Jace anyway—letters, numbers and symbols. "This is the language for creating web pages," she explained, glancing over her shoulder at him.

"Impressive," he murmured. "But a lot to accomplish between tango lessons, isn't it?"

Shay's face flushed again. "Um…"

"Tango?" London asked, looking between the two of them while still managing to convey that their conversation didn't interest her in the slightest.

"Never mind," her tutor said. "Why don't we show your father around upstairs?"

Again the girl obliged in a long-suffering manner. Ennui oozed out of her as she slowly moved from the computer and then led their small party down the hallway. Jace glanced into her bedroom and several empty ones, then another that appeared occupied. The bed linens were pure white and it smelled of Shay's scent, causing him to stride past quickly in an attempt not to remember how that particular fragrance had risen from his own skin in the steam of the shower just a few hours before.

They had a business relationship now, remember?

London guided him along the catwalk that was open to the foyer and living room below. At the other side of the house, she gestured to double doors standing open.

Shay spoke up. "The master suite."

He stepped inside, winced again. More gunmetal-gray walls accented with industrial lighting. Though the bed was huge, the mattress was perched on a wooden platform that hung from the ceiling using thick iron chains. A sitting room wasn't any more hospitable. The attached bath, while spacious, was as welcoming as an operating room.

Maybe the inhospitable environs would serve a good purpose, he decided. Under the circumstances, he'd be better off thinking like a monk, not a man.

Ignoring the headache beginning to throb at the base of his skull, Jace exited the room and addressed the hovering females. "I'm going to bring in my things," he said.

Shay appeared uneasy at the news. His daughter appeared unaffected. He might have said his hair was on fire or there was a snake in the shower and he'd bet she'd wear the same nonexpression expression.

It didn't help that he had no one to blame for that but himself. Fifteen years was a long time to go without having a relationship with your father.

When he'd learned of London's mother's death, he'd been in Qatar's capital city of Doha. Though he'd instantly called, she'd been mostly nonresponsive to his assurances that they'd both be back in the States soon. That then they'd sort out the future.

Not once had he considered bringing her to him. His work in the Arab country sent him to remote, primitive locations that made her presence impractical. To underscore that point, not a short while later he'd been in an earthmover accident, miles from the nearest village. One of the workers with medical training had tended to his injuries, but when his wits had finally unscrambled, he'd lost weeks of time and further opportunities to connect with his daughter.

It took him a few trips to haul all his gear from the car. He refused Shay's help and London drifted back to her computer. As he passed her, he noted she was modifying those lines of gibberish on the screen.

The truth couldn't have hit him harder. They were two people, he thought, who didn't know the same language.

Dumping his bags on the floor of his room, he battled the urge to punch something—the wall, himself for his own ineffectiveness as a parent, the memory of his effing unfeeling martinet of a father who hadn't given Jace a clue as how to proceed.

Each moment that passed only made it clearer that he'd never have a chance with London.

Or that maybe he didn't deserve one, because a lone wolf couldn't change its ways.

A soft footstep sounded behind him. The air suddenly charged and his next breath brought with it a faint note of sweetness. The nape of his neck itched. Shay.

His daughter's tutor. His employee.

"Dinner's at six thirty," she said to his back. "Can I get you anything before then?"

He turned, and at the sight of her warm beauty, memories of the night before slammed into his chest. Blood rushed to his groin as he recalled her fingers wrapped around him, the taste of her pale nipples as they hardened beneath his tongue, the quiet, low sound she'd made when he'd entered her. Jace's breath felt trapped in his lungs.

Hell. Damn. *Shit.*

Anger rose from the depths of his belly. How could this have happened?

How could one woman and one night so tangle his simple plan? But she had. It did.

Everything was turning into knots and snarls.

Not only was he certain he was fighting an uphill battle in forging some kind of understanding—if not a relationship—with his kid, but his notion of retaining a businesslike attitude also already felt as if it were failing.

His daughter was an enigma.

Having the hots for her teacher was no help at all.

LONDON JENNINGS KNEW she was a freak.

After a day like today, the knowledge weighed heavy as she slipped out of the house and into the lake-scented darkness. Though Shay usually insisted on having help with the dinner dishes, tonight she'd shooed London from the kitchen. Due to pity, probably.

Not every teenager had a dead mother.

Not every teenager had a father who'd arrived years too late.

Hunching her shoulders, she tried shrugging off thoughts of Elsa as she headed toward the water. In their first week at Blue Arrow Lake, Shay had assigned her to read *The Great Gatsby*. In Daisy Buchanan, London had seen her mother. Beautiful, careless, childish. Elsa had been effusive some days and distant others. She'd followed boyfriends to foreign cities for weeks at a time, leaving London behind with their housekeeper, Opal, who was near a million years old and hailed from Boise, Idaho.

When Opal had needed to return to the States to take care of her sick sister, Elsa had been forced to cut short her latest trip. Between Budapest and their flat in Kensington, a train accident had taken her life.

And brought Jason Jennings into London's.

She hunched her shoulders once more as she followed the shoreline, leaving behind their dock and the bobbing powerboat that Shay sometimes piloted. The only sound was the water lapping gently against the silty sand. It was midweek, and most of the houses along the lake were dark except for security lights. There wasn't another person in sight.

Still, London had a more private destination in mind.

Three estates away, a dilapidated boathouse sat beside an equally run-down dock. Brand-new structures were located fifty feet from them, and on a morning walk, Shay had speculated that the old ones would be cleared away soon.

Before that happened, London wanted to spend more time inside the damp-smelling walls of the small, square building. Though her tutor likely wouldn't approve, London had been hanging there for an hour or so almost every day. The padlock was broken and there were signs that she wasn't the only visitor to the place.

It was those signs that fascinated her most.

The evidence of other teenagers, she was sure of it.

With a push of her hand, London swung open the door and peered into the dark interior. Before, she'd only visited during the day. In the gloom she could barely make out the usual litter: empty cans of Red Bull, Snickers candy wrappers, cigarette butts, a few moldy copies of *GamerNews* and *People* magazine. Seating choices consisted of various mismatched cushions that leaked stuffing and had been tossed onto the ragged indoor/outdoor carpeting.

Merely being around the debris of American kids made her feel closer to them. It was as if breathing in air they'd also shared could gain her entry into their world.

Suddenly, a flashlight flicked on.

On a breathless squeak, London jolted back, nearly falling. Regaining her balance, she saw the yellow circle of light jump along the walls as the figure wielding the instrument clambered to its feet.

His feet.

"Sorry. I didn't mean to scare you," a male voice said. Then the beam shifted, illuminating a face.

Everything inside London went still: her heart, her breath, the coursing of the blood beneath her skin. She knew that face. That tall, lean body. It was a boy she'd seen around town, always with a pack of other kids, always in a casual pose, comfortable with himself.

Who wouldn't be comfortable with his tanned skin and his shock of dirty blond hair and with those very white teeth that seemed to be glowing like neon even in the darkness?

London swallowed. "I'm not scared," she said.

She saw his head tilt, like a curious animal trying to figure out something new. "You have an accent."

Not hardly! At least, she didn't want to have one. The British kids she'd run into once in a blue moon said she didn't sound like them. When she'd gone to school—and it was true that Elsa had not always been consistent on getting her to class—she'd attended an all-girl American school with American teachers.

Since she was twelve, she'd exclusively watched American television, determined to become what she considered the epitome of confidence and cool—the typical American teen.

"Cat got your tongue, England?" the boy asked.

"It's London," she was forced to admit. "It's my name…and also where I've been living." Since coming to Blue Arrow she'd been trying out different city names—US city names—to replace her own, as if selecting a new one would obliterate her otherness. But the minute Shay had started to explain that to her father today, it had seemed foolish. Babyish. Like believing in Santa or expecting visits from the Tooth Fairy.

Elsa had cleared up those misconceptions right away, despite Opal's protests.

"Huh," the handsome guy said now. "London…I like it."

Emboldened by the compliment—giddy!—she voiced a question of her own. "And you are…?"

"Colton. Colton Halliday."

Colton Halliday. London repeated the name in her head. It sounded like the name of a cowboy or a Wild West gunslinger. Very American and maybe even a tiny bit dangerous.

Though she didn't feel afraid around him, she'd been truthful about that. Just warm and excited and like she was poised to begin the life she'd been waiting for. Until this moment, she'd been the victim of everyone else's whims—her mother taking her to Europe, her father sending her to Blue Arrow Lake, Shay insisting on Gatsby and Shakespeare and that boring history book about Western civilization.

Colton slid down the wall so he was seated again. He set the flashlight beside him so its beam washed up the dingy wall and cast half his face in light, half in shadow. "What are you doing out here?"

She took one small step inside. "I live back that way." She made a vague gesture. "You?"

"Promise you won't tell?" he asked, though he didn't sound too worried either way.

"Sure."

"We local kids, you know, full-timers on the mountain, we have a few places, hideouts I'd guess you'd call them, where we go to chill. This is one of them."

Hideouts. London nodded, pretending a teen-only retreat wasn't completely beyond her previous sheltered—okay, freak—existence. "Just you tonight?"

"I had to get away from the parental units for a little while. They can be a pain in the ass, right?"

"Right." London dug her toe into the worn carpeting. "My mother's dead." Her hand clapped over her mouth. What was wrong with her?

"God." He twitched, then was silent a moment. "God, I'm sorry."

"No. It's okay. I…" Miserably embarrassed, she stepped back again.

"Don't go," Colton said. "I shouldn't have…"

His discomfort only made her feel worse. "It's okay."

"Come back in, I don't bite. You probably need a little downtime, too."

Dueling desires warred within her. To go, to stay, to allow him to bite her. Goose bumps burst in hot prickles all over her skin at the thought. Biting! She'd never even been kissed. Yeah, at fifteen, she was unkissed.

Total freak.

"So, you go to school down the hill or something?"

Down the hill encompassed every place that wasn't the surrounding mountains. London had learned that from Shay. "No," she said, coming inside so she could make her own slide along the wall. They were propped on opposite sides of the small structure, London situated closest to the still-open door. "I'm sort of being homeschooled at the moment. I have a live-in tutor."

Colton released a low whistle as he drew up his knees and draped his wrists over them. In the low illumination from the flashlight, she stared at his hands. They were long-fingered and bony-looking. Not like a skeleton, just…bony like a boy's hands. Like a boy's hands should be.

"How's that?" he asked. "A live-in tutor? No dozing off during class, I suppose."

"No." If pressed, she'd probably admit she liked Shay. Yes, there was the dusting and the vacuuming and the Western civ book, but the woman had also been tolerant of her name experiments—which seemed even stupider now that Colton Halliday said he liked *London*.

Shay paid attention, too. She was the only one to ever notice that when it came to bubbling test answers, London had a peculiar technique. The first time she'd turned in a score sheet, Shay had taken one look at the paper then tossed it back. "Love the long-stemmed rose," she'd said drily, noting the pattern London had made with her No. *2*. "Now put your efforts into answers, not illustrations."

"Finals are coming up at the high school," Colton said. "That's what my parents are on my case about. Studying. Hell, I can't wait for summer."

"What will you do then?"

"Hang with friends, swim, hike. I have a part-time job scooping ice cream, too. Gotta save for college… only a year away."

Meaning he was going to be a *senior* next year. That seemed way older than her.

"What about you, England?"

"I'm—" She stopped herself from blurting out *fifteen*.

"Hey, I thought you liked London?"

His grin glowed again, seeming to light up the whole room. "I like 'England,' too, since I came up with it. My special name for you."

Another riot of goose bumps bloomed over her body. "That's all right, I guess." It was better than all right!

"So…are you going to be around this summer?"

She shrugged, trying to play it casual. "Sure."

"Then maybe we'll see each other again." Colton rose to his feet. "I gotta go now. Chemistry homework due tomorrow."

London stood, too, pressing her shoulder blades against the wall to hold herself up because her knees felt wobbly as he drew near. "See you around, then," she said as he passed through the doorway.

"Yeah, see you." He turned, walking backward as he looked at her, the moonlight silvering his hair. "How old are you, England?"

"Seventeen," she replied, without a single betraying quaver in her voice. It didn't matter that it was a lie; it was her next foray into the life she'd been waiting to begin.

Fifteen-year-old London, who'd lost her mother and only just met her father, was an outcast, that freak she'd always felt like. But London, nicknamed "England" by a handsome, soon-to-be high school senior, was the master of her fate and the captain of her soul.

And surely, surely seventeen.

CHAPTER FIVE

SHAY BUSIED HERSELF at the sink, swishing the dishcloth in the soapy water contained by one of the mixing bowls she'd used in preparing the evening meal. The chicken enchilada dinner had gone okay, she supposed, and she was relieved that she and Jace—his real name—seemed to be of the same mind.

The mind in which the Deerpoint Inn didn't exist.

Or, at least, of the mind that they weren't the same two people who had spent a night there together.

If the three of them were going to share the house for the summer, Shay's relationship with London's father needed to be polite, professional and impersonal. Surely she could manage that.

Then, even with her hand buried in the warm water on a warm night, a cold fingertip trailed down her spine. She froze, her prey-sense kicking in. Someone was behind her.

Lifting her gaze to the window over the sink, she saw a man reflected in the glass. His height, his breadth, the very masculine mass of him seemed to press the air from the room. Her heart skipped as he strode inside on silent feet until only the expanse of the stainless-steel-topped island separated them.

Calm down, Shay admonished herself. *He's no predator. He's nothing to you, not even that attractive man at the bar who was so charming at dinner and so blissful in bed.*

As a matter of fact, he was the kind of man she wouldn't find appealing at all. Upon learning of his ex's death, he'd made exactly one phone call to his daughter and then left her in others' care—without another word for weeks. Sure, Shay was self-aware enough to know she had a chip on her shoulder when it came to paternal issues, but anyone would agree that Jace should have maintained tighter contact since becoming London's sole guardian.

"Where's the kid?" he asked now, his voice low.

The sound of it—damn—reminded her of the night before. His voice, both rough and soft in the darkness as he murmured against the skin of her throat, as he whispered in the hot shell of her ear. *Your breasts fit perfectly in my hands. Open your mouth for my tongue. Spread your thighs. Let me feel your wet heat.*

"Shay?"

She jumped, and shook herself free of the memories. That man was not this one. The lover had been attentive and generous. This…stranger was neither of those things. "London is in her room, I believe."

"Look at me, will you?" he said. "We need to talk."

No, they didn't. And looking at him, looking into those lion-gold eyes, wasn't going to put them on that all-important professional footing. Maybe tomorrow, with more time and distance since they'd shared kisses, breath, a bed, she would have her armor intact and her memories safely locked away.

Maybe she could fully face him then.

The harsh screech of the bar-stool legs against the

polished concrete floor scraped her nerves. He was sitting instead of going away, she thought with a grimace.

But there was an odd heaviness to the sound of his body dropping into the chair. Without thinking, Shay swung around, only to see Jace sprawled in the seat, his elbows on the island, his head in his hands.

"What is it?" she asked, alarmed.

"I'll be all right in a minute."

"Is it the elevation again?" She hurried to get him a glass of cold water. "Drink this down."

He didn't move. "No."

"Don't be an idiot," she snapped. "If you're afraid I'll think less of you if your machismo takes another hit, forget about it. I—"

"Already don't think much of me?" he finished for her, lifting his head.

He looked terrible. There were lines of pain around his eyes and he squinted as if the light were torture.

"Why would you say that?" she asked, ignoring her guilty flush.

His mouth twisted in a wry smile. "I caught the hint from those emails you sent."

Shay swallowed. Not only had she written all that stuff about dancing lessons and field trips to chocolate factories, but she also recalled subtly—or maybe not so subtly—expressing her opinion on absentee parenting. "You read them?"

"Finally. After I recovered."

Her eyes rounded. "Um…recovered? Recovered from what?"

"I need to get some pain relievers." He stood abruptly, the uncharacteristically clumsy movement knocking over the stool. At the loud clatter, he put both hands to his head as if to hold it together.

"Jace." Shay rushed around the island to right the seat. Then she urged him back into it, tugging gently on one elbow. "I can get it. Something special? A prescription?"

"No. Just a couple of the regular kind."

He took the tablets with the water and without argument. For a few moments he sat, eyes closed, just breathing. Shay gripped the metal edge of the island, watching him with concern.

When his lashes lifted, she could see some of the discomfort had left him. "Better?" she asked.

"Yeah."

"Are you going to tell me what's up?"

He shrugged. "Construction accident. I ended up with a badly sprained ankle and a concussion. For a time I found it difficult to think, read, communicate clearly. I still get headaches, obviously—tension brings them on."

Remorse flooded Shay. While she'd been sending snarky emails and thinking uncharitable thoughts, he'd been laid up thousands of miles away with serious injuries. Still… "There wasn't someone who could send an email for you? Make a call?"

"This was a lay-of-the land mission, four of us in the middle of nowhere. My interpreter-slash-fixer understood a limited amount of English and my Arabic is sketchy. Beyond blueprints, we had a difficult time making ourselves known to each other. So I concentrated on getting here as soon as I could."

Frowning a little, she drew closer, continuing to watch him with assessing eyes. Definitely better, but—

"Christ, I don't need a nurse. Stop hovering."

Affronted, Shay spun around.

"Wait." Jace reached out, but her arm slipped through his fingers. "I'm sorry. I'm not used to…"

Hot showers, Shay thought, with sudden understanding. Birthday celebrations. Depending upon someone else, if only for a glass of water and a couple of aspirin. "It's all right," she said, insult evaporating. "I'm going to make coffee. Would you like some?"

"Sure," he said. "Thanks."

Her back was to him as she ground the beans and fiddled with the settings on the coffeemaker. Silence grew between them as she pulled mugs from the cabinet and readied the cream and sugar.

Before she sensed a single footstep, heavy male hands closed over her shoulders. Shay jerked once, then stilled. When he wasn't hurting from a headache, she thought, the big man moved with such smooth grace. Unnerved by it, Shay placed her palms flat on the countertop and tried to calm her thudding heart.

"Shay," Jace said, bending his head so his mouth was close to her ear. "I'm sorry. Really."

She closed her eyes, willing herself not to lean into his warmth. A ripple of desire rolled over her skin, slid down her arms, over her breasts, her belly, her hips. God, she'd never felt like this, so aware of a man, so greedy for his touch.

She'd expected only one night with him, but now, now there was another possibility. There could be a summer of such moments, she thought, aching to feel his heat surrounding her, his weight on top of her, his thick column of flesh inside her again. Her eyes closed. There could be such a sweet, sweet summer. Yes, the fact that he was her boss was a complication, but if they could sort that out—

"Really sorry," he continued, "but your employment will be terminated early. Though I'll pay out for the full contract, of course, I'm giving you four weeks' notice."

"What?" Lust and longing had muddled her brain. She felt drugged with it and shook her head to focus her thoughts. "What did you say?"

"Four weeks' notice," he repeated.

The words splashed over her like icy water. Wrenching from his hold, she scurried to the other side of the island. "I don't understand."

"You do," he said, his gaze on her face. "After what happened between us..."

But that hadn't happened! Didn't he understand their unspoken agreement that Shay and Jace were different people than Birthday Girl and Jay? Except...except a moment ago she'd been a breath away from begging for his touch, his heat, his—

Embarrassment kindled her temper. "Wait. Let me get this straight. Are you firing me because of our night at the Deerpoint Inn? I don't think that's legal!"

He grimaced. "Well—"

"You're letting me go because of a...of a personal choice I made *on my own time*?" She was aware of the outrage in her voice. "Because I went to bed with you?"

"Jesus, Shay." He glanced behind him. "Can you keep it down?"

"No, I can't keep it down," she said, though she lowered her voice to an incensed whisper. "How dare you judge me?"

"I'm not judging. I'm—"

"What about you? You're a single dad but that didn't

stop you from indulging in a one-night stand, seducing a vulnerable—"

"Vulnerable, my ass." Jace strode around the island and had hold of her shoulders again. "Seduce, *your* ass."

"What are you doing?" she demanded, trying to pull out of his grasp.

"Explaining to you the problem we have," he said from between his teeth. "No, showing you the problem we have." Then he bent his head and kissed her, his mouth hard and punishing and...

Beautiful. Masterful. Irresistible.

Shay's lips surrendered to the pressure of his and then his tongue was inside, plunging to rub against her own, pulling back to toy with her, then sweeping back in again. Her body melted against the hard wall of his chest and she pressed her breasts to it and her belly to the heavy rise of his erection.

She tumbled into another bubble, still in Jace's clasp. It pulsed around them like a heartbeat. It was a refuge. A private shelter. Their very own place. To anchor herself there, she tucked her fingers into the waistband at the back of his jeans. He grunted, low in his throat, and fed more deeply from her mouth.

Then, in an abrupt, desperate move, he pushed her away. Shay felt the counter at the small of her back, and she leaned there, panting. His golden eyes were molten and she felt his gaze like a touch as it moved from her mouth to her heaving breasts to the heated juncture of her thighs. Her muscles clenched there, and he groaned, as if he sensed that sweet spasm.

"You've got to see..." He sucked in a quick breath. "This is a problem."

She crossed her arms over her chest to hide her

taut nipples and trembling hands. "Just…just stop kissing me."

He gave her a wry look. "'Cause that'll work."

"Jace—"

"No, I've made up my mind." He pushed his hands through his hair. "I'm moving up the timetable."

"Timetable?"

"I had a boarding school picked out for London come September. I know I was supposed to spend the next three months here, with her, with you, but obviously…" He shook his head. "I made a call. She can go to the summer session that starts in four weeks."

Shay gaped at him. "You can't do that."

"Won't she be ready? From those emails, I thought you said she was making great progress. Maybe I can get her another tutor at the school—"

"Jace, she needs time with you."

His face settled into stubborn lines. "Look, I don't know anything about her. I know even less about being a father and it's obvious it's too late for me to learn. Now that I've seen her, it's clear she's not interested in that kind of relationship with me anyway."

"You can't know what might happen over time—"

"A summer won't help."

"That doesn't mean you shouldn't try."

"No." He forked his hand through his hair. "Don't get me wrong. I don't blame her in the least, but…but no."

Shay wanted to scream, to cry, to throw something at him. Maybe if she quit now, walked out on the stupid man, he'd be forced to rethink his decision.

Or he'd retreat for four weeks and not engage with the girl altogether until it was time to pack her off to boarding school.

Still, perhaps it would be better that she go, especially as Jace had made it clear he wasn't interested in being around her, despite that scorching, seeking kiss. Shay could return tonight to her own place. Wasn't she accustomed to being alone?

A furtive movement over Jace's shoulder caught her eye. London, dressed in her usual dreary black, her presence moving along the hall like a shadow.

The girl didn't need to be ignored and left adrift, she thought, her heart aching. London needed an anchor. Something Shay had been providing the past months.

Four more weeks wouldn't be so bad, she decided. She'd take that time to do what she could for the teen… while taking care to save herself from any unreciprocated wishes or impossible dreams.

JACE AWOKE AT DAWN. Jet lag was a bitch, and so was the cold, cavernous master suite. He yanked on jeans, a T-shirt and a pair of running shoes and let himself out the back door that opened onto the wide deck that wrapped around the house.

The air was still, the sky a pale, pale gray. The green of the fir trees along the shore was almost black against the nearly colorless canvas. Mist rose from the lake, obscuring its surface. Resembling flying ghosts, the vapor skimmed across the water then shifted, driven by a slight breeze to return like second thoughts.

Jace jogged down the steps to the sloping lawn that led to the narrow beach and the dock there. The wooden structure was painted a deep blue with matching canvas awnings, and consisted of a short rock staircase rising to a platform that loomed over the water. From it, a gangplank angled down to the wide berth that contained the sleek powerboat he'd bought with the house. It was neatly tied to metal cleats and bobbed gently.

Where were the keys? he wondered as an urge came over him to take the thing for a spin. He could already feel the power of it in his hands and beneath his feet, a convenient vehicle for whisking him away from the tangled complications in his life.

But hell, this was a lake, wasn't it? A finite body of water that meant he was caught forever within its boundaries. Any trip would only bring him back to his starting place.

To London.

To Shay.

To those misgivings that continued to emerge from the troubled pool of his thoughts.

But no, damn it, he assured himself. He'd made a decision to cut this sojourn short. The right decision.

All he needed was a little caffeine to cement that certainty.

So he turned back to the house, only to find someone else was up, as well. In the kitchen Shay was at the counter. Once more she was occupied with the coffee machine, her back to him.

The overhead light picked out gold threads in her auburn hair. The color warmed the stainless-steel-and-cement kitchen, a flame that seemed to give the place some much-needed life. A simple white T-shirt hung from her slender shoulders to brush the waist of the soft, beltless pair of denim jeans she wore. They were cuffed at the ankle to reveal her small bare feet, her toenails painted a translucent pink. Through the windows, the same shade was washing the sky as the sun began to rise over the mountains.

Jace stared at the woman, the same feeling every time he saw her rising like those vapor ghosts on the lake. It went beyond wanting her—and he wanted her very much. Maybe because she'd made him smile and laugh and, most important, take himself a little less seriously.

Just as her presence enlivened the house, for those two nights at the inn, she'd made him feel a bit more human.

Shay suddenly broke the silence. "When are you going to tell London?" she asked, her back still turned.

He blinked. She'd been aware he was standing there… admiring? Clearing his throat, he shoved his hands in his pockets. "Tell her what?"

"About the change of plans." She turned and carried a full mug of steaming coffee in his direction. His hands automatically reached for it when she held it his way. "About the upcoming summer session at the boarding school."

"Uh…" For someone with such bright hair, her blue eyes could be so damn cool, he thought. They stabbed at him now like icy shards. "I'm not sure."

She returned to retrieve her own thick white mug, where bold red letters proclaimed Size Matters. Jace glanced at the side of his own. Biker Chick. Huh.

"If you're uncertain about that," she said, gazing at him over the rim of her coffee, "perhaps it isn't the right thing to do."

He took a swallow of the hot dark brew. "It's the right thing to do." Because he was the wrong kind of man and it was certainly the wrong time—as in, too late—to try to forge a real relationship with the teen.

Shay shrugged one shoulder. The wide neck of her

T-shirt slipped, revealing the lacy edge of a pale pink bra strap. Jace's belly, and then his groin, tightened. Hell. It took just that small glimpse of intimate apparel and semiprivate flesh to get his full sexual attention.

Tightening his hold on his mug, he glanced away, trying to distract himself and the instinct that was clamoring at him. *Snatch her up*, it said. *Throw her over your shoulder.*

In his bedroom, he'd toss her to the mattress, strip her bare, then fist his hands in her hair as he insinuated himself between her thighs. She'd be wet for him, and hot, and he'd lose himself in her and all the problems plaguing—

"What's everybody doing up so early?" a new voice asked.

Jace jolted, then glanced over his shoulder to see London shuffling into the room, the hem of a plaid flannel robe flapping around her ankles, her starkly dark hair hanging in her face. Even half-asleep there didn't seem to be any child left in her.

What did you expect? he asked himself. *Teddy bears and Barbie dolls?*

"What can I get you?" Shay asked now. "OJ?"

The girl tipped up her chin so her gaze could meet the tutor's from behind her swathe of hair. "Espresso?"

"I don't think so," Shay said, shaking her head. "Green tea? Or I can make you a fruit smoothie."

London spun around and it was then Jace noticed she was wearing slippers shaped like strawberries. Was there some little girl left inside her, after all? "I'm going back to bed," she said around a huge yawn.

"Classwork starts at eight," Shay called after her.

Her mumbled reply sounded sleepy.

"Why the hell do you suppose she bothered to get up?" he asked, bewildered.

Glacial blue eyes shifted once more to his face. "My guess?" Shay said. "To make sure you're still here."

Shit. Jace didn't know how to reply to that.

"It's why you should explain what's going on right away," the tutor continued. "Tell her about the school, the new timetable."

He stared into his coffee. "Maybe it would be better if it came from you."

She made a sound that was half laugh, half snort. "You're not paying me enough for that, big guy."

Double shit. He wasn't. "I could—"

"Save your breath. This is all on you."

"All right. Fine." And he knew she was right. What he didn't know was exactly how to explain it to London. Still, after a quick breakfast and a detour to his room, his determination got him to the upstairs study area in a timely fashion.

Or not so timely, he realized, when he saw London in front of a computer, already perusing what looked to be some complicated math problems on the desktop's monitor. It was 8:05 a.m.

He shoved his hands in his pockets as the girl and her tutor looked up. "At it already?"

Shay had an essay in front of her, a red pen poised over it. "London loves her quadratic equations."

The teen rolled her eyes—once again circled with that black somewhat disturbing makeup. "I don't love anything."

Jace had no adequate response. But he couldn't just walk away, either. "Do you mind if I hang out awhile?" His gaze went to Shay. "I'll keep quiet."

"Or not," she murmured, sending him a significant look.

Ignoring it, he pulled out a chair on the same side of the table as his daughter. While she continued to work, he drew a science textbook toward him and began turning pages.

At the scratch of pencil on paper, he looked over. London was intent on the numbers she'd transferred there. The computer monitor had changed to screensaver mode. Photographs popped onto the screen like rabbits from a hat before being sucked down again and another moved into view. Jace stared at image after image of his ex-wife.

After a couple of minutes, he became aware of London. Her head was up and she was as focused on him as he'd been on the screen. He floundered for something to say.

Finally, he cleared his throat. "Those are good. Very good likenesses of your mother. Did you take them?"

The girl nodded.

"She was a beautiful woman," he said. Though she looked more mature in the photographs than he remembered, of course, there was still that knockout figure, the beautiful flow of light brown hair hanging down her back and her vivacious smile.

"Is that why you married her?" London asked. "Because she was beautiful?"

His grin felt rueful. "It certainly didn't hurt. I was twenty-one."

"She was older, right?" the teen said. "Like, a cougar."

"No." He laughed and he glanced across the table to gauge Shay's reaction. She didn't appear to be listening, her focus still on the essay, the red pen moving along. "Your mother was only five years older than me. I met her when I was doing some moonlighting at her house—where she lived with her father."

London tilted her head. "'Moonlighting'?"

"A second job." He closed the science textbook and shifted his chair to more fully face the teen. "I had a day position, but I also made extra money by doing some building on the side…weekends and evenings." Hal Olson, the construction firm owner he worked for Monday through Friday, had promised if Jace could get some cash together he'd let him buy into a slice of one of the company's new projects. Canny as all get-out, but already feeling the ill effects of the disease that would finally take his life, the old man had tapped into Jace's ambition and unflagging drive.

For a long time he'd thought those same qualities had doomed his marriage. Later, he'd understood that Elsa's agenda had been part of the problem, too.

But when he was twenty-one… "I remember the first time I saw her. I was up on the roof of the garage, and she sped into the circular drive in her white convertible, her hair waving in the wind like a flag. She looked up at me, gave a jaunty wave and…"

"And?" London's prompt was oh-so-casual.

"And we ended up getting married." Though in his mind there'd been no hurry to get rings. He would have been content to date Elsa—yes, and bed her. Six months later, however, she'd come to him with the news of her pregnancy and the suggestion of a quick trip to Las Vegas. Jace had considered marrying the mother of his child the right thing to do, despite her father's fury.

"But then my mom went to London."

"Then your mom went to London. There were some issues with her family she wanted to get away from. And I...I had financial responsibilities in LA that meant I couldn't leave with her." By then, Hal Olson was clearly losing his fight with cancer and wanted Jace to take over the company, giving him a big piece of it so that he would keep Olson Construction in business. That way, Hal had ensured a future income for his young grandchildren.

"But I did come visit you," Jace said. "Do you remember that?"

London was looking down now, her pencil in hand as she drew idly on her paper. What did girls doodle? He was a swords-and-stacks-of-boxes kind of guy. These looked like tiny circles or maybe a bed of flowers.

"I think I've seen some photos of us together," she said, frowning a little. "Or maybe they're memories. I'm not sure."

"Every couple of months I came to see you, until you were about five." Things had gotten sticky with Elsa after that. She'd filed for divorce and then he'd taken the company international, which meant long periods of time in India, Vietnam, China. He cleared his throat again, wondering how much to say. "I should have kept up my visits. Your mom..."

"You don't have to say it." London glanced over, her voice lowering. "I knew my mom pretty well."

Shit. A kid shouldn't have to sound like that, like *she'd* been the adult in the relationship. He wanted to punch his own face again. At the time, he'd done what he'd thought was best, sending money, sending—

"Really, it's all right," the teen said. "She could

be lots of fun. Exciting to be around, you know? In a drama-rama kind of way."

Yeah, he knew. But he also knew that at this moment the kid sounded like she was a fifty instead of fifteen.

London had scribbled a field of flowers now. "And you know what? She was really good at picking books."

Everything inside Jace froze. If he moved, he thought he might crack in two. "Oh?" he managed.

"Mmm-hmm. Every month or so she'd give me two or three—some just out, others that were old but I'd never read before."

There was pain in his chest and pain at the base of his skull. They both throbbed in time to the dirge of his heartbeat. "That's…that's great. A nice memory. A very nice memory."

The computer screen had gone black now and Jace was grateful his ex's image was gone. He put his hand to the back of his neck and tried to massage away the discomfort.

"Jace?"

Masking a wince, he shifted toward Shay, who was staring at him from the other side of the table.

"Are you all right?" she asked.

No. He'd never be all right. But his relationships with those who should be closest to him had been a disaster for years.

This conversation was only more proof that he was better on his own. The lone wolf, howling at the moon, but at least hurting as few people as possible.

"Jace?"

Shay sounded more concerned. He couldn't look at her pretty face as it would only make the ache sharper.

"It's the altitude again," he mumbled. "I'll get some water and be right back."

No lie. He went for water. And then for fresh air. He took a few minutes to stretch out on a lounge chair in the shade on the deck, letting the gentle breeze flow over him.

He awoke sometime later, disoriented. The angle of the sun said he'd slept for hours. Damn jet lag. Someone had draped a soft throw over him. He fingered it. The loosely woven wool was the same color as Shay's eyes.

Tossing it over his arm, he got to his feet then made his way into the house. A note was left in the kitchen, he guessed in Shay's handwriting: "Sandwich for you in the fridge."

Another was propped on the table in the study area. "We're out walking." Bemused, he stared at the spray of daisies penciled in one corner. Shay's hand again, his daughter's drawing. Without his permission, his fingers reached out to snatch the small piece of paper.

"We're out walking," he read again.

Which meant he couldn't yet tell the teen about the change of plans. Something tight inside him loosened. He breathed in deeply, breathed out. As he shoved the note in his back pocket, he wondered why, if it were such a good idea to make a quick, clean break with his daughter, he felt such immense relief at the postponement of imparting the news.

CHAPTER SIX

LONDON HURRIED AWAY from the house, trying to leave behind her father and all thoughts of him, as fast as her feet could carry her.

He wasn't a bad guy, she supposed. Not pushy, and not too parental. Maybe Shay had already shared with him how London was doing with her schoolwork, but she was still glad he hadn't hovered over her shoulder that morning, eager to insert commas or double-check her computations.

They'd conversed about her mother, and that hadn't been so terrible, either. It was kind of interesting to picture Jace up on a roof, her mother catching his attention as she drove by. Her mother had been like that—eye-catching. London had seen other men falling all over themselves in order to get her mom's notice…and then try to keep it.

But Elsa had been like a hummingbird. Flying high, dipping low, never stopping in one place for long…or with one man.

So London didn't blame her father for the divorce.

And maybe it was London's own fault that being around him made her feel…juvenile. She'd had to clamp down on the urge to turn his way and grill him on what he recalled of her baby self. To ask him if he'd ever twirled her around, her legs swinging out behind her.

To wonder aloud if once upon a time she'd sat in his lap, her head against his chest, while his heartbeat was in one ear and his storytelling voice in the other. Was it a real memory or some silly ancient wish?

But it was dumb to dwell on that. She wasn't some little girl with a need for her daddy!

Mortified by the mere idea of it, London gave an extrahard shove to the door of the abandoned boathouse. The slivered wood swung open with a creak and crashed against the wall, setting a wrinkled piece of paper scurrying along the carpeting. She kicked at the sheet, sending it on another scuttle, then she plopped onto one of the tattered cushions.

With her toe, she caught the door then pushed it closed. Sunlight was strained through the chinks and cracks in the old walls, making the unlit interior murky. Though the day was warm, it wasn't too hot inside the boathouse, those same chinks and cracks allowing the lake breeze to worm its way in and cool the temperature. London drew up her knees and yanked the oversize black sweatshirt she wore over them. She propped her stacked hands on her knees and her chin on her knuckles.

A dark ball of teenager who didn't need anyone.

She wriggled her butt into the thin pad and stared ahead at nothing. Her bum was turning numb and despite herself she began mentally reviewing her Spanish vocabulary when the door swung open.

London's skin went hot beneath her clothes as she lifted her gaze to the backlit figure filling the entry. The sun dazzled her eyes, but she knew who had come to the hideout, interrupting her solitary interlude.

"England," Colton Halliday said in greeting.

She straightened, pushing her shoulders to the wall and shoving her legs out in front of her. Her fingers tugged at the stretched-out hem of her sweatshirt. "Um, hi. Fancy, uh, seeing you again so soon." Not for a driver's license and a car to go with it would she admit she'd come this way—ditching Shay in the process by insisting on a solo walk—with the vague hope that she might meet him here again.

And it was vague. While she'd only been to the place once at night—last night—she'd visited other times during the day and hadn't encountered a soul. Her breath caught as a brilliant thought flashed through her mind. Had he come in hopes of running into *her*?

Colton stepped inside, his leather flip-flops snapping against the bottoms of his feet. He wore with them a T-shirt, shorts and a faint shampoo smell. Leaving the door open so the light streamed inside, he looked about him. "Have you seen a wallet? I think I might have dropped mine in here yesterday."

Hopes dashed, London shook her head. No, he hadn't anticipated seeing her again. Lying about being seventeen hadn't made her a jot more interesting. Or maybe he'd caught on to her freak-ness. How could he not? Hadn't she spilled about her mother's death and then about being homeschooled?

She couldn't imagine what he'd think if he knew she'd been separated from her father for ten years. Well, yes, she could very well imagine. Colton would think...

Freak.

"That's some fierce expression you're wearing." He crouched beside her, then made a small cry of triumph. "There it is." One long tanned arm stretched out to snatch a wallet from beneath a ragged piece of beach towel. "Whew."

He stood to shove it in his front pocket, then dropped onto the floor beside her. "I would've hated to lose that."

Lost in her low mood, London didn't answer.

"Hey," he said, nudging her shoulder with his. "Is it something I said?" He lifted his elbow and pretended to sniff his armpit. "Do I stink or something?"

"No!" A smile tried tugging at the corners of her mouth. This close he smelled even more strongly of shampoo. His hair, she realized, was still damp from a recent wash. "Isn't it a little early for you to be out of school?"

"Minimum day. Played some pickup roundball once we got out, then when I was showering after, I remembered where I might have left my wallet."

London thought of him naked, water running over his skin, and felt herself go hot again. To disguise her blush, she tried pulling more of her hair over her face.

"You're pretty, you know," he said, all casual and cool, as if doling out compliments was something that came naturally to him.

"No, I'm not." How else was she supposed to answer?

He nudged her with his shoulder again. "Sure, you are. Though I'm not certain black is your best color."

Mortification sluiced through her and she hunched in on herself. "So you're a fashion consultant?"

He grinned. "Nope. Have a younger sister. Go to school with a bunch of other girls."

London sniffed. "Black is classic."

"Whatever." He shrugged. "But it's almost summer. Pretty soon it'll get too hot for jeans and hoodies."

It was too hot for jeans and hoodies now. Upon arriving at Blue Arrow Lake she'd realized that she didn't dress like the other girls—and that her dark makeup and dyed hair didn't make her fit in, either. But London hadn't a clue how to shop…and hadn't anyone to ask to go to stores with her.

Though she wanted so badly to be like any other American teen, she had no idea how to remake herself. A girl at her last school had dared her into the black hair and black eyeliner and mascara and she'd kept up with the style because…because…

Because it was something to hide behind.

The bright colors and limb-baring clothes the Southern California mountain girls wore wouldn't allow that. Short shorts with suede boots. Sun dresses with surfergirl sandals.

If she wore things like that, would Colton like what they revealed?

"England," he said, his voice serious, "things can't go on like this."

She glanced over at him. "Like what?"

"I usually amaze girls, you know. I don't make them frown. I hardly ever get the silent treatment."

Now she detected humor and it eased her discomfort a little. "Is that so? You amaze them?"

He nodded. "Absolutely. And with little effort. But you seem to be an especially hard nut to crack. Which means I'm going to have to bring out the big gun."

When he reached for his front pocket, she felt her eyes go buggy. "Wh-what?"

Peering more closely at her face, he started to laugh. "Geez, England. Not that. I'm going to show you magic."

That didn't sound much better, but she stayed silent

as he yanked out his wallet and withdrew a dollar bill. Then he made a big show of tapping it, straightening it, letting go of one end and then the other to flick it with his fingers.

"A single, right? Nothing more than a simple dollar bill?"

"Um, yes." She shifted her glance from his hands to his face. "You're really going to do a magic trick?"

"My one and only. Pay attention."

Dutiful now, London focused on the bill. He made a show of folding it this way and that, until it was a square. Then, with his other hand cupped beneath, he pinched it between two fingers. A quarter plopped into his cupped palm.

London blinked. "Hey..." She frowned. "Do it again."

"Say please."

"Please."

He slid his hands behind his back and then brought them forward again, the coin gone, the dollar straightened once more. For a second time, he squeezed a quarter from the folded bill.

"Let me see that," she said, reaching for the cash.

"Nuh-uh-uh," he said, holding it over his head. "Magicians never give away their secrets."

Too dignified to pout, she crossed her arms over her chest. "Then show me again."

At the third performance of the trick, she finally shook her head. "I give up. You *are* amazing."

His expression turned smug. "I knew I could make you smile."

And she was, she realized. Smiling. At some silly parlor game that would entertain a child. London yanked at her hair again, wishing she could disappear behind it forever. "I probably seem like some weird little kid to you. Who wears the wrong clothes and smiles at the wrong things."

"Hey—"

"You said I was a nut. A freak."

"Hey." He grabbed her hand, squeezed. "Hard nut to crack. It's an expression."

"I know that," she mumbled, her attention focused on her fingers. No, on his. Those long, bony, *boy* fingers.

This was a first. No boy had ever touched her. No boy had ever held her hand.

"You're not a freak," Colton said.

By degrees, her chin lifted, and her gaze shifted to meet his. Blue, blue eyes.

The room shrank.

Colton dropped her hand, jumped up. "Do you want to do something?"

London's heart felt like it was unloosed in her chest. "Do what?"

"I don't know." He glanced around, then paced to the door. His hands gripped the jamb and he stared out at the water. "Go for a walk. Or if we had access to a boat…"

Access to a boat.

London swallowed and got to her feet. Access to a boat was something a seventeen-year-old who lived on this lake would have. "You know how to drive one?"

He glanced over his shoulder. "Sure."

What had she thought last night? That she was the master of her fate. The captain of her soul.

She curled her fingers into her palm to savor the

memory of his hand in hers. Not a little girl. Not a freak. Seventeen. "Then let's go."

SHAY'S FEET STUTTERED as she stepped into the kitchen to find Jace standing by the sink, his gaze on something in his hand. He looked over, shoved whatever it was in his pocket and leaned against the countertop. His arms crossed his chest and she tried not to notice his masculine breadth and strength. But the raw power he exuded made her feel breathless and achingly female.

"Did you have a nice walk?" he asked.

A polite comment, so she felt compelled to answer it in a similar tone as she continued forward. "Yes, thanks." Leaving plenty of room between their bodies, she crossed to a cupboard and grabbed a glass. She'd top it off with the cold tea in the fridge then escape. Hide out in her room, where she planned to spend as much time as possible until the remaining weeks of her employment were completed.

"London's not with you?"

She briefly glanced over her shoulder. "She's fifteen, not five. I let her off the leash on occasion."

"Yeah. Well."

Even with her back turned, she sensed his eyes on her. She could feel the heat of his gaze on the top of her head, between her shoulder blades, along the bare length of leg that showed beneath her skirt. It was a swingy cotton thing, not especially short, but now even the backs of her knees felt too...bare.

With careful movements, she returned the pitcher to its shelf and took a breath in preparation for getting out of his company as soon as possible. Her hand clutched the glass, which was already starting to sweat. "You're feeling better now?"

Damn. The words just popped out of her mouth. She didn't want to engage him in further conversation. She didn't want to think about him or his headache or the bits of his life that she'd gleaned when listening to his conversation with London that morning. In order not to interrupt the moment, she'd played fly on the wall, but she'd taken in every sentence.

"Better. Thanks."

"That's good to hear." And because she meant it, she grimaced. Poppy was the soft heart in the family, not Shay. Why feel concern for the man who was canning her as well as walking away from the daughter he barely knew?

Every couple of months I came to see you, until you were about five.

He'd said that to the girl, though, and it implied there was more to the story—

No. None of that was her business.

The hem of her skirt flew up as she turned, ready to hurry away. Her free palm clapped the lifting fabric against her leg but she saw Jace's gaze had flicked to the inches of thigh the move had momentarily revealed. Ignoring the flutter in her belly, she began to step past him.

He caught her shoulder.

"Hey—" Her protest halted at the expression on his face. His brows were drawn together, and he stared out the window over her shoulder. "What is it?"

"Hell," he said. "Is that…? That's…"

Shay twisted her head, peering in the same direction. A boat was motoring away from the dock and out of the shallow cove. The berth that belonged to the house was empty.

Her jaw dropped. "Who...?"

Jace's expression turned grimmer. "If my eyes didn't deceive me, that's my daughter in that boat."

Then he took off.

"The *Fun & Games*? It can't be," Shay protested, trying to keep up with him as he pushed through the back door and crossed the deck. "She doesn't know how to drive."

He shot a glance at her. "There was a boy at the wheel."

A boy? Astonished, Shay froze, allowing Jace to pull away. Then she sprinted to catch up with him. "She doesn't know any boys," she said, already breathless.

He didn't bother answering as he pounded up the steps to the platform then down the gangway to the berth. At one of the U-shaped ends, he came to halt, stopping so abruptly Shay grabbed at his elbow to ensure his momentum wouldn't take him into the water. Shaking off her hold, he cupped both hands over his eyes and stared in the direction the boat had taken.

"Damn it." His head swiveled from side to side, then he raced back up the gangplank to the kayak chained to the coffin-sized metal dock box resting on the platform. "Where's the key to this?" he demanded, rattling the padlock.

"On the same ring as the boat keys," she said. They usually hung on a hook by one of the back doors. Despite his clear worry, the corners of her mouth twitched.

His expression turned ferocious. "Are you laughing at me?"

She swallowed her humor back down, though it was

hard not to picture him using a one-man craft and a paddle in an attempt to overtake a powerful outboard engine. "It was just a smile."

"This is no smiling matter. My daughter is out there with a...with a boat-jacker."

Shay seriously doubted that—hadn't he said she was with a boy? "Did she look like she was being coerced?"

"She's fifteen," Jace said again. He started rattling the padlock once more, as if he could open it with sheer force of will.

Stepping away from the noise, Shay pulled her cell phone from her pocket. London didn't pick up, but Shay imagined she might not hear the ring tone over the roar of the boat. With a glance at the muttering Jace, she made a second call.

Two minutes later, she shoved her cell away and waved to get his attention. "The lake patrol is on it."

His gaze shifted to her. "The what?"

"There's three or four boats on the lake at all times, watching for trouble and making sure the rules are enforced—like a private Coast Guard. It's a weekday, so there's little traffic on the water. They'll find London in no time."

He stared at her. "You think?"

"I'm sure. They patched me through, and the guys on patrol know the boat, the dock, the situation. Once they find the *Fun & Games*, one of the officers will climb aboard and pilot them back. Don't fret."

"I'm not fretting." His hands pushed through his hair and he spun to stare over the water. "I'm worrying."

"Because you're a dad."

His sidelong look spoke volumes. "That's where

you're wrong." He paced around the platform. "Do we just wait here?"

"Why don't we sit down?" He needed to dial his anxiety down a notch. There was a bar-height dining set on the platform and she pulled out one of the chairs. "You'll see. It won't take long."

He threw himself onto the seat and raked his fingers through his hair again.

Shay stared at the dark disorder and felt a pinch of guilt. "Maybe I should have put her on a leash," she murmured, perching on the chair beside his.

"No." He dismissed that statement with a slash of his hand. "This is not your fault."

"You know, teenagers typically do dumb things now and again."

He shifted his gaze from the water to her face then back. "Yeah, but her upbringing hasn't been typical."

Hard to deny, Shay decided. Instead she sat back in her chair, forcing herself to relax as she took in the blue sky, the sheltering mountains and the water that glistened in the sun, sparking silver and gold. In the distance, a sailboat scudded over the surface.

"It's like a postcard," Jace said, indicating his mind was running along the same line as hers. "Beautiful. But— Christ." He froze. "Can she even swim?"

He dropped his head into his hands, then looked up again to stare at Shay. "How come I don't know if she can swim?"

"*I* know," Shay assured him. "She's fine in the water. A strong swimmer."

"Yeah?"

"Yeah. My sister Poppy's fiancé has an estate near here with an indoor pool. She swims there with my nephew, Mason." Catching Jace's alarmed look, she hid her smile. "He's five. A real lady-killer, though."

He let out an audible breath. "All right. Fine." Some of the tension left his shoulders. "Your sister's engaged?"

"Yep." Shay thought of her black-haired, blue-eyed future brother-in-law, all elegance and sophistication. A panther to the lion beside her now. "Ryan Hamilton… you might know of him."

Jace's eyebrows climbed toward his hairline. "Ryan Hamilton the actor?"

"He produces now," Shay explained. "But yeah, the one that did TV and movies in his younger days. He has a place in LA and a second house here at Blue Arrow Lake."

"Whoa," Jace said, still sounding surprised. "Ryan Hamilton."

"What?" Shay asked, bristling. "You don't think a Walker is good enough for a rich Hollywood bachelor?" Her eyes narrowed, she glared at him.

"Wait a minute. Wait just a minute." Jace shifted from his chair to stand before her. "Now hold still," he said.

On instant alert, Shay froze. "Is it a bug? A flying bug? I hate those. Even dragonflies, ever since my brother Brett told me they were actually tiny witches on tiny brooms."

"It's not a bug, though I appreciate this little glimpse beneath Ms. Capability." One corner of his mouth tucked up, he brushed briskly at her shoulder. "There. All gone."

"What was it?" She frowned, looking around to see what he'd flicked away.

"That big chip on your shoulder," Jace said.

Her frown deepened.

"I never said or implied there was one thing wrong with a Walker," he continued. "It's not like I was born with a silver spoon."

But he had one now, a whole set she was sure, if the house behind them was anything to go by. "Okay," she grumbled. "It's just that…we don't like anything to tarnish Poppy's happiness. She's been alone since her stupid boyfriend ran off when he found out she was pregnant."

Jace twitched and Shay cursed her big mouth. That was a little too close to the current situation, wasn't it? Except…

But then my mom went to London.

But I did come visit you, Jace had said.

The exact circumstances between him and his ex were not known to Shay—and were none of her business, especially now that he'd terminated their employment agreement early. "Sorry," she murmured, training her gaze to her hands in her lap. "I didn't mean—"

"Have you ever been married?"

Shay shook her head.

"Ever fall foolishly into a relationship?" Before she could answer he said, "I did."

"It's none of my concern—"

"Maybe it is, because at the moment you're still London's tutor." He sighed. "I don't know how much you took in this morning when I was talking to her…"

Every word. But she'd pretended deafness in case her presence might stop him from sharing with his daughter.

"It's pretty clear now she had an agenda when she

began dating me," he said flatly. "Elsa, London's mother. At first I think she wanted to infuriate her father by being with a blue-collar guy like myself. Then she became pregnant—and our subsequent marriage allowed her access to her trust fund. That money was her escape from her father's home. To a new life in Europe."

He sighed again. "She was gorgeous, reckless, exciting. And, ultimately, too much for me to handle. For the first five years of London's life it wasn't so bad. I dealt with it by seeing her as often as I could. Then one time I arrived for a scheduled visit and Elsa and London had taken off to parts unknown. I rescheduled...same thing. I was traveling a tremendous amount for business and Elsa's games...they wore me down."

"That's terrible," Shay said.

His mouth twisted in a wry curve. "What is? That she made things difficult, or that I weighed that, considered the long hours I was putting in to build the business—not to mention my nonexistent parental instincts—and gave my ex-wife generous child support but full custody when she filed for divorce?"

Shay opened her mouth.

He spoke before she could. "I'm the bad guy, Shay. Don't think anything different."

"I don't." Lifting her chin, she kept her gaze steady and cool, her heartbeat steady and calm. This man wasn't going to get to her. He wasn't *trying* to get to her, that was true, so it should be easy.

Easy-peasy.

"So?" He pinched her chin, a teasing, almost brotherly touch. "I bared my past and you never answered the question."

"Question?" That "casual" touch distracted her. Goose

bumps tickled her neck and she felt her nipples tighten. She crossed her arms over her chest. "I've forgotten what it was."

His knuckle traced the edge of her jaw. "Did you ever fall foolishly into a relationship?"

Fall foolishly into a relationship? She stared into his golden eyes, mesmerized. Did one night at the Deerpoint Inn count?

"Better yet," Jace murmured, his curled finger making another light pass. "Did you ever fall foolishly in love?"

Shay pressed into the back of her chair, away from his touch, those eyes, that unnerving query. Fall in love? She shook her head.

"No?"

"Never." And it seemed both the safest and saddest admission a woman could make.

Jace's palm, rough and warm, cupped her cheek. "Shay—"

The dual sound of boat engines caught their attention. His hand dropped, she slid from her chair and he hurried down the ramp with long strides, Shay at his heels.

They stood at one end of the slip, watching two boats approach. London stood slightly behind the uniformed officer at the wheel of the *Fun & Games*, her head bent, black hair swirling, both thumbs on the keyboard of her phone. A second boat, with a bar of lights across the top, trailed behind.

Jace shoved his hands in his hair as Shay drew up beside him. "What the hell am I supposed to do now?" he muttered, though she didn't think he was expecting her to answer. He might have forgotten she was there. "I haven't a clue how to handle this, damn it."

When the prow of the first boat motored within shouting distance, Jace pinned his daughter with a stare. "London Jennings!"

Her head jerked up. Her black-lined eyes went wide.

The lion roared, in clear worry teamed with frustration. "You're grounded! You got that? *Grounded.*"

Shay's hand flew up as the words reverberated in her chest. The dock moved, the pontoons beneath it rocking with the waves caused by the oncoming watercraft. She staggered, unbalanced.

Moved, in the strangest way.

You're grounded, Mr. I'm-No-Dad had said. *Grounded.*

She should laugh. It was funny, wasn't it? A typical reaction from a nontypical father. But instead, she was worried. Those few words had done something to her, Shay realized. *Jace* had done something to her with the simplest phrase. What exactly that was…well, she had a very bad feeling that Poppy was no longer the only Walker sister with too soft a heart.

CHAPTER SEVEN

LONDON CLUTCHED HER phone with one hand and grabbed on to the side of the boat with the other as the lake patrolman piloting the *Fun & Games* pulled back on the throttle, further slowing their movement. They glided closer to the slip and she risked a second look at Jace. His expression remained fierce and he stood with legs braced, his arms crossed over his chest, his narrowed gaze glued to her face.

Uh-oh.

Had she heard right? Had he just shouted she was grounded?

Nobody had ever yelled at her like that before.

It had made her stomach jump, just a little, but that was nothing compared to the rolls and somersaults it had made after she'd climbed into the boat with Colton. It had been an easy thing to dash undetected into the house for the keys and even easier to hand them over to the tanned boy unwinding the mooring ropes from the cleats. Clearly, he knew what he was doing.

Next, they'd reversed out of the berth, cruised past the five-mile-per-hour buoys, then hit free water. There, he'd set the boat on "Fly."

At least it had felt that way to London. Though her stomach had somersaulted, her grin stretched from ear to ear. She'd sunk farther into the low-slung seat, the speed exhilarating. She was a bird, a plane, an untethered balloon. Then they crossed the wake of another powerboat, and the *slap-slap-slap* of the hull against the water had bounced her bottom against the vinyl. She'd giggled and Colton had glanced over at her, smiling.

So comfortable in his skin. Confident. He'd stood behind the wheel, one knee propped on the captain's seat. The wind whipped his sun-kissed hair into eggbeater disorder and London had wrapped an arm around her own waist in a secret self hug.

This moment was happening to *her*!

The delight had ended much too soon. There'd been the short burp of a siren. Flashing lights behind them. Head turned over his shoulder, Colton had frowned. A rooster tail of water shot behind the *Fun & Games* as he'd slowed to a stop.

The patrol boat had idled up alongside them. The men inside wore blue uniform pants, bright white polo shirts and navy ball caps emblazoned with the Blue Arrow Lake logo. Both of them looked straight at her.

London decided it was too late to jump over the side or slide under her seat. Colton was the one who spoke up, though. "Jim? Chris? Is there a problem?"

His familiarity with the two didn't settle London's jittery stomach. Their serious expressions didn't ease. "Are you London Jennings?" the oldest one—grandfather-age—asked.

"Um…yeah."

Then she'd wished she'd taken that swan dive into the lake when she'd had the chance. The man informed her that her father was concerned, told Colton the boat had been taken without permission and said they must return to the dock immediately.

Colton had sent her a puzzled look but agreed in an instant. The older man's manner had turned more kindly, it seemed to London, and he'd said he'd be taking the wheel.

"It's all on me," London had declared then. "This was my idea."

"Hey—" Colton had begun

"He didn't know." London had spoken over him, coming to her feet in the boat, despite its slight pitch and roll. She'd held back her hair with one hand and directed her gaze at the man in charge, meeting his eyes. "I told Colton it would be okay."

The head patrolman had nodded at that, then clambered into the *Fun & Games*. He'd directed Colton into the other patrol boat, telling him he'd be dropped closer to his home. The boy's protest had been cut off. "I'll handle it from here, son."

On a sigh, Colton had turned to London. "Are you going to be all right?" he'd murmured.

If only the mortification would kill her, she'd thought, right then and there. "Of course," she'd whispered. "But...but I'm really sorry."

He'd smiled, touched her nose and vaulted from one vessel to the other. As both boats powered in opposite directions, he'd flashed her a grin followed by a jaunty salute.

And she'd known she had to see him again.

Had to.

For the magic. For the freedom. To take the next step into her own life.

But did he want to see her again, too?

She'd spent the return trip to the dock on her phone. Before, she'd stumbled upon a teen relationship app.

Calling it up, she'd tapped on "How to Tell if He Likes You?"

Pay attention to what he does.

At the old boathouse, he'd worked to make her smile. He'd suggested they do something together. Before leaving her, he'd touched her. A nose tap, but *a nose tap*. That had to mean something.

Pay attention to what he says.

This gave her pause. He'd told her black wasn't her color. He'd suggested a hoodie and jeans wasn't her best look. She'd known that. She just didn't know what to do about it.

Now, the prow of the *Fun & Games* gently bumped the dock. The patrolman threw over one of the lines to a grim-faced Jace, who started tying it down. London looked to Shay, but she was smiling at the patrol guy in the other boat. He was idling close to where she stood on the dock, and he swept off his hat to scrub his hand over his crew cut. If he'd been closer, London wouldn't have been surprised to see him nose tap Shay.

She glanced over at Jace, saw he was now watching the conversation. His expression had gone from grim to foul. Interesting.

When her tutor let out a light laugh, London's gaze shifted back. Whether Shay noticed it or not, as she chatted, her hand was sifting through her hair. Its color was so pretty, the sun catching gold threads and bronze ones, too. Frowning, London held up a hank of her own. It seemed dulled by the same light.

Another laugh from Shay. Her head was tilted back and there was a sparkle in her eyes. Her lashes were long and curled, but natural-looking. Her outfit was simple, a thin white V-necked T-shirt, a knit skirt of blue-and-white stripes that clung to her hips and fell just above her knees. She was wearing turquoise flats that matched the stones hanging from her ears and the bracelet wound around her wrist.

She looked stylish. Young. Not as young as London, but not as old as London looked in her baggy black clothes and her black dead-head hair.

Still contemplating that, she let out a startled "eep" as her father lifted her out of the *Fun & Games* and set her down on the dock. "Well?" he demanded, planting his hands on his hips.

He was big. More than a little angry-looking.

But the anger barely registered as her mind was on other things. Colton. Their brief time together this afternoon. The app on her phone. *How do you know he likes you?*

The last piece of advice bubbled up in her mind. *Follow your heart.*

Jace made an exasperated sound. "London," he said. "What do you have to say for yourself?"

Follow your heart. She half turned, waved to get Shay's attention. "Hey, will you take me shopping?"

POST HIS A.M. mug of coffee, Jace paced the boundaries of the upstairs study area, stewing as he waited for London to join him. Yesterday afternoon, following her boat adventure, he'd been so nonplussed by her nonexplanation of her behavior that he'd marched off to his quarters to regroup.

At dinner, he'd told her they would have a meeting the next day, first thing.

Still striding back and forth, he studied the paper in his hand. It was a solid, short set of rules. No boys. No leaving the property without permission. No boys.

He was going to get the young female in his life under control.

The sound of footsteps had him spinning around. "Oh," he said to Shay. "You."

She gave him a half wave and started sorting the books and papers on the table. "Sorry. I'm just here to gather some materials so I can work on lesson plans in my room."

"You're not staying?" He figured he could use her support.

"Jace, it's a family meeting."

His gaze ran over her, diverting him for a moment. Once again, she was a spot of brightness against the drab backdrop of the house. There was that vibrant color of her hair, the sky-blue of the tank she wore with slouchy pants rolled at the hem. A delicate chain circled her ankle and tiny silver shells hung from the links. A matching bracelet looped one wrist.

He wanted to see her wearing only the jewelry, he thought, the wish striking deep. There'd be nothing else to hide her apricot skin, the gold-red of her hair, the pale pink parts of her that he'd only explored during a short shadowed night.

He wanted to discover her in sunlight. She'd be completely revealed then, under a cloudless sky, in summer temperatures that burned as hot as the lust she spiked in him. He'd stretch her naked on the beach, and cup the lake water in his hands to dribble it over her bare torso.

The cool liquid would pearl her nipples, pool in her belly button, run into the soft place between her thighs.

"Is there something wrong with the way I look?"

He jerked out of the fantasy. "What?"

"You're staring."

Clearing his throat, he shifted his gaze and willed his south-rushing blood to switch direction. *I was thinking,* he wanted to say, *about you. Nude. At the mercy of my touch.* He cleared his throat again and wrenched his mind back to business. He had called a meeting. There was an important purpose to it.

"There's nothing wrong with you," he said. "It's…it's just that it's all new to me, this father-daughter thing."

"I know." Shay hesitated. "Look…teenage girls… they can be vulnerable."

"Why do you think I'm going to lay down the law?"

She returned the papers she held to the table and leaned back against it. "I have an older brother. I remember Brett's teenage angst. It came out in punishing sports competitions with his friends, marathons of violent video games, the consumption of incredible amounts of junk-food calories."

Jace remembered late-night runs to the local pancake house with his buddies, where they'd battle to see who could eat the most orders of buttermilk pancakes deluged with syrup. "What are you trying to warn me about?"

"Girls can go inward. Tuck disapproval—or perceived disapproval, any kind of negative feedback, really—deep inside. They'll keep it too close. Think about it too much, too often."

Jace groaned.

"They might become quiet, and be shy about speaking of their dreams and their desires."

His fingers tightened on his sheet of rules, crumpling the paper. What did he know of a fifteen-year-old's dreams and desires?

Shay turned and scooped up the materials she'd set down a few moments before. "Tell London I took her Dickens book, okay?"

"Oh, no," he said, catching her arm as she began to sweep past him. "Now I really can't do this alone."

"Sure you can." She tugged, trying to escape.

Jace only drew her closer, pulling her sweet scent into his lungs. Her skin was warm and soft beneath his palm and she was close enough that he could get a peek at a little cleavage if he let his gaze drop.

Maybe she was afraid of that, because she yanked free of him and stepped back. "Jace—"

"I'm not kidding," he said, catching her hand. "I need your help." Holding up his paper, he rattled his list in her face.

"What's this?" she asked, slipping her fingers free.

"My rules. Tell me what you think."

She frowned, dumped the things she carried back on the table again and swiped the sheet out of his hand to peruse the three items he'd written. "You named one of these rules twice."

"Because it's the most important."

Her response was an extravagant roll of her eyes. "She's fifteen—"

"Exactly."

"Jace, it's natural for her to be interested in boys."

"On television. In books. From far, far away."

"You remember what I told you about Colton Halliday, her boat adventure companion of yesterday, right?"

"I stopped listening after you confirmed he has an X and a Y chromosome." It was almost true.

She huffed out a sigh. "I know him and his fam—"

"How well?" he asked.

"Very well. And if you don't trust me, think about the lake patrol. They're acquainted with him, too, and aided him in avoiding your wrath because they judged the boy blameless in the situation."

That was actually true, he thought grudgingly, though Jace wasn't sure that both officers had been exclusively focused on their jobs the day before.

"That younger patrol guy…"

Her brows drew together. "Chris?"

"On the short side, blond, couldn't drag his gaze off of you?"

"Chris." She frowned. "And he's plenty tall. He's just not built on your massive proportions."

Jace ignored that. "You dated him, didn't you?"

"That's none of your business."

Of course it wasn't, but what the hell. Jace tilted his head, watching a faint blush tinge Shay's cheeks. "You broke it off with him." Yesterday, she'd confessed she'd never been in love. Well, good ol' Chris couldn't say the same. He'd been staring at Shay as if she were the first meal following a long fast. "Too bad, because he looks like just your type."

Her blush deepened. "What's that supposed to mean?"

"He's Officer All-Good. Apple pie, Mom and eight hours of continuous, guiltless sleep every night. Not a solitary sin or single rough edge."

Annoyance snapped in her glacial blue eyes. "You say that like it's a bad thing."

Jace shrugged. "You tell me. You're the one who broke up with him." Why was he needling her? He had no idea, except maybe he wanted to get what she was doing to him under control, too, and because that worshipful expression on Officer Upright's face had rubbed Jace entirely the wrong way.

"He's very nice," Shay said, her tone prim.

"I get it now." He grinned. "You dumped All-Good because he's just *too* virtuous. Too respectful. Too polite."

"You're ridiculous."

"I'm experienced." Leaning near, he lowered his voice. "I know you good girls like your panties torn off on occasion."

Her eyes flared and her pink cheeks turned red. "You don't know what I want."

"I know exactly what you want," he said in that near whisper. "A family man who'll make the rounds at the end of the evening, checking the doors to ensure you and the little ones are safe. Then he'll slip into your bedroom and lock that door, too, so he can make uninterrupted monkey love to you until the clock strikes midnight."

She moved back, reclaiming her personal space. "You're wrong."

"Yeah?" His eyebrows rose. "Which part?"

Her next move startled him. She stepped close, going up on tiptoe to put her mouth near his ear. "For your information," she said, her breath blowing warm against his cheek, "on occasion I want that monkey loving to go on way past midnight and into the wee hours of the morning."

Heat shot up his spine. His libido ignited, firing his blood. He cupped her shoulders, ready to yank her even closer so he could take her mouth and then he'd—

"I'll be right there!" London's voice floated from the direction of her bedroom.

Jace dropped his hands as if they'd been burned. Shay, her expression somewhere between smug and saved, slapped his list of rules to his chest. "Good luck, big guy," she said, and left.

He didn't make a grab for her this time. If he were going to win against one of the females in his life, he had to get his head in the game—and Shay's presence directed his attention to the wrong effing head.

Seating himself at the table, he took a few deep breaths and put himself into CEO mode. He managed employees all around the world and was known for his effective, hands-on style. *Hell.* Glancing down, he flexed his fingers and tried dispelling the lingering sense of Shay's skin beneath his palms.

Prepare to run a meeting, he told himself. *Think of your agenda.* He studied his three-item list. *Time to take the lead.*

"Sorry I'm late," London said, rushing into the room. She had her tutor in tow. "I asked Shay to join us, okay?"

He wouldn't give either one of them the satisfaction of balking, but he avoided looking in the woman's direction. "No problem," he murmured as they pulled out chairs. When they were settled, he lined up his paper in front of him. "Shall we begin?"

"Let me go first," London said, whipping out her own sheet and placing it onto the table.

"What? I called the meeting—"

"And I have new business," she said, smiling. For the

first time he saw the excellent outcome of those ortho-dontist bills he'd paid. He was so startled by the effect, he just stared, which gave her an opening to continue.

"I want only a few things," she said.

"Wait a minute—"

"Don't I have the floor?" she asked, glancing over at Shay.

The tutor seemed to consider, apparently not in the mood to do Jace any favors. "Well…"

"This is a family meeting," he said from between his teeth.

Shay's brows shot up and she sent him a pointed look. *Isn't that what I said?*

It was imperative that he wrest back power. "London, you'll get your chance. But first—"

"I want a car," she said in a rush. "And a driver's permit, a boat driver's license—you can get those at twelve, you know—and a sailboat."

It took several moments for all that to sink in. "What?"

"A car, a—"

"I heard you." He rubbed at the pain starting to throb at the base of his skull. It wasn't a lingering effect of his concussion, he could tell, but instead your average, everyday, teenager-induced headache. "Anything else?" he asked, his tone dry.

"Now that you mention it." She turned her cheeky grin on Shay. "I have some old business, too. About that shopping trip…"

Control was lost, Jace decided on a silent groan. He crumpled his list of rules between his palms and threw the paper over his left shoulder like it was spilled salt. Maybe that would neutralize the trouble he sensed he was in.

CHAPTER EIGHT

SHAY SAT IN the passenger seat of Jace's car, trying not to release any more emotion into the already thick atmosphere inside the SUV. He drove along the road leading to the Walker family cabins, hands at ten and two, determination pumping off of him. In the backseat, London's usual strict pains to project pure boredom had been replaced with a distinct adolescent sulkiness. The moods of the two Jenningses tussled silently with each other, making the drive anything but relaxing. But years of feeling like a family gate-crasher had made Shay feel obligated to take on the role of smoother of choppy waters.

"Lovely day," she said, in an effort to perform her usual function.

Jace grunted. London didn't bother to respond, clearly still peeved about her father's plan.

Though the girl had hijacked Jace's meeting the morning before, he'd had a new scheme by evening. As punishment for taking out the boat without permission, he'd announced London was sentenced to some hard labor. And he knew just the place where she'd serve her sentence.

Shay had been astonished when he'd revealed his idea of putting in some hours at her family cabins—and also somewhat impressed that he'd remembered them.

"I owe you, remember?" he'd said in an undertone, and her mind had rocketed back to that bittersweet morning in her room at the Deerpoint Inn. She'd been standing at the window when he'd come up behind her to say good-bye and she'd never, ever expected to see him again.

But here he was, for a little while longer smack-dab in her life. She flicked a glance at him now, and experienced that same overwhelming rush of "oh, my" as that night when he'd slipped onto the bar stool beside her. It had been simple, from-inches-away female appreciation, with no expectation of how he would later kiss her, stroke her...and needle her, she remembered with a grimace.

Yesterday he'd used his sex appeal to knock her off balance.

I know you good girls like your panties torn off on occasion.

Still, it was possible she'd knocked him right back, she thought, with a smug little wiggle of her tush on the seat.

Jace's sidelong look felt like a poke. "What are you thinking about?" he asked.

Getting as good as I got. "Nothing much," she said, feeling cheerier. But uneasiness struck back as she spied the turn to the steep driveway leading to the Walker land. "I told you not to expect too much, right?" The last thing she wanted to hear was his assessment that the cabins were a lost cause.

Instead of answering, he glanced in the rearview mirror as the car climbed the hill. "Is that another of your boyfriends following us?"

Shay twisted in her seat, noting the unfamiliar sleek sedan on their tail. The sunlight on the windshield made it impossible to see inside. "I don't know who it is… and I don't have a boyfriend." Jace had been right about Chris's ex status. They'd dated months ago, though even now she couldn't articulate why she'd ended things shortly after they'd begun. He was what a mountain girl like herself should want.

Jace's SUV braked and she was out of the car as the other vehicle came to a halt behind them. Then a long leg emerged from the driver's side ending in an expensive pair of running shoes and Shay grinned, scampering over to greet the newcomer. He swept her into a hug and bussed her on the cheek. Then he held her away from him and beamed at her a million-dollar, movie-star smile that only widened her grin.

"Don't waste those megawatts on me," she said, shaking a finger at him. "I've already told Poppy yes, I'll babysit during your honeymoon."

He pulled her in for another great-smelling embrace. Shay didn't even pretend reluctance. When a man like this wanted to hold you in his arms, who would be silly enough to object?

The distinct clearing of a throat broke them apart. Glancing behind her, she saw Jace looming, his expression suspicious.

"I thought you didn't know this guy," he said.

"I didn't recognize the car. New?" she asked Ryan.

He shook his head. "I usually don't bring it up to the mountains." His gaze shifted toward the teen getting out of the SUV. "Hey…"

"London," Shay whispered.

"Interesting," Ryan murmured, then greeted the girl before reaching toward the other man. "You must be London's dad."

Shay performed the introductions. Any ensuing small talk was postponed as Mason emerged from the backseat of Ryan's car. He threw himself at Shay, who squeezed him hard. Next, he leaped in London's direction. Jace appeared surprised that the girl bent to give the small boy her attention, but Shay wasn't.

"What are you doing here?" Shay asked Ryan as her nephew tugged the girl toward the cabins. With a glance back at her, Jace trailed behind the children.

"Mason left his favorite baseball bat last time he visited. We're here to retrieve it while Poppy does some sort of in-home beauty treatment that she claims will scare me away if I'm there to witness it."

Without thinking, Shay reached out and clutched his wrist. "Nothing will scare you away from my sister."

He squarely met her gaze as if sensing her great need for reassurance. "Nothing will scare me away from your sister, Shay. You have my solemn promise."

She sighed, and told herself there wasn't a stinging pressure behind her eyes. Poppy deserved such devotion. It was what Shay wanted for herself—a man to belong to. A man who'd stick.

Then Mason and London—carrying the sought-after bat—returned, a bemused Jace still on their heels. The little boy jumped onto Ryan and clambered up his body. "Found it, Duke. Now we can go home to practice."

He boosted the boy onto his shoulders. "In a sec. I want to know what brings your aunt to the cabins."

Shay glanced between Jace and his daughter. "London and her dad are here to…look around. They might be able to help out a little—you know, with getting the cabins into shape."

Ryan's brows rose. "Poppy said you'd come over to the dark side."

She shrugged. "I told her I'd like to see the resort return to some kind of life, too."

"I wish you guys would allow me to invest—"

"God, no!"

He put up both hands. "All right, all right. I get it. Flatlander cash and Walker pride, a combination never to be tolerated."

Mason tugged on his hair and curled over Ryan's head to gaze at the man upside down. "Practice, Duke."

"Practice, son," Ryan said, swinging the child off his shoulders. "Say your goodbyes."

A few more moments of chatter and then boy and man were climbing into their car. Shay and Jace stood side by side as the pair prepared to leave. At the last second, Ryan rolled down his window and sent them a serious look.

"Watch yourself," he cautioned, then drove off.

"I think that was meant for me," Jace said. "It's kind of a kick to get that from the famous Ryan Hamilton."

"Get what?"

He smiled at her. "A warning against the dangerous power of Walker women."

Ignoring that, she spun around. "Ready for the five-dollar tour?"

London, already familiar with the area, went on an exploration of her own. Shay explained to Jace there were twelve cabins in all, the five ringing the clearing and seven others in more secluded locations tucked into the surrounding woods.

He peered up at the roof of the nearest bungalow and pronounced a need for immediate repairs.

"We know that," Shay said, "thanks to a late winter storm."

Then he pulled at one of the cedar shingles that covered the outside wall. It practically crumbled in his hand. "An easy fix. I can tackle problems like this and the roof. We'll give London a rake and she can start tidying up around the cabins."

"You don't have to—"

"This is my idea, remember? It will give me something to do—and get London's mind off of boys."

Shay decided not to tell him that there wasn't any working prescription for that, and instead followed as he made his way into the woods. "I want to see some of the other cabins," he said.

"Just keep following the path," she instructed, pointing.

Poppy had already reworn a narrow track that wound through the tall trees. Despite the shade beneath the boughs, the smell of sun-warmed pine permeated the air. Bugs hummed and birds rustled among the needles and leaves, but other than those natural sounds, it was quiet. Beautiful.

The Walker legacy. She'd missed it.

"So…" Jace mused as he continued through the woods. "Duke? What's with that?"

Shay paused. "What do you mean?"

"Why does the boy call him Duke?"

"Oh." She ducked beneath a feathery cedar branch in order to catch up with him. "When Poppy and Mason met Ryan last March, the boy tumbled head over heels for Ryan at the same time Ryan was doing the same for both my sister and Mason. Duke is a character from a movie Ryan starred in that Mason loves."

"Ah." Jace snapped his fingers. *"Gang of Spies."* He came to a halt in front of another of the cabins, one that had always been a favorite of Shay's. The A-frame roof had deep eaves that lent it a fairy-tale air. The trees that nestled around the structure filtered the light and gave it an almost buttery quality.

Jace seemed to be giving the cottage a serious study. "So…they bonded that quickly," he finally said. "Your nephew and Ryan."

"What they have is pretty special…" Her voice trailed off as she caught on to the significance of the question. Oh, she thought. *Oh.* Her instinct to soothe moved her closer to him.

Reaching out, she brushed Jace's back, the muscles stiff beneath her fingertips. "Mason's not a teenager. He's five years old. Like a small puppy, really. Very ready and eager to accept new people and new things."

Jace glanced down at her. "Are you trying to make me feel better?"

His golden eyes could mesmerize her, she thought, as she stared up at them. Heat gathered low in her belly and moved everywhere. "I'm…I'm not trying to make you feel anything."

That seemed to amuse him. Smiling, he lifted his hand, his touch ghosting over her cheek. "You're failing at that, you know. Big-time."

Failing? Or…

Ever fall foolishly into a relationship?

Whatever he read on her face had him moving away. Shoving his hands in his pockets, he turned back toward the cabin. "How'd your family snag this prime piece of real estate?"

She told him about the Walker ancestors. How they'd

traveled up to the mountains with their oxen and their pioneering spirit one hundred and fifty years before. About the ski resort it had been in contemporary times. "But my father—not the shrewdest of businessmen—made a bad financial deal. When a fire swept through and took out everything but this handful of cabins, there was no way to rebuild."

"Until now."

"Until Poppy came up with an idea to refurbish what we have left and market it as an upscale, very private and secluded retreat. Fancy sheets, gourmet food, but no phones, no internet."

"For the busy city folk who want a real mountain escape."

"Yes. One that's easy to reach, but very much away from it all." She glanced around, breathing in the clean air. "Maybe for harried businesspeople such as yourself, who are looking for a solitary, peaceful haven."

He made a low sound.

Shay turned to see that he was watching her, something…something new, and intense, in his golden eyes. "What?" she said, apprehensive, but determined to hold her ground.

Shaking his head, he approached until he was close enough that she had to tilt her chin to meet his gaze. His breath fluttered the hair at her temple, making her shiver, and that connection between them snapped into place again, the line taut, quivering, just like the muscles in her thighs and across her chest.

Transfixed, as unable to move as if she'd really been tied to him, she continued to stare upward. "Why are you looking at me like that?" she asked.

"Because before today, before this moment, I would

have said that's just the kind of downtime I'd like. I'm good at solitary, Shay. That's what I know. But looking at you right now, with the sun warming your hair and glittering in your eyes…"

Shay felt herself sway toward him. He caught her shoulders and his fingers tightened there, whether to push her away or draw her close, she didn't know.

"I don't feel so much like being alone," he murmured.

Nor did Shay. All her life she'd been on the outside, the observer, a step away from family, from being one of their tight circle. She moved into Jace now, her foot stepping between his so they were flush, body-to-body, the tips of her breasts against his chest, the bulge at his groin touching her belly. Another shiver tripped down her spine. Her kneecap brushed his and that simple touch felt as erotic as his tongue sweeping across her lower lip.

Which it was doing.

She moaned, her nipples tightening into a painful ache that was echoed between her thighs. Who knew that desire could hurt so much, she thought, her eyes closing. Who knew that the need to have more direct contact—nakedness, nudity, his flesh against hers, more, more, *more*—could be harsh instead of honey-sweet.

Her arms rose up to cross behind his neck. She tilted her hips, rocking in tiny increments against the aggressive jut of his sex, trying to ease herself. Every cell of her cried out to have that thick stiffness, all of her wanted it inside her again. To be part of her.

His tongue slid into her mouth. She moaned, sucking on it, and felt his hand sweep down her back, past her hip, to cup her bottom and bring her tighter against him. Her sex throbbed, and she slid her fingers into his thick, short hair, anchoring his mouth to hers.

Then Jace's head jerked up, breaking her hold. Panting, Shay stared at him, dazed, only to realize he was the first to sense impending danger. Now she could hear it, too, the sound of someone moving through the forest, not trying to be quiet. Still breathing heavily, Shay moved away, the back of her hand wiping her wet mouth.

Jace's gaze dropped there, flipping her stomach and causing her pulse to stagger like a Saturday night drunk. That's what he did to her—made her intoxicated with desire. "Stop looking at me like that," she hissed, fanning her face with both hands. Surely her cheeks were tomato red.

Then their attention was claimed by London, who appeared around the side of the cabin. She glanced up at it, her lip curling. "Well, this one's really a dump, isn't it?"

Jace scowled at her. "Where have you been? Don't think you can wander off when it comes time to work."

"Sheesh." The girl's brows lifted, disappearing behind a hank of too-black hair. "Why are you so grouchy?"

"Don't ask," her father muttered, then stomped off.

London looked at Shay, the question still in her eyes. "Oh, you know," Shay said vaguely, trying to smooth over the situation, "he probably needs a snack."

The girl's frown said she considered the excuse a pretty poor one, though she did start off in her father's footprints. Shay held back, glancing one more time at the cabin, seeing it through a stranger's eyes. "It *does* look like a dump," she muttered.

But the thought evaporated as her gaze shifted to the

spot where she and Jace had tangled. As she recalled the powerful force that propelled them together, as she relived the taste and burn of that prolonged, passionate kiss, her heart once again thrashed in her chest.

Her stomach felt like a dinghy adrift on rough waters.

It made her wonder how she would manage to soothe her own unsteadiness.

JACE LOOKED DOWN from the ladder he was using to reach and remove the rotting siding of one of the dilapidated Walker cabins. Across the clearing, London was raking brown needles into piles, though she kept stopping to adjust the work gloves he'd bought for her. Still, she was halfway-industrious, and he was glad to see it was too hot for her ubiquitous black sweatshirt. She'd abandoned it for the black T-shirt she wore beneath.

Shay was in even less. Hiking boots, cut-off shorts, a tank top. Work gloves protected her hands, too, as she retrieved the shingles he let fall and tossed them into a wheelbarrow. Naturally, the task caused her to bend over a lot, denim cupping the round globes of her ass.

Jace wondered if she'd go away if he told her just the sight of that made his dick hard.

Christ.

Fact was, she was driving him nuts. He couldn't be around her for thirty seconds without wanting to push her up against a wall and push his tongue into her mouth. After yesterday's blistering kiss, he'd looked forward to some sweat-inducing, muscle-tiring menial labor, imagining it would refocus his physical urges in another direction.

That was not happening.

He inserted the claw end of the short crowbar he held between the shingles. Barely a yank, and the wood crumbled into pieces and fell to the ground. Too late, he realized that Shay was right under him.

"Are you all right?"

"No problem." Sunglasses protected her eyes and she didn't seem to mind brushing debris from her crown of bright hair and off her shoulders. She looked up, a frown turning down her lips. "It's pretty bad, huh?"

"Pretty," he murmured, staring into her face. There was a flush on her cheeks and a sheen of sweat on her throat. Instead of leaping to the ground to taste it with his mouth, he forced his gaze back to the house and his mind off her lovely features and long legs.

Okay, he was thinking about her lovely features and long legs. Clearing his throat, he attacked again with the crowbar. When the next shingle fell, he remembered something he'd wanted to follow up on before.

"The dark side?" he asked.

She scooped up the shingle. "Say again?"

"The dark side. Yesterday Ryan Hamilton asked if you'd come over to the dark side."

"Oh. That." She gave him a quick glance. "Thirsty? Would you like a bottle of water?"

Suddenly he was parched. And curious because she was clearly trying to avoid the subject. "Yeah."

He came down from the ladder just as she returned with a sweating bottle from the cooler they'd brought along. "Thanks." Half of it went down in one go. "Dark side," he prompted, when she took her own bottle away from her lips.

She sighed. "Promise you won't think we're all crazy."

Crazy was his reluctance to climb back up on the ladder and put much-needed distance between them. Instead, he reached out to push her dark shades to the top of her head so he could look into her eyes, their cool blue icy and beautiful. "Go ahead and tell me."

"First you should know the Walkers aren't in agreement about what to do with this property."

"Obviously Poppy's all for the resort, as are you, it seems. Your other sister and brother...?"

"Claim the place is cursed."

He laughed.

"I'm serious," Shay said. "Family legend says one of the logger forebears did something—causes differ upon the telling—and he and his property were damned for all time."

Jace finished his bottle of water and tossed it into the wheelbarrow. When he looked back at Shay, she'd restored her sunglasses to their place on her nose. Hiding, he thought. Why?

"You can't possibly believe in a superstition like that," he said, climbing back onto the ladder.

"Maybe sometimes I do," she replied, her voice pensive.

He frowned down at her. "Why's that?"

"I told you about the fire."

"It's a constant threat in these mountains."

"I was here—at the property—when it happened."

That startled him. He found himself on the ground again, and when she turned away from him, he tugged at her elbow to bring her around. "Tell me," he said.

Lifting a shoulder, she stared down at her toes. "I was twelve. Accompanied Dell Walker—Dad—on a routine trip to do some maintenance work. He got out his tools…and I…I wandered off on my own, into the woods."

Some instinct made Jace glance up, his gaze searching for his daughter. Tension that was just beginning to tighten his neck eased when he saw her, digging through the cooler. She had to be roasting in all that unrelieved black, he thought. He looked back at Shay. "You were in the woods…?"

She hesitated, giving him time for second thoughts. Why was he grilling her? He had a load of his own problems and issues. Instead of excavating her past, he should be thinking of the job in Qatar that he'd promised to return to. Or he would be better served mining his brain for some persuasive words that would get his daughter to the boarding school he'd picked for her, without muss or fuss.

But Shay was inspecting the dusty leather toes of her boots again, her head down. Hiding once more. Second thoughts evaporated.

"You were in the woods…?"

"Summer storm," she said, her voice low. "Lightning. It's common enough for fire to suddenly break out."

"I've already experienced that myself," he pointed out. And would likely remember his nights at the Deerpoint Inn for the rest of his life.

"Dell—Dad—saw the flames crest a nearby ridge."

Jace lifted his head, taking in the craggy mountains ringing them. In his imagination, a line of fire topped a nearby peak and raced downward. "Jesus."

"Maybe if he could have taken off right away, driven to the highway quick enough to alert the fire crews…"

"But he couldn't leave you," Jace supplied. Of course,

the man had to gather his daughter before leaving the property. "That was a no-brainer—"

"I should have stuck close to him, instead of wandering off on my own."

"You couldn't know, *he* couldn't know—"

"But I know *now* how it turned out."

"You were just a kid, Shay. And it was a freak accident of nature."

"Not what happened afterward." She pinkied her sunglasses off her face and swiped a hand over her eyes.

His stomach jolted. Was she crying? He couldn't handle tears. But he couldn't escape up the ladder quite yet, either. "What went wrong next?"

She pressed a hand beneath her nose, leaving a streak of dirt on her cheek. Jace stared at it, his hands fisting, willing himself not to snatch her close in order to brush it away, stroke that smooth skin clean. He didn't like a single thing marring Shay—not her flesh, not her psyche—but he wasn't the kind of man who knew how to provide such tender service. That would be a kind soul, not a man hardened by a crappy childhood and then a solitary life.

Officer All-Good.

It killed him to think that, but it was true.

Shay started speaking again. "The resort amenities burned to ash, leaving behind only the cabins below the ski slopes and Dell's deep wish to rebuild."

"Okay," Jace said carefully.

She swiped beneath her nose again. "It wasn't possible. He was already in deep with an investor who refused to pony up another cent. There wasn't enough insurance, either. Dad didn't surrender, though."

Her head turned, so all he was given was her profile,

with its clean, delicate lines. "Within a year he'd died of a heart attack. Stress, we believe."

He opened his mouth to say—what? London called out instead.

"Can we eat?" she asked. They'd brought sandwiches in the cooler. "I'm starving."

Shay latched on to the idea and was already hurrying away from him. "Great idea. Let's set it up on the porch over there."

Jace followed slowly, mostly glad for the reprieve. By the time he mounted the steps to the picnic they'd made on the wooden floor, Shay was chattering away about the lessons they would begin on Monday. Naturally, London appeared less than enthused.

Warily, Jace eyed the tutor. The only time he'd known her to be a chatterer like that was the night she was drunk and floating her gloom balloon. He supposed she wished she hadn't shared the story of the fire and her father with him.

The day heated up as they ate their lunch. The food and the temperature made Jace lethargic and even Shay finally wound down. The three sat in semicompanionable silence, picking at the green grapes in the plastic bowl centered between them.

It was weirdly almost family-like.

The weirdness must have been catching, because London suddenly vaulted to her feet. "It's hot as hell—"

"Don't say hell," Shay corrected automatically.

The girl rolled her eyes. "The temperature's hot as h—"

"Don't say it," Shay warned again.

"Hot as hell." Jace met his daughter's gaze. "I've got no problem with that."

She gave him the second smile he'd seen from her since he'd returned to her life. Wow, he thought, he'd give her a lot of four-letter words for more of those. Which he supposed was additional proof he'd make a lousy parent.

"I'm going to cool off," she said, and leaped from the porch.

Jace's gaze followed her to a spigot and a curled hose nearby. London flipped on the water, and as the flow came out of the plastic, she bent down to thumb the nozzle. Then she lifted it overhead, creating a fountain of drops that rained down upon her.

"Nirvana. Heaven. Paradise," she yelled, her hair going even inkier as it became saturated. She twirled in a circle, going faster and faster.

Jace had started to grin at her antics, but the smile died as a memory sliced through him. That little park across from her mother's flat. London, a ragged doll under her arm, insisting they have a tea party on the grass. He'd played pretend with her, even lifting his pinkie while holding his make-believe cup like any proper Brit would do. Later, when he'd managed to make a chain of dandelions into a crown with his big fingers, he'd held her hands and spun, causing her short legs to leave the ground.

Jace, making his little girl fly.

He closed his eyes, willing the pain and the memory away.

But before it did, he got a face full of chilly water. His eyes shot open, just as Shay let out a shriek. Looking over, he saw she was dripping, too.

"London!" he yelled, and the second syllable was drowned by another blast from the hose.

She went after Shay again, of course. They both leaped to their feet as the girl cackled and kept on spraying. His gaze met Shay's. "You go right," he said.

"You go left," she answered.

They took on the kid together.

Retribution wasn't really all that painful. London was mostly wet already, but by the time they were done, she was a laughing, completely sopping mess. They were all cooler, however.

And Jace was feeling…almost mellow. Shit. Almost content.

He turned off the spigot and put his hands on his hips. "Enough goofing around. Let me finish the south wall and we'll say we're done for the day."

London gave an extravagant shrug. He glanced over at Shay, then felt his belly tighten as he took her in. She was as drenched as the girl, the thin cotton knit of her tank plastered to her skin. Oh, boy. Wet T-shirt contest all the way.

He could see the outline of her bra. Her nipples were taut points.

He grabbed the hem of his shirt. "Do you want my—"

"Heck, no," she said, waving him off. "It feels good."

Swallowing, Jace forced his gaze from her and his steps back to the ladder. London returned to her rake. Shay, her face turned upward, stood waiting for more shingles to come down.

Trying to tamp down his lust, he remembered her last words before lunch. He had to say something about that, didn't he? "I'm sorry about your father," he said.

She hesitated a moment. "One more little factoid about my past…Dell wasn't really my dad."

One more *little* factoid? "What exactly do you mean?"

"Money was always a struggle for the Walkers. Lorna and Dell went through a rough patch and Dell took off for a mining job in South America, leaving Mom behind with my brother and sisters. While he was gone, she…well, she had an affair and wound up pregnant with me."

"Ah." He hadn't a clue what to say, to do. "But Dell came back…?"

She addressed her bootlaces as she bent to retie them. "He did. By then the affair was over—my bio father was married and not the least bit interested in paternity rights, as he had other kids—so when Dell returned to the mountains a few months after I was born, he and Lorna patched things up."

"That was good?"

"Very good." Shay straightened. "Dell was still a dreamer and still lousy when it came to money, but my mother and he seemed to be very happy for the rest of their lives together."

"And you—"

"Oh, I've been happy, as well," she said quickly.

Too quickly, he thought, as he began stripping the siding once again. He remembered how much she said she disliked birthdays and now he supposed he knew why—they reminded her of the unusual circumstances of her birth. Clearing his throat, he paused to watch her retrieve the tumbled shingles. "Well, your secret is safe with me."

Wood in hand, she glanced up. "Oh, it's no secret."

"I'm sorry, I didn't mean to imply it's shameful or anything like that."

"Twenty-five years ago, small town, it caused a bit of a scandal."

He grimaced. "But that died down?"

"Well…like I said, small town." She tossed the piece she held into the wheelbarrow and swooped up another. "But my sisters and brother don't like it when I mention I'm their half sibling. The Walkers never try to make me feel separate from their family unit."

"Good for them."

"As a matter of fact, I hardly ever am referred to as a—" She lobbed the next shingle, then gasped. "Ouch." Blood welled on her fingers.

Jace leaped down. "Are you all right?"

"Only a splinter. I forgot to put my gloves back on." She drew out a sharp spike of wood and brought her finger to her mouth.

"Don't do that," he said, jerking it away, then drawing her hand toward him. In a trice, he'd wrapped the hem of his T-shirt around the wounded digit and put firm pressure on it to stop the bleeding.

They stood toe-to-toe, just as they had the day before in the woods, when he'd kissed her so greedily. As if he'd called her name, she looked up, her eyes widening as they took in his expression.

He probably looked as if he wanted to eat her up. Her scent was in his nostrils, her taste so damn available. His blood started that primitive *chug-chug-chug* through his system, his heart pounding like a drum in his chest. Call of the wild lust.

Closing his eyes, he tried ignoring the clamor. "Referred to as what?" he asked, recalling what she'd been saying before crying out. "What do you hardly ever get referred to as?"

"A bastard."

He jerked, his eyes flying open. "Shay—"

"Kidding," she said. Her mouth stretched into a grin, but the smile didn't reach her eyes.

Bastard. Scandal.

The Walkers never try to make me feel separate from their family unit.

It didn't take an emotional genius to know what Shay had just given away. A real secret, he thought. The fact that she did, indeed, often feel separate from that intimate family circle of her brother and sisters.

Uh-oh, Jace thought. Oh, damn, damn, *damn.* So much for that redirecting of his physical urges. He wanted to touch her even more now. Bring her against him, into the shelter of his body.

But not for carnal purposes. No, this was much worse. He wanted to gather her close to bestow something he was wholly unfamiliar with providing.

Comfort.

CHAPTER NINE

SHAY HUNG UP the dish towel and glanced over at Jace. After their day at the Walker property, they'd returned home and gone their separate ways for showers and downtime. Dinner had been pizza that he'd insisted on ordering. When she'd said she had a ball of whole wheat dough in the refrigerator and could whip up one herself in just a few minutes, he'd shared a look with London and said "whole wheat dough" in the same tone he might have used if she'd suggested a crust of garden snails.

His daughter had giggled.

Giggled.

Shay still couldn't get over it, nor the playful hose fight the girl had instigated after lunch. Clearly she felt comfortable enough to blast away at the adults in her life.

At her father.

She glanced over at Jace, who was standing in the adjacent great room. Hands in his pockets, he was staring out the glass doors at the lake. The days were getting longer and there was plenty of activity on the water, but it didn't appear as if he was taking any of it in. He looked like a man with a heavy weight on his mind.

He looked like a man too alone.

"So, today was a good day, don't you think?" she

asked, daring to interrupt the quiet. After pizza, London had wandered up to her room where she was likely reading—if the girl gave *A Tale of Two Cities* a decent chance Shay thought she'd find it hard to put down— or surfing the web.

When he didn't answer, she said, "Jace?"

He twitched and glanced around, finding her in the kitchen. Then he glanced around again, as if seeing the place for the first time. "What have you done here? Things look different."

Unsure of herself, she fiddled with the elastic bandage she'd wrapped around her finger. He'd retrieved it from the first-aid kit in Poppy's former cabin. She'd done the rest of the doctoring, insisting she didn't need his help, desperate to avoid any more of his touch. "Different, uh, how?"

Frowning, he gestured to the furniture, all of it in shades of gray. Then he pointed to the kitchen island. "Flowers. Color."

"Well, yeah." A dozen sunflowers popped from a vase she'd found in a closet. There had also been a stack of colorful throws there, and she'd draped them across the drab-colored backs of the couches and love seats. "You mentioned this place was butt ugly."

"You don't think so?" he asked, brows rising.

Her lips twitched. "I kind of did. But the view is incredible and it's growing on me. Especially with some warmer touches here and there."

"The master bed—the one hanging on chains…"

She shook her head. "Sorry, I can't think of a way to warm that up."

He stilled, sent her a pointed look, then turned his

attention back to the lake. "I'll forget you said that," he muttered.

Curses, Shay thought. Those words shouldn't have popped out of her mouth, not when she was determined to ignore the sexual undercurrent that seemed to continuously flow beneath their feet. Even when it bubbled and spit on occasion—as it had today, and yesterday and every day since they'd met—she was determined to avoid the burn.

Clearing her throat, she ventured back into conversation. "Like I mentioned, I think today went well with London."

He kept staring out the glass. "You really think so?"

"Yes." She strolled toward him. "The two of you seem to be getting comfortable together. I think she might be starting to like you."

He turned when she paused beside him. "More evidence of her bad judgment," he said, grimacing.

"Oh, come on." She nudged his ribs with her elbow. "You're not such a terrible guy."

"Evidence of *your* bad judgment."

"Stop—"

"I can see where you're going with this, Shay. I see that little dream you're concocting in your head."

She frowned. "I'm actually one of the cynical Walkers. A realist. Poppy is our romantic."

"You keep telling yourself that."

His dismissive tone annoyed her. "I'm looking at the facts, Jace."

"Which are what?"

"How about we start with this one—you've yet to tell your daughter that her summer with her father has been curtailed." It had made her hope he might be having second thoughts.

"I—"

"That you've yet to tell your daughter that you're sending her off to boarding school before you even get a chance to learn her favorite kind of animal, her favorite flavor of ice cream, what she wants to be when she grows up."

"Vampira?"

She gave him a disappointed look. "Maybe you'd like to stick around long enough to find out her real hair color, too."

"It's enough to know that the shade it is now isn't authentic. Thank you." Rubbing his knuckles against the short stubble on his chin, he glanced upward. "Thank you, God."

Stubborn man. Shay saw that she wasn't getting anywhere with him, but she couldn't let it go. "Please reconsider, Jace."

He rounded on her, his voice low, but with frustration bleeding through. "Reconsider what? I can't 'reconsider' the past, Shay," he said. "I don't know her. I haven't seen her for ten years."

"That will just take time—"

"Don't you get it?" His hands shot out to grasp her shoulders. "I can't 'reconsider' *my* past. What do I know about being a father? The one that made my life miserable is not a good example and history bears out I'm just as cold as he was."

She refused to be cowed, even though his frustration was clearly morphing into anger. "Listen to your gut, your instincts—"

"Fine," he ground out. "I'll listen to your advice. I'll

do exactly what my gut is telling me I should." With a quick jerk, he brought her up against him.

His mouth crushed hers. Shocked, she was like wood in his arms, until she felt the rough-soft brush of his tongue over the seam of her lips. Her body had no resistance to him—never had—and she opened for him immediately. At her instant acquiescence, the pressure of the kiss changed from punishing to tender, and he ate at her mouth softly.

Shivering in reaction, she moaned, and then he changed the angle of his head to kiss her even more deeply. Her heart pounded in her ears, every beat working against her, drowning out the natural warnings any woman might feel upon being the sexual focal point of such a virile male.

His mouth roamed over her face, and she felt the prick of his evening whiskers along her cheek, edging her jaw, at the soft skin beneath her chin.

Shay felt as if she were coming undone one stitch at a time, a lifetime of hems and seams being picked apart by a master. His arm was iron against her back and she leaned against it, giving him all her weight, trusting that he would hold her up.

Her knees were too soft to perform their usual function.

He swung them both around and now her back was to the sliding door. His body held her to it, and the disparate sensation of cold against her back and heated man against her front confused her senses.

One of his hands was planted on the door beside her head, the other found its way beneath her T-shirt. Her belly muscles twitched and her nerve endings jittered as he found her bare midriff. His mouth sought out a sensitive spot on her neck and she whimpered as he kissed her there, hotly, and his hand insinuated itself beneath the stretchy material of her bra. He cupped the weight of her breast and his thumb stroked over the tip that tightened at his ministrations.

Shay closed her eyes, intent on the feel of his hot lips exploring her neck and his rough hand playing at her breast. Her fingers clutched the sides of his shirt and she whimpered again.

Making a much deeper sound of need, Jace shoved up her shirt and pulled the cup of her bra below the hard and rosy point. He bent his head and touched it with his hot, wet tongue. Shay gasped.

With a muffled curse, Jace jolted backward, yanking her clothes back into place. Shay's hands fell to her sides and she reached for purchase on the cold, slick glass.

"What are you doing?" she asked, her head still muzzy from the drugging effect of his kisses and caresses.

"Proving my point." He was striding away from her, toward the front door. "Good father material wouldn't be making out with his daughter's teacher."

JACE WAS STILL breathing hard when he vaulted into his car and took himself away from the house. Without any purpose other than to calm himself, he gripped the steering wheel and drove aimlessly, working hard not to lead-foot the gas pedal. Why the fuck couldn't he keep his hands off of her?

What was it about the woman that made him burn for her mouth and her body?

When he felt more in control, he took stock of his surroundings. Near the town of Blue Arrow Lake, he noted. There was a tavern overlooking the water and its parking lot was only half-full. A beer sounded good.

Baseball was on the TV over the bar. He ordered a local craft brew and took his first swallow, ordering himself to further relax. Desperate for some peace, he didn't look over when a man sat on the neighboring stool. No sense in inviting conversation.

But the newcomer didn't take the hint. "Hey, there," he said in an easy voice. "Good to see you again."

Again? Jace glanced over, taking in a tall man with a ball cap pulled low over his eyes. "Who…"

Then the stranger half turned on his seat and Jace noticed the distinctive blue eyes. Ryan Hamilton held out his hand. "Sanity break?"

"How'd you know?" Jace asked, returning a firm shake.

"Single man comes back to the States, suddenly finds himself with a daughter and a woman—"

"A daughter and her tutor," Jace corrected.

Ryan shrugged. "In any case, big changes for you."

"Yeah." Jace brought his beer to his mouth. "Why are you out for a cold one alone?"

Ryan's smile went movie-star blinding. "I hate to even tell you, man."

"Why's that?"

He shook his head. "My mountain girl…she's really something."

"Maybe you shouldn't tell me," Jace said, amused by the other man's exuberant mood. "It sounds private."

Ryan chuckled. "It's just a little game we like to play."

Jace's brows shot high. "Um…"

The other man laughed again. "It's probably not as

salacious as you're imagining. Every once in a while, I say good-night to Mason, then head out for my solo beer. Poppy reads the boy to sleep and uses my absence to take a long bath. After, she puts on something silky just about the same time as I ring the doorbell."

"I thought Shay said she lives with you."

"Oh, she does. But in our little role play I'm the stranger who needs shelter from the rain." He picked up his beer to clink it against Jace's and grinned. "A slightly modified reenactment of how we met."

Interesting. It made Jace think of Shay, their night in the Deerpoint Inn, and then of what she might be doing now. A bath like her sister? *Shit. Do not go there.* He stared up at the TV, trying to put all thoughts of the tutor—naked, wet—from his mind.

"We'll have to get you and Shay and London over for dinner," Ryan said now.

Putting the three of them in a sentence like that didn't sit well with Jace. "Not sure if there'll be time for that," he said.

Ryan flipped off his hat, adjusted it back on his head. "Summer's long up at the lake."

"I won't be here all summer."

"Really?" Ryan looked surprised. "I thought Shay said—"

"I'm cutting things short. Getting London to her new school early, for a summer session."

"New school?"

"Boarding school. Then I'm heading back to work overseas."

"I'm sorry to hear that. We really like London. She's great with Mason." Ryan frowned. "That means Shay will be out of work."

"I'm paying her the full contract amount," Jace hastened to say.

"That's good." Ryan stared off into space. "She can help Poppy with the wedding, if she wants. And with the cabins."

"We were out there today," Jace said.

Ryan shook his head. "Poppy will be thrilled, but I've got to say I'm surprised."

"She's a hard worker," Jace defended. "London put time in, too."

"No, no, of course Shay's a hard worker. She's a Walker, isn't she?"

"I've not met any of the other siblings."

Ryan gave a wry smile. "Stubborn as mules. Full of pride. Poppy's the only open heart among them."

Jace frowned. "Shay said she was one of the cynical Walkers. I find that hard to believe."

"My girl is rainbows and unicorns...who for highly sentimental reasons wants to make something of that land. On the other hand, Brett, Mackenzie and Shay have been just as highly reluctant."

"That curse doesn't sound very cynical."

Ryan waved it away. "A colorful excuse if you ask me."

"What's their real reason, then?"

He shrugged again. "You'd have to press each one of them about that. They don't volunteer much...especially Shay, I think."

Jace should leave it alone. She was none of his concern. "Especially Shay?" he heard himself ask. *Shit!*

"Poppy says she has a place inside no one can reach."

Jace's hand tightened on his beer. He thought he'd found his way to it unknowingly, to the hidden, secret center of her, that night at the Deerpoint Inn when she'd told him about her aversion to birthdays. And the next night, too, when she'd allowed him into her bed. Today he'd discovered even more—when she'd made clear she felt a veil of separation between herself and her half siblings.

"Anyhow, we'll find a way to keep her busy when you and London go," the other man said cheerfully.

Jace couldn't share in his good humor. "She might miss my daughter."

"Don't worry, Jace. It seems to me Shay doesn't allow herself to get too attached to anybody."

"Wonderful," he muttered, regretting this grand idea he had for a sanity break. It hadn't brought him even a modicum of peace. Instead, now he was bothered by the uncomfortable idea that keeping herself so apart ensured his daughter's tutor might forever be alone.

It was the last thing, he thought he could say for sure, that Shay wanted.

AT SNAIL SPEED, London climbed out of her father's car. Only one foot had made it to the ground when he glanced over the roof of the SUV as he pulled lumber from the back. "Dawdling won't get you out of rake duty," he said.

She refused to rustle up the energy to glare at him. "I should have stayed back at the house. I have math homework and a paper to write."

He grunted, not even bothering with a real answer.

London released a long-suffering sigh. It was her second day in a row to work at the cabins and it felt like forever since seeing anyone within ten years of her own age. She might die of tedium. For a time it seemed as if her life had finally started, but now it had come to another dull standstill.

"Help me carry these pieces over to the first cabin," Jace said.

London slammed shut the car door and then sauntered to the rear of the SUV. She picked up one end of the eight-foot length of wood and dragged the other behind her, following Jace, who carried several pieces stacked on his shoulder.

He set his load down and then took in her own lackluster effort. Though his expression didn't change, London felt a small spurt of shame. She told herself to ignore it. If she didn't cooperate with good grace, then perhaps he'd give up this idea of penalizing her by working at the cabins.

Being back at the house might give her another opportunity to meet up with Colton.

"I'm going to get started replacing the window trim," Jace said. "Go fast, go slow, it's your job to get the remainder of the wood over here, then—"

"I can't pick up that rake again," she said, sure she would keel over if she had to once more wield that particular tool.

Her father stared at her for a long minute, and hope bloomed. Maybe he'd tell her to sit in the car until he was ready to go home. She'd curl up on the backseat and snooze the afternoon away. Or perhaps he'd let her call Shay for a pickup. Her tutor had the afternoon off, but if London put her need for rescue in dire terms, surely she'd give in and collect her.

"All right," he said. "You can be my assistant."

Great. London rolled her eyes. Although he wasn't an ogre—and had actually been marginally humorous the day before when he and Shay joined in the water fight—she didn't want him thinking she was interested in being pals. Still, she couldn't get the least bit enthusiastic about more raking, so she trudged back to the car to retrieve the rest of the wood.

He'd found a couple of sawhorses and set up a work area by one of the cabins. The window trim was moldy and peppered with holes. "Dry rot," her father commented, pulling it off with his hands. "See what you can get free."

London made a face. The work looked dirty and buggy. Slipping on her gloves, she moved to an adjacent window, got a grip and tentatively tugged.

"You're not picking flowers," Jace advised. "Get more aggressive with it, or use the crowbar."

Irritated by the criticism, London put a little muscle into it. With a satisfying crunch, the bottom trim piece pulled free. She glanced over and saw that Jace had arranged the parts he'd removed onto the grass, in the shape of a frame. "Why'd you do that?" she asked, pointing.

"We can use them as a pattern for the new pieces," he said. "Then we'll prime and paint them before nailing them back up."

That made good sense. London went back to work, following his example. "How'd you learn to do stuff like this?"

When he glanced over, eyebrows raised, she felt stupid. "Not that I care or anything," she muttered.

"My father."

"Yeah?" She bent to place another section on the ground. "He around?"

"No. He died a number of years ago. Emphysema,

from a lifetime of smoking." He looked hard at her. "You don't—"

"Gross," she said. "As if I want yellow teeth and black lungs."

"Good," Jace said with a little nod. "That's good."

"What about your mom?" she asked.

"Gone, too. She left when I was young, much younger than you, but I was notified when she passed a few years back."

So he'd been a motherless kid, too, though his mom had chosen to walk away. Maybe that's what had given him the idea it was okay to basically ignore her for a decade.

Not that she'd ever needed a daddy.

She'd practically raised herself. Their housekeeper, Opal, had always said London was the most self-sufficient person she'd ever known. It made her feel good remembering that.

It also made her think she should write Opal a letter or something. Their former housekeeper didn't know the first thing about computers, but she'd been sending London handwritten notes every week or so. Maybe she could ask for her chocolate-chip oatmeal cookie recipe. Then she'd get Shay to shop for the ingredients and one afternoon London would make the dough and the scent of them baking would lure Colton to the house after school…

She imagined the occasion in great detail. He'd rap on the kitchen door and she'd gesture him in with the spatula. Practically drooling, he'd walk toward the rack of cooling cookies, then he'd look over at her and stop dead.

Because she'd have on…what?

Not black. Not jeans. Not a hoodie.

A flirty skirt? Shorts? She always thought her knees were too knobby, but she couldn't be in pants forever. So it would be something in cherry red, maybe, or—

"Your maternal grandparents are gone now, too," Jace said, interrupting her mental fashion musings.

London blinked, coming out of her fantasy kitchen scenario to the sunny reality of the cabins. She narrowed her eyes at her father, not sure where he was going with this. "Yeah?" she asked, drawing out the word.

He cleared his throat, looked over her head, then looked back at her face. "So it's just you and me."

Uncomfortable with the thought, she shrugged. "I'm cool on my own. Don't need anybody."

He smiled, but it wasn't the happy kind. "You probably get that from me. I've always lived a lone-wolf life."

London considered that. He sort of looked like a wolf, she decided. Thick dark hair. Those eyes that were gold-colored. And he was big. Muscular. He probably could kick ass if he had to. "You ever fight anybody?" she asked.

"Uh…"

"Please," she said, rolling her eyes again. "I know that violence isn't the solution to anything. I'm just asking."

This time his smile appeared more genuine. "I'm swearing you to secrecy on this, okay?"

"Sure."

"Fifth grade. There was this kid who had older brothers so he was pretty good with his fists. He liked to call me 'Jace Butt-Face.'"

London hooted. "That is really lame."

"Yeah," her father agreed. "But I got sick of hearing it, especially when he followed me home from school yelling it at me when I was walking with these really cute girls."

She tried picturing it. "Were you big then, too?"

"Scrawny. But like all bullies, at heart my tormenter was a coward. So I stood up to him. He slugged me, I slugged back and I split his lip. When he saw the blood dripping from his mouth, he ran home crying."

"No more Jace Butt-Face?"

"He tried to nail me during dodgeball for the next year or so, but he didn't call me names anymore."

"Dodgeball is a barbaric game," London said, shuddering.

"You like sports? Different games?" her father asked.

"I play a little tennis." Or she did. But sweating too much made the liner around her eyes sting.

"Yeah? Maybe you should try out for the school team."

"I don't know," London said, frowning. "What time of year do they compete? I don't see myself clearing mountain snow off a court in order to bat a ball around."

Jace opened his mouth, hesitated, then looked away. "We'll find out the details. You can decide then."

They returned to the task at hand. Her father didn't try to keep the conversation going, for which London was grateful. She returned to her cookie-baking fantasy, trying on imaginary outfits in her mind that would wow Colton Halliday. *Seventeen never looked so good*, he'd say, and she'd play with her hair while talking to him like she'd seen Shay doing the other day.

It couldn't be black anymore, London decided, suddenly certain of that. For the past fourteen months she'd been coloring it "Obsidian Wing," and she was down to the last box she'd brought with her from England anyway. But what shade had it been before? She could hardly remember. Like Jace's—a dark chocolatey brown?

"What?" he said.

With a start, London realized she was staring at him.

"My hair…" she began, then hesitated, waiting for him to latch on to the opportunity to talk about her current shade. She knew it was as startling as it was disguising.

"Your hair…?" he prompted.

"I'm going to change it," she said, watching carefully to gauge his reaction.

He shrugged. "It's yours."

"Maybe I'll dye it Lady Gaga platinum. Or blue."

She sort of liked it that he winced. Then he nodded. "As I said, it's your hair."

"And I need some new clothes," she told him.

"Is this about that shopping trip you asked for?"

Maybe it was time to change tactics. She pasted on a winning smile. "I've been a good worker, right? And I haven't brought up a car or a boat in ages."

"I think it's been all of three days."

"See?" She waved her hand. "Forever."

"This is tough work," he muttered, then he sighed. "How about we make a deal? Shopping trip, yes, blue hair, no."

Oh, *win*! But London didn't give that away by beaming at him like she wanted to. Still, this dad-daughter thing was becoming more manageable by the minute.

Jace turned back to his work and she watched him pull out a pencil and mark a piece of wood. Then he made a cut with a loud electrical saw. He moved like an athlete, she decided. Maybe football? There was power in his arms and chest and she suspected that he might have gotten in other brawls besides the one he admitted to in fifth grade.

He looked like a man who could hold his own in a fight.

It made her feel a little…good? Proud? Protected.

When he brought out his pencil for another cut, she thought of something else. "You didn't ever marry again, did you?"

"What? No." He shook his head.

"Do you have a girlfriend?"

"I've been traveling a lot. I work long hours."

But even his daughter could see he was handsome. And if he had a girlfriend, then he'd have someone in his life besides London. After years of practically raising herself, she didn't think she could stand to be the sole focus of a father. Then she'd never get her own life going again.

"You should learn a trick." Her face went hot when he gave her a curious look. She shrugged a shoulder, trying to appear casual even as she heard Colton's voice echo in her head. *I'm going to show you magic.* "I heard it's a way to, um, get female attention."

"So, you're an expert on that?" he asked, one eyebrow winging up.

She shrugged again, not sure if he were teasing or not. "Well, I *am* a girl."

"And I already know a magic trick." A smile tipped up the corners of his mouth. "Shall I show it to you?"

"Okay." She sauntered closer, watching as he bent down and picked up a couple of sticks. With a penknife, he worked at them until each resembled a stubby pencil, complete with sharp point. Then he slid a piece of plywood onto the sawhorses to create a tabletop.

Next he placed the sticks horizontally on the surface, a few inches between them. "Okay," he said. "Watch closely as I count to eight." His right hand, palm down, covered one of the sticks. "One."

His left did the same with the other. "Two."

On "three" then "four," he flipped each hand over. On "five," his right fingers picked up the right stick and set it in his left palm.

With a suppressed laugh, she noticed it didn't remain in there, however. While his left fingers curled into a fist, she could pretty clearly see him fold three of his right fingers over to conceal the stick. On "six" he retrieved the remaining stick with his thumb and pointer. At "seven," he loosened his left hand to show—surprise, not—it was empty. With a note of triumph, he said, "Eight!" and released the two sticks in his right hand.

He glanced up to measure her reaction.

Though she sucked on her tongue to hold back more laughter, he must have detected it in her expression. "My sleight of hand is not so good?"

"Your sleight of hand is not so good." Not nearly as good as Colton's, certainly. *I usually amaze girls.*

"That's it, then," her father said, his voice thick with layered-on resignation. "I'm obviously going to be alone for the rest of my life. In my old age it will be solely up to you to heat my soup and hand me my walker."

The idea of it made her grin. Then he did, too, and they shared a moment of mutual…something, before London's misgivings came rushing in. Her shoulders hunched and she turned away, not wanting him to think she was happy about spending time with him or feeling friendly whatsoever.

Instinct and experience told her it was dangerous to let down her guard and like the man too much.

CHAPTER TEN

UPON RETURNING FROM the cabins in the late afternoon, Jace hunted down Shay. He figured she must be somewhere about, because her car was in the drive, though she wasn't in the house.

Standing on the back lawn, he shaded his eyes, and thought he detected movement on the dock. Bright colors, a beach chair... As he got closer, he saw that Shay was propped in a low seat, wearing—good God—nothing more than a swimsuit. *So much skin*, his libido thought, on immediate alert.

Jace almost escaped back to the house. But he had a request to make and hell, he was a mature man. Telling his baser self to calm down and remember that ogling her was not an option, he descended the ramp that led to the slip.

The breeze was up, scooping the lake's blue water into white-lace-edged waves that scudded across the surface. They rocked the pontoons that floated the dock, moving it in an easy rhythm. The accompanying liquidy slosh must have masked his footsteps because Shay seemed unaware of his approach.

So he allowed himself a brief moment to admire.

For a near redhead, her skin managed to lightly tan to an apricot warmth. A massive tube of sun protection sat beside her, he was glad to see, because it would be a crime for that lithe body to bear a burn. She rested in the low chair, arms on its arms, legs stretched in front of her. The suit she wore was two pieces, a pale blue that would match her eyes, which were currently closed. Tiny dots of perspiration sprinkled her small straight nose.

Bad Jace wanted to lick them away.

Of course, since he was a mature man, that idea was dismissed. Telling himself he'd used up his admiration allotment, he cleared his throat.

Her eyes popped open. Blinking, she looked at him, then felt around for her sunglasses. Once she slid them on, she sat up. "Is everything all right?"

"Why shouldn't it be?" He kept his gaze trained on her face.

"I don't know." She reached for the striped towel folded beside her and pulled it over her midsection. "How did your afternoon with your daughter go?"

His daughter. A person. No longer just a memory of his big hands trying to zip a tiny sweatshirt, or of coaching a small child on the finer points of keeping up with a melting ice-cream cone. Was it an act of fatherhood to lie about his occasional brawling, since there'd been a few bar fights after fifth grade? He only knew that making her smile had felt like winning a grand prize.

"I think the afternoon went well," he told Shay now, attempting to sound offhand about it, because this was a teen they were talking about. He might jinx things by being overconfident. "She wants new clothes and to change her hair color."

"Sounds like you talked," she said, picking up the tube of sunscreen.

"Yeah." It had felt like real conversation.

"Did you tell her about school?"

He frowned. "I'll get to it."

She'd squeezed out some lotion into her palm and was swiping it across her shoulder and down her arm. Jace followed the movement with his eyes as the scent of coconut drifted by him on the breeze. Wrenching his gaze off her skin, he stared out over the lake.

In the distance, sailboats glided across the blue water and he counted them. One, two, three. "So, will you do it?"

"Do what?"

"Take her shopping."

"Jace, you should go with her. Use the opportunity to get to know her further."

"We're talking shopping. She's not going to want me. She's already asked you, if you'll recall."

Shay huffed out a sigh. "Jace—"

"C'mon. I'll give you both free rein with my credit card."

Her shoulders stiffened. "I can't be bought like that."

Shit. He remembered Ryan commenting on the Walker pride. He tried defusing the situation with a smile. "Okay, how *can* you be bought?"

"Ha-ha." Then she stilled, seeming to consider something. "How about this? For every hour I'm out with your daughter, you spend one with her, as well."

He shook his head. "I've just been at the cabins with her two afternoons in a row. Believe me, while it might have gone okay, I guarantee she won't be enthused about palling around with me more."

Shay shrugged a shoulder. "Those are my terms."

Christ, it must be his day for negotiations. "She won't like more time with tools."

"Then do something she'll enjoy."

Like he'd know what that was. He dropped to the dock beside Shay, drew up his knees and scraped his hands through his hair. His instincts were completely at a loss when it came to doing right by the girl.

"How about driving lessons?" Shay asked.

"She's too young for a permit. I checked." Which was a huge relief, because he wasn't ready for a daughter behind the wheel of thousands of pounds of steel.

"The boat, then," Shay suggested.

Not the boat, either. Teen, moving vehicle… He glanced over at Shay to tell her as much, but she was back to applying the sun protectant. The slow process fascinated him. She was thorough about it, making sure every centimeter of her biceps, her elbow, her forearm was covered. He watched as she massaged the cream into the thin skin at the top of her hand and then into the web of each finger.

A sexual shudder rolled down his spine and he began to harden, even as she continued with those mesmerizing strokes. Up, down, around. More cream, more strokes.

Envy pierced his belly even as he called himself a fool. He was jealous of her hand, the lotion in her palm, the breeze, those pinpoints of sweat dotting her nose. Anything that was so close to her when he was not. He didn't know where this response came from, why she instigated it, how it was going to be when they didn't share the same space and air.

Would he feel relief? Would she linger on the edges of his mind like a ghost? Would he rub his own cock in the shower and pretend it was her, and wake up on bleary mornings imagining for just a moment he was back in the Deerpoint Inn with a birthday girl in her birthday suit?

"The boat," she said again. "It's a good idea."

"Fine," he heard himself say. Because it was impossible to resist her, he realized now. Anything she suggested, anything she allowed…he was going for it.

Anything she allowed…

Yeah. Up to and including that. For the rest of their time together, it was going to be up to Shay to apply the brakes. His sexual willpower was officially out of gas.

He was empty of any inclination to keep his distance from her.

If she crooked a finger, he'd be running.

SHAY CUT THE lessons short the next day for the shopping trip. She'd considered going down the mountain to one of the big malls closer to the coast, but there were numerous boutiques in the small community of Blue Arrow Lake and nobody needed to encourage her to shop local. She knew full-time residents required all the cash they could accumulate during the tourist season to keep afloat during the quieter parts of the year.

Begging had got her a hair appointment for London at a local spa. They also booked a makeup session for the girl. Once a new color palette was in place, then they'd be in a better position to shop for outfits. She'd given Jace a brief rundown on their plans and he'd extracted a promise that there'd be no blue hair.

It seemed London had agreed to that stricture.

Now as they walked through the doors of Half Moon Spa & Beauty, the girl's excitement was palpable. Shay tried tamping down on her own. She had no real stake in London's life. Her temporary role would soon be over and getting too invested and too attached would only end badly.

Just like Jace, the girl was a short timer in Blue Arrow Lake.

At the reception desk, she learned the man had made his own call to the spa. Despite her sputtering, the receptionist was adamant that he'd paid ahead for the works for both London and Shay. With the teen looking on, she found she couldn't be so ungracious as to refuse the services.

So they had side-by-side styling chairs.

"What are we going to do today?" The woman behind Shay's chair fluffed out her hair.

"I think she needs more gold highlights," London suggested.

Shay raised her brows. "Does that mean I get to choose your hair color?"

"Uh…" The girl bit her lip, betraying a lack of confidence that Shay hadn't seen before.

Her heart squeezed. "Would that help, London?"

Red rose up the teen's neck and infused her cheeks. "I don't really know…"

Shay turned to the stylist assigned to the girl, a reputed expert with color. "This is going to be a process," the woman said. "We'll first use a nonchemical stripper, then apply color after."

"Do you want it to be close to your natural shade?" Shay asked.

"I can't really remember what that was," London confessed. "Maybe kind of mousy brown."

The stylist patted her shoulder. "Don't worry about that. We'll get it near to the way it was, then warm it up with highlights and lowlights if need be."

London transferred her gaze to Shay. "Sounds perfect," Shay said, exuding assurance, warmed by the grateful look the teen threw her way. *Don't get attached*, she reminded herself again. *It's never a good idea to care too much.*

Hours later, they emerged from the Beach 'n' Ski boutique and decided to call it quits. But Shay proclaimed they couldn't make it to the house without some sustenance, so they dropped the bags in the trunk of her car then crossed the street to Oscar's Coffee, where they each ordered an iced tea and a pastry. They carried their fare to one of the small tables on the patio that bordered the sidewalk.

"Looking like we do," Shay murmured, "we should see and be seen."

London had an awkward moment as she made to sit in the wrought-iron chair. Her gaze jumped to Shay, who hid her smile.

"Put your things onto the table, then hold the hem of your skirt to the back of your thighs as you sit down—prevents a breeze from going where it doesn't belong."

The second try was the charm. "I feel like an idiot," London said under her breath.

"You don't look like one." Shay leaned back in her chair to once again scrutinize the changes new hair color, makeup and wardrobe had wrought. London's stylist—who'd tugged Shay aside to say Jace had included an enormous tip—was a miracle worker. The dull black was gone, replaced with a medium brown color laced with streaky, delicate highlights in bronze and blond. Layers were cut to accent the catlike shape of the girl's face and show off her big eyes.

They were no longer surrounded with raccoon rings.

Instead, subtle liner, shadow and mascara made the most of them. Her irises were a warm brown, with dashes of the gold that made her father's eyes so distinctive.

Sipping at her tea, London self-consciously tugged at her skirt.

"It's not too short," Shay promised, having made this declaration several times already. The dress was a racer-back style in a soft green knit, the color light at the bodice then deepening at the bottom. She wore it with flat bronze sandals in a modified gladiator style. Her fingernails had been painted gold, her toenails a deep bronze. Just a touch of bronze gloss colored her lips. Small gold hoops hung from her pierced ears and she wore three bracelets that were silk cord knotted with amber beads.

From beneath her lashes, London was watching the world go by, her gaze inspecting every passing teen. "Maybe I should have worn shorts," she whispered.

It was true that most of the kids in sight were dressed in T-shirts and cutoffs, but Shay had encouraged her to put on something dressier. "You have those, too. Clothes for every occasion."

"Hey, Shay!" A voice hailed from behind her.

She turned her head to see Megan Daniels, a high school senior whom she'd worked with to prep for the college entrance exams. The girl bopped over in a short lace skirt, tank top and rubber thongs. "How are you?" Shay asked.

Megan's grin went wide. "Counting down the days. College in less than triple digits!"

Shay smiled with her, then introduced London. The senior was friendly but was on her way quickly, after promising to send a postcard from San Diego, where she would attend the university.

"They all do that," Shay explained as Megan hurried off. "I help them get ready for entrance tests and when they move to their chosen school, they send me a card for my collection."

London sipped from her straw. "You've had a lot of students?"

"A couple of handfuls so far." The postcard idea had actually come from one of the moms. Just as with London, Shay made an effort not to become overly invested with the kids she tutored. They weren't *her* kids.

Just then, London made a small sound. Her body stilled and she stared across the street, her gaze on a clutch of high schoolers coming into view. Shay recognized Colton Halliday, a pal of his and three girls— two blondes and a curvaceous brunette. They paused on the curb, looking in both directions before stepping into the street.

"They're coming here," London said, a note of panic in her voice. "We should go."

"No," Shay protested. "Not when you look so pretty."

Biting her lip, London started to slink low in her chair. She put up her hand to shield the side of her face. "I'm not like them," she whispered. "They're so...so... effortless."

Oh, the anguish of fifteen, Shay thought, as London's obvious misery touched a tender spot inside her. When Shay was the same age, still reeling after that disastrous fourteenth birthday, it had felt as if everyone in the world had a comfortable niche but her.

"Listen." Leaning across the table, she spoke in a low

voice. "Sit up straight, pin on a smile, look like you're having the most fun ever."

London's eyes darted to Shay, then darted back to the group of kids that had almost reached the sidewalk. "But…"

She reached out and tugged the girl's hand away from her face. "Trust me. If you look like you're enjoying yourself, other people will want to get to know you. Hang around you."

Slowly, the teen straightened in her chair. She curved both hands around her cup and gave her attention to Shay, a pained smile on her face. "Do I look like I'm having fun?"

"I don't know. Do you have fun when someone pulls out your toenails with pliers?"

The smile turned more genuine. "That bad?"

"Now it's good." She glanced over London's shoulder. "They went inside."

Her shoulders relaxed a bit. "Do you think they'll come out to the patio?"

"Who knows?"

London played with the straw in her drink. "He probably won't even remember me."

"He might not *recognize* you," Shay corrected. "But you look wonderful."

"You think so?" She brightened, then again went on alert as the sound of chattering teen voices emerged—along with their owners—from the coffee place.

They did not find seats on the patio like London and Shay; instead they continued on their way, arguing over a movie as they walked along the sidewalk, drinks in hand. The girl let out a long breath, even as she gazed over her shoulder, watching the small group, her expression betraying how much she would like to be part of them.

Oh, yes, Shay thought. She absolutely knew that feeling of being the one stuck on the outside. "It's going to be okay," she told the girl.

London turned back around and the doubt on her face tugged at Shay. Fifteen. Such a vulnerable age. "How do you know?" she asked.

"Trust me," Shay said again, and when the girl returned a small smile, she knew she was sunk. Well, invested, which in this case could very well turn out to be the same thing. Maybe it was because she saw something of herself in London. Maybe it was the girl's particular combination of a smart brain and a poignant vulnerability. In any case, London had opened up something inside Shay that she usually—safely—closed off to just about everyone.

Which now left her feeling uncomfortably exposed.

CHAPTER ELEVEN

JACE RETURNED TO Blue Arrow Lake near sunset, after a day taking meetings and handling conference calls in Los Angeles. Keyed up from dealing with dozens of business details and driving through the Southern California traffic, he looked forward to a quiet evening. Loners needed their downtime.

As he turned into his drive, he blinked, surprised by the number of cars gathered there. Four. One he recognized as Shay's, then there was the luxury model that Ryan Hamilton had been driving a few days before. Two others were unfamiliar. A work truck with an extended cab and a rack for landscaping tools. Next to it sat a small sedan with a Maids by Mac sign on the side.

Company.

Shay's siblings, obviously. Pulling into the garage, he decided he wouldn't be able to avoid the ol' greet-and-grip. But immediately after, he'd escape to the master suite with a beer or two. He hoped they didn't intend to stay long.

As he pushed open the front door, however, he could hear talk coming from the deck that overlooked the lake, as well as smell the scent of meat on the grill. Shay had guests for dinner.

Fine. He'd still head up to his room after introductions and sneak down to the kitchen for a sandwich when the spirit moved him. It wasn't that he couldn't hold his own socially when necessary, but this time it wasn't necessary. Shay's siblings were never going to be more than strangers, really, to him.

Emerging onto the deck, it seemed as if his house had been invaded by a passel of them. His gaze circled the group. Shay wasn't in sight, and he only recognized dark-haired Ryan and the little boy that was his stepson-to-be. Two other women stood beside a man tending the barbecue. A teenage girl he'd never seen before, wearing a summer dress, poured lemonade from a pitcher into a plastic cup. Then she crossed to the little kid and handed it to him.

Since no one had yet noticed him, Jace considered avoiding the crowd altogether. Maybe he'd search out his daughter and see if she wanted to head into town for pizza. He was curious to see the outcome of her trip to the beauty salon. Lady Gaga platinum, he guessed, inuring himself to the idea. It had to be better than blue.

Then the teenager looked over, catching him still standing near the glass doors leading from the house. Hell, he thought, working not to scowl. Busted. He moved forward, determined to get the introductions over quickly, when his feet stuttered to a stop.

That teenager, the girl— *Jesus*. He could not stop staring as he began walking toward her again. Three feet away, he cleared his throat. "London?"

She lifted a self-conscious hand to her hair. It was a lustrous blend of colors, clearly professionally high-lighted, and looked both healthy and age-appropriate. Without the dark frame of the dyed stuff of before, and without the overkill in the liner and mascara depart-ment, her face looked…normal.

More than that. Very pretty.

And in that dress...*fashionable*, he guessed was the right word.

A honey-haired woman walked over to link arms with the teen. "Doesn't she look fabulous?" she asked, a smile on her face that also beamed from her wide gray eyes.

"Fabulous," he echoed. He held out his hand to the small and slender woman. "Jace Jennings."

"Poppy Walker," she said. "And I would have picked you out of a lineup to be her dad. There's a strong family resemblance."

Jace and his daughter glanced at each other, her expression as surprised as he felt. Before, she'd looked like...well, he couldn't say, because before this transformation her appearance had been disguised by all that habitual black.

It made him wonder what she'd been hiding from and why she'd decided to come out from behind her mask.

The other woman he didn't know strolled over to join their group. She was more Shay's height than Poppy's. Her hair was espresso-colored and she gave Jace the once-over out of eyes the same shape and icy blue as her youngest sister. Her handshake was strong. "Mackenzie Walker," she said. "Mac."

Ryan hailed him next, just managing to rescue Mason's lemonade as the boy nearly dropped it in his zeal to chase after a big dog that was beelining for the house. "Good to see you again."

Then Jace faced a man who was wielding a wicked-looking weapon. It took him a moment to recognize it as a grill scraper. It didn't take any time to recognize that the oldest Walker sibling was naturally reserved.

He was muscular, too, the kind gained by heavy, outdoor work that had also lightened his short brown hair. His gray eyes were very much like Poppy's and a scar cut through his brow to his hair. A second was a pale line across the bridge of his nose.

"Brett Walker." He transferred the tool to his left hand to meet Jace's right palm with his own. "And you're yet another flatlander who has entered one of my sisters' lives."

Jace didn't think he meant *flatlander* as a compliment. "On a temporary basis," he murmured, then looked about. "Is she here? Shay?"

Poppy nodded, frowning a little. "But has taken herself away, per usual. Even when we arrived with food and birthday cake in tow for her belated celebration."

"If you'll excuse me," Jace said, "I think I'll track her down." A beer still sounded good.

Brett passed off the scraper and locked steps with Jace. "I'll drag her outside if I have to," he told his sisters.

They found her in the kitchen.

Her brother continued into the room while Jace paused at the threshold. Her hair was its usual swirl of brightness, some strands cupping her chin, others kicking out at the back of her neck in a tousled style that seemed a little too close to bed head.

Sex head. Sex hair.

He should look away, but he couldn't. Not since their evenings at the Deerpoint Inn had he seen her in a dress. This one was sleeveless, deep blue and something about the flounce at the hem and the ruffle at the V-bodice struck him as deeply feminine.

That aspect called out to everything male in him

and he took a breath, his chest expanding. He was hyperaware of their gender differences: from the width of his palms and the length of his fingers, to her slender waist and the curve of her hips. His body tightened everywhere, preparing for action—to rush, to defend... to possess.

When she looked up from the cheese-and-cracker platter she was arranging, her gaze skipped straight past her brother and latched on to Jace's face.

Her skin glowed with a light blush that pinkened her cheeks and nose. That telltale sign of nerves seemed to heighten his senses. Even from across the room he thought he could smell a trace of her sweet perfume. His eyes couldn't miss the pulse speeding at her throat.

Brett halted midstride, glanced over his shoulder at Jace, then looked back at his sister. She didn't seem to realize her sibling was in the room. "Shay..." he said, drawing out her name.

She started, then jerked her gaze to her brother. "Oh, hey."

Jace waded through the electrified atmosphere to make his way to the refrigerator. He pulled out a beer for himself, then passed one to the other man without bothering to ask first. Brett accepted it as he studied his youngest sister. "We're waiting for you on the deck," he said, his voice mild.

"I wanted to put together some appetizers," she replied. Her eyes slid Jace's way then back down to the countertop. "Hello to you, too. Thanks so much for footing the spa bill."

"You're welcome." He took a swig of his beer, thinking he had only about ten seconds left before Brett Walker figured out that the charged air wasn't due to dryer static, but to Jace's pheromones and Shay's pheromones finding each other in the room and rubbing together like two sticks on the verge of starting a fire. A mixed pseudoscientific metaphor, he supposed, but it was the best he could come up with when his brain was distracted by all her beautiful bared skin, the apprehensive touch of her tongue to her bottom lip, the darting glance she sent him from beneath dark curly lashes.

Jace felt Brett's gaze swing to him, too. It must have worried Shay, because she snapped her fingers and called to him. "I've been meaning to ask you again, Brett."

With a last suspicious look at Jace, her brother returned his attention to her. "Ask what?"

"Remember when I texted you about my adoption papers?"

The other man lifted his beer and drank before answering. "I got a text about adoption papers?"

"Yes. Didn't you see it? I asked for your help in finding them."

"You want to talk about this now?" the other man asked, glancing at Jace.

"Before I forget," Shay said. "They must be among Mom and Dad's things, right?"

Brett took another swallow. "You'd think so."

"I want to locate them—"

"Not only did Dad have no head for numbers, but they both were lousy at organization, you know that."

"Still—"

"Untold grief, babe," he said. "Needle-in-the-haystack-level search and seizure and you know what kind of mood that puts me in."

She frowned. "Brett…"

He turned to Jace. "Speaking of moods, I heard you made Poppy ecstatic by doing some work out at the cabins." With a quick movement, he scooped up the platter of food and started walking from the kitchen. "I'm interested in hearing your opinion on the situation, given that you're a builder."

"Brett," Shay protested.

"Come along, little sister. Your party awaits."

Just like that, both Jace and Shay were effectively roped and dragged out to the deck. He could have broken away for the stairs, that was true, but when that notion occurred, he caught another glimpse of his daughter. At this moment, he didn't want to walk away from her. Or from Shay.

The unexpected party turned out to be no hardship. The Walkers had brought hamburgers and turkey burgers to grill as well as portobello mushrooms. Several salads and watermelon slices were available to fill the party plates—paper ones, with birthday balloons printed on them.

Instead of sitting at one of the larger patio tables, the group chose to arrange themselves on the more comfortable cushioned sofas and love seats. They all held their plates on their laps, except for Mason, who sat cross-legged on the deck in front of the coffee table.

The group talked, argued and laughed, and it pleased Jace to see that London often inserted herself into the conversation or was asked questions that started a new line of discussion. They liked his kid, ergo, it wasn't hard to like them.

The only thing odd was how Shay kept removing herself. She'd get up to retrieve something for one of the guests—more lemonade, another beer, a second helping—and then rather than returning to her place within the group, she'd sit outside the circle. Her perch might be a tall stool behind her brother. Another time she leaned against the glass-topped table they were using as a buffet, watching the action instead of immersing herself in it.

He wondered how much of that the others noticed or if they were accustomed to her withdrawing.

Finally, after birthday cake was served, he decided he couldn't sit still for it any longer. Without a word, he rose from his couch cushion. Shay stood by the deck railing, a faint smile on her face as she listened to Poppy attempting to pump Brett for information about his love life.

Jace grabbed her plate of barely touched dessert. When she made a sound of protest, he used it like bait to draw her back into the heart of the gathering. He pushed her onto the couch and then dropped beside her, returning the cake to her hands. At her puzzled look, he merely shrugged and half turned in order to ask Mac how she liked being her own boss.

As the night darkened, the outdoor lights switched on automatically and a light breeze came off the lake. Jace dragged a couple of patio heaters close, then returned to the couch as the siblings argued about the finer points of some long-ago childhood prank. Shay was part of the discussion this time, he noticed, gratified. London was engaged as well, in a game of Go Fish with Ryan and Mason.

He sat back, surprised by how relaxed he felt, even among the Walker clan. Perhaps because there was another Jennings in the group—his daughter. Perhaps because he enjoyed the brush of Shay's shoulder against his as she made some point with the wide arc of her arm. Accustomed to being at the head of a boardroom table or the leader of a team, being in the middle of things was…different. He'd never before experienced the camaraderie of family.

And for the first time in his life, he had a keen awareness of what he'd been missing.

HURRYING DOWN THE BEACH, London shoved her hands into the hoodie she'd pulled on over her sundress. The evening air was chilled and she still felt self-conscious in the shoulder-baring dress. Though she thought her new hair and clothes looked good, that didn't mean she felt comfortable *inside* the look.

She couldn't help but wonder what Colton would think of it. Her face went hot just imagining his eyes on her.

There was no guarantee he'd be in the old boathouse, of course, but this was her first opportunity in days to get away and find out. She figured she had less than an hour before her father or Shay would begin wondering about her whereabouts, so she took longer strides, ignoring the grit that got between the soles of her feet and her new sandals.

As she neared the dilapidated structure, her stomach twisted and she felt her palms go damp. Through the chinks in the walls, she caught the barest flicker of light.

It could be anyone, she thought, pausing. Maybe not someone safe.

She glanced around, aware the night sky lacked a moon and the stars provided little illumination. The glow from the house she'd left was far enough away that it didn't penetrate the gloom at this end of the deep cove. Curling her fingers together she took a step forward, and then another.

Steps on the road to her own life.

The door of the boathouse gave its usual creak when she nudged it forward. A single votive candle rested on the floor, surrounded by a circle of half a dozen seated people. Their faces were impossible to make out in the shadows.

"England?" a voice asked.

London's heart leaped, bumping against her throat. "Yes," she croaked. "Um…Colton?" She knew he couldn't see her clearly and it made her both relieved and disappointed.

"Come in, darlin'," another male voice said. "Are you as cute as you sound?"

"Sam…" Colton said, a hint of warning in his voice.

"What? We can use another female."

"Oh, yes, please." It was a girl's voice now. "Lessens the chance that I'm the one stuck in paradise with you, Sam."

"I beg your pardon—"

"They don't call you Snake-Tongued Sam for nothing."

All the kids except the one being teased laughed. London grimaced, worried for his feelings until he joined in. "All of you can sod off. Isn't that the Brit lingo, my new little friend England?"

"Her name is London, actually, and it's where she's been living," Colton said.

"That's very nice," Sam replied. "Why don't you come in? Do they play Seven Minutes in Heaven in London, London?"

Her fingers curled around the doorjamb and her

stomach twisted again. It sounded like a game and she didn't know the rules. "Um…no."

"That's okay, I'll explain it to you." She could vaguely make out his arm lifting and she heard a dull slap as his palm hit the carpet beside him. "Come sit by Sammy."

Another step toward her own life. She relaxed her fingers.

But as soon as she moved inside, a hand caught her wrist. "Right here," Colton said. "Next to me."

Then he introduced the other teens in the boathouse. It was dark enough that she wouldn't recognize them by day, but the girls were Janice, Marie and Bess. A third boy was John. She sketched a wave she realized they probably couldn't see. "Hi."

Sam slapped his hands together. "So…Seven Minutes in Heaven."

Colton spoke up. "We could do something else—"

"And leave our favorite Londoner, London, still ignorant of our American game?"

"So you know, I'm an American, too," London said. She hated being different. "What are the rules?"

"We spin the bottle." It was the girl who had spoken before, the one who London thought was named Janice. "When it stops, whoever it points to is party A. Party B comes with the second spin. Then the designated couple goes out for 'Seven Minutes in Heaven' under one of the big trees."

"What happens during the seven minutes is negotiated by the pair," Sam added.

"Negotiated?" London asked.

"Janice and Bess, for example, might choose to spend their seven minutes locked in an embrace I'd pay money to watch—" one of the girls threw something in Sam's direction and he ducked "—or they could decide to discuss the AP Lit final or possibly how impossibly irresistible I am."

London let out a silent breath. Talking with another girl. That didn't sound too terrible, did it?

"But it's common courtesy, if it's a boy-girl combo," Sam continued, "to exchange some wet sloppies and anything it leads to after that."

Wet sloppies? London pulled her sweatshirt closer around her.

"This is stupid," Colton declared. "We played this in junior high."

Did he think she wasn't mature enough for a kids' game? London straightened, unwilling to be the reason they halted their planned activity. "Sounds like fun to me."

One of the girls spoke next. "Okay, my turn to spin."

Though London's heart beat like crazy through the two-step process, the revolving soda bottle didn't point to her either time. When John and Bess left the boathouse to hoots and innuendo, they walked out with all the cool nonchalance London always wanted for herself.

Though the first thing she realized was that seven minutes could be an eternity. Sixty seconds or so in, Colton half turned to her and addressed her in a low voice. "Did you get into any trouble after the boat incident?"

She hitched a shoulder. "Not so much. My dad took me out to these crummy cabins and had me help him work on them."

"The old Walker ski resort."

"You know it?" She glanced over, but it was impossible to read his face in the dark.

"John and I saw you there."

She blinked. "When? Why?"

"We have another hangout. One of those cabins in the woods. It's a wreck, but we go there sometimes by mountain bike or trail bike to study or chill. I caught a glimpse of you when we were leaving."

"Oh." She tried thinking of something to keep the conversation going. "Well—"

"You should go home, London," he said, his voice almost a whisper.

Her face burned. "You don't like that I'm here."

"I'd rather see you at the library," he muttered.

The library? So now she was not only a freak but a nerd? "Wha—"

"I take my sister there on Saturday afternoons. Standing promise."

She stilled. Was he proposing something that was sort of like…like…a date?

Before she could ask him, the first seven-minutes couple breezed back in. Whether they'd kissed or discussed upcoming exams, London had no idea. Preoccupied with trying to figure out the truth of Colton's Saturday afternoon remark, she hardly paid attention until Sam said, "I got London!"

She jerked in his direction. "Me?"

"The bottle's looking right at you," he said.

Glancing down, she saw that its glass neck was pointing at her.

"I'm setting the timer on my cell," Sam said, his tone cheerful. He stood and in one stride was to London. He bent down and circled his hand around her upper arm, and then she was standing because she didn't know what else to do.

She couldn't balk now, right? Unless she wanted to look like an uncool, weirdo baby who could never fit in. The other girls would snicker and Colton would instantly be aware she was nowhere near seventeen.

Plus, there was still the negotiating, right?

It's common courtesy, if it's a boy-girl combo, to exchange some wet sloppies and anything it leads to after that.

London tried to imagine a wet sloppy with Sam, a complete stranger to her. Maybe she could tell him she'd never been kissed—

She couldn't tell him she'd never been kissed!

One glance in Colton's direction only gave away his stiff posture, but she couldn't see his expression and he didn't say anything as she and his friend exited the boathouse. The air was cool against her hot face as they exited the boathouse and she hunched in her sweatshirt, wishing for her jeans and her black hair and the protection of thick mascara and eyeliner. Nobody could get close to her when she wore them. She was safe from everyone and everything.

"Let's walk up the beach a little ways," Sam said, with a vague gesture in the direction of her house. "I know this private spot…"

"Sure." The farther they went, the more of the seven minutes would be eaten up.

Too soon, however, he took hold of her elbow and tugged her toward a stand of evergreens. Her mouth went dry as they stepped beneath the sweep of one tree's branches. It was even darker now and she pressed her shoulder blades and the palms of her hands against its rough bark.

"So, what's your pleasure, London?" Sam asked.

He sounded friendly enough, she supposed. Except that didn't stop the whine in her ears and the nausea in her midsection, and the way her ribs were tightening on her heart.

His hand reached out. She flinched, even though it didn't quite touch her, and crowded closer to the trunk of the tree. Panic was overtaking her, which was silly, because she could just tell him no. She could push the branches out of the way and return to the boathouse without being gone the full seven minutes.

Return there humiliated.

Then the sound of her name caused her to start. "London!" she heard in the distance. "London!"

"I—"

It came again, louder, loud enough to goose her into action. *"London!"*

"I have to go," she told Sam. "I really have to go."

Then she rushed through the branches, her arms in front of her like a heroine in a scary teen movie, and ran in the direction of the voice. His voice.

Her father's.

"London!" a different voice called. Closer.

Still moving, she glanced over her shoulder. Colton was just an inky outline on the beach. In the darkness, she couldn't be much more than a shadow herself. "Are you all right? I was coming for you."

Gratitude spilled through her. He'd been worried! But then her dad called her name again and she needed, for whatever crazy reason, to be near him right now.

"My dad," she told Colton by way of explanation, and then she continued running in the direction of home.

Jace must have heard her thudding footsteps, because suddenly she could make him out hurrying in her direction. London tried to slow her momentum, but her feet couldn't find purchase on the combination of sand, dirt and pine needles, and she fell into her father's arms.

They closed around her.

"Are you all right?" he asked.

She heard his voice rumble through his chest. An old memory resurfaced, at least she thought it was an old memory. Jace holding her, talking, and her listening to the sound instead of the words.

"London?"

She swallowed. "I…I spooked myself." It was true.

"Well." He patted her back. It might have been a little awkward, but she didn't mind. "You're safe," he said.

Yes. Whether that made her a weirdo baby or not, his arms made her feel just that way…

And she had to admit to herself that at this moment they were the only ones she wanted around her.

CHAPTER TWELVE

THOUGH SHAY CONTINUED to enjoy the conversation with her sisters out on the deck—it was centered around plans for Poppy and Ryan's upcoming marriage—she kept one eye out for Jace and London. The girl had disappeared more than half an hour before, saying she was going to walk down to the dock, but when she hadn't returned and couldn't be spotted in the vicinity, Shay had whispered her concern to Jace.

He'd shot to his feet, murmured an excuse and absented himself from the party.

"What do you think, Shay?"

"Hmm?" She glanced around, saw Poppy had her eyebrows halfway to her hairline. "Did you ask me something?"

"I was begging for your help with wedding stuff. Since you won't be tutoring London all summer—"

"How do you know that? *She* doesn't know that." Shay whipped her head around, relaxed when she saw her brother, Ryan and Mason occupied with another card game. The little boy hadn't overheard.

"Jace told Ryan. I haven't said anything to London about it."

"Please don't," Shay said. "Jace is trying to find the 'right time.'" She put finger quotes around the word. "I keep hoping he'll change his mind."

"If he doesn't, I've got plenty to keep you busy."

Shay opened her mouth, intending to tell her sisters about another plan she'd been toying with, one that would make her unable to do much hands-on wedding work. But she hesitated. They wouldn't like it, so it might be better to present them with a fait accompli, if that's what she finally decided to do.

"Uh-oh." Mac narrowed her eyes and pointed. "That's Guilty Face. I'd know Guilty Face anywhere. What are you hiding?"

"I don't have Guilty Face," Shay said, struggling not to squirm. "You're..." Her attention snagged on the pair climbing the steps to the deck. London continued on inside the house, ruffling Mason's hair along the way. The little boy followed.

Jace, on the other hand, returned to where he'd left his bottle of beer and finished it in one long swallow. Shay rose and crossed over to him.

He looked perplexed. "What's wrong?" she asked.

"I think she might have hugged me."

Shay drew back.

He grimaced at her reaction. "Yeah. Surprised me, too."

"What happened?"

"Saw her running on the beach, back this way. She fell against me and that's when I think I got a hug."

"Did she say why?"

"Maybe it's my scintillating personality," he said, his voice dry.

"Hey, my personality is much more scintillating than yours and I've never gotten a hug."

He smiled a little. "She said she was scared by the dark and the sound of the wind in the trees."

"I'll go check on her," Shay said, and hurried into the house, passing Mason on his way back out. Jace was the first one to say he was lacking in instinct when it came to the girl, so she figured he wouldn't be insulted that she wanted to see London for herself. The teen was in her charge, after all.

London was in the kitchen, forking up another piece of cake. She glanced up when Shay strolled forward. "Good," she said, around the bite of old-fashioned white cake with chocolate frosting that Poppy had made from scratch.

"Save some for breakfast."

London goggled. "We get to have cake for breakfast?"

"Nope." Shay grinned. "Most important meal of the day, and all that. But after lunch, I'll be fighting you for what's left."

"I can work with that," the teen said.

Trying not to be obvious about it, she gave the girl a once-over. Her hair was a bit windblown and her color was up, but she seemed all right. Though the truth was, London was a pro at hiding her feelings.

It was why her next move surprised the heck out of Shay. The girl drew something from her pocket. "I have a gift for you."

"Oh, London…"

She held out a small tissue-wrapped item. "Late birthday present and a thank-you."

"For what?" Shay asked, unwrapping the paper. "Oh!"

"I saw you looking at the bracelet in that boutique this afternoon and bought it when you were in the dressing room. I thought it would remind you of the day you took me from an ugly duckling—"

"You were never ugly!"

"—to a swan."

It was indeed a swan featured on the bracelet. The band was two thin pieces of gold wire connected at the center by a polished, carved piece of flat white stone the size of a quarter. She ran her fingertip over the "feathers" that had been etched into the surface. "It's lovely," she said. She'd always loved swans. There was a pond near the village where a few pairs made their home. "You know," she murmured, "they mate for life."

Shay looked up at the girl. "Thank you so much. I'll treasure it. Though you shouldn't have spent your money."

The girl shrugged. "I've been stashing it away when Poppy and Ryan pay me to babysit Mason. By the way, he wants me to have a sleepover with him tonight at his house. Do you think that would be all right?"

"I suppose so. But check with your father—"

"I asked him earlier. He said it was fine. And that way Poppy and Ryan can go on a hike in the morning and I'll get paid for watching Mace and it will be win-win for everybody."

Still, Shay hesitated. "You're very patient with Mason, and we all appreciate that. But you know you don't have to hang with him like you do, right?"

The girl licked the last of the icing off her fork. Then, eyes on the plate, she set the utensil carefully across it. "I don't mind. I think he loves me." She glanced up. "He tells me so all the time anyway." Her mouth moved in just a hint of a smile.

It sank like an arrow into the center of Shay's chest.

There was so much secret pleasure revealed in that gentle curve that her heart hurt with it. The lonely teen was clearly delighted to be the object of the little boy's affection—probably because she was thirsty for it.

No mother. A father who cared but didn't know how to draw her close. Shay thought of Jace's baffled expression. His "I think I got a hug."

And a tutor... Shay drew in a sharp breath that caused more pain as realization bit deep.

A tutor who, just like Mason, seemed to have fallen for the girl herself.

It's true, she thought. *I love this kid. Every prickly, contradictory, sweet and sour aspect of her.*

And she hadn't the first idea what to do about it.

FOLLOWING THE PARTY, there wasn't much cleanup to do beyond balling torn birthday paper and washing a few platters. Shay took care of those chores alone, her mind on London and how much she'd come to care for the girl.

It wasn't like her, she thought.

With all the students that had marched through her life—the ones she'd coached for the SAT or quizzed on science terms—she'd learned early not to let herself stay awake at night worrying about their Friday mornings in Biology or their Saturdays sitting down to a college entrance exam. She liked them, of course, and wanted them to succeed, but she didn't *care* about them.

Not liked she cared for London.

She'd miss her eye rolls, her snarky, under-breath comments, her sudden insights into classics of literature. When the girl had declared yesterday morning that *A Tale of Two Cities* was the best book *ever*, with an expression on her face that said she might have shed a tear or two over poor Sydney Carton, pride had swelled.

Hanging the dishcloth over the handle of one of the mammoth ovens, Shay blew out a breath and told herself that there was no reason to regret that pride or the warm feelings she had for the teenager. Nothing bad would come from them, right?

When London went away to school, Shay could keep up with her. Emails. Facebook messages.

Surely there was nothing ominous or tragic about letting a child a little way into your heart.

It was just…out of character. And that made her feel uneasy.

As a distraction, she let herself onto the deck. The lights out there had been extinguished and she breathed in the cool dark, the fragrance of pine and clean breezes in the air. It was the mountain scent, a heady elixir that had sustained generations of Walkers. She wondered if she'd wither without it.

Closing her eyes, she shoved that thought away. Take in the peace, she told herself, and listen to the night. In the distance, lake waves slithered against the silt, rocking the boat so the ropes holding it down creaked like crickets. Skitters and scurries betrayed the nocturnal critters going about their business in the trees surrounding the house. She was so attuned to the natural world that the soft clap of a quiet step on the deck behind her sounded like a gunshot.

She started and whirled, only to see Jace moving toward her. He'd changed from the slacks and shirt he'd worn earlier. In jeans and a T-shirt, he came to rest at the rail beside her, and stared into the darkness.

"Nice evening," he murmured.

She'd thought so, before he'd arrived and scuttled her peaceful moment. "I should go—"

He cursed, ducked, cursed again as a handful of dark shapes flew close to their heads. "What the hell? Night vultures?"

She couldn't help but snicker. "No."

"Seriously." His head tilted back to examine the sky. "What were those?"

"Bats."

"Yeah, right."

"I'm not kidding." Glancing around, she saw a trio break from a nearby tree. "Bats," she said, pointing to them.

Jace let out a low whistle. "And we're without Vampira for the night."

Smiling, she nudged him with her elbow. "No Vampira anymore."

"You're right. Thanks for that. She looks great."

"She's a great kid."

As that comment settled between them, a previous one struck her…too late. Much too late. *We're without Vampira for the night.*

London was gone. Shay and Jace were alone.

Maybe the same thought occurred to him, too, because he suddenly stilled and that now-familiar tension began humming in the air. She slid a glance sideways, noting his gaze was fixed on the lake.

"Did I mention how beautiful you look tonight?" he asked, his voice quiet.

The compliment shouldn't have sent a warm thrill coursing through her, the slightly rough edge to his voice shouldn't have felt like the stroke of a man's palm down her naked back. She tried suppressing a shiver as the muscles low in her belly tightened.

"Thank you," she said, and sounded breathless.

"Shay." He still didn't look at her as he let out a long breath. "This is going to be up to you."

She didn't need to ask what he meant by *this*. The possibility of another night together pulsed in air that was suddenly as thick as the blood coursing through her veins. Her limbs felt heavy, her body drugged by the desire that expanded with every inhale.

She glanced at him again, not sure how she felt about his latest declaration. "I made all the moves at the Deerpoint Inn."

His head turned, and he smiled at her, forcing her to grip the rail so her weakening knees wouldn't fail her. "I won't fight you off this time," he offered.

Oh, God.

Another night sounded so tempting, she thought, as the cool air raised goose bumps on her heated skin. She felt electrified, every cell zinging, every nerve on alert, her whole body primed to once again feel the touch of her secret lover.

It was only supposed to have been that once, a birthday treat. But why not? Why not a second time? Especially when she was considering a tremendous life change that would be anything but an indulgence.

Jace turned to her now, and his hand cupped her cheek, his workingman's palm wide and slightly scratchy against her burning flesh. Just that simple caress was enough to abolish all counterarguments. Still, she wasn't quite ready to surrender. "You said this was up to me," she whispered. "No fair touching."

His thumb gave her a tantalizing stroke. "I think I've

pointed out the flaws in my character before." But his hand moved away.

She snatched it in hers, pulled it back, nestled her face against him and closed her eyes. Breathing in, she tried slowing her heartbeat, but it clacked against her ribs, a runaway train that she couldn't control. What she wanted, how fast she wanted him, was unseemly, she thought. Nothing like the sexual appetite of the pre-Jace Shay Walker, who strolled the straight and narrow so that people wouldn't be reminded of her scandal-ridden beginnings.

His other hand sifted through her hair and her scalp prickled, another part of her coming alive thanks to his touch. "God, I want to do everything to you," he said, the dark promise in his voice sending another erotic charge down her spine. She shuffled closer, her body pressing against his so that the heavy jut of his arousal surged against her belly. Between her legs she felt swollen and achy. He nudged her again and her breath hitched, her orgasm hovering only a quiver away.

"But slow," he murmured as if reading her mind. A wicked smile turned up the corners of his mouth. "So slow you'll despise me before I let you come."

He was teasing, she knew, but she wanted that, too, she thought. That sounded safe.

Please. Make me despise him before this is through.

JACE SLID HIS hands down Shay's slender back to cup her bottom. He fit her more snugly against him, then bent his head to take her mouth. She tasted hot and sweet and as his fingers tightened on her soft flesh, he ground his mouth on hers, ravenous for her.

Which made him instantly ease up.

She was delicate, slender, and he was a big man. It was his nature to want to use his physicality, but he'd promised to go slow, and the way to do that was not to hold too tight. Not to possess, just pet.

He drew his lips away from her mouth, taking a feather's path to the hollow behind her ear. His tongue dabbed there and then he nipped the small lobe, her shudder his reward.

Her hands clutched at his shoulders, but he ignored the urgent clasp to take another meandering route down her neck. Every instinct urged to bite, suck, mark— God, primitive stuff!—but he merely skated his lips against the tender skin, feeling it move beneath his mouth as breath stuttered in her throat.

That this beautiful woman wanted him...

He lifted his head, struggling for calm. Her eyes were closed, he could see the fan of her lashes against her cheeks and he dropped tiny kisses on each eyelid, trying to convey how much her desire undid him.

His mouth once again found hers and he trailed a hand up her spine to find the tab of her dress's zipper at the middle of her back. He drew it toward her waist in tiny increments, until she gasped and pulled away.

"Not here," she said, her tone alarmed. Her hand pressed to the bodice to keep it in place.

He kissed her temple, her forehead, the downy softness of her left eyebrow. "The bats won't mind."

"Someone could drive by in a boat," she said in a stage whisper.

Smiling a little, he glanced over her shoulder at the dark and tranquil lake. "Why would anybody come to our end of the cove at this time of night?"

"Jace."

"All right, all right." He took her free hand and drew her through the glass doors. Once inside, he continued toward the great room. The lights had been dimmed here, and he stopped beside the couch, unable to go another inch without tasting her again.

This kiss was rougher, he allowed himself just a little of that, his tongue aggressive against hers. She melted into his body, both sets of fingers clutching his waist. Her bodice sagged a little and one skinny strap dropped toward her elbow. He cruised his mouth along the curve of her neck and scraped his teeth against the refined bone of her shoulder. There was so much elegance in her design that he wanted to stretch her onto a flat surface and have his way with her limbs, her arched feet, her slender hands, examining each part of her with the avid interest of a builder.

He'd take her fingers into his mouth to learn their shape. Bend her knees up, then out, her soles pressed together so he could admire the erotic, feminine angles and the soft folded secrets between her thighs.

His hands drifted down to the hem of her skirt, finding the bare skin of her legs. He touched her there, the fabric catching on his wrists as he drifted his fingertips over sleek warm flesh toward her panties.

She moaned when he found lace, traveled farther, then dipped both hands inside the stretchy material to cup her bottom, bare palms to bare flesh. She shuddered against him and lust flooded his body, steeling his muscles and causing his skin to burn.

He dropped onto the sofa cushions, pulling her over him. Their mouths fused and he steeped himself once again in her taste, his hands flexing in resilient flesh. Her hips rocked, pushing into his palms, then pushing against his hard cock. Jace groaned, his control beginning to unravel.

Switching positions, he began to draw down the scrap of lace.

She helped, yanking up the hem of her dress, then her eyes flew open. "Wait! I can't do it here."

He ignored her batting hands. "No boats, darlin'."

"Your daughter sits on this couch," she said, gaze boring into his.

"Hell." The idea was nearly a lust-killer "Okay. Fine. Up you go." He had Shay on her feet and began to hustle her toward the stairs, the master bedroom his intended destination. Then he halted. "Double hell."

"What?" Her hair was disheveled, her mouth slightly swollen, her cheeks a delicious pink. If they didn't get somewhere horizontal soon he was going to ravish her standing up.

"*I* can't do it on that fucking bed with the chains. I'll flip us both over." He shot her a look. "So it's your room or nothing, baby."

"But…but…we'll have to walk past London's."

"Close your eyes," he ordered, swinging her up in his arms.

She laughed, burying her face in his neck until he nudged her door open with his foot. The room was lit by a small bedside lamp and he took in the flowers in the short vase beside it, the soft throw draped over an easy chair in the corner, the white and fluffy lace-edged duvet. A photo of Mason stood on the long dresser and he paused to flip the frame facedown. "We're officially a no-kid zone now," he said.

She giggled, then pressed kisses to his throat, raising his temperature and spiking his lust. But he lay her against the covers and backed away to gaze on her in the faint golden glow of the lamp. Her skin was luminous, her hair gleaming with color and life. She was a candle, bringing radiance to the bleak dreariness of his soul.

What a ridiculous flight of fancy, he told himself, dismissing the idea as he watched her eyelids drift lower until her lashes brushed her rosy cheeks. Her fingers opened to clutch handfuls of the silky material of her skirt, inching it upward. "Take off your clothes, Jace," she whispered.

"Sure," he said easily, though his gaze was riveted to the flesh she was slowly revealing. "And you take off yours."

Instead of complying with her request, he remained still as Shay drew the dress up her slender body. There were the lacy panties, the color of flesh, and a matching strapless bra that cupped her breasts like he wanted to. Once the fabric was pulled over her head, she blinked, finding him there, staring at her half-naked form.

"You're still dressed," she said with a little frown.

"I told you I'd make you despise me," he said, teasing her again. Then he gestured with his hand. "Go ahead. I'm watching. Waiting."

Her eyes widened and her fingers tightened on the dress she still held. He saw the struggle on her face, and wondered if she'd take up his challenge.

A long moment passed. He didn't exhale until her gaze shifted to his. She held her hand over the side of the bed, uncurled her fingers and let the dress fall.

His cock twitched, every iron inch of it. As her fingers drew slowly down the center line of her body, his lungs seized. She circled her navel with a fingertip, drew it across the horizontal line of her panties, then to the center again so she could retrace her way back toward her breasts.

Jace fisted his hands, trying to keep them under control, though they itched to travel that same path with a hotter, heavier touch in order to rend the fabric covering her flesh so he could have all that he wanted of her.

Grasp. Take. Possess.

But this was the game he'd determined, and he held himself immobile as she drew her palms to the sides of her breasts and then inward, stroking herself over the lacy bra. He swallowed past the tightness in his throat, his mouth drying as he saw that her nipples were tight now, poking up in invitation.

Still, he didn't move.

Not even when she sat up and her hands reached behind her back. He saw the instant the bra was unfastened, the lace beginning to release its hold, but she caught it against her, one arm crossing her chest.

Jace groaned, his cock damn uncomfortable in its denim prison. "Shay..."

"Is there a problem?" she asked, one eyebrow arched as she kept her breasts from his gaze with her cruel hand holding the fabric to her skin.

"I want to see," he muttered.

And she smiled.

The seductive warmth of it hit him like a blow to the chest and he swayed on his feet. Her compliance in this little game, her confidence in this moment was a gift, he realized. A gift to him that was almost unbelievable.

Trust.

No one—no woman—had ever trusted him like this.

In another slow movement, Shay slid the lace away, revealing the perfection of her breasts. Her arm moved like a ballerina's to release the bra. It floated to the ground on top of her dress.

Every one of his muscles was strung tight. His avid gaze consumed her, all those inches of glowing, apricot flesh, the tight tips of her nipples, the triangle of material that was her only covering now. She drew her thumbs along her hips and looped them in the narrow sides of her panties.

She hesitated.

He broke.

One minute he was by the side of the bed, the next, he was on it and yanking that scrap of lace down the length of her smooth legs. Then he crawled between them, desperate, and held her open while he leaned down for his first taste of her.

At the last instant he remembered—*gentle!*—and he corralled his voracious hunger for her. Breathing in the creamy scent of her arousal, he just looked at those beautiful glistening folds flowering for him.

His.

But he reined that in as well and bent his head, his tongue moving in short brushstrokes, opening her there, exposing the little nub that he caressed with the very tip of his tongue.

She cried out, one hand spearing in his hair, the other curling into the duvet at her side. He slid his palms under her bottom, tilting her hips so that he could play with her like a tender delicacy that had to be licked, sipped, savored.

Too soon she was moaning, her whole body tense. He lifted his mouth from her.

"Jace…" It was nearly a wail of protest.

He pressed a kiss to her stomach, glanced up to meet her eyes.

"I despise you," she said, her tone earnest. "I really do."

Chuckling, he crawled up her hot body, her legs twining his hips. "Not enough," he said, then he closed his mouth over her breast, drew up so only the nipple was between his lips and gave a pull.

A *gentle* pull.

She banged on his shoulder with her fist, which made him want to laugh again, but then it was just so good to have that sweet, hard tip in his mouth and he filled his hand with the other breast, cupping and caressing.

Her fist banged again. "I loathe you," she said as he moved his mouth along her soft skin to the other nipple. He toyed with that, too. "Loathe you," Shay said again.

He smiled against her flesh then drew his mouth along her collarbone, up her neck, to meet her lips. She opened for him instantly, drawing in his tongue, sucking on it hard as if to show him how it must be done.

He was steaming beneath his clothes, his body primed for her. Forking his hand in her hair, he tilted her head for a different fit and kissed her, completely, adding a touch of ravish, then backed off before lust overcame him.

"I'm too heavy for you," he murmured, but her limbs cinched down on him.

"No, I like your weight." She pressed her mouth to his jaw, bit him there. "I'd like your *naked* weight better."

Giving in to what they both wanted, he did a one-arm push-up, using the other hand to yank at his T-shirt and lift it over his head. Then he lowered to her, his chest brushing the hard, ruched tips of her breasts. Her head turned to the side and she moaned, her fingers trailing along his spine. They insinuated themselves under the waistband of his jeans and the elastic of his boxers.

He shuddered.

"Please, Jace," she whispered in his ear. "I want you. I need you."

Hauling in a breath, he moved down her body again. He peppered kisses over her breasts, his tongue swiping just the crests of her nipples. "I abhor you, Jace," she said as he made his way back down to the wet, soft center of her.

She cried out when he tongued her there. He gave her more friction this time, playing with the small nub and pinching it between his lips. She was panting, her neck arching, her hips curling toward him. He went on one elbow to watch her lovely, lovely face as he insinuated a finger inside her. Then two.

Her eyes widened, her gaze snapped to his. He began to move them, in slow circles and tender thrusts. Her heels dug into the mattress and he turned his face to kiss the inside of one knee, and then the other.

With his tongue, he wrote his initials there.

She made a sound, low in her throat. "I detest you," she said. "I loathe you, I abhor you. Do you hear me? I *despise* you."

And then it was time. He lowered his head, found her clit with his mouth and sucked firmly. At the same time he thrust deep inside the heated clasp of her body. Three fingers.

Her body jerked, once, twice, again and again. He rode it out with her, letting up by degrees, until she was no longer coming. Just quivering.

Lifting his head, he saw the dazed look on her face. He slowly pulled his fingers from her, heard her squeak of protest. Her muscles were still clamped around him. "Relax, baby," he said, caressing her hip while he worked the buttons of his jeans with his other hand. "You'll need to be able to let me in."

She made another inarticulate sound and her eyes drifted closed. Good. It gave him time to regain control and to grab a condom from his room.

He was gone for twenty seconds. Upon his return, she opened her eyes and reached for him with one languid hand. Naked, he kneed onto the mattress. She lay as he had left her, sprawled in a sated abandon that brought forth a new tenderness.

A renewed resolve.

Still stay gentle.

It took time to work himself inside her. She writhed with each slow increment and he watched carefully for true discomfort. "Ease up, Shay," he whispered to her. "You want me in, don't you?"

"Yes," she said. "Oh, God, yes."

He moved his hand between them, massaging her there, caressing the place they were joining. His cock slid deeper. She moaned, lifting into him, but he held her hip down. "Let me do all the work."

Bending his head, he sucked at her nipple, rhythmic and steady, and felt himself breach another inch. Another. Another. Until they were sealed, his hips to her pelvis, his cock sheathed by her tight heat.

His eyes might have rolled back in his head.

Then he was moving, small movements again, rocking, not driving. Sweat burst over his skin as he held firm to the reins. When he felt his grasp on them slipping, he stilled, then began again.

Her legs slid up his thighs, her ankles crossing at the small of his back, chaining him to her. Gritting his teeth, he continued the sweet rock, completion just evading.

"I hate you," Shay said, a demand in his ear as she lifted up to him again. "I hate you, I hate you."

Her body began shuddering as the climax hit her. He let it pull him over, his bigger frame quaking with the goodness of it. "Shay," he groaned as she clutched at his shoulders, the scrape of her nails wringing another pulse from him.

"I hate you," she said, one final time with feeling, just as her body went limp.

"I know," he replied, collapsing into the pillow.

He hated himself, too, for not realizing by holding back that he'd failed to slake his need for her. By not using this opportunity to possess her body, he now only wanted to have her all the more.

And they could have nothing past this night.

CHAPTER THIRTEEN

SHAY AWOKE ALONE and was grateful for it. Smelling coffee, she wrapped herself into a robe and made her way to the kitchen. Sun streaming through the wall of windows warmed the concrete floor beneath her bare feet. On the counter sat an empty mug beside the full carafe of coffee staying warm on the maker's element. Next to the mug was a note: "Out for a run."

More relief. If she hurried, she should be able to leave the house before Jace returned.

The place felt too empty without the buffer that was a teenage girl. And too full of memories from the night before.

She'd retrieve London right away, Shay decided, and use the short drive to shut the door on the compartment where she was keeping every recollection of her nights with Jace in bed.

One cup of coffee and a quick shower later, she headed out the long driveway and turned onto the lane. Humming a purposefully cheerful tune, she rolled down the window and let the warm morning air flutter the ends of her hair. It was going to be all right, she told herself, as the car passed through sunlight filtered by the pines and oaks that lined the narrow road. Last night had not been a monumental mistake.

Not if she put all thoughts of it—and Jace, who had a starring role—from her mind.

Then she spied a half-naked man running toward her.

Her stomach jolted and her foot touched down on the brake. Though she'd been next to his bare skin between sheets twice now, seeing Jace during the day, in a pair of nylon shorts and nothing else but running shoes, was a different experience altogether.

His brown hair was darkened and spiked with sweat. More of it rolled down his neck and glistened on the broad expanse of his chest. She didn't know the names of all the muscles that her eyes were drawn to, but they rippled on his torso and flexed in his powerful arms.

He jogged to her open window, and his fingers curled around the opening. When he bent at the waist she found herself staring at his pectorals and the dark dusting of hair between them that thinned into a line, which disappeared beneath his shorts. She remembered what it was like to be pressed against that wall of hot man, to have what lay beneath that nylon, the sleek steely heat of it, brushing her belly and penetrating between her thighs.

Her face burned. Jerking her gaze up to his, she managed to paste on a smile. "Uh…hi."

He studied her face. "You all right?"

"Oh, sure." She waved a hand. "I'm off to Poppy's. I'll bring London back."

He frowned. "I was planning to do that. I thought she wanted to stay until after lunch."

"It's probably best I get her sooner," Shay said, looking away before she got caught like a fly in the honey that was his golden eyes. Before she begged to drive him home so they could take a sexy, soapy shower together.

"Smart move."

She glanced up, saw the glint of resigned humor in his eyes. He might not be thinking of shared showers, exactly, but he understood why she was taking this line of defense. Despite the pleasure-soaked hours they'd spent together, that compelling attraction between them continued to pulse.

She hesitated. "And I'm going to tell Poppy no more sleepovers."

He was silent a moment. "Yeah."

"So, okay, then," she said, her voice bright. "I'll just—"

"Shay." He cut her off, his hand moving to her hair to give it a light stroke. "Should I apologize?"

"Certainly not," she scoffed.

"You don't feel I coerced—"

"Certainly *not*," she repeated, embarrassed to be having this discussion. "The situation arose…" Oh, now her cheeks had to be scarlet.

His mouth twitched. "That's for damn sure."

"We're two adults," she said, struggling on gamely. "We acted on impulse, which we're allowed to do. Now it's over and we go about our business."

"No regrets?"

She gazed out the windshield, eager to be on her way. "Not a one."

And she meant it, she reminded herself, as she left Jace behind in her rearview mirror. Last night had happened, now it was done and Jace would no longer have a place in her head.

Poppy was already at the open door of Ryan's immense house, which was styled as an Italianate villa. At first Shay had been dismayed by the sight of it. Walkers didn't have money and weren't much impressed by what it could buy, but she'd feared her sister and nephew might feel out of place there once the three had decided on a future together. But now the walls were filled with smiles and a small boy, love and a big lunk of a dog, and it felt like a home.

In a floaty cotton skirt, tank top and flip-flops, her sister waved as Shay climbed out of the car. "Hey, there."

She held up her hand as if shielding her eyes. "The sun on that ring's gonna make me go blind."

Poppy grinned as she glanced down at the rock on her left finger. "Best part of this engagement deal."

"I heard that." Ryan stepped up, looking down at his fiancée.

She turned her sunny smile on him and when their gazes met, Shay felt a decided snap, like two of Mason's Lego blocks fitting together. The elegant, movie-idol features of Ryan Hamilton softened and he leaned down and kissed her ear, and maybe whispered in it, too, because Poppy's cheeks went pink.

Shay told herself that watching them didn't cause a little ache, just below her breastbone. She was delighted for her sister, of course. Having a man like Ryan Hamilton was everything her sister deserved.

"Come in, come in," Poppy urged. "Mac's here, too."

Shay passed into the house and waved at Mason and London on her way to the kitchen. The two kids, engrossed in a video game, barely looked up. Mackenzie, however, welcomed her by pouring a mug of coffee. "We were just talking about you. Are your ears warm?"

Ryan had stopped off in his office, so it was only the three sisters in the kitchen. They each took a seat on one of the bar stools drawn up to the granite-topped island. Lifting her brows, Shay looked between Poppy and Mac. "Do I want to know why I was a topic of conversation?"

Mac, never one to pull any punches, didn't this time, either. "Jace Jennings."

Shay tried to pretend she misunderstood. "London's father was the topic of conversation, then."

Mac gave her a pointed glance. "Okay, you and Jace Jennings."

"Shh." Shay glanced around the room, in case one of the kids had snuck in. "Let's not have this conversation."

"Why not?" Poppy asked. "If I recall, you and Mac had just such a one with me a few months ago. So sure you were that I'd make a mistake and fall for Ryan."

"Look how well that turned out," Shay muttered.

"It turned out very well," Poppy answered, her smile smug. "So I'm not here to give you a lecture full of warnings like you two gave to me. I'm just being nosy."

"I'll give the warnings," Mac said.

A loud groan sounded in the room. Startled, they looked at each other and then over to the doors leading to the terrace, where Poppy's big shepherd-Labrador mix, Grimm, had just flopped over on his side to bask in a patch of sunshine. Shay laughed. "The dog speaks for me."

Mac frowned. "I only have your best interests in mind. We know the potential consequences of short-term flings—"

"I think so, Mac, since I *am* one of those consequences."

She had the grace to look ashamed. "Sorry. I know you're usually so careful—"

"Too careful," Poppy said. "You've got to put your-self on the line sometimes."

Shay rolled her eyes, borrowing one of London's favorite ways of expressing herself. "There's nothing going on between me and Jace."

"Well, I like him," Poppy said. "He's been working at the cabins."

"Yeah." Mac's eyes narrowed. "What's up with that?"

"He wanted to get London doing something besides schoolwork," Shay explained.

"Okay," Mac said. "But why the cabins?"

Shay glanced at Poppy, then back at her oldest sister. "I happened to mention the land to him. And I happened to mention that I'm with Poppy. I think we should make a go of the cabins."

Mac's jaw dropped.

Shay kept talking, glad they were off the subject of romance. "I know we don't have much seed money—"

Her sister snorted. "You mean, no seed money," Mac said.

"I have a sort of plan about that." Shay thought of the offer she'd been considering and wondered again about floating the idea with them now.

"We're not taking on any investors," Mac warned. "Particularly flatlanders. You better not be talking to Jace Jennings about—"

"No investors. Nothing to do with flatlanders."

Mac studied Shay, her expression suspicious. "Why haven't you spoken up about this before? You've been as anti-cabins as me and Brett."

"No," Shay corrected. "I've mostly said nothing."

"Well, how come?" Mac demanded.

"Remember?" Poppy said, her voice quiet. "She's implied her opinion doesn't matter because she's not really a Walker."

"For God's sake," Mac answered, glaring at Shay. "You really piss me off when you talk like that."

Her big sister's irritation didn't stop the facts being the facts. "Yes, but—"

"Anyway, all of this is just a distraction," Mac declared.

Oops, Shay thought. She'd noticed.

"Yes," Poppy agreed with another of her happy smiles. "Let's talk about Jace some more and why he looks at you like he's in dire need of utensils."

Shay grimaced. "You two are like Grimm with a bone, do you know that?"

"Just saying." Poppy's smile went wider. "I saw romance in the air yesterday evening."

Mac frowned at her. "You aren't helping, Miss Rose-colored Glasses."

"Your scowls aren't working on me," Poppy said, still bubbling with glee. "I even have high hopes for you and You Know Who."

Mac froze and the cold look in her eyes scared Shay a little. You Know Who was code for the town's wild boy and Mac had once been wild about him. As far as Shay knew, nobody had heard about him or from him in years.

"He's probably lying in a ditch somewhere," Mac muttered.

"If so, it's a waste of beautiful male flesh."

"Did I hear 'beautiful male flesh'?" Ryan strolled into the kitchen and headed for the refrigerator. "Are you women talking about me again?"

Now they all rolled their eyes, then laughed. Shay took this as her cue to extract herself from the conversation and from the house. "Well," she said, rising, "I should collect my charge and take her home."

"Not before you do me a big favor and agree to go to dinner with me tomorrow night," Mac said.

Shay hesitated. Not that dinner alone with her big sister would be so unpleasant, but... "Only if Jace is not one of the topics of conversation."

"Oh, she can practically guarantee that," Poppy said as Ryan came behind her. In a natural move that made Shay want to sigh, her sister leaned back against her fiancé. He dropped his hands to her shoulders and rubbed lightly.

"Ask her who else is going to be at your dinner table," Poppy continued.

Shay turned to her oldest sister.

Mac's expression was lousy with innocence. "It will be a double date. You get Chris."

"Chris Seeger?"

At Mac's nod, she groaned, louder than Grimm. "He's a great guy—"

"And you're not hung up on anyone with the initials *J* and *J*, so you have no reason to refuse," her oldest sister said.

Shay groaned again, then thought of Jace—even though she didn't want to think of Jace—and remembered the concern on his face when he'd asked her if she had regrets about their second night together. Did he doubt she was telling the truth when she asserted she was without remorse? Humiliating thought.

If she proved to him she was moving on, then he'd be absolved of any residual guilt. She'd be able to finish her assignment with London, her head held high. Then there was the additional bonus of getting her big sis off her back.

"All right," she said with ill grace. "I'll do it."

Maybe a date would give her something else to focus on besides the golden-eyed man on the way out of her life.

IT NIGGLED AT JACE, how comfortable Shay seemed with the reality of their situation. Though they'd been intimate—on two separate nights—now that his daughter was back in the house, the woman treated him like a piece of furniture. It had been two days since they'd had that evening alone and he'd been waiting for her to come after him with a dust cloth.

He scowled as he watched her wield a can of polish now, her summery skirt riding up the back of her tanned legs as she bent over the coffee table to rub it clean. "I thought I told Leonard to engage a service to do that," he said.

Straightening, she glanced at him over her shoulder. "I canceled it. It wasn't my sister's business that was hired, but some big company from down the hill. Waste of gas to get them up here."

"She speaks," he murmured. They'd barely exchanged three words before now.

She turned her head again. "What?"

"Nothing." If he complained about being ignored, he'd sound like some sulking high school swain.

Now she moved toward the kitchen, and he followed. "Call Mac, then. Give her the business."

"I know how to clean. As a matter of fact, I work for my sister when she can use me."

That had him scowling again. He didn't like the idea of her cleaning up a stranger's messes.

As if she sensed his disapproval, she spun around. "All work is good and honorable, Jace."

"I know, I know," he grumbled. But thinking of her vacuuming some other man's house made him think of her as some other man's wife.

Which shouldn't bother him at all.

In the kitchen, she put the polish and cloth away in the broom closet and crossed to the sink to wash her hands before pulling sandwich makings from the refrigerator. London was applying herself to schoolwork at a stool pulled up to the stainless-steel counter. Maybe the place was growing on him, because the kitchen seemed almost homey now, with the bright spots of Shay and London in colorful summer clothes.

A big vase stuffed with some daisy-like things sat near his daughter's elbow. It looked nice.

He watched Shay make sandwiches. She already knew that London liked mayo and he liked mustard and neither one of them wanted tomatoes on their turkey-and-Swiss. Cut-up carrots and celery sat in water in the fridge and she plucked some out to put on each plate.

Had she cut up the vegetables herself, too?

Of course she had. It was just another of the domestic skills she'd mastered. Motherly stuff. Wifely stuff.

Why did he keep thinking of that word?

Because she'd been doing all the cooking, that's why. With the exception of the day her siblings came over, she'd put together every meal with little help from him except clearing and some cleanup. She probably wasn't talking to him because she thought he was taking advantage of her.

Cleaning, cooking, taking care of his kid.

"Why don't I take you two out to dinner tonight?" he said on impulse. "I saw there's a Thai place—"

"You guys go," London said, not looking up from her paper. "There's a pizza in the freezer. I'd rather eat that and read my book."

He glanced over at Shay. Her back was to him as she put some utensils in the dishwasher. "No need for Thai or frozen pizza, either. I have a casserole all ready to go."

Of course she did.

She really was Ms. Capability, wasn't she? He'd called her that before and every day she proved it even more. Experienced tutor. Handy at all household tasks. Fabulous cook. Able to have fantastic sex one night and pretend that it never happened the next morning.

Grr.

After lunch, Jace insisted that he and London do the dishes. He told Shay to relax on the deck. "Read a book," he said. "Page through a magazine."

He found her out there once the kitchen was put to rights. She was reclined on one of a pair of loungers under the shade of an umbrella. With sunglasses covering her eyes, he couldn't be sure, but he thought she was asleep.

So he tried to be as quiet as possible when he took the second chair. The lake was a deep blue and the power-boats cutting across it were far enough away that their motors were merely a distant hum. A sailboat cruised by at the mouth of the cove, a peaceful sight.

Jace didn't feel the least bit serene, however.

He could go inside, look over some plans he'd brought with him, or scrutinize the details of some pending proposals, but neither sounded interesting. Rolling his head, he studied Shay.

After a moment, her mouth moved. "Is there something the matter?"

Hell if he knew, though it seemed messed up that he had this odd need to keep her talking to him. About what?

His daughter, of course, the only point that Shay would allow they had in common, he was sure. "I, um, have been thinking over how to tell London about starting at the new school."

Shay sighed. "You're going to have to do it, Jace. The sooner, the better."

"I know it."

"You also know…" She halted, pushed up and swung around so that she was sitting, her feet flat on the deck. She shoved her glasses to the top of her head and met his gaze.

She was so pretty. So damn beautiful.

"Do me a favor." Her arm stretched out and she placed her palm on his hand. "Reconsider."

He covered her hand with his free one, he couldn't help himself. "I can't, Shay."

She tried to slide away, but he firmed his hold. Her fingers felt so delicate in his, and right. It was so fucking wrong that it felt so fucking right.

"You mean you won't." Her expression turned from frustrated to sad.

He'd do anything in his power to take that unhappiness from her face, but he had no ability to become the kind of father and family man that Shay was thinking of. It wasn't in him, by nature or by experience.

"I'm sorry," he murmured.

"Then tell her tonight," Shay said, and this time she escaped his grasp.

He should. He would. With Shay by his side, it didn't have to be terrible. "At dinner. When the three of us are sitting down."

She stood up. "Sorry, but I won't be there. I have a date."

"SHAY WENT OUT on a date?" London said. "Who with?"

"I didn't ask." Jace set a dinner plate filled with food in front of his daughter. "It was none of my business."

"Maybe it was that guy she was smiling at on the boat that day."

He took his own seat, poked at the layered chicken, cheese and tortilla casserole that smelled great. "Maybe."

"Or some famous movie-star friend of Ryan's. He knows everybody." She scooped up a bite of the steaming mixture. "I could call Poppy and find out."

Chewing on his own forkful, Jace decided the kid needed to get off the topic of Shay and her mystery date. It was going to spoil his appetite for the delicious dinner in front of them. As he searched for a new subject of conversation, his conscience reminded him he shouldn't avoid the important subject of London's future a moment longer.

"It appears you like Mexican food," he observed instead, watching her dig in with enthusiasm.

She nodded. "I've only had it since I came to Blue Arrow. Our housekeeper, Opal, she made mostly meat loaf and mac 'n' cheese. And something she called turkey tetrazzini that had chicken, not turkey."

"Ah."

London made a face. "It had peas in it."

Jace mimicked the face. "I hate peas."

"Peas suck."

They looked at each other with new interest. Jace decided to try a compliment. "I like your hair." He gestured with his fork. "And that shirt is a pretty shade of blue."

"It's teal," she said, her head dropping so he couldn't see her face any longer.

Had he embarrassed her? What else sucked was his inability to connect with his kid. "London—"

"I don't like bananas," she said, flicking him a glance.

He blinked. "Me, either. And mangoes make me itch."

Her head came up and her eyes rounded. "They make me itch, too! I only found that out since I came here, too. I never had a mango when I lived in England. Opal was pretty much an apples-and-oranges kind of person."

Jace hesitated. "Your mom…she didn't introduce you to other foods? Take you out to restaurants? Cook for you?"

Without all the excess makeup, he found London's expressions easier to read. She looked uncomfortable now, her gaze sliding away from his.

"You can tell me the truth," he said, putting down his fork. His interest in food was diminishing with every second his daughter appeared uneasy.

"She liked me to go shopping with her sometimes," she said, addressing her plate. "But she wasn't very good in the kitchen. And, you know, she traveled a lot."

So had Jace, so he couldn't even fault the woman for that. But hell, he'd assumed—which made a you-know-what of him—that Elsa had taken a more active

role in raising their daughter. Sighing, he speared his
hand through his hair and felt the dull throb of a headache start up between his eyes. "I didn't do right by
you," he admitted out loud. "My father wasn't much of
one—or much of a human being for that matter—so I
don't know squat about being a dad. I didn't think you
weren't missing out by not having me around—but I
should have done more anyway."

She was moving her food around her plate. "I told
you it wasn't bad, remember? Mom could be fun. She
was always getting me those books."

Those books. Jace pinched the bridge of his nose.
Fuck. Those books.

"Yeah," he said. "Still…I'm really sorry—and I
know those words don't change the past. As for the future, though…" Now was probably the time to segue
into the whole going-away-to-school deal. "I promise
to always do what I think is best for you."

Her head jerked up, and she pinned him with
chocolate-brown eyes. "*I* know what's best for me. Don't
forget I'm fifteen."

Fifteen. So many years he'd lost. So many years he
could never make up for…even if he could figure out
how to start doing so. "London—"

"Can I be excused?" she asked without waiting for
his answer. She carried her plate to the sink and set it
inside.

Jace considered calling her back, making her sit once
more. Then earning her wrath by telling her that her
life was going to change again. Shortly.

And he found he just couldn't do it. Not yet. Not
tonight.

She scampered out of the room. In the distance, he

heard her bedroom door close. Jace put his elbow on the table and his head in his hand, telling himself now he could enjoy the quiet and the familiar sense of being alone. Still unsettled, however, he rose from the table and crossed to the window over the kitchen sink. Staring out it, the lake was a dark patch of serenity in the near distance. An owl—at least he assumed it was an owl—hooted, for whatever reasons owls hooted.

It should be peaceful. Strange, though, that tonight this loner felt he was more abandoned than at ease.

CHAPTER FOURTEEN

SHAY LET HERSELF into Jace's house and walked straight to the alarm control box to enter the code on the keypad. She switched off the porch and foyer lights, leaving the downstairs in nearly complete darkness, and headed for the stairs. As she crossed through the living room, Jace's voice came from the shadows.

"Shay?"

She paused, then turned, able to just make him out, sprawled at one corner of the couch.

"How was your evening?" he asked, his low voice sending the nerve endings along her spine skittering.

She wasn't about to tell him it was boring at best. "Wonderful." Though he likely couldn't see her smile due to the lack of light, she pasted one on anyway.

"You look beautiful."

Her brows came together. Her little black dress and strappy heels surely were just smudges in the darkness. "Your carrot intake must be up if you can see much of me right now."

"Hair in loose waves. Dress is black and sleeveless. Square neckline, poofy skirt, sash thing that you tied in a big bow at the front of your waist. You're lucky you didn't break an ankle in those high heels."

Shay smoothed the "poofy" skirt. "All right, what's your secret?"

"I have a thing for your legs. So I watched you out the window when you left, in hopes that you'd be wearing something just that revealing."

"It's not revealing!" Yes, the hem ended above the knee, but inches south of any overexposure.

"Well, I appreciate the wealth of bare skin anyway. Thank you."

Did that require a "You're welcome"? Should she be polite after he'd basically admitted to going voyeur on her? Not that she hadn't done her share of sneaking looks at him. He'd been running shirtless again that morning and she'd only pretended to read behind her sunglasses once he returned. He'd strolled onto the deck where she was perusing the newspaper and she'd watched him with avid eyes as he downed a bottle of water in one go, his throat muscles working.

"How come he didn't pick you up?" Jace asked.

"Let's talk about your evening instead, shall we? How was it? Did you tell London—"

"That I'm packing her off to school then heading back to Qatar for months of work? No. But we did discuss our mutual aversion to peas."

"Nobody else in your company can take over the management of the project there?"

He was silent so long, she figured he was thinking of something else besides her simple question. Then he began speaking again and confirmed it.

"We actually did connect, I think, just a little, until I got the fifteen-year-old version of 'You're not the boss of me' and 'I know what I'm doing with my life.'"

Shay winced and moved closer. "She was on her own a lot in London, I think."

"Yeah, I'm getting that. It doesn't make me happy in

the least, but I don't know what the hell to do about it. I can't wind back the clock and make her five again."

She sat in a chair adjacent to the couch, almost close enough to touch if she reached out an arm. "You could stick close, Jace. Be there for her now."

"I don't deserve her," he muttered, then jolted forward to prop his elbows on his knees and scrub his face with his big hands. His head turned her way. "So, did he kiss you?"

"Chris?" Damn, she hadn't meant to bring the other man into their conversation.

"It was him, then," Jace said. "Did he kiss you?"

She wasn't going to talk of kissing, not when that only made her crave Jace's kisses, Jace's touch. Remembering the sensation of his whiskers against the skin at her throat and the inside of her knees, she rubbed her suddenly damp palms against her dress.

"I think you should give him another chance," Jace said.

Caught up in her own thoughts, she figured she must have missed something. "Who? Give who a chance?"

"Officer Upright. Officer All-Good. You look nice together."

It hurt to hear him foisting her off on Chris. "You're not the boss of me," she said, keeping her voice light. "I know what I'm doing with my life."

"I'm serious," Jace said.

"You're seriously trying to direct my romances?"

"We're just having a conversation."

She blew out a breath. "Look, he's a great guy—"

Jace winced. "And has a really good personality? Admit it, Shay, that isn't a bad thing. Not to you. Not *for* you. I can see you being happy with him."

Frowning, she crossed her arms over her chest. "Would you like me to predict the kind of woman you'll settle down with?"

"As if that's going to happen," Jace scoffed.

"I say it will," Shay said airily. "In the not-so-distant future, you'll be back in LA to check in with your headquarters and touch base with your daughter. One night you'll stop in at some bar for a drink—"

"A seedy bar with darts and pool or a fancy bar with high-class call girls looking to pick up clients?"

Shay's brows rose. "There are really bars with high-class call girls hanging around?"

He laughed.

"And how do you *know* they're high-class call girls and not just some regular women wanting a drink out?"

"I've got a sixth sense. So, which is it?"

"It's the bar at your hotel and there are no call girls in sight," she said, her voice prim. "There's a woman in a business suit at a small table and since there's no other seats open in the place, you ask if you can take the one beside her."

"And she'll agree, just like that?"

"Believe me, Jace, she'll agree, just like that."

"Huh. Go on," he said, gesturing.

"Like you, she travels a lot for business. Sales trips to sell, um…greeting cards."

"What kind of greeting cards?"

"The funny ones that you give your girlfriends for their birthdays, all about purses, martinis and hot men. Also the ones with really cute animal photographs that you send to maiden aunts and elementary-age nephews."

"Is she successful?"

"Yes, but she's tired of airports and body scanners—

she doesn't look her best in black-and-white—and would like to find the right man so she can talk herself into finding a new job that doesn't require a suitcase."

"Okay. I'm sitting next to this woman. Then our eyes meet and she tells me it's her birthday—"

"It's not her birthday. But your eyes meet, and well… it's history." She was tiring of the game. She didn't want to picture Jace with some cool blonde or sultry brunette.

"Okay…" He drew out the word. "I'm not sure I can take your word for it. Does she know how to cook? Does she mind cleaning? Most important, will she like someone else's kid?"

Shay shook her head. "You don't care about the cooking and cleaning. You're perfectly capable of doing them yourself or trading off doing them with Greeting Card Woman. As for London…she can win anybody over."

Shay went silent, fingering the swan bracelet on her left wrist while trying to ignore the ache of losing the girl's presence in her life. "Jace, she's special. You know that, right?"

"I do," he said, his voice low. "And I see that you know it, too."

Clearing her throat, Shay went for bright again. "Bowled over by love, you'll rearrange your life to cease almost all the travel—except for jaunts you can do as a family—and find a lovely home by the beach to move into."

"Will we keep this place as our lake getaway?" he asked. "Or perhaps I should find a way to do most of my work from home and decide to live in the mountains 24/7."

"I don't know." She shrugged.

"That way we might run into you and your stalwart

lake patrolman. I can see it now, little Shays and little All-Goods following behind you like ducklings."

Her heart shrank at the idea of running into him and Greeting Card Wife. As silly as it sounded, since she'd conjured the woman herself, it was…unbearable to imagine looking up one day and seeing a smiling Jace saying hello to her like the one-time tutor that she'd been. Probably not even remembering they'd also once—twice—been lovers.

"I won't be here," she said, impulse driving her to the decision. She'd been considering it for months.

"What are you talking about?"

"It looks like I'm going away. For a while." Maybe longer, who knew?

"Going away where?" Jace asked slowly.

"I have a college friend. She teaches English at an exclusive private school in France—Nice, actually. She's been after me to join her."

"Leave the mountains? Leave your siblings?"

"I'm sort of doing it for them." She thought of the day of the fire, Dell Walker's roughened voice shouting her name, the devastation the flames wreaked on the property, Dell's subsequent death. *If only she hadn't wandered off!*

"The position comes with lodging and the money's amazingly good in relative terms. I could send lots of it home to help rebuild the cabins." While it wouldn't make up for the loss of her siblings' father, it would be something.

"You'd go away." Jace sounded…puzzled? Bothered?

"Yes." As long as she'd been considering this plan, it had made her sad to think of leaving, to not breathe in the smell of lake-scented air and sunlight on the pines every day. But now, now she thought it might be for the best. Blue Arrow Lake would never be the same for her once Jace and London Jennings left.

SHAY TURNED ON her pillow, only halfway into a restless sleep. Then she stilled, something warning her of a presence in the room.

Not one she was afraid of, however.

Turning again, she saw Jace approaching her bed.

"Is something wrong—"

"Shh," he said, placing his finger over his lips. Then he lowered to the edge of the mattress. She sat up, too, feeling less vulnerable when he wasn't looking down on her.

"What's going on?" she whispered.

He reached toward her, let his hand drop. "Couldn't sleep."

She frowned. "Do you need help warming some milk?"

Smiling a little, he shook his head. "And a warm shower didn't work. Not a cold one, either."

He'd hoped a cold shower might work.

She knew why, of course. It had come into the room with him, the powerful sexual magnetism that made her draw up her sheets to cover her breasts. She wore a nightshirt, something not the least bit sexy, but it was thin enough that he'd be able to detect her tight nipples poking against the fabric.

A shiver worked itself down her back and she bit her bottom lip, trying to think of what to say, what to do. Earlier in the night she'd made up Greeting Card Wife. She'd told him about her plans to go to Nice.

Both had kept her from dropping into a healthy sleep.

And now it seemed he was equally affected.

Still… "Your daughter is only a room away."

"Snoring," he said, his voice nearly soundless. "I checked. Not to mention we both already know I'm a lousy father."

"I don't like to think I'm a lousy tutor—"

"She won't know anything about this. We'll go to the Big Bed O' Chains."

How could he make her want to laugh at a time like this? And long for him. And yearn to be in his arms.

"I'm lonely tonight, Shay."

They were magic words. She was lonely tonight, too. Sometimes she thought she'd been lonely her whole life, despite her siblings, her mother, her adopted father.

Maybe he saw all that on her face, because he reached toward her again, and this time his palm cupped her cheek. Without thinking, she nuzzled into it, breathing him in. He smelled so good, a masculine, clean, almost salty scent—which she giddily mused might be testosterone—that she wanted to chase all over his skin with her mouth.

She pressed a kiss to his rough calluses and heard him draw in a sharp breath. Then he shifted and gathered her close by using his strength to lift her out of the covers and into his lap. His mouth covered hers.

This was magic, too.

Pleasure seeped into her from the kiss. When he slid his tongue across her lips, she opened for him, let him explore inside with gentle forays. While he had showered, he hadn't shaved, and the stubble surrounding his lips abraded her skin, a light scratching that she wished to feel in so many other places.

He was a mind reader, she thought as he made some

sound and pressed his cheek to hers, then drew it over her jaw and down her neck. "I'm not supposed to want anybody like this," he said, and she felt the words more than heard them.

"Then go away," she suggested, knowing he wouldn't.

Instead, his arms tightened on her and he rose, moving to carry her over the threshold like a bride in a gown printed with sleeping puppies and kittens. Her hands linked behind his neck even as she tried dredging up the will to refuse him.

They were in his room with the door locked when he let her down, the bottom half of her body sliding against his. Heat was gathering under the soft cotton knit of her nightwear and she clutched at the sides of his T-shirt to prevent herself from flinging off her own garment in wanton abandon.

Jace closed his fingers over her shoulders. The room was dimly lit by light streaming in from the attached bathroom. "Did he kiss you?" he asked again.

"It doesn't matter." She wasn't trying to be coquettish. The truth was, she couldn't remember. Nothing of the evening out had made an impression on her, not when her mind had been back at the house, on Jace, on her and Jace together.

"I want to know if he kissed you." His golden eyes narrowed and she could see he was both serious and seriously turned on.

It thrilled her, that note of possessiveness in his voice. Was it bad of her? But she couldn't help it. Maybe because she didn't think anyone had ever wanted her with that kind of...of intense passion.

The idea was dizzying.

"Shay—"

She cut him off by lifting to her toes and grinding her mouth to his. One of his hands slid from her shoulder to the back of her head. He speared his fingers through her hair as he ate at her mouth, the kiss one of ownership…on both sides. Shay tightened her hold on him and pulled his tongue into her mouth, sucking on it until he broke away from her to drag in a rough, ragged breath.

He pressed the side of his face against her temple, and she slid her hands under his T-shirt to the burning skin of his back. He groaned as she explored the heavy muscles there, and it aroused her unbearably to feel them bunch beneath her palms.

Emboldened by his obvious pleasure in her touch, she found the hem of his shirt and started yanking, trying to bare his magnificent chest. But he was tall and still holding on to her and she growled in frustration as she tried to make the shirt magically disappear.

His laugh was low, amused. "Wait, honey," he said. "I've got this." Then he half stepped back and reached one hand between his shoulder blades to grasp the cotton and pull it free.

She stared. She'd been stealing glances at him after his half-naked runs, and now she could trace the contours there with one fingertip: his pectorals, his abdominals, those incredibly sexy angled indentations at each hip that disappeared beneath the waistband of his jeans.

He flinched when she drew a faint line just above the denim. "God, Shay," he said, and she saw his hands fist at his sides. "You want to kill me, don't you?"

What she wanted next…she decided to show him. Dropping to her knees, she grasped the top button of his pants. He groaned, his whole body tensing, and she saw the thick column beneath his zipper jerk beneath the heavy fabric.

Shay wanted to see that naked, too.

He went absolutely still as she worked at unfastening. Beneath the denim he'd gone commando, and he was hot and incredibly hard in her hand as she drew him free. Above her, he breathed in and out in rough pants and she glanced up to see his eyes were fever-bright and that color edged his cheekbones and the bridge of his nose.

Still watching him, she leaned forward to draw her tongue around the silky head.

He gasped, his eyes closed, and one hand shot out to brush the top of her hair. She drew him into her mouth, wetting the sleek skin as far as she could take him. His fingers tightened in her hair, not directing, just holding on as she took up a soft, sucking rhythm.

She shuffled forward on her knees to take more, catching the material of her nightshirt beneath them, causing it to tighten over her breasts that felt so heavy, almost too full. Her eyes closed as she moaned around the column of flesh in her mouth. The intimacy of the act was causing something to come undone inside her. She was heated, molten at her core, but some brand-new sensation was swirling in her chest and rushing through her blood, something wholly unknown to her.

Jace's fingers tightened again, the small pull a delicious little pain that raced across her scalp. As she moaned again his other hand caught her arm and he pulled her up.

"Hey—" He silenced her protest with a kiss, deep and erotic, and she swayed into his body, his broad chest holding her up.

Then he was moving forward, using his strength to herd her toward the bed. She stumbled a little on her feet, and he swung her up again, only to lay her against the covers like precious treasure. Standing over her, he stared down, and the look of him set her heart thumping against her ribs. His features were hardened by desire, his bare chest moved up and down with heavy breaths, his arousal jutted forward through the open placket of his jeans.

She remembered Poppy saying he looked at her like he needed utensils and she saw it now, that hungry gaze, the greedy need on his face that matched the same simmering in her belly and below.

Nothing could appear more primitively male. He was the victor, she the spoils. The conqueror and the maiden. It was every single romantic, erotic fantasy she'd ever had...

And it was Jace.

His magnificent body and golden eyes. His delicious weight that came down on top of her. She parted her thighs as he tilted his head and found the perfect angle for another long, inebriating kiss.

His hands moved, drew up her nightshirt and flung it away. She pressed up, arched her naked breasts against his chest, her nipples rubbing into the crisp hair there.

Jace's mouth lowered again and sipped at her skin. He tongued her neck on the way to her breasts and he sucked and toyed with them, murmuring praise. *You're so beautiful...perfect...you taste like flowers...lift up while I take off your panties...oh, there you are...so soft, so hot.*

Shay didn't have legions of lovers to compare him to, but she'd never had a man speak to her like this during sex. His words slurred together a little, like he was getting drunk on the taste of her flesh. He circled her navel with his tongue, he bit lightly on the curve of her hip, he lifted one hand to examine her fingers and his mouth rubbed over each joint.

It was as if he were cataloging her, inch by inch, and it seemed to take her to a higher plane, to a cloud maybe, where she floated in a sexual haze.

"Have you ever," he said, moving up to drop kisses on her temple, her hairline, the side of her nose, "seen a fairy house?"

Her neck arched as he rubbed his whiskered chin against it. "Fairy house?"

"Mmm." His lips touched the side of her breast. "Years and years ago, an old lady who knew I liked to work with my hands requested I make her one."

Now he was focused on his thumb, lightly circling her tight nipple. The close attention made her feel flushed and shivery.

"Well," she managed to say, "you are very good with your hands."

He glanced up, smiled.

It made her shiver again. She sifted her fingers through his hair. "Tell me about the fairy house."

"You make them with natural materials. Moss, bark, acorns." He took her hand from his hair, kissed it, then placed it, palm up, on the pillow beside her head. The other hand received the same treatment. "The one I built for Mrs. Sugarman was about yea big." He pantomimed a rectangle, smaller than a shoe box.

Now one fingertip drifted lazily down her center line and her legs moved restlessly. "What did she do with it?"

He tugged on the soft curls at her center. "She had me set it outside, of course." His glance met hers again. "To attract a fairy."

She tried imagining it, this so-masculine man creating such a small piece of whimsy.

Leaning down, he spoke into her ear. "You inspire me to make another, Shay. I'd construct it using eucalyptus bark for walls and layered maple leaves for the roof, soft moss as a rug for the floor. Inside I'd place a bed of petals plucked from summer roses."

"To give to me? A present?"

"Oh, no." His head lifted so he could look into her eyes. "I'd keep it for myself. Find the ideal spot in my yard, wherever that might be, and set it out…in hopes of luring you."

Shay's heart stopped, then it started moving again, a flurry of beats that pushed a new, dizzying, euphoric feeling through her bloodstream. Her skin flushed hotter and she couldn't move as he placed a kiss in the cup of one palm, and then the other.

"My sweet fairy," he murmured. "If I was a different man, I'd do just about anything to capture and keep you."

The words soared, wheeled and turned inside her head. *My sweet fairy. I'd do just about anything…*

Then he was over her, his erection already covered by a condom. The blunt tip of him pressed against her soft center and she was so turned on that he slipped inside with little resistance, despite his big size. But he pressed forward in increments, tiny little nudges that made the possession a long, delirious process of exquisite yielding.

Shay was dizzied by all of it, the delicious, gratifying penetration, the heat in his golden eyes, the sound of his voice, murmuring to her again. *Oh, baby...tight... take me in...you're incredible...hot...so hot.*

Finally, he was fully seated and she closed her eyes on a moan. It was as if he'd reached some place that had never been touched before. Another chemical cocktail poured into her bloodstream, some brilliant, electrifying combination of adrenaline and champagne bubbles she'd never experienced.

It both exhilarated and alarmed her. As he started moving, his hips surging in a purposeful rhythm, more euphoria coursed through her. There must be another name for it, she thought, something that would cover all this...this physical sensation and stunning intimacy.

But she didn't know what that would be...

Unless...

Jace slid his hands beneath her bottom and tilted her hips, allowing him to slide inside her another elemental increment. She gasped, and he filled her mouth with his tongue as he began another devastating kiss.

Her arms came around him and he shifted, so they lay on their sides. Both heads on the pillow, her top thigh propped on his, his body still thrusting, joining deeply with hers. Not conqueror and maiden now, but equals, man and woman.

Jace and Shay.

And then she knew what this feeling was, this thing she'd never felt before. It was—oh, God—it was love.

She was in love with him.

The knowledge stunned her. Scared her.

And yet, her body still moved with his, its commitment made to the act of love, and when he slid his hand between them, his fingers toying with the slick surface of her clitoris, she arched into the touch, letting it take her over the falls and into the deep.

Where she heard a final echo of his voice like the sensation of cold water closing over her head. *If I were a different man...*

LONDON DIDN'T HAVE to do much arm-twisting to get a ride to the community library on Saturday afternoon. Shay was heading out to run some errands and said she'd drop her off and pick her up an hour or so later. Since Colton hadn't specified exactly what time he brought his sister, London could only hope that she'd encounter him there.

She tugged on the ends of her denim shorts, and Shay glanced over from the driver's seat. "You look cute," she said.

The compliment eased London's self-consciousness a little. The outfit was similar to things she'd seen the teens around town wearing. Paired with the denim shorts was a lacy short-sleeved top in white that had a little swing to it around the hemline. With them she wore these half boots she'd loved the minute she saw them. They were a natural-colored leather and lug-soled, with lace insets on the calf portion. A pretty version of a hiking boot.

As Shay pulled to the curb in front of the library, London flipped down the overhead visor and checked out her face in the mirror. Her highlighted hair hung smoothly around her face. The makeup had stayed where she'd put it—as she'd been shown by the stylist at the salon. A touch of taupe shadow and pink blush. A thin tracing of dark brown liner around her eyes and a light coat of mascara. Berry-colored lip gloss.

With a casual "See you later," she stepped onto the sidewalk.

The path to the door seemed like a mile, but her life was all about walking forward now, not waiting for things to happen to her. Though her legs still felt too bare, she forced herself not to tug on her shorts again. As she reached the entry, a pair of girls exited. She was grateful to notice they'd rolled the hems of theirs to even greater heights. The white triangle ends of the front pockets showed below.

Once inside, London realized she didn't know quite where to go. It was an expansive space with shelves of books, rows of tables topped with computers and several seating areas made up of comfortable-looking chairs with nearby racks of magazines and newspapers. In one corner a giant Winnie-the-Pooh hung suspended from the ceiling, which she figured denoted the children's area.

Knowing to avoid that, London wandered in the opposite direction.

As she passed through stacks of cookbooks—Dewey call number 641, a piece of trivia she filed away to surprise Shay with later—she saw a knot of teens gathered at another cushioned seating area. Her feet stuttered and her stomach did a little pancake flip. Colton was there, along with another boy she thought might be his friend John, as well as a couple of girls.

John glanced her way but his gaze bumped right over her. Of course, she thought, he didn't recognize her. She wouldn't have guessed his identity, either, except she'd gotten a closer look at him when he left the boathouse with Bess the other night.

Swallowing, she directed her attention to the row of

colorful books, pretending an avid interest. There were two devoted to broccoli alone. Who knew?

Still half facing the shelves, she slid a gaze toward the kids again. Colton was only getting cuter, she decided. He had on a ragged pair of shorts that hung low on his hips, his leather flip-flops and a white T-shirt that emphasized his golden tan. His sandy hair was more sun-streaked than ever. He shoved his hands in his pockets, and she noted the ropy muscles of his arms.

It hit her all over again. *Almost a senior in high school!*

Maybe he felt her regard, because his head suddenly jerked her way. Caught, she could only remain still and wait for his reaction. But...

There was none.

Yes, his gaze momentarily seemed to take her in, then one of the girls said something and he returned his attention to the group. It was almost as if...as if...

He hadn't recognized her!

She didn't know whether to be insulted or delighted.

Or what her next move should be.

Uncertain, she turned back to the broccoli books, going so far as to pull one free. Her fingers idly turned the pages, though she didn't actually absorb a single recipe.

A voice murmured close to her ear. "I'm never eating pancakes that look like *that*."

She clamped down on the urge to jump. "Green is not a good color for pancakes," she agreed, trying to appear calm as she shut the book and reshelved it. "Hi, Colton."

He smiled. "Hi, England. It took me a minute to realize it was you."

Her hand lifted. "I changed my hair."

He stepped back to survey her from head to toe. She fought not to squirm. "You look good."

"Thanks." She shifted a shoulder.

"You made it back to your house okay?"

He was talking about the Seven Minutes in Heaven night. Though it still embarrassed her to think of it, she was relieved that she'd gotten out of kissing Sam. *Wet sloppies!*

"I heard my dad calling me," she said, shrugging again. "We had some people over." London liked the sound of that. *We had some people over.* It gave the impression that she and her dad were a kind of...kind of a social team.

"Do you want to meet my sister?" Colton asked. He was talking in a library voice, though it seemed as if this place was more relaxed than some. Even from here, she heard murmuring coming from the cluster of teens.

Shay cast a glance at them. She could hardly refuse, she supposed. Hadn't she just been happy to impress him with her social abilities? "Sure," she said with another shoulder hitch.

They walked together toward the group. "Amy, this is London," he said upon reaching them. The girl he addressed was short and slender and she had braces with alternating blue and yellow rubber bands twisted around them. When she smiled, the effect was bright and sunny.

"Hi," she said, her expression open and friendly.

She was reintroduced to John, another boy, Phil, and a girl who looked a little older than Amy. They called her Peach and she tucked her hand into Phil's bent elbow, clearly laying claim.

Colton gave the others a short bio of her and the fact that she'd been living in London garnered a few questions. Phil had gone there on a visit with his parents and had developed a passion for fish and chips. He'd liked visiting the Tower.

When that line of conversation petered to nothing, he, John and Colton exchanged glances. "We out?" Phil asked.

"We're out," Colton confirmed. "See you later, Ames," he said to his sister. Then he gave London a two-finger salute. "'Bye."

She could only stare as he turned and began to walk off with his friends and Peach. *Wait!* she wanted to call. *I came here to see you! To talk to you!* Sweat pricked at her hairline as she struggled with the dilemma. Would she look desperate if she ran after him?

But how could she let him get away?

"So, how do you like living here?"

Amy Halliday's voice broke into London's thoughts. She glanced at the girl. "Um…okay?"

With another flash of her blue-and-yellow smile, she sat on the armless couch and patted the cushion beside her. "You can sit if you want."

London hesitated, torn. What she wanted was more time with Colton, but she didn't think it would do to be impolite to his sister. Chewing on her bottom lip, she perched on the couch, watching as the other teens strolled through the exit. When the door closed behind them, disappointment swamped her.

An elbow nudge drew her attention to Amy again. "What?"

"I asked you about school. Are you going to enroll at Arrow High?"

Still thinking about the missing Colton, London shrugged.

"It's a good school. I'm a freshman and I work on the literary magazine. Would you like to do something like that?"

"Maybe."

Her less-than-enthusiastic response seemed to drain some of the vitality from the other girl. An awkward silence welled between them. London thought she'd die of embarrassment. Here was this girl being nice to her—Colton's sister!—and she couldn't even keep a conversation going.

No one would ever want to talk to her.

She'd never make friends.

Then she recalled something Shay had told her the other day, after the salon. *Look like you're having the most fun ever.* It was supposed to make people want to be around her.

Ignoring another rush of embarrassment, London tried altering the expression on her face. Lifting her lips, she swiveled her knees so she faced the other teen. "So," she said, "you really like school? What are your favorite subjects?"

The questions might have been lame, but her interest must have seemed genuine enough that Amy began talking. She was a chatterbox, London decided, but in a good way. Fifteen minutes later, she knew more about the other girl than she possibly knew about herself.

And they clicked. It was weird and almost as exciting as being around Colton, except it was easier because it was a girl. They both shared an interest in reading, the singer-songwriter Clarita and boys, though London didn't spill a word about Colton.

As Amy shared her plans for the summer and beyond, London felt the smile on her face widen and knew it was as authentic as her usual frowns. Had she made a friend? She thought so, and was feeling happier about it by the second.

Until the subject of school came up again. "Being the new girl is going to suck," London said.

Amy was already shaking her head. "Nope. You're my project now. By September you'll know all my friends and you'll have people to eat lunch with and you'll probably recognize at least one person in every one of your classes."

Sophomore classes, London thought. She'd have to find a way to explain to Colton she was a seventeen-year-old sophomore. As Opal had always warned, even little fibs could create tangled webs.

"Why are you frowning now?" Amy said, her expression perplexed. "I've solved all your problems. Next year is going to be great."

London couldn't help but smile again, though she reminded herself she didn't have to depend on other people to make her life what she wanted. Yes, it might be really nice to have Amy at her side, but London was still the captain of her fate, the master of her soul. When the time was right, she'd broach a few subjects with Jace. Number one on the list would be Arrow High School.

Because it was decided. Vital to the whole entire rest of her life was going to school with Amy and Colton Halliday. It would suck worse than peas ever could if that didn't happen.

CHAPTER FIFTEEN

BECAUSE JACE KNEW he was destined to disappoint his daughter—and had let her down in the past—he found himself having trouble refusing her anything. In the past few days he'd taken her out on the boat on three separate occasions and allowed her practice minutes behind the wheel, which had surely sliced years off the span of his life. He'd also been persuaded to let her steer his car down the long driveway once, but she'd scared herself into tears believing she'd barely missed hitting a squirrel that had dashed across the asphalt. When she declared she was done with automobiles for the time being, Jace had blessed the speedy little creature, which hadn't been in jeopardy for even an instant.

This morning London had given him big eyes while requesting the chance to attend the matinee of a popular movie in Blue Arrow's small theater. As the alternative was spending more time filling his day by avoiding Shay, he'd readily agreed.

Only to find out they were going to be a party of three.

But that was all right, he told himself as they walked from the back deck toward the dock. The teen would provide an adequate buffer. And it wasn't as if Shay had been clamoring to spend one-on-one time with him, either. Since the night after her date, when he'd brought her to his bed, she'd been keeping her distance, as well.

Only something else to feel guilty about.

On a silent sigh, he glanced over at the woman, sighed again. Complete avoidance might have been the better choice, because there was no way to ignore the beauty of the bright sunshine glinting off her russet-and-gold hair. What she wore shouldn't be so irresistible, either, being just a T-shirt and cropped jeans, but the sleeves of the shirt were loosely knitted or crocheted or something, so they played peekaboo with her delicate shoulders. The same kind of crochet was inset into the sides of her formfitting pants, from hemline to knee.

He should never have gone to bed with her that third time, he decided. Everybody knew there was something about threes…right? God, did three times establish a habit?

It felt like a habit. An addiction. Ever since he'd walked her back to her room in the early morning hours—like some boy seeing her from his car to her front door—he'd not been able to get her taste and fragrance and feel out of his head.

At the dock, he swung open the metal door leading onto the boat, then held out a hand to help London and Shay step on board. There were slips near the village where they could tie up for the afternoon, and taking the overwater route to the theater was the quicker option. Both females ignored his proffered palm and clambered easily inside. He released the lines then manned the pilot's seat to reverse and pull away.

There was more traffic on the lake than he'd seen before, signaling the imminent arrival of the summer season. People paddled one- and two-man yellow-and-red kayaks in shallow water. Stand-up paddleboarders hugged even closer to the shoreline. Sailboats navigated open water while powerboats dragging skiers and wakeboarders zipped by, creating wakes that scudded against the hull of the *Fun & Games*.

"Do you know how to do that?" London asked Shay, pointing to a young woman flying by on a single ski.

"I haven't in ages," Shay said, over the thrum of the motor.

"I want to try." London looked over at Jace. "I saw a water-ski school not far from the movie theater when we were out the other day."

"They don't start operations until later in the summer," Shay cautioned.

He felt her glance but didn't meet her eyes. Just another reason he'd been avoiding her. She wanted him to break the news to his daughter about their imminent departure from Blue Arrow and he kept procrastinating.

Putting off the day when London would look upon him with new dislike.

Once docked on the other side of the lake, he purchased three tickets to the movie, ignoring Shay's attempts to press money on him. Then, snacks in hand, they turned into the theater, the stadium seating half-lit as advertising played on the screen. Fortune shined on him when their progression into their chosen row put London between him and Shay.

The girl didn't pay attention to either one of the adults, and instead hunched over her phone, thumbs hip-hopping over the keyboard. He glanced over her head and his gaze snagged on Shay's.

The small smile she sent him opened a wound. She was so fucking lovely it hurt.

Tossing some popcorn into his mouth, he focused his attention on the screen. An ad for soda appeared and he instantly regretted forgoing that sixteen-ouncer he'd considered. Maybe they did contain subliminal "buy" messages as had always been rumored.

Suddenly London shot straight in her seat. He glanced over, saw her attention was riveted by a group of girls rounding the corner into the main aisle. They were looking about, as if deciding where to stake their claim. One teen's gaze roamed past London, then zoomed back. She waved, the smile breaking over her face revealing a full set of braces.

"That's my friend I met at the library," London said. She glanced down at her phone. "Amy wants me to sit with her. Can I?"

"Uh…"

His daughter's eyes narrowed. "I'll be right over there," she said, pointing to the lower row where the friend and others were seating themselves.

Jace looked them over. They were the safer gender. He supposed there weren't drugs and alcohol in their Junior Mints and soda cups. "Go ahead," he said. "Just don't disappear once the movie's over, okay? We'll meet in the lobby."

She was already scrambling over his knees, her Milk Duds in hand. Left with the tub of popcorn, he put it on the now-empty spot between him and Shay. "Help yourself," he said, nudging it toward her.

"Oh. You're talking to me now?"

Stalling, he took up another handful of popcorn and threw it into his mouth. Post-munching, he glanced over at her. He had no reasonable—or even grown-up—explanation. And it was ridiculous to spout dumb excuses. "I've been an ass."

"Something like that," she said. "Blowing hot, blowing cold…"

He sighed. "It's just that…that I still intend to blow past."

"Understood." Her expression gave nothing away.

"I know I've gone about this all wrong." Especially when what would have felt right to his horny self was to have her next to him each and every night.

"Hey." She smiled. "You seemed to do all right with the Big Bed O' Chains."

Her lighthearted response eased him, and he grabbed up the bucket between them and switched into the empty seat. "I was feeling like high school with that space between us. Teenage buddies sit that way at the movies."

"I've always wondered about the practice," Shay said. "It makes no sense that you can slap each other's butts during sports but insist on personal space when the lights go out."

Jace shook his head. "We're a peculiar gender."

"I'll say."

He chewed on more popcorn, then regretted it, his mouth now desert dry. Without meaning to, he stared at Shay's bottle of water that sat in the holder between them.

"Go ahead," she said.

"What?"

"You're thirsty. We can drink from the same bottle."

He hesitated.

"For goodness' sake, Jace. We shared spit. We can share some water."

"Don't bring up the sharing spit." He shot her a glance. "Please."

"You're trying to forget about it?"

"I'm trying to be a gentleman and restrain my more caveman urges." His hand curled around the bottle. "Belatedly, I know."

"Oh." Stiffness drained out of her and she relaxed into her chair. "I thought…I thought you were maybe mad that I wasn't the one to hold off or…" She shrugged. "Something."

Shit. He really had screwed things up. "I'm not mad at all, unless at myself. Damn it, I…I like you, and that might make this situation even stickier. It's why I've been spending most of my days mentally kicking my own ass. I've taken advantage of you more than once."

"Is that what we're calling it now?"

"Shay—"

"I told you before. I'm a grown woman who has made her own choices. And by the way, I like you, too."

Though the words sounded like good ones, he still had an uneasy feeling in his gut that he wished he could blame on the greasy popcorn. "I—" He broke off, his gaze homing in on some action below. His daughter and the other girls she'd joined were sitting in the middle of a row. London had been positioned at the end so there were empty seats beside her.

Now the one directly adjacent was occupied.

He leaned forward. "Who the hell is that?"

Shay looked over at him, then followed his glance. "Oh," she said, a smile in her voice. "That's Colton. You know, Colton Halliday."

Jace narrowed his gaze. "My daughter is at the movies with a boy."

"A boy happens to be at the same theater as your daughter."

"I don't think I like it," he said, frowning.

"It will be okay, Protective Papa." Reaching over, she covered his hand with hers.

"You're being the voice of reason." He figured his tone of voice communicated he resented that fact.

"It's what friends are for." Her smile lightened his concern.

It could light the whole damn theater. The world.

It sure as hell did something great for him.

He shook his head, resigned to the blurred lines in this relationship. Friends. Lovers…ex-lovers. Whatever. Turning his hand, he caught his fingers with hers, keeping their connection. No longer concerning himself with maintaining distance.

LONDON BARELY STOPPED herself from bouncing in her seat in excitement. Her plan had worked! At the library, she had exchanged cell numbers with Amy. When the other teen had texted about seeing a movie this afternoon, oh, she'd wanted to go! She might have talked Shay in to dropping her off and picking her up at the theater, but she wasn't certain about her dad, so she'd come up with a different strategy.

Awesome.

She glanced over to the empty seat beside her. Colton had been there a moment ago, a total surprise to her that he'd shown up. He was gone now, to the snack bar, *but he said he was coming back.*

And he'd asked her if he could get her something to go with her Milk Duds!

Though she'd said no, being willing to spend money on her was almost like a date, right?

Amy rattled the candy in her box. "Want to swap a Mint for a Dud?"

The mint would make her breath smell nice. "Sure." They made the exchange.

Then Amy glanced over her shoulder. "So that's your dad?"

London looked, too. "Yeah." He'd taken her place next to Shay and was drinking from her bottle of water.

"He's cute."

"You think?" She stole a second glance. Cute was Colton, a boy. London didn't mind admitting, though it was just to herself, that her father was actually handsome. Not like a movie star, like Ryan, Poppy's fiancé, but in a more rugged, hand-me-a-hammer kind of way. Though Shay's brother, Brett, and her dad didn't look at all alike—their coloring was different—both he and Jace gave off the sense they could compete on a survival-of-the-fittest game show and win.

Her dad could build a shelter, she was sure. Find food and water. It made her feel warm inside to think he could protect her from weather or bears or…whatever stuff life dished out.

Though she only wanted to rely on herself, she remembered. And she certainly didn't want Jace micromanaging her. She wasn't five years old like Mason.

Amy leaned over to sip from the straw in her soda, which was sitting between them. "Does he like Shay?"

"Who?" London asked, blinking.

"Your dad."

"Oh." She shrugged. "Sure he likes her, I guess. She's a good cook. Men always like good cooks, right?"

"My dad is the one who cooks in our family. My mom makes good pies, though."

It reminded London of her planned cookie baking. Opal had recently sent the requested recipe. On a sigh, she descended into a little daydream. Cookies studded with chocolate chips cooling on racks. Colton stopping by. Maybe she could ask him to stay for Shay's enchilada casserole and save the cookies for dessert. She'd wear that cute dress from the boutique, the one that tied at the shoulders...

Amy was peeking up the rows again. "I think he likes-her, likes her." She wiggled her brows. Giggled.

"What?"

"I think your dad likes Shay like a man likes a woman, not a cook."

London frowned. "He said he doesn't have a girl-friend—"

"Yet," Amy said, giggling some more. "What would you think about that?"

Something churned in London's belly. She put her hand there, rubbing at the ugly, almost-sick feeling. If her dad gave his attention to someone else, who would build her a shelter? Who would find her food? Who would keep her safe from bears?

She shook her head, trying to dash the silly thoughts away. For one, hadn't she always done a fine job taking care of herself? For two, even if her father liked Shay, that didn't mean she would care for him back.

Though she didn't like the idea of his heart being broken, either.

Sliding down in her chair, she cast a look back, hoping they wouldn't notice her staring. They were relaxed in their seats, their heads turned toward each other, their expressions… What did she know about grown-up romance and what it looked like?

Her mother's boyfriends had mainly stayed out of London's way, so she didn't know if there was a particular manner in which an interested adult party should behave.

As she watched, Shay's gaze shifted from London's dad to look directly at her. Busted! She widened her eyes and smoothed out her forehead, going for innocent, when the woman gave her a little smile. Then an encouraging, though subtle, thumbs-up sign.

The acknowledgment made her feel…good.

Shay always made her feel good, even when she was making her dust the furniture or fold her laundry. While London saw her dad as capable, Shay made *London* feel capable.

Smart and responsible.

She thought of that thumbs-up again. Cared for.

Sliding a little lower, a different daydream entered her head. A table set for dinner. Flowers in the middle, those pretty place mats that were the color of the lake, a selection of yummy food. Not a pea in sight. People gathered around ready to eat. Her dad, Shay, London.

A real family.

Colton landed in the seat next to hers just as the lights went out. She hardly noticed, her focus on the new dream building in her mind.

WATCHING THE GAGGLE of teenagers at the ice-cream parlor, Shay smiled to herself. London had done it. She'd found her way into a social group and she looked as if she were having the time of her life.

When she and Jace had met the girl in the lobby after

the movies, she'd begged for the chance to join her new friends for a treat across the street. Jace had said yes, and they'd gone straight there, to find the other kids sitting in a booth, each wearing expectant, hopeful expressions. "Oh," London had said, a shadow of guilt crossing her face, "I kind of promised you'd spring for sundaes."

That's what Jace was in line to order and pay for now.

Since his back was turned to her, she allowed her gaze to linger on him. He was dressed in mountain-casual: a beat-up pair of chinos, a short-sleeved, rumpled sport shirt, tails out, and some boat shoes that might have been rescued from the bottom of the lake. The labels were luxury, she guessed, but he wore them with a casual air that she recognized from the other wealthy visitors to the Blue Arrow resort area.

She glanced down at her leather sandals and remembered she'd purloined them from Poppy's closet. Knowing her thrifty sister, they were likely from a local resale shop.

When Jace moved, her gaze went with him. He strolled to the teen booth, where he propped a number on the table as well as a thick stack of paper napkins. It was such a dad thing to do that hope surged.

Perhaps it made her as optimistic as the irrepressible Poppy, but Shay hadn't given up on the idea that Jace would change his mind. Instead of sending London off to boarding school and heading back to Qatar, he'd adapt his lifestyle, stay in the States and be an on-site father to his daughter. No more solitary ways.

She caught the pointed once-over he now gave the lone boy in the group, Colton, who was squeezed between London and another girl. Shay pressed her lips together to hold back her grin. Despite what Jace thought, it appeared to her he had the paternal instincts for the job.

With a nod to the teens, he turned and made his way to the small table Shay had commandeered. When their eyes met, her heart did a little bump-and-grind and she redirected her focus to the marble-topped table, determined to disguise her reaction. It wouldn't do for him to guess she'd fallen in love with him.

The man who was intent on "blowing past" her.

In moments since that night he'd talked of building a fairy house for her, she'd tried dredging up some righteous anger about that. How could he do this to her—find his way into the heart she'd kept inviolate forever—and then calmly take his leave?

But she'd known it was his intention from the very beginning. She'd never expected him to be long-term in her life, from the night she'd turned to him in the Deerpoint Inn bar and blurted out it was her birthday.

Now Jace pulled out the chair across from her, its metal legs screeching against linoleum. "Why the sad face?" he asked, dropping into the seat and setting another plastic number on the tabletop.

"That sound," she lied. "Like fingernails on a chalkboard."

His eyebrows rose and he studied her face as if trying to detect the truth.

She dipped her chin and fussed with her hair to distract him, apprehension prickling along her spine. If he was intent on reading her mind, it might be better that she resign and leave the house immediately, she thought, in a little rush of panic. When he left, she'd only have her pride, and she was hanging on to that, by God.

Laughter from the teen booth erupted, and she looked over, relaxing as she saw London grinning along with the rest of them. The girl had never looked so happy. The days of raccoon liner and asking to be called Elko or Des Moines seemed like a lifetime ago. She'd stay, Shay decided, she'd stay as long as possible with the teen to ensure those old insecurities wouldn't return.

She glanced over at Jace, noting he was watching the teens, too, wearing his own half smile.

Her gaze shifted away from him again, lest she be caught mooning over something she couldn't have.

Maybe her feelings for him would evaporate, she thought, desperate to find something to hang on to besides the anticipation of heartbreak and loss. Surely that was true. He was her first love and everybody knew first love never lasted.

But then her mind leaped to her sister Mac and You Know Who and she wanted to stab herself.

"So…"

Jace's voice pulled her back to the present.

"Now that we're pals and everything," he continued. "France?"

"What about it?" she asked, stalling.

He linked his fingers on the table. "Where'd the idea come from?"

"My friend, and former college roommate, Dee, she's half-French and her uncle runs the school." Shay had once been thrilled with the mere idea of visiting her there, saving for a time when she'd use it as a home base and travel throughout Europe for a number of months. But her bank account didn't expand all that quickly and when Dee floated the notion of an actual teaching position with an actual, regular and fairly generous salary, she'd begun thinking beyond a vacation.

"What's the other Walkers' opinion on you leaving the mountains?"

She shrugged. "They like Dee. When we were in school, she used to come up here in the summers."

His golden eyes narrowed. "Brett, Mac and Poppy don't know, do they?"

"They will." She waved a hand. "And they want me to be happy."

He sat back in his chair, stretching out his long legs. "Is leaving your family, leaving this place you love, going to make you happy?"

"Poppy's happy. She's been splitting her time between LA and Blue Arrow."

"France is a hell of a lot farther than Los Angeles. You're not going to be bopping over for a quick chat with your sisters or to see Mason whenever you get an urge."

Mason. That was a low blow. She adored her nephew. "It doesn't have to be forever," she said. "A year. Maybe three." Mason would be well into elementary school then.

"The money's good," she added, when Jace just looked at her.

"Which you're going to invest in the cabins."

She lifted her chin. "That's right."

"I'll be interested to hear what your sisters and brother have to say about that. Whether they think your sacrifice is worth it."

"Sacrifice! It's *France*. Cheese, chocolate, coffee, baguettes. Wine."

His expression remained skeptical. "Who are you trying to convince—me or yourself?"

Lucky Shay was able to avoid the annoyance of answering when a server came up to their table with two sundaes. Hot fudge for Shay, a banana split for Jace.

She was happy to dig in and drop the conversation altogether.

It took several bites of ice cream, fudge, whipped cream and nuts to begin to eradicate the bad taste the discussion had left in her mouth. It was the cherry that finally did the trick and for good measure, she stole Jace's from the top of his dessert when he happened to glance over at the feasting kids.

He looked back at his banana split, then at her just as she popped the little red orb into her mouth. "You! You stole my cherry."

"I'm sure that was gone long ago," she said, chewing with relish.

"You are a bad girl," he said, frowning at her.

"Never." She laughed. "Not until the night I met you."

"I know it," he said, looking arrogant and smug and so very male. "But you're going to have to pay for swiping the cherry, darlin'."

Before she could do any more than smile at his mock-threatening tone, he'd swiped up a fingerful of whipped cream he then deposited on her nose.

"Jace!" She grabbed her napkin, going cross-eyed as she tried cleaning off the mess.

Then they both laughed and were still doing so when they noticed London standing nearby, staring at them, a bemused expression on her face.

"What's so funny?" she asked, her gaze darting between them.

"Your father is very rude," Shay said primly, only to be rewarded by another dab of whipped cream, this time on her chin. "Jace!"

"Shay!" he mimicked, grinning at her. But he leaned close with a fresh napkin to clean her face himself. "And you missed a bit here," he said, running his warm thumb over her nose.

He was so near, she was breathing in that salty, soap-clean scent of him. Her heart started to hammer and she felt a flush spread up her neck. She pushed his hand away, afraid she'd do something inappropriate like crawl into his lap if he didn't stop touching her. "You should see what your daughter wants," she said, looking over at the girl.

London was still watching them. "Not so weird," she murmured. Then glanced over her shoulder at her pals and back to Jace. "Could we order a couple of drinks?"

He pulled out some money and handed it over. She danced away.

"I feel like I'm a wallet," he groused, though she could see he was smiling again as he watched London chatter with the other kids.

"You're a father," Shay said. "Same thing."

He continued to observe the teenagers and his eyes narrowed when Colton playfully blew the paper wrapper from his straw into the girl's face. "I'm trying to keep an open mind about that kid," he muttered.

She hid her smile. "So what about you?" she asked. "Were you so dangerous at sixteen, seventeen?"

He took his eyes from the booth and gave a sheepish shake of his head. "Probably not. At that time I had chores at home and a part-time job, so I didn't have a lot of opportunities to get into too much trouble with girls."

"Ah." That only came later, she supposed.

"But I had thoughts," Jace said darkly.

Shay leaned close, whispered, "So you know…girls do, too."

"Don't tell me that!" He sent an alarmed look over his shoulder. "Do *not* tell me things like that."

She grinned. "I know this crash course in parenthood is difficult—"

"Look, I'm going to do what's best," he said, his expression turning serious. "I promised London that. I promised myself that."

"You'll do what you *think* is best," she countered, but then went back to her sundae. They'd been having a nice afternoon and she didn't want to muck it up by overselling her point.

They traveled back to the house, everyone in good spirits. London spent the boat ride texting, surely communicating with her new friends she'd only left minutes before. Jace cast his daughter a quick glance, and Shay thought he might say something disapproving about that, but she could see him think better of it.

He's learning, she thought. *You've got to know which battles to pick and when.*

She caught his eye, mouthed "Good job," and they shared a moment of silent communication.

I'm not a complete idiot, he told her.

She held up both hands in surrender. *You're right.*

Once back at the house, she found she was chilled and went upstairs for a sweater before returning to the kitchen to do some dinner prep. She could hear Jace and London murmuring as she approached the entry, and she slowed her steps to give them a longer chance to converse in private.

They're bonding, she thought, not feeling the least bit of shame as she shuffled forward to eavesdrop.

London was speaking. "…I saw the way you two are together."

Jace's reply was unintelligible.

"I don't not like it, you know," London said. "Shay's cool. Like, really cool."

Shay smiled. That was heavy praise from the fifteen-year-old and it made her stupidly happy. Who said eavesdroppers never heard good about themselves?

"I'm glad she was here for you," Jace said, his voice a quiet rumble. "For us."

Hah! *Us.* That did sound like bonding!

"So I was thinking…" London sounded more hesitant than usual. "Remember when you told me you didn't have a girlfriend?"

Shay held her breath.

"I remember."

"Maybe Shay should be your girlfriend," London said quickly. "My friends, they kinda wondered about it and I thought at first it was weird, but now…now I don't think it's weird at all."

Jace was silent. Shay couldn't imagine what his expression might be.

"I don't need a mom or anything like that," London continued. "But that doesn't mean we couldn't be…I don't know…like a family. The three of us."

The three of us. Like a family.

There was another long beat of silence, then Jace's voice rang out, adamant. "That's not going to happen, kid. Okay? Never going to happen."

CHAPTER SIXTEEN

RIDICULOUS HOW JACE'S statement had hurt so much. Shay tried to talk herself out of the pain, knowing he only spoke the truth she'd already accepted, but it remained there, a tight and thorny constriction around her heart. That her love for him was going to somehow evaporate seemed even sillier a hope now.

So she soundlessly let herself out of the house. Getting away for a little while would do her some good, she hoped. An opportunity to regroup and then return in a happier frame of mind.

Gas prices were too high and conserving money too important for aimless driving. She considered escaping to Poppy's, but she couldn't face her sister's sunny and romantic disposition right now. Mac would take one look at her and spot trouble Shay didn't want to explain.

So she put the price of a gallon out of her head and drove slowly along the narrow mountain roads, idly checking out the magnificent lake-view homes, while resigning herself to being miserable without company. Then she spotted a familiar truck through a pair of open wrought-iron gates.

She tapped the brakes, then steered to the side of the road, tucking her small car on the shoulder between an oak and an aspen. Down the long flagstone-covered drive, she saw a man squatting by a lush flower bed.

Letting herself out of the car, she decided that a chat with Brett just might settle her down.

As a man, she doubted he'd detect a disturbance in her force, but he would make a fine distraction. They could talk about baseball or something.

She called out to him when she was still some distance away. "Hey, how about those Dodgers?"

He looked up, then rose to put his fists on his lean hips. He wore ancient jeans, work boots and a T-shirt, and leather gloves covered his hands. "Since when do you give a shit about anything professional sports-related?"

"Maybe I'm expanding my horizons," she said, noting how light his hair had gotten thanks to its constant exposure to the sun. Women paid a mint for those kind of highlights. "That wouldn't be a bad thing, would it?"

He narrowed his gray eyes. They looked a little eerie, their color almost crystalline against his tanned face. "What's the matter?"

"Nothing." He wasn't supposed to notice! "Not one teeny tiny itty-bitty thing." That was probably overkill.

His eyebrows rose. "God, you're a terrible liar."

"Am not," she protested, then hesitated. "I am?"

Smirking, he shook his head. "Just like I said."

Shay frowned. Not that she had any career ambitions to become a con artist or anything, but it seemed like an ability to spout some believable prevarications would be a useful skill. "I don't know why I'm just learning this," she said, glaring at her brother. "It seems like something you might have shared earlier in our lives."

He snorted. "What were you going to do, practice?"

"Well, I don't know. Maybe…yeah?"

Brett shook his head again. "Lord save me from

women." He bent over to pluck a weed from the loamy earth. "Something's wrong. Is your nightmare bugging you again?"

He was the only one she'd ever told about it. Since the fire that had wiped out the ski resort, she'd relived that day in her dreams. Smelled the fire, heard the roar of the flames, saw Dell Walker, covered in ash, his voice hoarse as he shouted.

And in the nightmare she was frozen as she had been that day, feet rooted as a licking, crackling, destructive monster raced toward her.

Brett straightened again. "Shay?"

She opened her mouth, but was saved from having to answer when a car turned into the drive. It was a low-slung luxury convertible—Shay knew zip about makes and models—and it was driven by a young woman with a wealth of dark hair that tumbled in waves past her shoulders.

When she braked near where Brett and Shay were standing and pushed her oversize sunglasses on top of her head, Shay discovered she was jaw-droppingly gorgeous. Golden, sun-kissed skin, dark-lashed brown eyes, a small straight nose and a pretty mouth that was curving in a smile. "Hi, Brett," she said warmly, her gaze shifting between Shay's brother and Shay.

He muttered something that might have been "hello."

Surprised, Shay looked at him. While he wasn't the most gregarious guy in the world, and had been on a brood since getting out of the army a few years back, his attitude right now was borderline rude.

The woman in the car spoke to Shay. "I'm Angelica. Angelica Rodriguez." Her gaze slid back to Brett. "Is this your girlfriend?"

Brett grunted. It could have meant anything.

Shay stared at him. "I'm his sister," she said. "I'm Shay Walker."

Angelica's smile, already radiant, brightened like a sunbeam. "Nice to meet you."

"Nice to meet you, too." It was impossible not to respond to the woman's open expression and innate friendliness.

The woman turned her attention to Shay's brother again. "Brett, I have your check at the house. When you're done, just knock on the kitchen door and I'll give it to you. I have some cold lemonade, as well. Freshly made."

"It'd be better if you mail the payment."

"But—"

"You've got an envelope, don't you? A stamp?"

Angelica didn't lose the pretty smile, but she pulled the sunglasses over her eyes. "Sure. Okay. 'Bye." The dark lenses shifted to Shay. "Again, nice to meet you."

"Yes," Shay said. "I…" But she was talking to air because the other woman was already accelerating away. She rounded on her brother. "What was that about? Are you getting off on kicking kittens these days?"

Brett strode toward the back of his truck and began unloading the power mower. "Don't worry about that useless piece of fluff."

Shay's eyes bugged out. He never talked about women like that. "How horrid. You have three sisters. What if some guy said—"

"Just leave it alone, Shay."

She glanced down the driveway in time to see Angelica climb out of her car. That bounty of dark hair waved halfway down her back. "She's very beautiful."

"Her mother's a former supermodel—Brielle? Her father's got more money than God. Angelica used to model herself when she was a child, but then got too fat or wasn't tall enough. Something like that."

Shay's head was about to explode. "Too fat? That's—"

"She told me so herself."

"Huh." As Brett wheeled the mower toward the swathe of grass in the front of the house, Shay couldn't help but speculate. Angelica had shared with him about her life. Angelica was making him homemade lemonade. Brett was unusually hostile to the lovely woman.

Brett, like all men, she concluded, could be a raging idiot. "You—"

"If this is about Angelica, there's nothing more to say." Sighing, he glanced over at her. "Can you let it go?"

"Maybe," she said, giving in.

Her brother retreated to his truck for a gas can. "You didn't answer me about the nightmare." Over his shoulder, he sent her a look of concern. "Are you doing okay?"

Her irritation with him disappeared. She didn't know what was going on between him and this Angelica, and he was closemouthed enough that she'd likely never learn, but he was a good man at the core. A caring big brother.

Yes, she'd miss sweet Mason and the camaraderie of her sisters when she left the mountains, but being away from Brett would be a hardship, too. He might be too macho for his own good and hardheaded as well, but when push came to shove, he'd never let Poppy, Mac or Mason down.

She'd insist they take a family photograph before

she left Blue Arrow. She had a zillion snapshots on her phone, but she wanted something more formal—a portrait. It would include Ryan, too, because once he married Poppy, he'd be as much a Walker as Shay was, really.

"Shay?"

Brett's prompt pulled her from her thoughts. "Sorry. What?"

"Nightmare," he said in a patient tone.

"Not a problem." She waved a hand. "And I'm not lying," she added, when he narrowed his eyes.

"Okay. But just so you know, the whole family was aware it was you who broke Mom's favorite pitcher, despite your straight-faced denials and your lame attempts to fob it off on the cat." He grinned.

She decided to ignore his remark. "You should do that more often—smile, I mean. You're a very handsome man." Definitely getting a professional photo, she decided. Then she'd impress all her new French students with her beautiful big brother. She'd get two copies—one for her teacher's desk and one for her room. She'd hang it on the wall, where she could see it every morning when she woke. Thinking of that reminded her of something else she'd like to take with her…those papers she'd considered framing.

"Brett," she said, "I really want to find my adoption documents."

"Shay," he replied, shaking his head.

She frowned at him. "I'll do the searching. And while I'm at it, I'll organize everything. Wouldn't you like that?"

He gave his attention to the gas can and the mower,

filling the tank carefully. The acrid smell rose into the air, causing her to blink away a sudden sting.

"Come on, Brett," she said. "Why the reluctance?"

On a sigh, he set the can down at his feet. Then he strode over to her, placed his hands on her shoulders and looked into her face. "Shay…" He glanced to the side as if gathering his thoughts.

Alarm made her stomach clutch. "What is it?" she whispered.

He met her gaze, his expression kind. "There are no papers."

"What?"

"Mom and Dad…they intended to. You know Dad, he was big on intentions. But the whole deal…going to a lawyer, drawing up the documents, it would cost money."

"But why did they say…"

"Like I said, intentions. But the fact is, they didn't think it was really necessary. Because Mom was legally Lorna Walker when you were born, it says 'Walker' on your birth certificate. You know that. So there was really no need to do anything further."

She stared at him. There was every need! Those papers—that she'd believed had been real—in her mind had partway closed the gap that existed between her and the rest of her family. And now she knew they were just a daydream.

A connection that didn't exist.

She felt…like she didn't know who she was anymore.

Swallowing hard, she backed out of her brother's hold. "I have to go."

"Shay…" He moved toward her but she scooted farther away.

"I've got to…got to…"

Get away. Get a hold of herself.

The very intention she'd had when she left Jace and London. Running back to her car, she ignored her brother calling her name. Before he could catch her, she had the car started and in gear, and she accelerated away.

Without thinking, she drove back to the house on the lake. It was where her things were, she told herself, as she braked in the driveway. She'd take a shower, put on some pajamas and hide away for the rest of the night. Jace and London could rustle up their own dinner.

Surely things would look better in the morning.

When she opened the front door, Jace came rushing toward her. "Thank God," he said. "I've been phoning but then I realized your cell is upstairs in your room—I could hear it ringing there."

"What's the matter?"

He ran his hands through his hair, leaving it looking as agitated as he seemed to be. "London."

Shay's hand went to her throat. "She's hurt?"

"No. Yes. Fuck. I fucked it all up."

She grabbed his arm. "What *is* it?"

"I told her the plan," he said, rubbing the heel of his palm against his forehead.

"She didn't take it well," Shay said, her heart aching for the girl.

Jace's expression turned bleak. "She ran off and hasn't come back."

LONDON SAT ON the dirty carpet in the boathouse, huddled in the corner with her sweatshirt pulled over her legs. How could the best day she'd ever had become the worst day so quickly?

It had turned dark just as she ran out of the house. There was moonlight tonight and she kicked herself for not taking the boat keys. She could have jumped into the *Fun & Games* and gone…where?

These four walls would have to do. She planned on staying here forever. Jace would be sick with worry— hah!—and when they found her body someday then he'd feel like a total jerk and the whole world would know what a lousy human being he was.

The rest of his life he'd be sorry. Karma would bite him in the butt and he'd lose all his hair and get a pot- belly and develop a limp and have to move into a nurs- ing home where the only food they would feed him would be peas! Breakfast, lunch and dinner—peas. And each time they were served to him he would think of her and how he had done her wrong.

There was the scuffle of footsteps outside the little shack. She drew farther into the corner, hoping it was just some random resident taking a walk. If it were teen- agers looking for more Seven Minutes in Heaven, she was going to have to find another hideout in which to pass her final days.

"London?" a voice whispered. "Are you in there?"

"Ames," Colton said. "Just push open the door and see if she's inside."

"I don't want to scare her," Amy hissed. "Why are you so bossy?"

London didn't know whether to laugh or cry. "I'm here," she said.

The door creaked open and two people were silhou- etted in the entry. She waved a hand. "This way."

"What *is* this place?" Amy asked, venturing inside. "It's disgusting."

"It's not so bad," London said.

Amy turned to her brother. "You hang out here? How come you never told me? How come *I've* never been invited to hang out here?"

"You're too young," he said dismissively.

Before Amy could say something that might make London defend her, thus revealing her true age, she waved again to get the pair's attention. "What are you guys doing here?"

"Shay called," Colton said. "We said we didn't know where you were, but after I hung up, I thought I'd give this place a try."

"You didn't tell them I might be here, did you?"

"No," Colton replied. "I didn't say anything to anyone. Amy and I told our parents we were going out for milk."

"We still need that," Amy said. "I want milk with the pie Mom made. Apple with the crumb topping."

London's stomach churned on its emptiness at the thought of food. She'd not had dinner before running away. Sticking her hands in her pockets, she searched for leftover gum or mints. Nothing.

Amy traipsed into the dark room and slid down the wall to take a spot beside London. "It smells like mildew in here." She bumped her shoulder against London's. "Are you going to tell us what happened?"

"Parents suck."

Colton propped himself against the opposite wall and crossed his arms over his chest. "Yeah. At one time or another. It's inevitable."

"I'm going to have five children," Amy said. "Two

sets of twins and then the baby. I refuse to dress the twins alike, however, which just goes to show that as a parent I will *not* suck. As a matter of fact—"

"Ames?" her brother said.

"What?"

"Shut up," Colton said. "England, tell us what happened."

It poured out of her then. How she'd come to Blue Arrow Lake to get prepared to enter an American high school and that Jace let her assume it was going to be high school here. Until tonight when he'd told her it wasn't going to be as she'd imagined at all.

He'd looked her straight in the eye when he imparted the news. It had taken a moment for his words to sink in, but when they did she knew they were no joke. He'd flinched when she yelled, but he hadn't backed down, not when she yelled some more and not even when she stomped her feet like a spoiled two-year-old.

So then she'd gotten control of herself and tried reasoning with him, but he had reasons, too. When she couldn't move him, she'd opted for moving herself out of the house as fast as her legs would carry her. She was never going back.

"My father's signed me up for a boarding school," London told her friends now.

Amy scooted to face her. "Why?"

"Oh, it's a great school, he claims. Has a stellar computer science department, which he knows I'm interested in."

"That…that doesn't sound so bad," the other girl said. "I mean, if the computer science stuff is your thing."

"I'm enrolled in the summer session, which starts soon."

Amy gasped. "Summer school? That really does suck. Everybody knows that the only structured summer activity that's any good is if you go to something like space camp or drama camp, or I heard of this camp that's set up like a government and you run elections and—"

"Ames," Colton said. "Shut *up*." Then he dropped to the ground, to sit cross-legged opposite London. "What's your dad have against public school?"

"Nothing in particular I know of," London said. "But he's going to be working off and on in Qatar—"

"Where?" Amy asked. "Is that in Northern California?"

"It's in Western Asia," Colton told her. "God, Ames, for a girl on the honor roll you can be really dim."

"Geography is next year," his sister said, sounding insulted.

"Never mind," Colton muttered. "So your dad needs to find a place for you to live and to go to school, is that right, England?"

"That's what he says. Where he works in Qatar is very remote…he's building some sort of solar energy facility."

"That's green," Amy offered. "Green energy is good."

"I don't give a flying whatever about green energy," London muttered.

"I'm sorry," Amy said. "I don't always know the right thing to say."

"That's okay." London yanked her sweatshirt more firmly over her knees. "You're being nice. Thank you."

"So what are you going to do?" the other girl asked.

"I'm not going. Not to the school and not back to the house."

"You're going to run away?"

London shook her head. "I'm going to stay here. After a few days without food or water, I'll just fall asleep and my body will become mummified."

Beside her, Amy shivered. "A mummy? That creeps me out."

"And it will make my father very sorry."

"I like that part," Amy said. "But wouldn't it be better not to be hungry or thirsty? I'm sure he'll still be sorry you're gone."

"I don't even have my wallet with me. And I'd have to sneak into town to get to a grocery store." She put her head on her knees. "Starving is the only way."

"No, no it's not," Amy said, her voice getting excited. "I can smuggle food to you! I'll slip a bunch of stuff in my backpack and bring it after school. Granola bars and some of those juice pouches and I don't know... what do you keep saying is the perfect food, Colton?"

"Snickers bars."

"That's it! We have a bunch of them in the freezer. They'll never be missed."

"Maybe by me," Colton put in.

"Oh, shush," his sister said. "So you'll have plenty of sustenance. I can bring you some blankets, too."

"Amy, I can't have you do that."

"Of course you can. You know I love a project, right? I told you that. And I told you that you were the one I was going to dedicate myself to this summer." She took in a breath. "Now, what else? We need to think of some way for you to shower..."

"She can use the lake," Colton said. "You've got a ton of those little hotel shampoos in your bathroom, Ames."

In the dark, London couldn't see his expression, but there was something in his voice…

"Perfect," Amy told her brother. "And for laundry—"

"How did the local Native Americans do it?" he asked. "I'm sure we learned about it at Lake Elementary School."

"Hmm…" Amy seemed to be thinking back. "I believe they first made reed baskets, then they…well, I can bring you a plastic basket or a mesh bag or something. When they washed, didn't they beat the clothes on a rock?"

"That's how I remember it," Colton said helpfully.

Feeling hopeless and miserable, London lifted her head. "How long do you think we could keep me hidden away?"

"Until you're eighteen, of course," Amy replied. "And then you can emerge from the boathouse and do anything you want. But *I* think we should write a book."

"Good God," Colton groaned.

"You shut up this time," his sister said. "We'll write a book about your time in hiding, London. It'll kind of be like Anne Frank—"

Colton groaned again. "Minus the Nazis and the Holocaust."

"I don't think I should compare myself to Anne Frank," London said hastily. "It's not anywhere close to the same thing."

"Well, of course," Amy answered. "We wouldn't put that on the back cover or anything."

To get the other girl off the subject, London brought

up something else. "How are we going to communicate? I don't even have my phone with me."

"Oh." Amy went silent a moment. "Let me think…"

"Smoke signals?" Colton asked, helpful again. "Maybe you could train a homing pigeon, Ames."

"Don't be silly," Amy said. "Really, Colton, you come up with the dumbest ideas."

"Amy—" London began.

"I've got it." The other girl snapped her fingers. "I'm going to break into your father's house and get the things you need. Your wallet and your phone and… we'll make a list. I'll sneak out of my bedroom tonight at midnight. Then after I've gathered your stuff, I'll bring it to you here. When you hear two hoots like an owl, you'll know it's me."

London stared at her. Even in the darkness, she could see the teen was serious about taking on this adventure. It made London feel thirty instead of fifteen, because she couldn't even entertain the possibility. Not when it involved her new friend wandering around at midnight doing illegal things.

With a sigh, she looked over at Colton. "It's not going to work, is it?"

"It's not going to work," he agreed.

Amy made a worried noise. "But—"

"I'm going to have to go back," London said.

Colton nodded. "You're going to have to go back."

"Wait," Amy protested.

"No, he's right," London told the other girl. "I can't ask you to do those things."

Amy was silent a long minute. "Well, you can ask me to write to you at the boarding school. I'll do it, real letters. That would be cool."

"That would be," London agreed.

"And there's still some time before you have to leave," Colton added. "We'll hang out some more."

For a moment, her misery subsided. Maybe he'd hold her hand again. Maybe she'd be in a boat with him again, flying, and they'd exchange glances and it would be her and an almost-senior sharing boy-girl secrets that until now had seemed so mysterious. There would be more movies and maybe real dates and she'd consider it Seven Years in Heaven if he would be her very first kiss.

"London?" Amy said, shaking her out of her brief reverie. "Is it a plan?"

"Yeah." She got to her feet as did the other two. What other choice did she have?

As she approached the house alone—she'd told the Hallidays to go home, promising to text them ASAP—she didn't even bother dragging her feet. The place was lit up; it looked to London as if someone had switched on every bulb, in the closets, kitchen, bathrooms, deck. She stuck to the shadows at the side of the back lawn, but when she reached the stairs, she stepped into light as bright as day.

"London!"

Glancing up, she saw her father come running. "Are you all right? Where'd you go?"

"I took a walk," she said, and without another word, began trudging upward.

"You were gone for hours. In the dark. We were worried." He kept pace with her, forking his hand through his hair. "I called the police."

His concern left her unmoved, she told herself. "Maybe they should arrest me," she said, and heard the snotty tone in her voice. "It's probably against the law for me to have my own mind."

"London." Jace sighed. They'd reached the deck and he put his hand on her shoulder.

She shrugged it off. "Look, I'm back. Okay? And I know I'll have to do what you say. But I don't like it… and I certainly don't like you."

He jerked as if she'd slapped him. Then he sighed again. "I realize I should have told you right away. I screwed up. And I'm…sorry. I'm a piss-poor father."

"That's the first thing you've said tonight that I agree with." She swept past him into the house.

Inside, she found Shay hurrying toward her. "I thought I heard your voice. Are you all right?" Poppy followed behind her.

London looked past Shay. "Is Mason with you?"

"Past his bedtime. I came to talk to Shay only to find out that you went MIA."

"I took a walk."

"We were so worried—" Shay began.

"I needed some time to get used to the fact that I still don't have my own life. That everything that happens to me is at someone else's whim." She glanced over her shoulder to see Jace had remained on the deck. He was leaning against the railing, staring out at the lake.

Poppy's brows rose. "You've got some ideas of your own?"

"Of course I do. But he—" she jerked her head toward the deck "—doesn't listen to me."

"Well," Poppy said, drawing nearer so she could tuck London's hair behind her ear, "you're not going to just give up, are you?"

CHAPTER SEVENTEEN

SHAY STARED AT her sister, groaning inwardly, then sidled closer. "Don't give her false hope," she murmured, for Poppy's ears only.

The other woman acted as if she didn't hear her. "Sometimes life kicks us in the head," she said, and shot a quick but meaningful glance at Shay.

Crap. Brett had called her.

"But you can't lie down," Poppy continued. "Because Walkers aren't whiners."

London made a face. "I'm not a Walker."

"I'm making you an honorary one," Poppy said. "If Mason has his way, you'll marry him someday, which will make you my daughter-in-law."

"Mason," London said, and her mouth curved in a ghost of a smile.

"So let me tell you about one of the Walker ancestors—Hortense."

This time Shay groaned out loud. "Not that old saw."

Poppy shushed her. "Now Hortense raised chickens, and sold the eggs for spending money. To do so, she had to travel over the mountains to the next town."

"On her mule," Shay added, "named Persimmon."

"Lemon," Poppy corrected, "because of its sour disposition."

London put her hand to her mouth and made a sound that might have been a smothered giggle.

Poppy shot Shay a triumphant glance. "So there was Hortense, on her mission over the mountains. An especially important mission, because she was going to use her egg money to buy tatting—a kind of lace—for the gown she was sewing to wear to her upcoming wedding."

"London," Shay said, "ask Poppy why the very accomplished chicken-raising, egg-selling, dress-sewing, mule-riding Hortense didn't make her own lace."

London pressed her lips together, as if holding back more laughter. "What she said." With her gaze on Poppy she indicated Shay with her chin.

"Because," Poppy answered, "Hortense only had three fingers on her left hand due to a childhood accident. For your information, it's very difficult to tat with eight fingers."

London blinked. "Is that true?"

Shay shook her head. "Remind me to give you a lesson on the segment of American folk literature known as tall tales."

Poppy looked affronted. "Granny swore on her mother's grave."

Gesturing with her hand, Shay said, "Carry on."

"So on her journey to the next town, Lemon stumbled and broke his leg. Hortense, loath to see the poor animal suffer—"

"Though maybe not quite as sad as she might have been due to its sour disposition."

"—shot the animal dead. Then Hortense continued on her way, on foot, alone, for two days and two nights."

"Here comes the best part," Shay said to London.

"That's right." Poppy beamed at them both. "Once Hortense reached her destination, she successfully sold the eggs and bought the tatting."

"Then walked back home and married her man?" London guessed.

"No," Shay said, trying to keep a straight face. "She fell for some guy who bought her a root beer at the general store. Ended up eloping with him and got married in her dirty, travel-stained dress. They resold the lace in order to pay the fee to the justice of the peace."

"I love that story," Poppy said, smiling again.

Shay shook her head. "You're kidding, right? What is the moral of it, do you suppose?"

"Don't give up," Poppy answered promptly.

"How about 'Hortense was a floozy'?"

"She made the most of every situation," Poppy countered.

"Some other poor man ended up with a broken heart," Shay pointed out.

But London was laughing now, which Shay thought might have been the real reason behind her sister's sharing that family legend. Poppy brushed the teen's hair from her forehead, in that effortless maternal manner she had. "Why don't you start a conversation with your father," she said quietly. "Who knows where it might lead?"

London glanced behind her, to where Jace continued to stand on the deck, his pose pensive. "Do you think it will do any good?" she asked.

"No promises," Poppy answered. "But I don't think it can hurt, do you?"

The girl shrugged, seeming to think about it. After

a few moments, she squared her shoulders and headed back outside.

The two women watched her go. "I'm guessing," Shay said, when she saw Jace turn and greet his daughter, "that part about life kicking you in the head was for me?"

"For you both." Poppy faced her. "Brett called me."

"I figured."

"He's the only one of us kids who knew that those papers were…"

"Fantasy," Shay said flatly.

"Dad told him before he died. He and Mom honestly didn't think not having them would make any difference—and it doesn't make any difference."

It does to me, Shay thought.

They both went silent. Then Shay shoved her hands in her pockets. "I learned one important thing from this kick in the head, Poppy."

Her sister's brows rose. "What's that?"

"Secrets are destructive." She glanced out to the deck, where London and Jace appeared to be in conversation. "You should know I'm going to take that teaching position in Nice."

Poppy's brows drew together. "The one your friend Dee is always dangling like a carrot?"

"Yes. It's good money. I'll send most of it back and you'll invest it in the cabins."

Her sister frowned. "Shay, don't leave because of that. We'll find another way—"

"There's other reasons." Shay's gaze drifted to the deck again. "I need to get away."

Poppy glanced over her shoulder. "Oh." Her voice

filled with understanding. "Have you done it, then? Have you fallen in love?"

She lifted a shoulder. "I really like London a lot."

Poppy gave her a pointed look. "Try again, little sister."

"Okay, I love the girl," she admitted. Then she inspected her sandals, pretending a fascination with them. "Maybe her father, too."

"I wish you didn't look so miserable about it."

"He's not interested in anything…you know. Permanent. I'd be stupid to believe that's going to change soon. Or for me."

Poppy sighed. "We all make ourselves fools for love, I'm afraid. It's part of the deal."

Shay looked up. "You and Ryan aren't fools."

"I worried I was one when I fell for him—you even warned me about it, remember? But still, I put myself on the line. And I didn't give up when he pushed me away."

"He certainly didn't hold you off for long, either," Shay said drily.

Poppy grinned. "Because I'm stubborn, another wonderful Walker trait. And I kept my heart open, even when I thought I would lose him."

"But that's you. Always openhearted."

Her sister touched her arm. "To find true love, to become a partner with a man, you'll have to strip the locks off yours, Shay."

She didn't want to tell Poppy she was terrified that she already had…unlocked the darn thing and offered it to a man who would never take it up.

WHEN HIS DAUGHTER let herself back onto the deck, Jace didn't speak right away. There was more to be said between them, he knew that, but he'd screwed up earlier and would be more cautious this time. He didn't know if she'd ever buy why he thought this was the best decision, but he had to give it a try.

When the silence between them turned awkward, he glanced over. "Do you feel like telling me now where you were and what you did?"

"No."

"All right." He looked over his shoulder at the two women inside the house. "But you did scare the bejesus out of Shay. Poppy, too."

"And you?"

"I told you I was worried."

"You called the police on me."

"I didn't call the police *on* you. I called the police because I wanted help finding you."

"Will they give me a ticket or something?"

"No. But they're building up quite the file. First joyriding in the boat and now this."

Her head whipped toward him and she looked aghast. "Really?"

"No." He ruffled her hair. It was soft and as light as feathers. "I'm teasing."

She smoothed the tangles he'd left behind, a frown between her brows. "Don't mess with my hair."

The boy in him wanted to do it again, but he held himself in check. "I beg your pardon," he said, very polite. "Especially since I'm so glad it's not blue."

She peeked at him from under her lashes. "Who knows what color might strike me as interesting when I'm in boarding school?"

He refused to give in to panic…or blackmail. "Who knows," he said mildly. "But maybe you'll run it by me if you think about making a drastic change. We're going to be Skyping. Sending emails. You'll be able to text me whenever you want."

Her head came up and her eyes widened. "You…you want to be in contact with me?"

The sting of a thousand lashes struck him and he knew it wasn't nearly enough punishment. "I'm not losing contact with you again."

"Promise?" Her voice sounded incredibly young.

Five thousand more strokes strafed his skin. "I promise."

Her eyes narrowed. "I thought you said that where you'd be working in Qatar was very remote. What if I can't reach you?"

There was that, Jace thought. He'd just have to make the long trip into Doha often, to make sure he was available if she needed him. "We'll make sure you can," he assured her. "And I'll be returning to the States, um, I don't know, every month, to check on you."

Had he just said *every month*? It would mean rearranging his team, giving more control to one of his managers—maybe even hiring another. But money wasn't an issue and he couldn't renege on this new promise. His conscience wouldn't let him. The way he was coming to care for this kid wouldn't let him.

He glanced over his shoulder, saw Shay still talking with her sister. If he came back to Southern California every month he could see her, too…but no, she was going to France. Fucking faraway France.

Looking back at his daughter, he noticed she was scowling. "What's the matter now?"

"I don't like the idea of you 'checking' on me." Lifting her hands, she put the word in scare quotes. "I'm fifteen, remember?"

"Yes." *So old.* This time when he reached out, he stroked her hair instead of tousling it. "How about we call it something else…something simple. Visiting?"

"But not just to make sure I'm keeping up with my homework or not dyeing my hair green. It needs to be more of a sharing thing. You tell me about your work, what you're doing. I tell you about school, what I'm doing."

"Okay."

That sounded much like the conversations they'd been managing to have at the dining table here at Blue Arrow Lake, with Shay directing, or prodding, or initiating, whatever was needed. Those had been the most entertaining meals in his memory and he'd miss them when he was eating alone again, going over plans and running numbers for the latest phase of the latest project.

Back in the rat race.

Back on the hamster wheel.

For some reason he thought of the fantasy future Shay had concocted for him. *Bowled over by love, you'll rearrange your life to cease almost all the travel— except for jaunts you can do as a family.*

He rubbed at his forehead, disturbed at how good that sounded. But he was incapable of loving like a family man should know how to do. Not only had his old man been a lousy example, but the early failure of Jace's own marriage and the way he'd walked away from his daughter had also proved that.

"Jace," London suddenly said.

Jace. He realized, with another pang, that she'd never called him Dad. Who could blame her? "Yeah?"

"I know it was you who sent the books."

Going still, he stared at her. She was leaning against the railing, her gaze on the lake, where the reflection of the moon rippled on the water. "Books?" he asked, cautious.

"The ones that came every month. How…how did you pick them out?"

"You told me your mom—"

"I don't know why I said that." She shoved her hands in the kangaroo pocket of her hoodie. "I just wanted to…I don't know."

To hurt him, he thought with sudden insight, like she'd been hurt. "It's all right," he said. "I understand."

She threw a quick glance at him. "When they came in the mail, Mom handed them over, or Opal. No one hid that they were from you."

He was glad about that. It seemed like such a small thing to do—but had been important to him, too. His best memories of his little girl had been reading to her and because it was clear she'd loved books, he'd sent her a packet of them every month.

London looked over now. "I have a hard time picturing you browsing the children's and teen section at a bookstore, though."

"I did, actually."

"No!"

"Yes. Some that I picked were my own favorites."

"Willie Wonka? The BFG?"

He smiled. "And *Harry Potter*, of course."

"But there were lots of…well, I guess I'd call them girl books."

"I made a contact. A retired librarian. She's helped me with recommendations over the years."

"Mystery solved," she said. "I've been wondering."

And it seemed as if asking the question showed she trusted him a little. He couldn't express how glad that made him feel. "Do you want to know another secret?"

Clearly intrigued, her brows rose. "Sure."

"This has gotta be hush-hush. Seriously messes with my man cred."

"Man cred?"

"Man credibility. None of the guys will ever invite me into a football pool again if this gets out."

Her lips twitched. "Do I have to cross my heart?"

He held out his little finger. "Pinkie swear."

When she hesitated, he explained what he meant. Pain knifed into his heart when she curled her much, much smaller digit around his. "Do I say anything?" she asked, looking up into his face.

"On pain of death," he answered solemnly.

She giggled. "On pain of death."

Then their hands unlinked, and he surprisingly, keenly, felt the loss. Jace leaned close to his daughter. Whispered, "I bought double sets."

She frowned, then her face cleared. "Of the books?"

"Yep. I read them right along with you. I do a lot of traveling, I spend a lot of nights alone, so they came in handy. Even those 'girl' books." He mimicked her scare quotes.

A smile lifted the corners of her mouth. "We...we sort of had a book club."

"We sort of did." He hesitated. "And we can again... would you like that?"

Her smile broadened, showing her pearly whites,

then she bit it back. At fifteen, he knew, she wouldn't want to show too much enthusiasm for anything. Particularly when it came to him.

But when she said, "I would like that," it felt as if the heavens had opened and even though it was still night, that a brilliant beam of sun bathed the top of his head and the breadth of his shoulders.

Shay's voice echoed in his head again. *Jace, she's special. You know that, right?*

And he also knew that even though it was the best thing to do, it was going to be damn rough to walk away from his daughter again.

EVEN THOUGH THEIR time at Blue Arrow Lake was running out, London's father hadn't given up putting in hours at the Walker cabins. He said he liked the chance to work with tools instead of spreadsheets and blueprints. Shay went with him in the afternoons, which had left London free to hang out—usually with Amy. Sometimes with Amy and Colton.

Today she'd been roped into helping at the old ski resort herself, though, because Mason had called, begging to see her. Now he and Poppy had gone home and she was supposed to be meeting Amy and one of her friends in the local hideout in the Walker woods…the most remote and dilapidated cabin. Arrow High was out for the year now, and the girls were planning to get there via mountain bike.

London had kept quiet about the local kids using the old place. So far, the Walker family had been focused on the most easily accessible cabins in the clearing. When they started rehabbing the rest, the teens would figure it out, she was sure, and abandon their use of it.

Grabbing a water bottle from the cooler they'd brought with them, London waved to get Shay's attention. She was on a ladder, cleaning gutters, while Jace was inside one of the other bungalows doing something that involved loud electric sawing noises.

"What's up?" Shay asked, wiping her sweaty forehead with the back of her wrist.

"I'm going for a hike, okay?"

"Do you have your phone?"

London patted the front pocket of her shorts.

"We don't always have the best signal strength out here," Shay warned. "A text will go through if a call won't, though."

"Got it."

"No more than an hour, okay?"

London waved again and headed into the surrounding woods. It was cooler here than in the clearing, and it smelled like clean earth and warm leaves. She trailed her fingers over the barks of the trees as she wound around them, a sort of goodbye.

A squirrel zipped past and scampered up a pine and she watched his ascent, until he paused on a branch, looking down at her with bright eyes. He chattered, his tone scolding.

"I'm moving along, see?" she said, strolling past his tree. "And I'll be gone altogether soon."

The thought made her footsteps drag. She shuffled through the decaying leaves and dried pine needles and wondered what she'd be doing a month from now. Six months from now.

What someone else directed her to do, of course.

Sighing, she kicked at a pinecone and watched it fly. It reminded her of that boat ride she'd taken with

Colton, when she'd felt the air rush past. That day she'd thought her life was about to begin.

Now she was back to being a fifteen-year-old freak, anticipating becoming the new girl at a new school.

A fifteen-year-old freak who had learned to drive the boat herself, though, she thought, brightening a little. And maybe not so much a freak, because she had better hair now and better clothes and best of all—a friend in Amy. Maybe Colton, too, though she'd hoped that might turn into something more.

That wasn't going to come true, either, she supposed. Time had practically run out.

She was moving on to the next school, never kissed.

Up ahead was the cabin that the kids used as their hideout. She'd discovered it before and when Colton mentioned it knew instantly the one he meant. As she approached the bungalow, she frowned. No mountain bikes were parked outside. Instead, a dusty and battered lean motorcycle stood braced on its kickstand.

Hesitating, she slid her hand in her pocket and fingered her phone. "Ames?" she called out. "Amy?"

From around the corner of the cabin came Colton. "Oh," she said, putting her hand over her heart.

"Sorry, didn't mean to scare you."

"No, you didn't." How could he, looking all wind-blown and tall? She didn't know if he'd worn braces like his sister, but his teeth were perfectly even, perfectly white.

He was so perfect.

"I was expecting Amy."

"Yeah. Last-minute babysitting job." He dangled a plastic grocery bag in his hand. "I told her I'd bring the books she wanted to give you."

"Thanks." Feeling oddly shy, London moved forward to grab them. When she was closer, she could smell a hint of that shampoo he used. It reminded her of the other times they'd met at the boathouse and she realized this was the first time they'd been alone since she'd been introduced to his sister.

Something fluttered to life in her belly.

"How's it going?" Colton said. He crossed to a fallen log and dropped onto it, resting his elbows on his knees.

He wore a pair of jeans. Another white T-shirt. Instead of flip-flops he was wearing a pair of work boots.

She gestured to them. "I've never seen you in real shoes." Then her face burned. What an idiotic thing to say!

But Colton didn't seem to mind. Stretching out his legs, he tapped the toes together. "When I'm out on my motorcycle, it's the rule." His mouth quirked. "See, I don't get everything I want, either."

London nodded, unsure what to add.

"Am I getting the silent treatment again?" he asked, smiling. Then he patted a spot next to him on the log. "Sit. You're giving me a crook in my neck."

London did as directed, and set the bag of books by her feet. Amy was a big fan of the fantasy genre and was lending her the first three volumes of one of her favorite series.

"I'm glad we have this chance to talk alone."

Her head turned toward him, belly fluttering again. "Oh?"

"I wanted to thank you for making sure my sister didn't follow through with her harebrained schemes the other night."

"You wouldn't have let her."

"Yeah, but she would have felt bad that way. It's better that you nixed the idea."

She felt her mouth curve. "I couldn't see myself writing that Anne Frank–inspired book."

He laughed, then shook his head. "I know. She's supposed to be smart, but I don't really see it myself."

London shrugged a shoulder, still smiling. "She has good taste in new friends," she said. "And big brothers."

Oh, God, she thought, panicking a little. Where had that come from? And why had it come out sounding a little...flirty?

Colton was looking at her no differently than a moment before, however, so that was good.

Or was it?

She swallowed, trying to ease her suddenly dry throat. Here she was, alone with the boy of her dreams, for possibly the very last time.

And she'd never been kissed.

This might be her final opportunity to be kissed by Colton.

Wiping her damp palms on her denim shorts, she tried thinking how she could make that happen. What signals must she send to get him to take the hint?

First, she was too far away. Trying to be as smooth as possible, she wiggled her butt on the log and then feigned pain. "Ouch," she said, jumping to her feet. She rubbed her back pockets and noted with a combination of nerves and satisfaction that Colton's gaze was following the movement.

It jerked up to her face and he cleared his throat. "You're hurt?"

"Just a knot or something." She reseated herself, this time right next to him. "Better here."

"Yeah. Good," he muttered.

London did not know where to go with this next. She had zero experience, freak that she was. Perspiration prickled under her arms and she hoped her deodorant wouldn't give out. Her mouth still felt minty fresh, though, thanks to the gum Mason had shared with her earlier.

The birds were the only ones interrupting the silence. London stared at her knees and prayed for inspiration. "So about that Seven Minutes in Heaven game," she said, out of nowhere.

Her face burned again. Why had she brought that up? She was not only a freak, but also an idiot. And if she'd had a hoodie she would have crawled inside it like a sleeping bag, zipping herself inside.

"What about it?" Colton asked.

"You've played it a lot?"

"In seventh and eighth grade a few times. We were bored that night and Janice thought it would be funny to do it again."

"Ah."

"I wouldn't have played it at the boathouse, though."

She glanced over at him. "No?"

"I didn't think you should have, either," Colton said. "Especially with Sam."

Was he jealous? And why did he say he wouldn't have played? Did that mean he wouldn't have played with *her*? "What's wrong with Sam?"

"Nothing, except you don't know him."

"So…you only kiss people you know?" She looked at him from under her lashes.

He shrugged. "London…"

"How well do you think one should know the people

one kisses?" She could feel the heat of his body all along the side of hers and all she could think about was what it would feel like *against* hers. What his lips would feel like when they touched hers.

Where had all the oxygen gone? Didn't trees and plants make the stuff?

Gathering up her courage, she looked at Colton again. He was staring down at her, a question in his eyes.

But he'd not answered hers. "I said, how well do you think one should know the people one kisses?"

"I guess…I guess it depends," he said slowly.

"How about me and you?" She was going to win a prize as the bravest girl in the universe. "Do you think we know each other well enough?"

He leaned away from her, a crease digging between his eyebrows. "I'm not sure what you're getting at."

And he called his sister harebrained! London clasped her hands together, trying to decide what hint to lay down next. But the free hour she had was running down, her time at Blue Arrow Lake was nearly gone, and if she spent one more day without a kiss from a boy she…would…die.

Taking a deep breath, she put her hands on his shoulders, lifted up off the log a few crucial inches and…

Planted her mouth on his.

His lips were warm and a little chapped and she smelled his shampoo and grape soda. His muscles were rigid beneath her palms, his whole body seemed to be as still as a statue, and she hadn't the slightest idea what to do next.

She knew about tongues and wet sloppies—which didn't sound so icky when Colton was involved—but should she just poke it in there? And why wasn't he doing anything, including kissing her back?

A wave of humiliation rolled up from her toes. She scrambled away from him, staring at him in sudden horror. "I'm sorry, I'm sorry."

He rose off the log, both palms up in the air. "No, it's okay. I should have said something. I didn't know... I didn't think..."

Where were the predator drones when she could use one? Right now would be a good time for something to drop from the sky and annihilate her. A prick of tears stung the backs of her eyes, but she told herself she could not cry.

She began backing away. "I've got to go."

"England, wait. Wait just a minute."

Shaking her head, she kept her feet moving in the opposite direction. "I've got to go," she repeated.

"I have a girlfriend," Colton said.

London's spine smacked into a tree, halting her movement.

"She's taking a semester in South America. She'll be back next week." He ran his hand through his hair. "I made promises."

"Of course you did," London said. "I'm so, um, happy for you both." Then she whirled and ran through the forest. A fifteen-year-old who had kissed, but who still had never *been* kissed.

A freak.

CHAPTER EIGHTEEN

JACE MET UP with Shay at the cooler they'd filled with cold drinks and brought to the cabins. He lifted his arm to dry his sweaty face on the short sleeve of his T-shirt. "Hot today," he said.

"Summer," she replied as if her mind were a million miles away.

It had been like that for the past couple of days. A preoccupied Shay walking through each morning, afternoon and evening with shadows under her eyes. She lifted her hand to take a swallow from her soda can and Jace's stomach tightened when he saw a deep scratch on her forearm.

He grasped her wrist, bringing the wound close for an inspection. "How did this happen?"

"What?" She blinked at him, glanced down at the line of dried blood, shrugged. "I don't know." Turning her head, she looked around as if the source of the scratch would stand up and salute.

He tamped down his concern. It was a minor hurt, after all, but he couldn't like her preoccupation. Pouring water from his bottle over the scratch, he took a longer study of her face. "You shouldn't be up on a ladder when you're so distracted."

She blinked again. "What?"

"Shay." He dropped the empty bottle and dried her

skin with the hem of his T-shirt. "I know you aren't sleeping well. I hear you puttering around at night."

"Strange dreams," she said, slipping her wrist from his grasp to inspect the broken skin herself.

"Something has happened," he said. "Or something has changed."

Her gaze jerked to his face, then jerked away. "Nothing's happened. Nothing's changed."

It was her own fault, he decided, that he wanted to keep pushing her. From the very first she'd let him into her private inner self, the core of her that her family thought she kept unknowable. When she'd shared her dislike for birthdays and later revealed more fully the discomfort she felt with the circumstances of her conception, she'd planted the seed that grew into this... caring.

It wasn't something he was comfortable feeling—concern, worry about her well-being—but she'd hooked him. So now he wanted to know what was troubling her. *That's what friends are for*, she'd said to him at the theater, and friendship was a two-way street, damn it.

"Let me help," he said. "Tell me what's going on inside that head of yours. Maybe I can do something."

"No."

Her refusal spiked his temper and he plunged his hand into the cooler's icy water in an attempt to chill it down. He pulled a second bottle of water free. "I don't like seeing you unhappy."

"It has nothing to do with you."

He eyed her, noting the edge to her voice. "That sounds like it has everything to do with me."

She rolled her eyes.

"You get that little bit of body language from London. So you know, it's just as annoying when you do it."

The observation startled a laugh out of her. "I'm not surprised. I wonder how long it will take me to drop the bad habit?"

Jace reached out to touch her hair. It sifted through his fingers like warm rain. "Ryan once told me you wouldn't let yourself get close to London—but I think he's wrong. You'll miss her."

Shay hesitated a moment. "I'll miss her."

"Is that what's bothering you?"

"I'll get over that. I'll get over all of it."

All of it? He frowned at her, disliking when she turned away from him so he couldn't see her face. Their time together was coming to an end and he hated the idea of leaving her in this odd state of—he didn't know. Yes, he could stop prying, but, damn it, he'd like to do right by Shay.

"What do you need to get over? Can I help? Let me help." He was practically begging.

"I'm fine—"

"You're clearly not fine," he said, temper snapping, and his hand shot out to turn her toward him again. "I'm not going to give up until—"

"Until I admit how stupid I am?" Temper had lit her eyes, too.

He pulled her closer. "You're not stupid. Never that." His palm caressed the curve of her shoulder. "What is it, honey?"

"I—" She bit her lip.

"You…?"

Snagging the unopened bottle of water out of his free hand, she stepped away. She gave great attention to unscrewing the cap. "I thought there were adoption papers."

"Huh?"

"I was told, since I was a child, that Dell Walker formally adopted me."

"Okay." He remembered her asking her brother about the documents. "And…it's not true?"

She nodded. "Brett's known for a long time. He said Dell meant to go through with it—the adoption—but it cost money and so I guess he put it off and then…"

He thought she swallowed back a sob. "And then he passed away?"

"Yes." She rubbed one hand over her face. "My brother and sisters say it doesn't matter. Of course they're right."

But it did matter. It mattered to her.

"Oh, honey," he said, reaching to take her into his arms.

She jolted back. "Don't touch me. I can't have you touching me right now."

The panic in her voice put him on a new alert. "Shay," he said. "That's not all, is it?"

"Leave me alone." Again, that panic.

"You can tell me anything."

"Not this."

The misery on her face made his gut turn itself into a pretzel. He *had* to do something for her. He *had* to make whatever it was right. Determined, he reached for her again just as his daughter came rushing into the clearing, her face red, her hair disheveled.

Jace's gut twisted tighter and he lurched forward. "Are you okay? Are you hurt? What's happened?"

London ignored his questions and turned her tear-filled gaze toward Shay. "I'm fifteen," she said. "I'm fifteen and I've never been kissed!"

While that didn't sound like a calamity to Jace, clearly there was some subtext that he was missing. He glanced at Shay and she returned the look, her eyebrows rising.

She wasn't getting what the tragedy was, either.

"Um…" Jace said, at a loss. "Would you like a soda?"

His daughter sent him a withering glance. "Wh-what will that do?" she wailed, and then launched herself at Shay.

The story that poured itself out in words and tears took some time to make sense to Jace. When he finally absorbed the salient facts, his fingers curled into fists. "I'm going to kill that kid," he declared.

London turned in the circle of Shay's arms to stare at him. Shay did the same. "No!" they said at the same time.

His daughter turned back to Shay. "I shouldn't have told you," she said, hiccupping between each word. "I would have told my friend Amy, but she's Colton's sister—"

"Of course you couldn't tell her," Shay soothed.

"I'm so h-humiliated. Nobody in the whole world has ever felt so ashamed."

Shay patted her back. "I know it feels that way right now."

"What if I see him again? I'll have to throw myself in front of a car if I see him again."

"Then he'll know he hurt you. Better to keep your chin up, swing your hips and smile."

London lifted her head. "S-swing my hips?"

"It's a female thing," Shay said, her lips curving just a little. "I'll demonstrate later."

"Is it kind of like pretending you're having the best time ever?"

"It's exactly like pretending you're having the best time ever."

Another shudder ran through London. "Maybe I can do that." She wiped her palms over her wet cheeks. "This is awful, though. What must he be thinking?" She burst into more tears.

Instead of answering, Shay drew her close again. The girl laid her head on the woman's shoulder. "R-remember how you t-told me that time it was g-going to be all r-right?"

Jace didn't know what to do, so he just stood there watching as Shay smiled, her eyes closing. "Yes. And it's going to be all right now, too." She pressed a kiss to Jace's daughter's hair.

That kiss felt like a dart to his heart.

Minutes passed as London's crying came in fits and starts before tapering off at last. "I'm g-glad I told you," she said finally, looking at Shay, her lashes spiky and wet.

"All girls know how it feels to be rejected. It's a sad truth of life that you can like a boy—like him *a lot*—and he might not return your feelings. There's nothing you can do to change that. You can only put on a pleasant front and fake it until you make it."

London hiccupped again, sighed. "I wish *he* hadn't heard," she said with a quick glance over her shoulder.

Ouch, Jace thought, another dart. That *he* was him. Shay met his gaze over his daughter's head. He twisted his mouth in a wry smile, shrugged. It was no more than he deserved. "I think I'll take a walk."

When his daughter whipped around, alarm written all over her face, he held out both hands. "Not in the same direction you came from."

Her shoulders relaxed.

He turned, took two steps away, then, without giving himself a chance to change his mind, spun back. "London."

Her gaze was wary as he approached.

He cleared this throat. "You're wondering what that rat—"

"He's not a rat," she said quickly. "He didn't ask for me to kiss him."

Jace nodded. "Okay, we'll give him a medal."

"Let's not go that far." A ghost of a smile warmed her sad face.

It might as well have been the most brilliant rainbow to ever grace the sky. "Anyway," he said, "you're wondering what Colton thinks."

She shrugged.

"As the only one here with the male mind-set, I think I can actually clue you in."

Another shrug.

"I'm betting he feels sorry that he hurt you or somehow gave you the wrong impression, but he's going to swagger a little bit, as bad as that may sound."

"Why?" Her brows rose over her pretty brown eyes.

"Because this afternoon a smart, beautiful and funny girl gave him something special."

New tears welled.

"Now don't go getting any ideas about the indiscriminate handing-out of kisses," he said with a pointed look. "But take my word for it. Any boy would be beyond flattered to be kissed by you."

He wasn't prepared for what came next. Lightning would have surprised him less. Instead it was a hurricane, a girl force that flew right into his arms. He closed them around his daughter as she wept against his shoulder. His heart felt like it was crying right along with her.

Happy tears.

Because, he knew, he hadn't failed in this instance. He'd finally done something right for a female in his life. He'd finally done something right for his daughter.

SMOKE TASTED LIKE ash on Shay's tongue. When she looked up, through the dense trees, it colored the sky with a strange reddish-gray, like a slap morphing into a bruise.

Usually the woods were full of noises, skittering birds, humming insects, the scolding chatter of squirrels and blue jays, so that she never felt alone, even on solo hikes like this one. But now it was silent except for the papery sound of the wind moving the leaves of the oaks. The branches of the cedars and pines were moving, too, but silently, as if desperate not to attract attention.

She glanced at the sky again, disquiet growing until it filled her chest, nearly suffocating her. The fire was too close.

Getting closer.

Spinning, she tried orienting herself. This was Walker land, her family's legacy, and she knew it like other kids knew their backyards. But it looked different to her now, the trail at her feet seeming to erase itself as a small flurry of ash rained down.

She reached out to steady herself on the solid trunk of a tree. Was it vibrating with apprehension, or was it that her hand was shaking? By her foot, an alligator lizard poked its pointy snout from beneath a ragged fallen leaf and she jumped in surprise. It jumped, too, then disappeared into some nearby undergrowth.

It gave her the idea that it was time for her to get going, too.

But which direction?

She turned in another circle, trying to establish her bearings, as more gray flakes sifted down on her. Maybe if she called out, her father would find her. But she'd wandered far from his truck and the inner surface of her lips felt as if they were pasted to her teeth.

Her mouth couldn't form words, even if someone was near enough to hear them.

In the distance, a new sound. Shay stilled, her head tilting this way and that to better identify the noise. *Crackle, snap, pop*, like breakfast cereal amplified.

Like flames.

Disquiet turned to pure terror. It was so absolute, so all-consuming, that her reaction must have come from some prehistoric part of her brain. Without conscious command, her feet scrambled on the dirt and decaying leaves and she began to run.

The monster was chasing her, she knew that. It was roaring, its breath hot, its anger now whipping the branches of the trees so they lashed her face and scraped at her bare arms. Each inhale brought in more heat and the dark taste of danger.

"Shay!"

She heard her name, though it was nearly lost in the

monster's voice and the sounds of her harsh, frightened breaths.

"Shay!"

Though her mouth opened, nothing came out. She was strangled by her own fear.

"Where are you, Shay?"

She didn't know. Or she did. Hell. It had to be hell, which the books said was a burning place of fire and torture. Demons. The flames at her back, her feet skittered to a halt as one of those terrifying creatures came toward her, lurching through the trees.

It was huge, a hulking shape, with gray ash blanketing its body. Black covered its face and it had icy, crazed eyes that bored into her. Baring its teeth, it reached for her.

Jolting back, she gasped, torn between a faint and a scream.

The demon's black claws found her flesh, bit into her skin. She screamed and over her cry she heard it speak.

CHAPTER NINETEEN

JACE WASN'T SLEEPING. After his daughter's emotional upheaval, they'd packed up and returned to the lake-front house. She'd taken a shower and a nap, and then eaten dinner. After, instead of opting to hang in her room reading or playing on her computer, she'd sat in the great room and watched TV, wrapped in a throw the color of sunflowers.

Another of Shay's additions, he supposed.

Both he and the tutor had joined London, their gazes fixed on the big screen. First it was a singing show and then a dancing show and then a cop show and then the news. He hadn't absorbed any of it, from "Don't Stop Believin'" to the next day's weather forecast.

His job hadn't been to be entertained or gain information. He'd been there to offer any support London might need.

Finally, he and Shay had traded looks. Though his daughter's eyes were still owl-wide, he'd made the traditional noises about bed, sleep, have a good rest.

The females in his house had retired to their side of the upstairs.

He moved to his, but found himself getting up and making the rounds every twenty minutes or so, as if guarding against an enemy invasion. Ridiculous, really, because there was no way to protect London from the slings and arrows of growing up.

But if she woke up in the night, well, he'd be on alert, ready to do…something. Make her a bowl of ice cream. Wrap her in that yellow blanket again. Tell her a thousand more times she was beautiful and smart and he couldn't believe he was lucky enough to have a daughter with her humor and resilience.

That he was proud of her.

Of course, he hadn't said anything about his pride or good fortune. He was so goddamn new at fatherhood he felt as if there were land mines and booby traps everywhere. What if he said the wrong thing? Did the wrong thing?

Where was the fucking map to all this? People who said men wouldn't consult such things or stop to ask directions had never known a solitary-minded bachelor who'd suddenly become a full-time father.

In cotton pajama pants and a T-shirt, he padded downstairs, wandering the first floor. There were more flowers on the kitchen countertop, a low bowl of pale blue glass—the exact shade of Shay's eyes, he thought—centered on the dining room table, an orchid arched from a ceramic pot on the table in the foyer.

Heading back the way he'd come, he spied a stack of textbooks on the bottom stair. He hefted them into his arms on his way up the steps. In the area used as a schoolroom, he placed the books on the table.

It was then he heard it.

A moan of distress. A muffled cry.

Galvanized, Jace rushed to London's room, but before he even had his hand on the knob, he knew it didn't come from her. Another plaintive, almost eerie noise lifted the hairs on the back of his neck and he hurried toward it.

Toward Shay.

Her door pushed in soundlessly. It was near-dark inside, but he'd been wandering the house without lights so he easily zeroed in on her, her hair a deep shadow against the white pillowcase.

Her head thrashing back and forth, she plucked at the covers. "No…" she moaned. "No, no."

He crossed to her, and took a seat on the edge of the mattress to brush her hair from her face. "Shay," he whispered. "Wake up."

But she was deep in the nightmare, her legs moving as if she were running, one hand coming up in front of her face as if to ward something off. "Don't, don't, *don't*," she cried, each iteration of the word getting louder.

"Shh," he said in a low murmur. "Shh, shh. You're safe."

Her eyes popped open, the horror in them revealing that whatever she saw in the nightmare was now in the room. She opened her mouth, inhaled a breath.

Jace put his hand over her lips to prevent the imminent scream.

She thrashed as he gathered her close, pulling her free of the tangle of covers to carry her out of the room. "Shh," he said again, his mouth against the damp hair at her temple. "It's me. You're safe. Let's not wake London. Shh."

Halfway to his room, her struggles abated, replaced by silent tears. "You're okay," he whispered to her. "I'm here. You're safe. It was just a bad dream."

Crossing the threshold, he kicked the door shut with

his foot. Then he sat with her on his bed. Still shaking, she curled in his lap, her face pressed to his chest. Murmuring nonsense, he stroked her hair, her shoulder, whatever parts of her he could reach.

His day to stanch tears, he thought, as the wetness from her cheeks turned into a damp patch on his T-shirt. Eventually, her body quieted, but he continued with the soothing strokes. When her head tipped back, he looked down at her.

"Better?" he asked, smiling a little.

She nodded and made to move off of him, but he tightened his arms around her. "A little longer," he said. "For me. I was worried about you for a while there."

"It's a terrible dream," she said, her voice raspy from crying.

He cupped the back of her head with his palm and pressed his lips to one downy brow and then the other. "I could see that. Want to talk about it?"

She hesitated.

He found himself almost annoyed by her reluctance. She was holding back again and they didn't have secrets from each other! He'd been so smug about how she'd opened up to him, and now she was resurrecting her barriers. Still, if she told him it was none of his damn business, he couldn't very well protest.

Really, why should she share with a short-timer in her life?

But then her voice echoed in his head. *Girls can go inward. They might become quiet, and be shy about speaking of their dreams and their desires.* Sue him, he was going to press her again.

He rubbed at her damp cheek with his thumb. "Maybe the nightmare will go away if you tell me about it."

"I've never told anyone…not in detail."

"Turns out I'm becoming a good listener." At least better than he had ever expected of himself.

She glanced up at him. "You are," she said, her voice low.

"Let's get more comfortable." Before she could change her mind, he drew both of them toward the pillows, and arranged them so he was sitting up and she was curled into his side. With a gentle hand, he drew her head into the cup of his shoulder. "Look how perfectly you fit," he whispered against her hair.

Her hand rested over his heart and she curled her fingers into her palm. He placed his own over that small fist, insinuating his thumb into its center to unfurl her digits once again. She sighed.

"How does it start?" he prompted.

"The fire at the resort," she began.

It was a recurring dream that she'd had since childhood, she explained. She was again in the woods at the base of the ski mountain, exploring alone while her father took care of some routine tasks up at the lodge. She'd been there many times before.

"But I wandered far that day, even though Dell had told me to stay close to where he was working. I was daydreaming, lost in my own twelve-year-old little world when I smelled the fire."

It was something all the mountain people grew up knowing to fear, she said.

"In the dream I freeze, just like I did that day. I knew I should get back to the truck, but I couldn't figure out which direction to take."

Jace stroked her hair, and when he felt her shiver,

he pulled the covers over them. "Then I could hear the flames," she whispered. "Greedy. Burning the forest."

The ghostly tone of her voice triggered a chill along his spine. He hitched her closer. "How close did they come to you?"

She shrugged. "At the sound, I began to run. In real life and in the dream. It's a monster at my back, chasing me, and I tear through branches and over rocks and I'm sure it's going to catch me, consume me…"

"You're safe now." His hand returned to stroking her hair.

"In the dream I think I'm in hell, and not only is there the fiery monster at my back, but a dark demon rushing toward me, covered in ash. I can't retreat because I'll be burned. I can't avoid the demon's claws, either. Just as it grabs hold, I scream, and over that sound, the creature speaks." Rolling away from him, she sat up. "Then I awaken."

Shay forked her hands through her hair, and glanced over at him, clearly embarrassed. "Maybe that helped. Because it sounds pretty garden variety on the retelling."

Having heard and seen her reaction to it, the nightmare didn't seem garden variety to Jace in the least. "How often does it occur?"

She shrugged.

"Do you have any idea what triggers it?"

She shrugged again.

Jace rubbed his palm over his jaw, the nighttime bristles making a scratchy sound. "What does the creature say, Shay, when you scream?"

Her head turned toward the bank of windows as if seeing more than the blackness of the night beyond the glass. "In real life, it wasn't a creature at all, of course. It was Dell, who'd seen the fire and was out looking for me. He'd been working on some machinery and he'd gotten grease on his hands and on his face. The fire had rained ash on his clothes."

"Okay." Jace shifted on the mattress and touched her shoulder. "What did Dell say to you?"

"He said…" Clearing her throat, Shay's fingers clutched the sheets that were pooled at her waist. "He said, 'Girl, you'll be the death of me.'"

Then she looked at Jace. "And I was, you know. I was."

He frowned. "What are you talking about?"

"If I'd stayed near like he told me to, we would have been able to get help sooner. The resort would have been saved. The stress of losing it is what killed him."

"Shay…" He had to think of how to put this. "The words that were spoken, you have to know he was just expressing his worry. It was an utterance of the moment."

"It's what I remember. And relive in my dreams."

"You were a blameless little girl. Surely you can see that? Nobody holds you responsible for what happened at the resort."

She stared down at her lap. "Part of me understands that, I suppose. Then I remember… There are no adoption papers."

Ah, he thought. That was the crux of the matter.

"Words have power," Shay murmured.

And the lack of them had power, too.

She lifted her hands to her face, scrubbed. "I'll go back to my room now. I appreciate you pulling me out of that."

What else could he do but watch her climb from the bed? In a sleeveless, light cotton gown that floated about her knees as she walked toward the door, she appeared fragile and beautiful and he wanted to shelter her forever. But if he held her again he might not ever let her go and she deserved someone who could give her all she needed.

The security of family and belonging that was a hole in her that needed filling.

A man who had the temperament and experience to provide both.

She paused, her hand on the doorknob, and glanced at him over her shoulder. "Thanks, again. I owe you one."

"Shay," he said, before she could leave him.

"Yes?"

"Your parents? Did they tell you they loved you?"

"My mother—"

"Remember those words. Treasure them."

She frowned. "I—"

"They're special. I know, because no one's ever said them to me."

Shay's eyes widened. Her mouth opened. She started to speak, then apparently decided against it. With a tight nod, she was gone.

Jace had yet to move when he saw the door swing open again. Shay stood in the entry and he could sense emotions waving off of her: uncertainty, determination and something else he couldn't name.

He sat up straighter. "Shay?"

"You should know…" She shook her head, began again. "I need to tell you something. There's something you need to hear."

"What?"

On slow feet she came toward the bed. In the light-colored gown, she looked like a ghost—no, an angel. She halted at his bedside and he could see she was trembling.

"Shay," he said, worried. He caught her hand. It was icy.

"What I'm going to say…I know it won't change anything."

He nodded, though he couldn't guess what she was talking about.

"My last day with you and London…it's tomorrow."

"That's what you wanted to tell me?"

"No, it's something different."

Frowning, he tightened his hold on her fingers. "Well, tomorrow's too soon. I'm not taking her to school until next week."

"Nonetheless, I've decided tomorrow's my final day. I have a last assignment to go over with London in the morning. Then—"

"We had plans to return to the cabins in the afternoon. I need another hour or so to finish repairing that mudroom roof. And I'll need your help."

She hesitated. "Okay, the cabins. *Then* I'll be moving out."

"There's no need—"

"In a minute, you'll know it's the right decision." She slipped her hand from his and perched on the edge of the mattress. Her shoulders rose on a deep breath.

"You're scaring me," he said, trying to lighten the mood. "Is this where you confess—"

"I'm in love with you."

He'd heard wrong. "What?"

"I fell in love with you," she said quickly. "Sometime between my birthday and watching you beginning to bond with your daughter, I fell in love."

"Shay—"

"I love you, Jace. I wanted you to hear that. I wanted you to know it."

Dumbfounded, he stared at her. *I fell in love with you. I love you.*

A wild feeling surged from his toes, through his heart, all the way to the top of his head. It was... triumph. With something else beneath it, that felt like the push of powerful wings. Awe.

I love you.

He reached for her, but she scooted away and rose to her feet. "It's a goodbye gift. Now that it's given, I'll go."

Go? She thought she could share that with him and then *go*?

He had her in his arms before she made the door. With his foot, he kicked it closed once again even as he bent his head and took her mouth in a searing kiss. Her hands pushed against his chest and he thought he might have to let her leave, after all, but then she slid them up to wind her arms around his neck. She opened her mouth, welcomed his tongue, pressed her nubile body against his.

His cock was already hard, his balls drawing tight.

He strode for the bed.

Desperate to have her, he dropped her to the mattress. The hem of her gown was drawn up nearly to her hips, exposing a tiny triangle of lace panties. He stared at it, sucking in deep breaths, trying to find a modicum of control.

Every other time, he'd worked hard to be gentle with her. His conscience urged that again. But it was losing the war with this carnal need to hold her, have her, possess her in every way he'd restrained himself from before.

I love you.

He tossed off his clothes. Maybe she saw the raw intent on his face, because she cast him a wary glance and rose up on her elbows. "Too late," he rasped, putting one knee on the bed. Then his hands grasped the neckline of her gown and he tore the garment in two.

She gasped, her breasts moving up and down in shocked, unsteady breaths.

His gaze traveled her body, clad in panties and tattered fabric. His heartbeat hammered against his ribs and the erotic charge of what he'd just done fired up his blood. Curling his fingers in the elastic top of the tiny bikinis, he tore them off her, too.

Lust crawled over his skin, maddening him.

He came down on top of her, his mouth finding her nipple. As he sucked with strong pulls, his hand found the other breast, and he shaped it, fondled it, tweaked and pinched the other nipple.

She writhed under his weight, moaning and arching into him. Her hands found his hair and her nails scratched his scalp. His tongue laved the other nipple and then he bit her there. She cried out again, her hips jerking high.

I love you.

The words echoed in his head as he ran his mouth along her smooth skin, over her ribs, to her navel, then to the succulent flesh between her legs. They fell open for him and he pressed his palms to the hot, soft skin of her inner thighs as he tasted the pleated layers of wet flesh.

He trailed the tip of his tongue to her clit, circled it, circled it, his gaze going to her face as he felt her tense and tighten. Release broke over her in a strong, sharp wave and he watched the beauty of it, of her, as her head dropped back and her thighs quivered in his grasp.

"Go again," he said against her and continued lapping.

"No, I can't…I won't…"

"You will." He slid two fingers inside her hot channel and licked her again, nudging her clit with his nose. She was protesting, but her voice was nearly inaudible and her body was already lifting to his mouth. Her inner muscles clenched and unclenched and clenched again on his invading fingers.

He felt the next orgasm begin to coil inside of her.

"Oh, God," she moaned. "You shouldn't…I'm afraid…"

"Not of me," he said against her. "Go over."

"No." She thrashed in his hold, the movements weak. "Not like this. Not just me."

"Go over."

"No."

Her refusal broke his restraint. He became a man possessed and possessive. Crawling up her body, he ran heavy hands over her delicate lines, making a blueprint in his mind of every curve and every hollow. He buried his face in her neck and opened his mouth to taste the skin of her shoulder.

He moved down again, blind with desire, his mouth finding her nipple so he could suck there again. His fingers drove between her legs, spearing her softness. His thumb flicked at the hard nub at the top of her sex.

She jolted once more, cried out, but then her fingers circled his wrist. "I'm too close," she said, trying to pull him away. "Not without you. Please."

At that last word, he lost the last of his control.

Lurching up, he flipped her over on the bed. The remnants of her gown were still clinging to her and he ripped at the cotton again, tossing the pieces from her body. Then he exposed the nape of her neck, and pressed a hot, hard kiss there, the same place he'd put his mouth that morning when he'd said his first good-bye.

His hand slid under her hips and he lifted, canting her body so he could wrap himself around her. His knees edged between hers to open her for him. She moaned, her cheek against the sheet and he knelt over her to run his hands along her shoulders, down either side of her spine, over the round curves of her ass.

Breath was heaving in and out of his lungs as he took in the primitive sight of her, positioned for his penetration. Ready for his thrust.

Donning the condom made him suck in air between his teeth, the sensation of the latex sheathing him almost unbearable, he was so aroused. He ran his hand down her spine again, trailing it along the cleft until she jerked into his touch and her wetness bathed the ends of his fingers.

I love you.

The memory of her saying the words struck his heart like a hammer hitting a gong. His body quivered and he dropped over her, covering her tender and delicate loveliness with his harder, tougher muscle and bone. He grasped his cock and fit it to her opening.

"Shay," he said, and thrust to the hilt.

They both went still, then she made a sound, plaintive, beautiful, and backed into him, offering every inch of herself. He pushed forward into the wet and clasping heat and his mind spun away as instinct and want took over. Desire made a beast of him and he gripped her hair in one tight fist while the other hand crept around her hip to find her again, that scrap of flesh that was standing hard and ready.

He toyed with it even as he continued to drive himself inside her. She'd be sore, he'd probably already left bruises, but those thoughts were pounded to dust by the primal imperative of making his mark.

On a gasp, she surged back into the cradle of his hips, taking him to the root. She writhed there and he held fast, letting her muscles milk the climax from him. He strained under the power of it, quivering like an animal covering its mate.

Then he emptied…and for the first time in his entire life he felt filled.

When he could move, he rolled away from her and fell to his back. Glancing over at her still form, worry rushed in. "Are you all right?"

"As long as I never have to walk again," she said, sounding drowsy.

Her spent voice motivated him to make for the bathroom. He returned with a warm, wet washcloth and a soft towel that he worked over her body with all the gentleness he hadn't used before. Then he pulled one of his T-shirts over her head and pushed her arms through the sleeves.

"I need to go back to my room," she murmured.

"Anything you want."

He carried her there and tucked her into bed with

great care. He kissed her forehead and then her mouth and he knew she was already half-gone. As he watched from the doorway, she turned to her side and curled up. He stayed a few minutes, watching her sleep, her hair spread out on the white pillow. She looked like a fairy taking a nap in a snowdrop.

"If I was a different man," he whispered, repeating the words he'd said to her before, "I'd do just about anything to capture and keep you."

CHAPTER TWENTY

"CAN I GET you water?" Shay asked, hand up to shade her eyes as she addressed Jace, who was perched on the roof of one of the cabins. It was the first time she'd seen him that day. He'd gone ahead to the Walker property while she and London finished going over one final essay. They'd driven up after lunch.

"Great. Thanks."

She tossed him her best bright smile along with a cold plastic bottle. He caught it in his left hand, then scanned the vicinity. "London?"

"Cleaning windows as you suggested yesterday." With her thumb, she indicated the cabin across the clearing.

He lowered his voice. "How do you think she's doing today?"

"Okay. We made plans to go shopping again before she leaves Blue Arrow."

"Did you tell her you were moving out of the house?"

"I did."

"How'd she take that?"

"What fifteen-year-old wouldn't like to hear her daily schoolwork has—temporarily anyway—come to an end?" The girl had accepted the news with her old nonchalance. Shay was the one who'd decided on the shopping plan so she could spend additional time with London…a plan that naturally excluded her father.

"And you. How are you doing today?" Jace asked.

She sent him another sunny smile. *Pretend you're having the best time ever.* "I've got a clothes-and-makeup expedition penciled on my calendar. What's not to be happy about?"

"Shay…"

Another smile eluded her. "Of course I'll miss seeing London every day, though. I already told you that."

He descended the ladder, his movements startlingly quick for such a big man. His hands cupped her shoulders. "I want to know how you're feeling after…after last night."

Keep your chin up, swing your hips, smile. "Great," she said with more false cheer even as she stepped out of his hold. "And isn't it a beautiful day?"

At least that wasn't a lie. The sky was a hard, rubbed-crayon blue. Sunshine beamed bright but not too hot. The air smelled of healthy pines and warm dirt. It was a mountain day for memory books.

And one of her last for a while, because she had that upcoming date with France.

Determined to keep her composure, she turned, eager to assign herself a task as distraction. "I'll just—"

"Shay." Jace caught her elbow and turned her back. "Last night…"

A flush crept over her skin and she wished she could bury it and herself under a rock. What had gotten into her? Why had she admitted she loved him?

Because just as he'd never had birthday cake, he'd never heard the words before. And it had seemed miserly of her to hoard the phrase. There was something about it, she'd found out, that just begged to be shared. Poppy was right. People became fools for love.

It was like a bulldozer or a snowplow, with an engine that had the power to drive over shame and through embarrassment.

Jace cleared his throat. "I worried—I was rough."

She stared at him, another blush painting over the first. What had come after she confessed…well, that was something for another memory book. Her secret, X-rated one. "I'm fine. It was fine."

"'Fine'?" Jace quirked an eyebrow.

Her mouth went dry as she recalled the way he'd used his strength. Turning her, yanking her up, thrusting his hips with masculine, arousing, incredible intention. It had thrilled her. "I liked it," she whispered.

He studied her, his gaze moving over her face. "I'm concerned you might be, uh, sore."

"I liked that, too."

His golden eyes turned molten, and her belly jumped. What had gotten into her? Had she been drinking truth serum?

"Shay—"

"Could we talk about something else?" Or how about not talk at all?

He shoved his hands in the pockets of the rattiest pair of jeans she'd ever seen. The knees were more bare than thread and one sleeve of his T-shirt was gone, exposing the wicked etch of his biceps.

She averted her eyes from it. "Is there something you'd like me to do?"

"Reconsider France."

"What? I meant here, at the cabins. Aren't I supposed to be assisting you?"

"You're running away."

"I don't know what you're talking about. You know why I'm going. The money's—"

"It's not about the money. You're letting this idea that you're not a real Walker put a wedge between you and the rest of them, even though feeling part of their circle is your deepest desire."

"I don't know how you can make those judgments about me," she said, feeling too exposed by his diagnosis. "You're a stranger—"

"I'm no stranger, damn it, and you know it."

"Yes, you are—"

"You told me you're in love with me, Shay. It's like when you save someone's life. It makes you responsible for them forever."

Her jaw dropped. "That's not true. And I'm rethinking the whole love thing. Because you're a bully and a…and a bad father and you're more of a coward than I could ever be."

"I've copped to the bad father," he said, his eyes narrowing. "I've never been afraid to admit to that."

"That's not what makes you a coward." Her throat was tightening and she felt a sting of tears behind her eyes. *Keep your composure, Shay!* But her emotions were getting the best of her. "You claim I'm running away, well, you should take a look in the mirror."

His mouth tightened, then he sighed. "Shay, I don't want to fight with you—"

"Maybe I want to fight with you." She stepped forward, so they were toe-to-toe. "Maybe I want to tell you what a jackass you are."

"I think I've copped to that before, too."

Oh, he was trying to be the cool one now. But Shay

wasn't going to allow him to deflect her ire with a cloak of calm. "Your daughter needs you."

"I'm no good—"

"Then get good! Figure it out. If you can build a structure, then you can determine a way to build a family with that wonderful girl who shares your DNA."

He narrowed his eyes. "Where are the plans? Can you tell me what the production schedule is? What kind of heavy equipment will I need?"

She stared at him.

"That's what I'm familiar with. You see how this is different? I have no idea how to even lay the foundation."

"No. Yes." She waved her hand. "I don't care about the stupid metaphor—"

"It was your stupid metaphor."

"Fine," she said, throwing up both arms. "Let's go with it. You already have laid the foundation. London told me about the books you've shared over the years. *That's* the foundation. The short time you've spent with her here in the mountains…those are the bones of the first floor."

"The frame."

"Whatever. The point is, you've got to keep building."

He shook his head. "If I do it wrong, it all falls down."

"Don't do it wrong." When she saw him about to protest, she held up her hand. "What if she already loves you, Jace? You just told me that's like saving someone's life. It makes you responsible for them forever."

"I'll be responsible for her. I'm not shirking that."

"Then don't shirk when it comes to loving her, either," she said.

His face was a mask of frustration. "What the hell do I know about that?"

Before she could answer, the sound of cars coming up the steep drive had them both pivoting. It was her siblings, she noted, half grateful and half annoyed by the interruption.

"I wonder what they're doing here," she murmured, glancing at Jace.

He seemed less surprised at their arrival than she. Frowning, she headed toward her brother and sisters as they piled out of their cars. Ryan accompanied Poppy, of course.

"Hey, what brings you here?" she asked as they moved forward as a group.

Poppy's gaze shifted to Jace, then moved back to Shay. "I told the others about the progress made. We came to see."

Shay released a long breath, and tried to appear as if she hadn't just been arguing with the man beside her. "That's right. Among other things, Poppy's cabin—the one she used before she and Mason moved to Ryan's— is nearly habitable again," she said, addressing Mac and Brett. "Roof repaired, et cetera."

Poppy beamed. "Isn't that great?"

Brett wandered over to inspect the work. He climbed the ladder, gave a whistle, then returned to the ground. "Appreciate what you've done, Jace," he said.

"Shay and London have put their time in, too."

As the two men began to talk of the particulars, Ryan moved to join them, while Shay's sisters sidled closer to her. "How are you?" Poppy asked.

"Terrific. Fabulous. Never been better." She pasted on another of the smiles she'd been working on all day, determined to hide her upset. If Mac was the feisty sister and Poppy the optimist, Shay had always excelled at self-containment.

Until Jace, she thought. Until he'd destroyed her secure inner walls.

"We heard you're moving back to your place," Mac said.

Who had passed along that little nugget? "It's time." It would seem small compared to Jace's lake house, but it would suit her until she moved to France.

"And we heard you're planning on taking that job Dee's offered," her oldest sister continued as if reading her mind.

Shay glared at Poppy.

The other woman widened her eyes. "You didn't say I couldn't tell."

"I didn't say you could, either," she grumbled.

"Are you running off because of him?" Mac asked, nodding toward Jace.

Shay exploded. "Why is everyone suddenly accusing me of running?"

Her sisters exchanged glances. "Well, uh, hurriedly changing the subject, we have something to show you," Poppy said, taking her by the arm. "Inside my old cabin."

"I know what's inside your old cabin," Shay said, resisting.

Mac tsked. "You're usually easier to get along with than this."

"I didn't like making waves or getting people mad at

me before," Shay said in a bad-tempered voice. "Now I don't care."

"I love this new you," Poppy said, grinning. "But come along anyway."

With ill grace, Shay allowed herself to be escorted into the bungalow. Behind her, she heard Jace making noises about returning to the roof to finish up, but Poppy's will was formidable and when she insisted that both he and London join them, that's just what happened.

"Sit," Mac said, and pushed Shay onto the sofa in the living area. Everyone else took up places around her.

Wary, she glanced about. "This isn't an intervention, is it? Because I'm pretty certain I can't give up those dark chocolate-covered caramels."

"It's a movie," Poppy said, whipping a DVD out of her purse. "All about you."

"Is this going to be embarrassing?" she asked, warier still, as her sister handed over the recording for Ryan to insert into the player.

"Of course not," she assured Shay, then said, "oops!" as the first image popped onto the TV screen.

Shay shrieked. "I'm naked!"

"You're a baby, on a blanket," Mac said. "And your butt was cute."

She thought she heard a "still is," whispered by a male voice in her ear, but she ignored the remark and slumped lower on the cushions.

"What is this?" she demanded, as music burst through the speakers. A lively tune to accompany photos of her in a stroller, a crib, eating rice cereal in a high chair.

"We wanted to give it to you for your birthday, but the guy who was doing the editing for us was running behind," Poppy said with a significant glance at her significant other.

Ryan raised his hand. "Sorry, Shay. I've been spending too much time with your adorable, affectionate, effervescent…"

They all groaned, even as he spoke over them.

"…dog-in-law—or is that nephew-dog? Anyway, Grimm."

Poppy threw a pillow at him just as the images changed from solo to sibling shots. There were all four of them, at Christmas, Easter, Halloween, first days of school.

The next photo showed a mess in the kitchen and all four kids covered in dough. "That's the time Brett decided to make cookies," Mac said.

"He used the blender and forgot to put the top on," Poppy explained.

Shay grinned, remembering, and then grinned wider as the still shots changed to video of her big brother teaching her to ride a bike.

"You broke my big toe when you steered the two wheels over my foot," he said.

The movie ran on, a combination of photos and camcorder footage, a chronicle of her growing-up years. No, she thought, of *their* growing-up years. But the film editor—Ryan—had managed to put Shay at the center of everything.

And she couldn't miss how her brother and sisters were always there behind her, or to pick her up, or to lead her forward. The point wasn't lost on her.

As the movie ended, she closed her eyes, tight, then opened them to look at each one of her siblings. "Thank you. I love it. But you should know I've never doubted you guys."

"You've doubted something recently," Brett said. "We hope this puts that to rest." With a flourish, he handed over a rolled piece of parchment, tied with a ribbon.

Mac leaned close. "One of his exes does calligraphy. Personally, I'm surprised she didn't use her talent to slash his tires, Mr. New-Girl-Nightly, but he sweet-talked her into doing this for you."

"Sweet talk?" Shay asked, brows rising as she slipped off the ribbon. "Brett knows sweet talk?"

"I know, I know. I think it consists of 'Hey, baby, you wanna?'"

The parchment was the size of a legal document and the lettering was beautiful. She stared at what it said, her eyes beginning to burn. The sting made it impossible to read. With one hand she swiped at her eyes.

"I'm having an attack of something akin to fuzzy-screen syndrome. What does it say?"

"It's an adoption paper," London said. She came to look over Shay's shoulder. "It looks very official and declares you a Walker through-and-through. It's signed by everybody, even Mason."

Shay hiccupped a watery laugh. "What about Grimm?"

"He's got some slobbery kisses he's saving up for you," Ryan said.

Overwhelmed by sudden emotion, Shay passed the document to Mac and covered her eyes with her hands. Then she curled over her knees, trying to prevent the sobs in her chest from breaking free.

Mac patted her back. "It's okay."

"Walkers aren't whiners," she answered, her voice muffled.

"I think you should go ahead and let the tears flow. You're the only one of us who's a pretty crier," advised Poppy. "Except for Brett, of course. He's beautiful when he cries."

Shay sensed another pillow being thrown. "And even more beautiful when he's angry," Poppy added.

Then there was no help for it. Shay was laughing and crying and she had to jump up to hug each of her loyal, generous—while sometimes exasperating—Walker siblings.

Maybe her composure was shot, but at the moment it seemed a small price to pay.

WATCHING SHAY WITH her siblings calmed some of the disquiet Jace had felt since leaving her alone in her bed the night before. Certainly it made him glad he'd called Poppy early that morning to put a bug in her ear about her sister's low mood. Turned out they'd already had plans in the works—the DVD and the adoption paper— but made the decision to deliver them ASAP.

The DVD was being replayed and the woman who loved him was smiling again even as she blotted fresh tears with the heels of her hands. He smiled, too, his gaze on the screen as she grew from infant to woman. So beautiful.

Movement by the cabin's front door caught his eye and he turned, just in time to see London let herself out. There was something about the set of her shoulders that put him on alert. He glanced back at the Walkers, loath to leave the scene—he'd had a hand in engineering it, right?—but his feet made the decision for him.

A few minutes behind his daughter, he exited the cabin.

Looking around, he didn't see her at first. Perhaps she'd returned to her task in the other bungalow, he thought. But then his gaze caught on the bright green shirt she was wearing with shorts. London was steadily making her way up the steep, weed-covered hill north of the woods and cabins. During the heyday of the resort, it was the location of the ski runs. According to Shay, there had been chairlifts, a rope tow for little kids and a lodge at the top—all lost in the fire.

Eyeing London as she picked her way up he reconsidered following her. A teenager needed her space. But his gut was talking to him again, urging him to go after her and he started to hike.

Ninety seconds into it, he was sweating. Darn kid, he thought, grimacing. If she wanted to go for a walk, the forest would have been a more comfortable meander. Without the shade of pine, oak or aspen, the sun beat down without mercy. The thick soles of his work boots dug into the soft dirt okay, but every once in a while he'd hit a patch of broken rock and take a brief slide backward.

His hand shot out to brace yet again, just saving himself from an awkward nose-plant. He sent another glance upward, raising the silent question. *Kid, why not the easy path?*

Like the one he'd always taken with her, his conscience murmured. He'd walked away in the past and now he'd arranged their future lives in order to avoid much of the direct fathering. But was it his fault, damn it, that he lacked a decent paternal figure to model another way? For a lone wolf like him, what other route was there?

Finally at the top of the hill, he paused to catch his breath. London stood several feet from him, her back turned. As he approached, he felt a deep clutch in his belly seeing her poised so close to the edge of a precipitous drop.

It was hardwired into the genes, he supposed, to protect the young.

Unwilling to startle her, he didn't try to disguise the sound of his footsteps moving through the drying grasses. She glanced over, and he could read the unhappiness in her expression.

Shit, he thought. *Shit.*

As he came to a halt alongside her, she tipped up her head, her gaze on a red-tailed hawk that sailed overhead and then floated on the up currents coming from the canyon at their feet. Miles of wilderness were spread out before them: craggy mountain ridges, deep ravines bristling with evergreens, silty narrow valleys.

"Quite a view, huh?"

His question hung in the air a second before falling to the ground like a stone. God, he thought, spearing his hand through his hair. Yesterday he'd believed he'd made a tenuous connection with her, but now it felt as if they were back at square one.

He was no good at this.

Shay's words echoed in his head. *Then get good. Figure it out.*

Once again forking up his hair with his hand, he wondered if her voice would be in there for the rest of his life. *I love you. I'm in love with you.*

He squeezed his eyes shut, the memory of her sharing that with him mainlining more shock and awe into his bloodstream. Last night, it had driven him to lay claim to her in his bed. Today, he felt no less ownership.

Just something else he didn't deserve.

Opening his eyes, he took in his daughter's profile. She continued to contemplate that hawk still surfing the wind. It wasn't a stretch to imagine the creature enjoyed the play—rising, floating, soaring—as an exercise in self-determination.

It should come as no surprise that London would envy that independence. After all, she was no longer a little girl, but a teen just a few short years from adulthood. Sighing, he struggled with what to do. He'd failed the girl before...

But that didn't give him a license to fail her again.

He cleared his throat. She shot him a quick look.

"I have this idea," he said. "An offer."

Her brows rose. "What kind of offer?"

So suspicious. "I thought I'd give you three wishes. *Reasonable* wishes," he added, when her eyes flared wide.

Tucking her fingers in the front pockets of her shorts, London tilted her head as if trying to puzzle him out. "Why would you do that?"

He shrugged, deciding it would be unwise of him to admit he was looking for a window into her head and heart. As well as a way to make her at least a little happier. "I'll pick one and make it come true."

"No." She frowned. "In stories, the picker gets to have all three wishes—the benefactor's only contribution is to provide."

"This is a different kind of story."

"Figures," she muttered.

Ignoring that, he continued, "Tell me your wish number one."

Her long-suffering sigh rolled right off his back. "Indulge me," he said, prodding his daughter.

Her gaze shifted from him to the mountaintop view. "I don't want to leave here," she replied, sweeping her arm to indicate the breathtaking surroundings. "This."

It didn't exactly surprise him, but... "At the risk of seeing Colton again?"

"I have a solution to that problem," she said. "Keep my chin up, swing my hips, smile."

Was that what Shay had been doing this afternoon? He recalled her cheery attitude. *Fake it until you make it.*

He despised the idea of Shay faking anything. It had been his privilege to see inside her private self and the idea she was papering over that now felt all kinds of fucked-up. Pinching the bridge of his nose between two fingers, he returned to the matter at hand. "What's your second reasonable wish?"

"Go to a regular school like a regular student. Public school, where they have proms and a tennis team and a literary magazine. Amy says at hers there's a green energy club."

"You're interested in green energy?"

She shrugged. "I looked up what your company is doing in Qatar. I'm thinking maybe I should learn more about it."

Jace rubbed at his chest. Hell if the kid didn't touch him at the oddest times. Book clubs. Green energy. The idea that she wanted to be "like, a family" with him. Well, with him and Shay.

Shay.

He pushed the thought of her from his head and instead focused on reasonable wishes. Unfortunately, while the first two London had asked for might seem reasonable to her, they were beyond his power to grant. He was going overseas, she was slated for boarding school.

There was only one shot left. Of course, like an idiot he'd set himself up for failure, hadn't he? If on this third round she posed something equally undoable from his perspective, then he'd prove himself once again to be lousy dad material.

He was boxed into a corner with only himself to blame.

With an air of fatalism, he turned to face his daughter. "Wish number three?"

She looked down, using the toe of her sneaker to draw something in the dusty earth. Probably an image of him, he decided, impaled by something painful. "This is difficult," she mused.

Naturally, choosing between either skewering him with a sword or cleaving him in two with an ax wasn't easy. "Go ahead," he said, between gritted teeth. "I'm all ears."

"Maybe…" Her head came up and she looked at him with her big brown eyes. "Maybe you can teach me how to do that magic trick."

Dumbfounded, Jace stared at her. "You're taking it easy on me."

She shrugged. "Could be."

"I'm terrible at that trick," he pointed out.

"Yeah." A smile hovered over her mouth. "So maybe it's something we can practice together."

He clutched at his heart again, this time the feeling not a touch, but a blow. She *had* actually cleaved him with an ax—but with the kind of ax that was giving him a second chance with her. *Something we can practice together.*

Once, when he was helping his old man with a home remodel, he'd been standing in the kitchen and given a sledgehammer and the direction to remove an exterior wall that the resident abhorred. For a big kid loaded with testosterone, it had been a match made in heaven. He'd swung the shit out of the tool, breaching all the way to daylight with the first hit and the sunlight bursting through the hole had nearly blinded him. Yet he'd swung again and again and again.

It felt like he was the wall now. And it was London with the sledge, busting his old barriers so that a new day could come in.

His daughter, in her way, had extended her hand to him.

He stared at her, aware if he similarly reached out that his former solitary life was going to change. Mistakes would be made. The path wouldn't always—would maybe never—be completely clear. But if he took the chance, the magnificent sunshine would surround them and he could have summer all year round.

It turned out to be such a simple decision.

"Yes," he said, his voice hoarse. "To the mountains, to regular school, to the magic trick."

Her eyes went round. "I get all three?"

"You get more." Jace paused a moment, then said the words that had been walled up inside him for fifteen years. "I love you, London." With that, he pulled his daughter into his arms, enfolding her against him. He pressed a kiss on the top of her hair. "I love you."

"Jace," he heard her whisper against his shirt, then, "Dad."

Above them, the hawk keened a wild cry that sounded, to Jace, full of joy.

CHAPTER TWENTY-ONE

SHAY WALKED HER siblings to their cars, her face aching after so many smiles. Her sisters and Ryan were waved off first, leaving only Brett. Jace and London were nowhere to be seen.

Risking permanent cheek damage, she grinned at her brother. "Thanks. That surprise was really nice of you guys."

Brett shrugged. A yellow butterfly fluttered past his nose and then came back to settle on his shoulder. He froze, appearing bemused as it slowly pumped its wings as if it had all the time in the world and her brother was the gentlest of souls.

"The average butterfly has a life span of two weeks," she told him.

"Yeah?" Her brother continued to contemplate the insect. "'Gather ye rosebuds' and all that, my friend," he said softly, speaking, she presumed, to the still-calm yellow fellow.

But the knowledge struck Shay that her love affair hadn't lasted much longer than a butterfly enjoyed the sunshine. It made her melancholy, and yet she was still glad she'd gathered flowers when she could. Her throat tightened.

Inside I'd place a bed of petals plucked from summer roses.

"Since we're sharing trivia," Brett said, "there's a moth caterpillar that will wait thirty years before forming a cocoon and becoming an adult."

"Huh." Shay was impressed. "It's got you beat on that becoming an adult thing."

He laughed, which pleased her, since he had a tendency to brood, but it disturbed the butterfly. The insect rose from his shoulder and made its way toward the woods. Brett's gaze followed it, and he sighed. "I admit it's beautiful here."

"It's worth saving," she said.

Instead of answering, her brother changed tactics. "What's up with you and the flatlander? Mac is muttering in dire tones."

"Mac always mutters. I think 'Dire' is her middle name."

"Still, you're going to France."

"You guys say it like I'm going to the guillotine. The French Revolution was over long ago."

"I'll take your word for it. But we don't want to lose you."

She had to clear another obstruction in her throat. Oh, she'd miss him. "I think I just need some time away."

"Try a walk in the woods. Have you done that recently?"

With Jace. She shrugged. "Maybe I will."

"Well, gotta go." He gave her a soft punch in the arm.

She clapped her hand over it and screeched as he meant her to. "Ouch!"

"All's right with my world," he said, and turned to his truck, whistling.

By the time he'd driven off, Jace and London had

not reappeared, though his SUV was still in its original place. *Try a walk in the woods.*

She would follow that advice, she decided, and strolled out of the clearing. It was unlikely she'd come back here before making her way to France. It would remind her too much of Jace and London. Though she supposed she'd forever hear a hammer stroke and think of him. Or glimpse a girl with a coltish stride and wonder how London was doing.

Instead of dwelling on the Jennings, as she followed one of the old trails she returned her thoughts to the DVD and the "adoption paper." Both made her smile. Still, neither assuaged that smear of guilt she felt on her soul. Dell Walker had been a kind and generous man—albeit not perfect, as no one was—and she'd let him down. *You'll be the death of me.*

Although she was sure that those last words were ones he wouldn't want her to linger over, the fact was that they were seared by fire and fear in her mind.

She'd reached the A-frame cabin where Jace had kissed her the first day they visited the property. At that time, though the attraction had been palpable, her heart had remained her own.

Where had she gone wrong? What had been the first wrong move? She supposed it started with that tipsy talk about her birthday. Before then, she'd always been so secretive about her dislike of the day. After that night, her inner self had unfolded, revelation after revelation spread out for him to see. Now he knew everything, from the circumstances of her birth to the circumstances of the fire and Dell's subsequent death.

He knew about her love for him.

It no longer seemed to matter that she'd shared that,

too. When he was gone, she'd be miserable without him and London. If she'd kept her counsel, it wouldn't have made a whit of difference.

She should head back now and find them, she decided. But Brett's butterfly—or one just like it—suddenly appeared before her, zigzagging in front of her face before darting farther into the woods. On a whim, she followed it, aware she hadn't gone this far into the forest since the day of the fire.

Then, though, she'd actually gone much farther. Beyond the last of the Walker cabins. She'd turn back when she came to the twelfth, she promised herself. It would be good to check on it. Poppy said at her one and only inspection months ago that it seemed to be a haven for wild animals and maybe the kids in the area. Everybody who grew up in the mountains knew—since it was a tradition from time immemorial—that teens would find their secret gathering places.

She hiked to the more secluded cabins, trying each doorknob to ensure they remained secure. There was the expected peeling paint and dislodged shingles, but other than those, all appeared well.

Finally, there was only one left, a quarter mile from the second-to-the-last. As she approached, pushing through branches and over creeping ground cover, her foot caught on a root and she fell to the ground, crashing through some dried branches to land just a few feet from the cabin with a loud "oomph."

Given that she thought herself alone, she didn't hold back the litany of curses that fell from her lips as she picked herself up. Bending over to inspect her scraped and bloody knees, she heard running steps from the back of the cabin and then the catch of a small engine.

A dirt bike, she guessed, a popular mode of transportation for the mountain kids.

Her head lifted, and through the trees, she saw movement. Two boys, it appeared, riding tandem and taking off in the opposite direction.

Well, Poppy had been right. Kids were using the cabin.

Shay would have to find a way to lock it tight. Tradition or no, it wasn't smart for the kids to do their squatting on Walker land. It was remote enough to be a real danger if someone got hurt.

Straightening, she directed her attention to the condition of the bungalow. Not good. The door was ajar, and listing on its hinges. Windowpanes were broken.

Moldering was the only word for it. A single breath might blow it down.

And as she took in one herself, she smelled it.

Her heart seized. Her muscles froze. Four letters blasted across the surface of her brain, a neon-styled warning.

Fire.

The scent of it, coming from the direction of the cabin, was like a paralyzing drug. Shay turned so cold she wouldn't have been surprised to see snow. But that would have been welcome. Snow could put out flames.

Instead, it was summer. There was wind. Both two more ingredients that added to the recipe for disaster.

That last thought broke her free from inertia. With her heart pounding again, she fumbled for her phone in her back pocket. "Come on, come on," she muttered to herself.

When it finally slid from the confines of her pocket, she dialed 911.

And did not connect.

Cursing the spotty mountain cell coverage, she tried a second time. Same result.

Then, knowing a text had a better chance of getting through, she sent one off to her brother. But he'd driven away, she reminded herself.

Jace, presumably, was closer.

She texted him, too: Fire at the twelfth cabin. Help.

But she had to do more. Even if neither of the texts went through, professional assistance was a long way off. She didn't dare lose a chance to prevent the spread of fire from destroying the remainder of the Walker legacy. She had enough blame on her shoulders.

Though flames were not yet apparent, the burning smell was stronger. Gathering her courage, she raced forward and slipped inside the structure.

Her feet stuttered to a halt. The floor of the cabin was littered with refuse: dried leaves, soda cans, a few beer bottles. In one corner was a pile of old blankets and a ragged sleeping bag. In the opposite, dumped onto the upturned lid of a battered metal trash can lid, lay thick bundles of used lined paper. Six discarded three-ring binders were tossed nearby.

The pages were just beginning to flame.

At the sight of them, Shay froze again and a flash-back dropped over her like a burlap sack. As in her nightmare, fire crackled and hissed at her back. Terror had her firmly in its grip and she stood, rooted to the ground, ready to be eaten alive. The smoke stung her eyes and filled her nose and tears cascaded down her cheeks as she waited to die.

Then she heard her name. She jolted, her head whipping around to find the source. There was nothing but the wall of flames behind her and the enclosing woods around her. Which way? Where to go?

Then she was running, tripping on her feet, getting lashed by branches. Her name again. The demon came into her line of sight, rushing toward her, mouth open, arms out, claws reaching.

She screamed as it touched her. Pulled her close.

"Girl, you'll be the death of me." It was her father!

Relief tore the sobs from her chest. She clung to him, for the first time believing she might survive, after all.

He swept her up in his arms as she continued to cry. "We've got to get to the truck," he said in her ear as he began running through the woods.

Still shaking with fear, Shay held on tighter.

Dell Walker didn't halt his stride. But he spoke to her in soothing tones. "You're safe, honey. Daddy's got you. Daddy loves you. We'll be fine."

As he ran toward the woods, Jace scanned the sky. There wasn't a sign of smoke. Yet.

He looked back to yell at his daughter, standing by his SUV. "Stay there," he shouted. "Unless you have to—"

As she dangled the keys he'd handed her, he shut his mouth. He'd given her enough instructions

Except she doesn't really know how to drive, a panicked voice in his head said. That couldn't be helped now, he reminded himself as he plunged into the thick stand of trees. He'd managed to reach Brett by phone and the other man was on his way back to the cabins.

Maybe the land really *was* cursed.

Jace tripped over a rock and stumbled, cursing under his breath as he regained his balance. Unsure of the danger Shay was facing, all he could do was speed in the direction of the twelfth cabin.

Follow the trail, Brett had told him over the phone. *And hope that it's not grown over.*

London had been the one to assure Jace he could find the place. The farthest cabin was where she'd had her non-real-kiss encounter with Colton. "You can't miss the path, Dad," she'd said. "It's narrow, but you can't miss it."

Dad.

His daughter, again showing the way.

Still, the distance seemed interminable. His breath sawed in and out of his lungs and he kept expecting to draw in the stench of burning wood. It only made his legs pump harder. He thought of Shay's nightmare, of the flame monster and the ash demon and her trembling in his arms. Everything inside of him yearned to shelter her, protect her, keep her forever in the secure circle of his embrace.

He wanted her to belong to him, and him to belong to her. Like a family.

Sweat rolled into his eyes and he didn't bother swiping at the sting. Instead he sent out a mental message to her. *I'm coming. I'm coming. I'm coming.*

His heart jolted when he detected the first whiff of smoke. He gazed wildly about, but had yet to see flames. Then he thought he spied the crumbling cabin roof through the foliage ahead. Adding an extra burst of speed, he shoved through needled branches. His foot caught on something and he soared through the air like a low-flying Superman, to land flat on his face a few feet from the open door to the rickety cabin. He lifted his head.

Shay was standing just inside the open doorway, her back to him.

He sucked in a sharp breath, relief spurting through him until he realized she wasn't moving and beyond her there were flames rising. Fear knotted his guts and he shoved to his feet.

"Shay! Shay, baby."

As if in a trance, she turned to him, blinking.

There was dirt on her face and both her knees were skinned. Blood trickled down her shins.

And the flames behind her continued to rise.

He grabbed her elbow to pull her from the cabin. "Honey, get away. Go stand over there."

As he tried to move back inside, she clutched at his shirt. "He loved me, Jace." Her expression was serious, her words earnest. "I remember now. He said he loved me."

"Well, I love you, too, but that won't mean squat if we turn into crispy critters." Breaking her hold, he ran back into the structure.

Smoke was filling the place, billowing gray-brown clouds of it. He coughed, glancing around to see what he had to work with. *Shit.* Did he have anything else besides spit?

Shay pushed past him. "Hey—" he said, trying to catch her. But he missed and she disappeared into the bank of smoke. "Hell," he muttered, starting after her, but then she was back, her arms filled with what looked like ragged blankets. She dropped some at his feet and unfolded another, which she began to use to beat out the flames.

He followed suit, and both of them were coughing, tears streaming down their faces as they continued to attack. Jace saw the corner of Shay's blanket catch fire and he yanked it from her hands to stomp on the flames with his boots. His pulse was going crazy and at the sight of embers flying around the room like lethal insects he was fucking filled with terror. If one landed on Shay's clothes or hair...

"Enough!" he shouted at her, turning to pull her from the cabin. The building could burn, the whole forest could burn, the mountain itself turn to ash. He didn't care about anything but Shay. Nothing could happen to her now. Not on his watch.

He pulled at her arm, but she wrenched away and went back to battling the fire with a new length of blanket. "You go!" she yelled without looking at him. "I'm saving this. I've got to save this."

And, fuck, he knew that she did. As much as he wanted to drag her away from danger, as much as his own instincts were clamoring to leave now because there was little time before the flames spread, Shay Walker had allowed him to see inside her so that he was certain of one thing.

This salvation would be her redemption.

His acquaintance with that inner core of her meant he knew she must see this through.

As he picked up the remaining blanket, he wondered if it would have been better if they'd remained strangers.

Ten minutes later, it shocked the hell out of him to realize they'd won. Shay stepped back, her blanket falling at her feet, as he stomped through the pile of ash to make sure there was nothing left to reignite. Then Brett leaped through the doorway, a fire extinguisher in each hand.

He skidded to a halt, taking in the situation. "Out," he said, speaking the obvious.

"Toss me one of those," Jace ordered, and he doused the detritus of the fire with the foam.

"What the hell was burning?" he asked, to no one in particular.

Shay's breathing was ragged and her face was covered with muddy soot. "I think it was kids torching a years' worth of homework assignments."

Jace lifted the hem of his T-shirt to wipe his face, examined its ashy state and decided against it. "Your sister saved the day," he told Brett. "Should we call the fire department? Tell them the danger's passed?"

"Yeah," he said, yanking his phone from his pocket. "Shit. No coverage."

"That's what happened to me." Shay sank to the floor as if too weary to stand another moment.

"I'll text London. She has a signal at the clearing and can make the call." He grimaced. "Though I'd better get back there, just in case they want to hear it from an adult."

"You go ahead," Brett said. "I'll let Shay catch her breath and then we'll follow."

Jace looked at his soot-covered battle partner. She had her bloody knees drawn up. Her arms circled her shins and her eyes were closed. As he watched, they opened, their icy blue rimmed with red. "Thanks," she said. There was a relieved peace about her that acted as a parachute to his adrenaline crash.

"You're welcome," he said. "We'll talk, okay?"

Her eyes had already closed again. "Sure."

But then she didn't come home.

Brett sent a text telling Jace that he and London

should go ahead and return to their house. He and Shay would meet with the fire inspector, who was coming out to inspect the damage.

As the dinner hour approached, London received a text from her tutor, instructing her about where to find fixings for a meal. She told the girl she'd see her later.

Jace didn't hear a word from Shay himself and he noted that "later" was pretty damn vague. It started to piss him off.

As he slung a couple of plates on the kitchen table for himself and his daughter, she looked across at him, her eyebrows rising. "What are you going to do?"

He ratcheted down his temper. "About what?" he asked.

She shrugged. "Everything."

"We'll figure it out." He looked around the house he'd originally considered butt ugly. "Do you like this place or should we find another in the area?"

Her eyes lit up. "We're really going to stay?"

"We're really going to stay. I still might have to make the occasional business trip—I'll rearrange things as best as I can—"

"Maybe I could bunk with Poppy and Ryan when necessary…and you know, do some babysitting for Mason." She sounded enthused. "Or Shay could come back…"

Shay had to come back.

He worried she wouldn't for the rest of the meal and until London took herself off to bed. She said, "Good night, Dad," and wasn't that a kick in the ass? He smiled and ruffled her hair and she complained about that so he did it again.

But then he was alone as night settled around the

house. He sat in the living room nursing a beer. The only lights he'd turned on were those on the porch and in the foyer, just like Shay's date night.

And just like her date night, he was sitting in the dark living room when she let herself into the house.

"Shay," he said as she passed his still body.

She jolted, put her hand to her throat. "You scared me."

"Sorry. Are you all right? I didn't hear from you and was worried."

After a moment's hesitation, she perched on the chair adjacent to his spot on the couch. "I should have called to thank you again. Brett and I went to Poppy and Ryan's, Mac brought some clean clothes over for me and we all had dinner together, talked."

"Ah."

She hesitated. "I guess I should let you know I'm not going to France."

He decided against a touchdown boogie, though it was a near thing. "Is that right?"

"I told you about my dad—"

"You said you remembered him telling you he loved you."

"After he found me in the woods. I'd forgotten in the…in the trauma of it all, I guess."

"I'm glad you remembered."

"Yes." Even though it was dark, he saw her bend her head, stare at her hands clasped in her lap. "So, I'm not going to France. I'm staying in the mountains. My brother and sisters and I discussed it over dinner. I fought for the land today and because of that…I finally feel like it's my land now, too."

"Shay Walker," he murmured.

"Yes." He could hear the smile in her voice. "Shay Walker."

They sat in silence for a long moment. Then she spoke again. "How did things go here?"

"It's been pretty quiet since my daughter hit the sack. By the way, we've decided to make a go of it, London and I. Regular school, full-time father."

"Jace!" She swiveled to fully face him. "What changed your mind?"

"Hard to pinpoint just one thing." Though the Walkers figured into it pretty heavily. He wanted that kind of connection for his daughter, with her.

"I'm so happy for you both."

"About that happiness…I've been sitting in the dark contemplating the kind of woman I'll eventually settle down with."

"Oh." She sounded nonplussed. "You seemed so sure that wasn't going to happen."

He shrugged. "Not with Greeting Card Wife."

"Well, I think she was perfect for you," Shay said in an airy tone.

"I don't want a woman I pick up in a bar."

He heard her offended sniff.

"I want a woman who picks *me* up in a bar."

The atmosphere in the room changed in an instant, becoming charged with wariness and uncertainty. Had she closed her heart to him already? "Shay?"

"I'm still here."

And because of that, he was plowing forward. "It's probably not fair to you, what I want. God knows I'm fumbling my way into fatherhood and I'll probably make a hash out of being a husband."

There was a long pause. "Nice alliteration," she finally said.

"Thanks, I've been practicing that. Is it...is it softening you up at all?"

"For what?"

"To take me on. To become part of my family. To belong to me and London like we'll belong to you."

He heard her breath catch.

"I considered doing the noble thing and leaving you free for Officer Upright, but it turns out I'm not so chivalrous. I want it all, and I won't have it all if I don't have you."

Another long pause. Then she whispered, "I...I want it all, too."

More sunlight shined on his heart. He knew what she was hinting at. "I love you, Shay. I'm in love with you."

"Why? When?" There was astonished delight in her voice.

The sound of it nearly broke him. He was up and he drew her up, too, so he could enclose her in his arms. "I think it started with those smart-ass emails. And I was certain when I saw your naked baby butt."

She shoved at him, but he held firm. Then she tilted her head. "Hey, wait. I remember something else. You told me you loved me at the cabin today."

"I did. And I was a little annoyed that you didn't appear to notice."

"There was a lot going on at the time." Her hands curled around the back of his neck and she toyed with his collar in a proprietary way that he found, frankly, adorable. "Will you make me a fairy house?"

"A new one every year," he promised.

She buried her face in his chest. He stroked the back

of her hair. "What are you thinking now, my lovely one?"

She lifted her head. "That I'm going to make you very happy."

Frowning, he tapped her nose. "That's my line."

"We'll share," she declared.

And looking down at the wonderful woman in his arms, Jace Jennings knew that was going to be the best way to live the rest of his life.

EPILOGUE

LONDON LOOKED HERSELF over in her bedroom mirror, retucking a lock of hair in her updo and fussing with the strapless bodice of her prom dress. Though she'd danced the night away, the gown still looked perfect.

There'd been quite a lot of "discussion" around the Jennings dinner table about what was appropriate for an eighteen-year-old to wear to a dance just weeks before high school graduation. Her father had some ridiculous notion involving sleeves and high necklines. Shay had talked him around.

London figured he'd actually given in because she was not going with a date, but with a group of her girlfriends. They were in her room, too, now, chattering and checking on their own dresses and makeup. The limo had dropped them off not more than ten minutes before and at any second their guests would arrive for the postprom party.

Shay had suggested they volunteer to host that bash, that way avoiding her dad objecting to London going to an all-night event. Sure, now he was complaining about having to chaperone until morning, but he liked to pretend he was grumpy.

Since marrying Shay, he was really quite malleable.

In the distance, the doorbell rang. "People are here!" London said to her posse. Since the other four were still fussing with their lipstick, she went downstairs by herself. Glancing in the kitchen as she passed, she saw her father and stepmother in a lip-lock. No wonder they hadn't heard the bell.

They were even more crazy about each other—if that was humanly possible—now that Shay was a week shy of her due date. London was getting a little brother *and* a little sister. She'd decided on a college down the mountain but close by in the LA area, just so she wouldn't be too far from taking part in the raising of the new members of her family.

Wearing a smile, she turned the knob.

Her fingers strangled it when she saw who was standing on the front step. Colton Halliday.

Yes, it was his rangy figure, his tousled sandy hair, his half smile. Though she'd seen him on occasion— Amy was one of her closest friends—they'd both taken great pains to avoid each other.

It hadn't been that hard over the past three years since he'd been going to college in Colorado.

But she was almost a college girl herself, not some gauche, freaky fifteen-year-old, so she should be able to handle this moment with a modicum of sophistication. "Hello," she said.

"Hello," he replied. "Did you have fun tonight?"

"Sure. Because it was, well, prom."

He nodded. "Yeah, prom."

She remembered his senior year he'd gone with his girlfriend, the one who had been studying abroad when she first met him. They'd broken up before college, however. His love life was a mystery to London now.

As was why he was here. Surely he wasn't one of those college guys that showed up at high school parties, she thought with an inner grimace. That would be such a disappointment.

"Um, would you like to come in?" she asked, because she figured she must.

"No, no." He held up a small duffel bag that was in one hand. "Ames left her overnight stuff at home. I volunteered to bring it over."

"Oh!" She was glad they were both spared the embarrassment of an unexpected, *older* party guest. "I'll take it."

The transfer went off without a hitch.

Colton Halliday remained on her doorstep.

She raised a brow. "Is there anything else?"

"Yes," he said, stepping forward. He cupped her face with one big hand, bent his head and kissed her.

It wasn't the first time she'd ever been kissed, but after a second she couldn't remember any of those that came previous. When he moved back, she gripped the door to avoid toppling over.

He was grinning at her.

She was just happy to realize she was still breathing.

"Are you going to be around this summer, England?" he asked.

England. A nod was the best she could do.

"Me, too. Want to go to the movies next Saturday night?"

Another nod.

He continued to grin. "It's a date."

Then he jogged down the steps and disappeared just as a gaggle of classmates came pressing through the still-open door. One girl, who'd been new this year and Amy's senior project, looked over her shoulder then at London. "Who was *that*?"

Her past? Her future? London smiled at her friend. "Just some guy I know."

She pulled the other girl toward the kitchen where food and drink awaited. Her dad looked up as the crowd surged into the room. "Everything okay?" he asked, smiling as he walked to London.

"Everything's fabulous," she answered, going on tiptoe to kiss his cheek. It was prom night and college was coming in September and possibilities were opening up all over as she took these first real steps into her own life—the life in which her dad and Shay would always have her back.

Master of her fate, captain of her soul, certainly. But never alone and never lonely. "Love you, Dad," she whispered, and he drew her close.

"Love you, too," he said, his voice gruff. "Love you always."

* * * * *

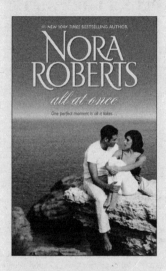

REQUEST YOUR FREE BOOKS!

2 FREE NOVELS
FROM THE ROMANCE COLLECTION
PLUS 2 FREE GIFTS!

YES! Please send me 2 FREE novels from the Romance Collection and my 2 FREE gifts (gifts are worth about $10). After receiving them, if I don't wish to receive any more books, I can return the shipping statement marked "cancel." If I don't cancel, I will receive 4 brand-new novels every month and be billed just $6.24 per book in the U.S. or $6.74 per book in Canada. That's a savings of at least 22% off the cover price. It's quite a bargain! Shipping and handling is just 50¢ per book in the U.S. and 75¢ per book in Canada.* I understand that accepting the 2 free books and gifts places me under no obligation to buy anything. I can always return a shipment and cancel at any time. Even if I never buy another book, the two free books and gifts are mine to keep forever.

194/394 MDN F4XY

Name	(PLEASE PRINT)
Address	Apt. #
City	State/Prov.	Zip/Postal Code

Signature (if under 18, a parent or guardian must sign)

Mail to the Harlequin® Reader Service:
IN U.S.A.: P.O. Box 1867, Buffalo, NY 14240-1867
IN CANADA: P.O. Box 609, Fort Erie, Ontario L2A 5X3

Want to try two free books from another line?
Call 1-800-873-8635 or visit www.ReaderService.com.

* Terms and prices subject to change without notice. Prices do not include applicable taxes. Sales tax applicable in N.Y. Canadian residents will be charged applicable taxes. Offer not valid in Quebec. This offer is limited to one order per household. Not valid for current subscribers to the Romance Collection or the Romance/Suspense Collection. All orders subject to credit approval. Credit or debit balances in a customer's account(s) may be offset by any other outstanding balance owed by or to the customer. Please allow 4 to 6 weeks for delivery. Offer available while quantities last.

Your Privacy—The Harlequin® Reader Service is committed to protecting your privacy. Our Privacy Policy is available online at www.ReaderService.com or upon request from the Harlequin Reader Service.

We make a portion of our mailing list available to reputable third parties that offer products we believe may interest you. If you prefer that we not exchange your name with third parties, or if you wish to clarify or modify your communication preferences, please visit us at www.ReaderService.com/consumerschoice or write to us at Harlequin Reader Service Preference Service, P.O. Box 9062, Buffalo, NY 14269. Include your complete name and address.

ROM13R